# KONA SNOW

## A BIO-TERROR THRILLER

## BOOK TWO

BY

# TERRY FRITTS

*ECHO
PARK
PRESS*

Books by Terry Fritts

BIO-TERROR SERIES

*TAKA*
*KONA SNOW*
*KAPU ʻĀINA*
*(Forbidden land)*

The Kevin Bridges Spiritual Warfare Series

*BROTHERHOOD OF THE DIVINE*
*SEVEN OF THE CROSS*

*Kona Snow* is Book Two in the bio-terror series featuring the Hawaiian Islands. It primarily takes place on the Big Island, Kauai, and Oahu. There are also some exciting action scenes in Russia, Thailand, and Japan. *Taka*, Book One in the bio-terror series was released in November of 2006. *Kona Snow* is a more complex story and adds several new characters. Book Three in the series, *Kapu ʻĀina (Forbidden Land)*, is a non-stop thrill-ride that shouldn't be missed.

This book is a work of fiction.

Second Edition Published by Echo Park Press LLC 2009
First Published by Echo Park Press 2007
*Copyright © 2007 by Terry Fritts. All rights reserved.*
ISBN-13: 978-0-9791514-2-2
ISBN-10: 0-9791514-2-2
**www.echoparkpress.net**

Library of Congress Control Number: 2009940324

**Cover photo: © G. Brad Lewis / volcanoman.com.**

**Back Cover background photo of blooming coffee trees (Kona Snow) by Gail and Ken Hennig, former owners of Redbird Kona Coffee**

Manufactured in the United States of America

# ACKNOWLEDGEMENTS

Writing a novel requires an intensive amount of research and I love to do research, but I cannot always do it alone. I want to thank the following people for helping me--Berch Papikyan for help with questions about Russia, Roger Hull for the Japanese scenes, my son-in-law Brandon Beirne for Navy and military information, Bo Adler for his Thailand input, Melanie Balasbas for Pidgen, Gail and Ken Hennig, former owners of Redbird Kona Coffee, for the information on growing and processing coffee, and most of all Mike Corwin who always asked me the right questions and researched answers to my questions.

The chapters about Russia were inspired by our two humanitarian trips to Russia through KidCare International, a USAID non-profit organization. I would like to thank our group leader and friend, Fred Illyan, who showed us all the sights in Russia that tourists should see as well as those sights tourists never get to see.

On Kauai I want to thank the Princeville Resort for providing me with a great place to stay while I was writing parts of *Kona Snow*, especially the action scene in the lobby. It is a fabulous and inspiring resort with one of the best lobby views one could imagine. I would also like to thank Kauai Coffee Company for the information and great coffee they supplied.

On Oahu I would like to recognize the Hawaii Prince Hotel Waikiki where I stayed while writing portions of this book and where I had Jotty stay in one scene. It too is a great hotel.

On Molokai, I want to thank the clerk at the Molokai Coffee Plantation and the owner of the Big Wind Kite Factory and Plantation Gallery for taking the time to tell me about many of the local issues on Molokai.

On the Big Island I have to thank the Hilton Waikoloa Village for all their support, especially the first book signing in the Malolo Lounge, and for providing a wonderful source of inspiration for my books. I also want to recognize the Waikoloa Marriott, whose pool area and beach are one of my favorite spots to sit in all of Hawaii. I do have to say I am a little disappointed in their trend away from the Hawaiiana theme of the hotel.

On Catalina, I would like to thank the Busy Bee Restaurant that will no doubt be surprised to see that they play a minor part in

*Kona Snow*. I also want to thank the Glenmore Plaza Hotel for allowing me to wander their hallways as part of my research.

I want to thank Echo Park Press for believing in me as an author and Booklines-Islander Group for distributing my books in Hawaii. I also want to thank David Cook at instanthawaii.com.

Of course I want to thank G. Brad Lewis, volcanoman.com, for the great cover photo and Gail and Ken Hennig for the photo of the Kona Snow used on the back cover.

Most importantly, I want to thank my editors--my wife Pauline, my daughter-in-law Jennifer Boen, and the man I call the finisher, Gary Corwin.

As always I need to thank my family, especially my wife Pauline and my daughter Katy.

GMOs are a mystery that needs to be better researched and regulated. The names of the chemical companies used in *Kona Snow* are made-up, but most of what I said about the companies and their products are fact. Take the time to read labels so you know what you are putting in your body. And please, don't stop drinking coffee--Kona Coffee is some of the best coffee you will ever enjoy.

Terry Fritts is an author and musician who resides with his wife Pauline in Claremont, CA. They often visit Hawaii and travel the world to research his novels. You can contact Terry at: tfritts01@aol.com

# KONA SNOW

## BOOK TWO

*Laura,*

*Thanks for your support*

# KONA SNOW

## Chapter One

**"Pull!"**

The fluorescent orange disc exploded into a thousand shards as a thunderous crack erupted from Jim's gun. The flakes drifted in the wind and then disappeared from sight as they were churned into the tumultuous wake created by the massive twin turbines that powered the cruise ship *the Grand Maui*.

"Superb shooting," declared the English aristocrat standing next to Jim. "That makes twenty-two hits with no misses for you my dear fellow. Even if I am perfect on my next four shots, I won't be able to match your score." "Damn!" he grunted under his breath. Lord Farrelton was not used to losing at anything.

"Yep," Jim said lazily in his elongated Texas drawl. "I reckon that's just about two thousand dollars you now owe me there, Lord Farrelton." Jim smiled wryly as Lord Farrelton shook his head in disbelief.

"I still cannot believe that…that thing you call a shotgun... was able to out shoot my Kreighoff. My custom grade K-80 cost me over 25,000 pounds and is supposedly the best competition skeet shotgun made."

"It is a mighty fine looking piece of weaponry," Jim said, nodding his head in agreement. "But I am rather partial to this here old Winchester," he said as he held up his Model 97 pump shotgun. "She may not be the prettiest thing to look at," he continued, "but she has sure got me out of many a scrape, and even won me a little money and pride along the way."

Lord Farrelton was speechless, which was rather unusual for one of the most prominent and outspoken members of England's House of Lords. Lord Farrelton and his beautiful wife Katherine, along with a contingent of servants and security personnel, were spending several days aboard *the Grand Maui*. The trip was an appeasement to his wife, Katherine, for having to put up with all the official trips her husband had to make lately. This was his third trip to the Pacific region as head of the Intelligence Committee of The

1

Ministry of Defense. More importantly, he was there representing his privately held company, Hydrogen Solutions, as it tested military applications of his company's research findings.

"There's no doubt that you too are a mighty fine shot, my dear Lord Farrelton." Jim had a hard time properly acknowledging Farrelton's English title. It made Jim feel like he was pray'n in church every time he addressed Farrelton, but he knew it was the proper thing to do. "Now if you are a real gamblin' man," proposed Jim, "I'll give you a chance to win back those dollars you owe me. Let's shoot another round of trap, but this time I'll use my six-shooters instead of my shotgun to knock them little orange discs out of the sky and you can continue to use that mighty fine looking Kreighoff shotgun."

"A very intriguing proposition there, Rikey," Lord Farrelton responded. "I would indeed love to see you shoot some skeet with those six-shooters that you have strapped at your side."

"I'll even keep them holstered until you yell 'pull'," interrupted Jim, "and I'll alternate hands."

"I am sure you would," continued Lord Farrelton, "but as foolish as I may appear, I know when I have been hustled and I know when its time to pay my wagers and put my gun back in its case. You are undoubtedly a more superior shooter than I could ever hope to become and I am certainly pleased it is dollars and not pounds I owe you. Thank goodness your economy is in such a shambles. It has decimated the value of your dollar. The British pound has never been worth more."

As if the exchange rate would make any difference to Lord Farrelton's bank account. He and Lady Katherine were one of the few aristocratic families in England allowed to retain their titles and all the perks that went with those titles. The British taxpayers had grown tired of supporting the enumerable titled families throughout England and demanded the advantages that accompanied the titles of Baron, Count, Lord and Lady be rescinded. Most of these aristocrats were still allowed to use and were referred to by their titles, but no longer benefited from the tax free status or the government subsidized staff that catered to their every need that such a title once guaranteed.

"Well sir," Jim responded, "then I would be honored if you and Lady Farrelton would join me in the bar and allow me to buy drinks to celebrate my victory and your good sense."

Lord Farrelton could only laugh and shake his head at Jim's impertinent comment. Usually he found this typical impetuous American trait rather tedious and annoying, but how could anyone not like a fellow as honest and sincere as Jim Rikey.

"Can you really shoot skeet with those six-shooters?" questioned Lord Farrelton.

Instantly Jim yelled out, "Pull, pull, pull, pull, pull, pull." Six of the clay-like discs went flying in all directions. In a flash Jim pulled the six-shooter from the holster on his left side. He fanned the hammer of the Colt 45 with his right hand as he held the trigger down and swung the revolver from left to right. The six discs seemed to explode simultaneously in clouds of orange dust as Farrelton's staff, along with a small crowd who had gathered to watch the match, roared their approval with applause and yells of "Bravo".

Jim just looked up and gave the crowd that Texas "Aw shucks, it was nothing" grin. He turned to Lord Farrelton who, along with the crowd, continued to applaud. "Had I used my right hand, I would have shot them in the order they came out. My left hand is a touch lazy."

Jim smiled as he shook Lord Farrelton's hand. The two gentlemen surrendered their guns to the ship's range marshal and watched as the marshal carefully emptied, cleaned, and stowed both men's guns with equal care and expertise.

Forty years ago, shooting trap from the rear deck of a cruise ship was a common occurrence. Many a first class passenger brought along his treasured skeet shotgun to compete for fun and, more often than not, for considerable sums of money with his fellow passengers. That tradition has all but died on today's commercial cruise liners. *The Grand Maui* is one of the few cruise ships to still offer that experience. But it doesn't come cheap! No longer are the passengers allowed to stow their weapons in their cabins. The ship employs an arms expert who carefully inspects and cares for the weapons brought on board. The cruise line also contributes a substantial amount of money to several animal rights organizations. One in particular took issue with the lead poisoning of the ocean creatures from the shotgun pellets fired at what now are biodegradable fluorescent orange discs made out of fish food. For the most part, these non-profit organizations tended to leave the Hawaii Cruise Lines alone.

Money does talk!

Jim made arrangements to meet the Farreltons in an hour at the Volcano View Lounge. That would give both the men a chance to wash the gunpowder residue off of their hands and faces. It would also give Lady Katherine and her handmaiden time to freshen up.

Jim felt like a fish out of water aboard *the Grand Maui*. This was not his idea of a fun way to spend a week of vacation time. Jim had hoped to head back to Texas this week to visit his ranch in Abilene. It had been several months since he had been back there. He needed to handle some business with the sharecropper who farmed his property and the family who was renting his farm house and taking care of things. He also had a hankering to drop by and visit his old girl friend, Susan Tyler, in College Station. That is, if he had time! Actually he was going to make time to do that. She had given him quite a welcome when he dropped by a while back looking for information about Spencer. Spencer was her ex-husband who had worked for the Red Summit and was killed by the Red Summit just as Jin tried to rescue him from the terrorists. Susan and Jim had continued to keep in touch and her letters made it vividly clear another such welcome awaited Jim whenever he decided to drop in. Unfortunately, or as Jim hoped maybe it would become fortunate, his trip to Texas was not to be at this time. Jim had promised Haruko he would follow up on some questions she needed answers to. She had been an integral part of the counter-terrorism team when they supposedly crushed the Red Summit's terrorist plot in Los Angeles. The only way to get those answers was if Jim was aboard *the Grand Maui*. Haruko could not let go of her belief that it was Taka Matsuura who was the true leader of the terrorist group the Red Summit. Her bosses at the National Police Agency, as well as the FBI, had made it clear when Minoru was killed in Los Angeles, that the Red Summit ceased to be a legitimate threat as a terrorist organization. Taka was no longer to be considered a suspect or even a member of The Red Summit. Haruko disagreed with this official position with every fiber of her existence. At least in private! She had learned that, if she were to keep her position in the Japanese National Police Agency, she had to keep such beliefs to herself. Speaking of them would only give one of her assistants the ammunition they needed to have her job. That was how Haruko had convinced Jim to use his vacation time to do a little detective work for her. Actually, she knew Jim would jump at

4

the chance to help her out. Jim had moved to the Big Island to continue his own follow up investigation of the incidents which had occurred there with Minoru. And besides, Jim still desired Haruko and would do just about anything she requested if he thought it improved his chances of being with her. Haruko knew this but felt no guilt in using Jim's desire for her to get the information she needed. She would do anything to prove Taka was indeed the true power behind the Red Summit.

Taka and Niki Matsuura had cruised on *the Grand Maui* for their honeymoon. According to Haruko, Ono Saito, as he was known in Japan, was the journalist from Tokyo who had been writing stories about the Taka Matsuura controversy. He had received information from both the photographer and the chef who both worked on board *the Grand Maui* regarding some very strange behavior Taka and Niki had exhibited while on board. They both spoke almost as if there were two Takas who had been on board the ship during the cruise. Haruko had accompanied Ono to the Big Island to hear firsthand of this information. Jim had to admit there must be something to these claims, because the ship's photographer was killed in a fire that consumed his file of photos aboard the ship just a day before he was to meet with Ono, who then also died under very mysterious circumstances the very next day. The ship's head chef disappeared the morning after the fire, the same day the journalist died. "A strange coincidence indeed!" Jim said softly to himself. He couldn't understand why these events were not followed up before but, then again, things were moving pretty fast at that stage of the investigation with the big shootout at the Waikoloa Hilton and the one up at David Paleaka's Ranch. Then the whole Red Summit saga seemed to come to an abrupt end with the killing of Minoru in Los Angeles. At least the governments of both Japan and the United States wanted it to come to a conclusion.

Since coming aboard, Jim did get a look at the passenger manifest for the cruise when the fire occurred. He was not surprised to find Minoru had joined the cruise in progress and then left rather abruptly after the fire. He of course wasn't the only passenger to leave at that time, but Jim knew it had to have been Minoru who set the fire that killed the ship's photographer. There was no doubt some sort of cover-up was the intended goal. But was it intended to hide information about Taka or hide information about Minoru? That was still the question. And what had happened to the head chef? So far from what Jim had been able to find out, Hiroshi Kurosawa, the chef, had abruptly left the ship claiming some family emergency back in Japan. There were rumors from some of his assistants that he was working as a head chef somewhere in Southeast Asia, possibly Thailand or Malaysia. He did have a cousin who used to work at the Aioka Steakhouse somewhere near Tokyo. The cousin may know more about Hiroshi's whereabouts, but none of the ship's present chefs even knew the cousin's name. "That's something Haruko needs to check out," thought Jim. It also had to have been Minoru who killed the journalist Ono Saito, even though the Federal Aviation Administration claims the helicopter crash was an accident due to pilot error. Jim would do a little more follow up by questioning members of the ship's crew who were present when Taka and Niki took their honeymoon cruise. He wanted to find someone who may have spoken with the head chef or the photographer about their suspicions. Typical police work! Something Jim didn't care much for, but something that needed to be done. Jim fired off an e-mail to Haruko telling her what he had found out and promising to look into things further. He would call her later in the week. But right now, Jim had to put on his fancy duds and head to the Volcano Lounge to entertain British Royalty. Sometimes Jim couldn't believe the things he would do for Haruko.

One thing was for sure--Jim cleaned up very well! When he had on his country gentleman formal wear and entered the room, every head would turn to stare. It was no different today as he entered the Volcano Lounge on the upper deck of the ship. Almost in unison all heads turned to watch Jim as he strode through the lounge with his loping Texas gait making his way to Lord Farrelton's table. The Lord and his Lady were two of the few in the crowded lounge who did not turn to stare as Jim came towards their table. He did draw the attention of Lord Farrelton's security men, but it was their job to always know who entered a room. It was Lady Katherine's handmaiden, Emma, who caught Jim's attention as he approached the table. She, along with the security personnel, was sitting at a table just to the right of Lord Farrelton and Katherine. Jim was struck by her incredible beauty and wondered why he had failed to notice her before. She wore simple makeup and dressed conservatively. Her job

6

was to make sure Lady Katherine was the focus of attention in the room, not her. Her plain attire, however, could not hide the fact she indeed had a terrific body. Jim took notice and it was obvious to those who were looking that Emma took quite an interest in Jim as she watched his six foot five frame make its way towards Lord Farrelton's table.

"Howdy ma'm, gentlemen," Jim greeted Emma and the security men as he passed their table. Up until that moment, Emma did not realize she had been staring at Jim as he approached. She blushed and was too flustered to respond, but did manage to nod her head politely in response. Emma's social faux pas did not go unnoticed by the security men. They all smiled broadly and were sure to tease Emma later about her uncomfortable, but oh so telling, lack of response and her infatuated stare.

"Lord Farrelton, Lady Katherine, it's so nice of you to allow me to join you for a drink." Jim spoke as he joined the couple at a table near the window. The Lady Katherine nodded as her husband stood up to shake Jim's hand.

"Rikey, I'm not accustomed to losing at anything, but I also know when I've met my match. Please allow me to buy you a drink." As if on cue, Lady Katherine rose and excused herself as she went to join a group of other women at a table across the room. Emma was quickly at her side and accompanied her to the new location. Lord Farrelton noticed Emma's furtive glance towards Jim as she accompanied Lady Katherine.

"A jolly fine rogering from that one I bet," Lord Farrelton said to Jim. "I think she fancies you. Remind me to formally introduce you later." Jim hadn't heard that expression before but he was pretty sure he knew what it meant. And he definitely liked the idea.

"Rikey, I haven't been totally honest with you," Lord Farrelton began. "I wanted to get you alone to commend you on that great job you did of dealing with that terrorist group, the Red Summit, last year. You know that Minoru fellow killed a couple of our Brit security people before he took on you Yanks. I am very grateful you recovered that tainted material and kept it from widespread distribution. That could have been tragic."

Jim was at first taken aback by the information Lord Farrelton had regarding The Red Summit case. It was obvious he had been briefed by United States government sources. He knew a lot, but obviously he didn't know everything, and Jim was damn well sure not going to fill in the blanks. Especially about what happened to that tainted lipstick.

"Well, thank you sir," Jim responded. "But there were a lot more people than me involved in that case."

"As I understand," the Lord replied. "I hear that Jotty fellow with the FBI got a bit of a promotion recently."

"He was made head of the Far East Counter Terrorism Division for the FBI right after that Red Summit affair."

"So you haven't talked to him much recently then I take it," Lord Farrelton responded.

"Well, I'm kind of busy here in Hawaii taking care of Farm Service business. I haven't been back to the mainland for quite a while and I'm not much for calling on the phone for idle conversation."

"And dare I say, you have also been doing a little work for the FBI following up on some unfinished business with that whole Red Summit affair," Lord Farrelton added. Jim remained quiet. "Your friend Jotty has been appointed as the Assistant Director of Asian Affairs at the National Counter-Terrorism Center in McLean, Virginia."

"You mean Jotty doesn't work for the FBI anymore?"

"As I understand it," answered Farrelton, "it is more like he is on loan from the FBI to the Center. It seems the NCTC has had trouble attracting qualified personnel to fill its ranks."

"That sounds a little more like a punishment than a promotion to me," Jim replied in an amused tone. "From what I hear, they are still looking for a boss for that place."

"I've heard that issue has been resolved, or at least is about to be," replied Lord Farrelton. "I'm sure you will be hearing about it soon."

Jim didn't doubt Lord Farrelton's information was accurate, though possibly not totally complete. It was also no wonder Jotty hadn't called Jim to talk about his new job. He was probably a little embarrassed about the whole thing. Jim wondered if Haruko had heard about Jotty's new assignment and, if she had, why she hadn't told him about it. Jim knew that, like himself, Jotty talked to Haruko at least once a week on the phone.

8

The two gentlemen continued to exchange small talk for a while, then joined the table of women across the room. The conversation was brisk and the drinks flowed freely so no one seemed to notice the cruise ship had been dead in the water for at least twenty minutes. That was until Lady Farrelton saw one of the ship's shore boats had been lowered into the water and was trying to pull alongside a dive boat which seemed to be doing large circles in the water. What looked to be two divers attached to ropes were laying face down being pulled along by the dive boat in its fixed circular pattern.

"Whatever do you think is going on over there?" enquired Lady Katherine to no one in particular.

Her question did refocus everyone's attention to the activity taking place about a hundred yards off the port side of the ship. After a moment Lord Farrelton spoke up.

"Rather peculiar, wouldn't you say, Rikey?"

"I don't wish to upset anyone, but those do look to be two bodies being pulled along in the water by that dive boat." Jim responded.

"Oh dear," Lord Farrelton exclaimed. "Perhaps I should call the Captain to see what the trouble may be. Waiter!" Lord Farrelton demanded, "please get me the Captain."

"Yes sir, at once sir," the waiter responded as he scurried away.

"It appears a couple of the chaps on the shore boat have made it onto the dive boat. Looks like one of them is the ship's doctor," Lord Farrelton continued.

A crowd had gathered by the window to watch the drama unfold. Suddenly a panicked doctor appeared at the rail of the dive boat and waved frantically for the shore boat to pull away. Which it did but, instead of coming back to *the Grand Maui,* it moved in the opposite direction and stopped about a hundred yards further past the dive boat. The dive boat had stopped circling and now set rocking in the swift current waters as the anchor held it fast. The crew member who boarded the dive boat with the doctor now pulled the two floating bodies to the boat. The doctor leaned over to examine them, but suddenly jumped back, grabbing a gaff and pushed the two bodies away from the boat. He and the other crew member moved to the front of the dive boat as far away from the cabin deck as possible and began talking rapidly into their radios.

"Where's the Captain?" Lord Farrelton said loud enough for everyone in the lounge to hear. He turned to one of his security men and snapped. "Go find out what is going on now!" Instantly, the security man was out the door and the remaining two security guards were on alert. Within twenty seconds, he was back with one of the ship's officers.

"I am afraid you and Lady Katherine must come with me at once," he said in a calm controlled voice.

The Lord and Lady knew better than to question that tone of voice and immediately the entire entourage headed for the door.

"I'm very sorry, but the helicopter will only hold you, your wife, and two members of your security team. The others will have to stay aboard."

A look of panic came over Emma's face. Lord Farrelton was quick to notice.

"Emma, let me introduce you to Jim Rikey. He works for the FBI and solved that nasty little mess with the Red Summit last year. He will take good care of you until we can get you off the ship."

Emma knew better than to question what the problem was, but knew it wasn't good.

"Nice to meet you, ma'm. You have no reason to be concerned. I am sure this will all work out in no time at all." Jim said trying to comfort her and put her at ease, but not being too successful.

Emma tried to force a smile as the Lord and Lady were whisked out the door. Moments later a helicopter was seen heading away from the boat and towards the island. Two other coast guard helicopters could also be seen heading towards *the Grand Maui*. As the passengers watched from the various decks on the ship, two men in white bio-hazard suits were lowered onto the deck of the dive boat. The doctor and other crew members were sprayed with some type of chemical and both put on yellow bio-hazard suits. Next a basket was lowered from one of the helicopters and both men were lifted into the second helicopter and it headed off towards the islands. The two men in the white suits began spraying the same chemical they had sprayed on the crew members on the rest of the ship. By this time another helicopter, a military one, was now hovering over the scene and a coast guard cutter had arrived in the area and now seemed to be spraying the shore boat and its crew as well. "Will everything be alright?" Emma asked Jim softly. "I'm sure it will be alright for us, but I can't say for sure for those men out there. Obviously there was some kind of contamination on that dive boat which must have killed its crew and made the ship's doctor mighty concerned," Jim responded.

Just then the first officer walked into the lounge and several passengers rushed to him for an explanation. He calmly explained to them how the men on the dive boat had died of what appeared to be some kind of infection and, to be on the safe side, *the Grand Maui* would remain at sea until doctors from the Center for Disease Control on the islands checked out the ship. It should take no more than a day, he assured them.

There were several moans of disgust from the passengers, but they all realized that if there was a problem they wanted it solved and they demanded the best possible care. These were people with money who were used to the best. The Hawaiian Cruise Line would not disappoint them, the officer reminded them. If they were unhappy, amends would be made.

The first officer then approached Jim. "Mr. Rikey, the Captain wishes to speak with you on the bridge. Would you please follow me?"

"I will, but only if this lovely lady may join me. You see Lord Farrelton put me in charge of her well being," Jim replied, smiling at Emma.

"Of course she can come along," the officer responded politely, although he knew the Captain wished to speak to Jim privately. The three of them headed out of the Volcano Lounge and towards the bridge. Meanwhile, a large naval ship had arrived on the scene. Divers in white bio-hazard wet suits attached cables to the dive boat and it was winched into a holding platform in the rear of the naval vessel. They did the same with *the Grand Maui*'s shore boat. This ship seemed to be designed for just such a task. Two helicopters also arrived on *the Grand Maui*. Several doctors and technicians exited the helicopters with an array of detection equipment. It wasn't necessary for them to wear the bio-hazard suits. The cause of the infection had already been determined and all of these men had been inoculated for it. As had Jim.

The Captain was on the radio when the three of them entered the bridge. It was a hub of activity with crew members scrambling to make preparations for the arriving medical teams as well as the flurry of complaints from the well-heeled clientele. Before the first officer could introduce Jim and Emma, the Captain approached and was already speaking.

"Mr. Rikey, a pleasure to meet you. I don't mean to be rude, but I must be brief and to the point." The Captain did not wait for a reply. "Lord Farrelton has informed me of your FBI credentials and past experience in dealing with anthrax. He also informed me you are in Hawaii for that very reason. Well, it appears we have found your anthrax. Though I was informed you have been inoculated, we have been ordered not to allow anyone to leave the boat until tomorrow after the medical teams has had a chance to look things over."

"And to see if anyone else starts to show symptoms or lesions, no doubt!" Jim responded coolly.

The Captain continued, "you, of course, would be allowed to leave to begin your investigation if you choose."

"I appreciate that, Captain, but there is not much I can do until the medical team isolates the strain. I did promise Lord Farrelton I would look after Emma until she could rejoin him and Lady Katherine."

"Lord Farrelton thought as much and informed me to allow you to stay in his Presidential Suite so you could be near Emma's room and also keep an eye on their valuables until his security team arrives tomorrow when the ship receives medical clearance." The Captain was smiling as he told this to Jim.

"I have already had your things moved to his suite and the valet is packing his and Lady Katherine's clothing and possessions as we speak. Both your cabin and the suite have been provisionally cleared by the medical team, pending no further discovery of anthrax."

The Captain was pulled away by one of his crew members and as quickly as the conversation with the Captain had started, so it ended. Jim and Emma were escorted off the bridge and left standing on deck as panicked passengers raced back and forth with crew members at their sides trying to keep them calm. Emma was still trembling and the agitated passengers around her did nothing to help calm her shaken nerves.

12

"Looks to me like you could use a drink!" Jim said to Emma. "You know there is really nothing to worry about. If anthrax spores had gotten on this ship, we would know it by now. Especially if it's the strain I think it is," Jim continued.

"Quite reassuring," Emma responded facetiously. "I dare say you could use a bit of help at making a woman feel at ease." Emma blushed when she realized the implication of what she had just said.

"I reckon that's something I had better work on then this evening." Jim responded with a grin. "So why don't I start by getting you that drink and some dinner. We both have on our fancy duds, so we might as well get some use out of them and head out for some dinner."

Emma smiled and laughed. "You certainly have a rather peculiar way of stating things, Mr. Rikey."

"Well, ain't that funny," Jim replied, stressing his Texas drawl for all it was worth, "I was think'n the same thing about the way the words came out of your mouth. And please, ma'm, call me Jim."

"Only if you stop calling me 'ma'm'."

They both laughed as Emma grabbed Jim's arm and they headed into the dining room, both anticipating an unforgettable evening, and just quite possibly a 'jolly fine rogering'.

# Chapter Two

**Yuri Vladimirovich Rastsanov** was a second generation and, according to his father, a second-rate genetic scientist. His father, Vladimirovich, (sons are identified with their father's name), had worked for the Russian government on top secret projects throughout the Cold War, experimenting with ways to create bio-weapons that would only affect specific genetic markers found in certain ethnicities. For the most part, his experiments were considered failures, for they led to no tangible weapon. Science had not yet been able to differentiate DNA strains to a point that would allow specificity to such a degree. However, it was his research that laid the groundwork for the generation of scientists to follow and take up his challenge. Yuri, unfortunately, seemed to lack the skills to be one of these researchers who would further his father's quest. It was not so much that he was a second-rate geneticist as his father believed, but more probably due to his second rate values and personality. Yet Yuri was no fool! When Vladimirovich became deathly ill, Yuri secreted away much of his father's private notes regarding genetic alterations. These notes were the only thing of real value his father owned. Communism had seen to that! Yuri knew that someday these notes would enrich his life enormously. At least that was his hope. Yuri always thought he deserved more than what he earned and he was determined to have it.

Yuri attended graduate school in the United States. He earned his doctorate in genetics at Kansas State University. While attending KSU, Yuri was part of the team that patented the research which led to flea control products for pets. The compound is placed on the pet where it is absorbed into the bloodstream. When the flea bites the pet and sucks in the affected blood it becomes sterile, incapable of reproduction, thus ending the cycle of fleas. At least for a few months until another application is needed. Yuri envisioned a way to make the process permanent, needing only one application. However, the company that funded the research at the university thought it a much better idea to require the pet owner to continually spend money in keeping the fleas away. This lesson in capitalism was not lost on Yuri.

When Yuri returned to Russia, he was assigned to the genetics research lab in Perm where his father had worked for so many years.

Yuri's lab was in the above ground building at the facility, unlike his father's lab which had been several floors below ground. It was just one of many research labs hidden around the Perm area.

Perm is in the Ural Mountains, about a twenty-five hour train ride East-Northeast of Moscow. It is the sixth largest city in Russia and, up until about fifteen years ago, only U.S. intelligence agencies and the people who lived there knew it existed. It appeared on no maps and its presence was denied by the Russian government. The reason behind the secrecy is that Perm has always been the center of arms manufacturing for all of Russia and much of the world. Almost all Russian missiles, tanks, artillery, MIG jets, and nuclear weapons were manufactured in or around Perm. In fact, Perm is still the home of a booming weapons industry. Only now the industry is, for the most part, privately owned and sells its missiles primarily to the United States. Actually, it will sell to any country or person willing to spend the money. What is not generally known is the extent of the chemical and bio-weapon research and manufacturing still happening in Perm. Unfortunately, for the people in Perm and the surrounding areas, there is no government oversight concerning contamination of the environment. Especially the pollution of the rivers! The Kama River, once thought to be one of the largest rivers in Russia, empties into the Volga which in turn empties into the Caspian Sea. It has now been proven the Kama is larger than the Volga. Therefore, it is the Volga that now empties into the Kama River, though it is doubtful Russia will acknowledge the fact publicly. The Kama is capable of handling the largest ships and Perm has several ports located throughout the city. Besides now being the largest river in Russia, it is also one of the most polluted rivers. The weapons industry has laid waste to the river. There are stories by the local fisherman, who sell their daily catch along the roadsides or in the market bazaars, of mutated fish with multiple tails and even some with two heads. But of course the government is quick to denounce there is any such pollution problem. A few years back a Japanese industrialist offered to clean up the Kama River around the Perm area on the condition that he be allowed to keep all of the junk collected from the clean-up operation. The Russian Government quickly refused the offer and the Japanese were discouraged from making any further such offers. So the Kama remains one of the most industrially polluted rivers in the world.

Yuri was assigned the task of developing a more nutritious and disease resistant potato. This was not a difficult task based on the knowledge and experience he gained in the United States. Yuri's genetic modifications proved highly successful though not necessarily profitable. Not only had Yuri produced a more nutritious potato, resistant to pests and diseases, but his genetically modified potato practically would never spoil. It proved to stay edible for two years or more without any significant loss in nutritious value, taste, or quality. Great for a Communist-based economy and for an area with such a limited growing season, but not good if you are looking to make a profit on your potatoes. It was an amazing breakthrough in genetic modification. A breakthrough the Russian Government thought it best to not share with the rest of the world. That proved to be a wise decision! The potatoes were given to prisons and orphanages in and around the Perm region. The children and adults who ate them were carefully monitored with a multitude of tests given twice a year. It became immediately evident in the early stages of the trials that an unforeseen side affect of the genetic modification was a massive increase in the sperm production of the males who ingested the potatoes. Yuri was told to remedy that problem before the orphaned population skyrocketed. Using the notes from his father's experiments, Yuri was able to determine what caused the unwanted side affect. Using some of the aspects of his flea control research in the USA, combined with his father's notes, Yuri was able to adapt the modifications using state of the art DNA manipulation to completely reverse the virility affects of eating the genetically modified potatoes. His new GMO (genetically modified organism) still had all the desirable properties of his original creation, but now negatively altered the reproduction system of all males who consumed them. Once the GMO potato was consumed, the male who ate it would forever be unable to produce male sperm gametes, thus creating a future male gendercide for all who ate his GMO potatoes. The Russian Government was quick to realize the value of Yuri's research and his laboratory went from the ground floor to the fourth sub-level of the Perm research facility. However, before the significance of Yuri's findings was realized by the Russian government, Yuri recognized the money to be made and contacted a fellow research scientist from Kansas State who now worked for Monarch Chemicals.

For a rather large sum of money placed in a Swiss bank account, Yuri supplied Monarch with some of his fundamental genetic research that led to the development of several of Monarch's products including their New Breed potato. A potato that caused the death of any insect that ate it, but yet considered fine for human consumption. The potato even had to be registered as a pesticide, but no labeling was necessary for its sale to consumers. The chemical companies made sure of that.

Yuri saw the value of his research, as well as the value of keeping the bulk of it proprietary. At least the part he wasn't yet ready to sell. The less information he could give to his superiors the better it would be. Yuri learned how to slowly dole out his research information to keep his superiors satisfied, while at the same time use that information to upgrade his lifestyle. Yuri had seen the spoils of living large in the United States and wanted it for himself. The government wanted to keep Yuri happy and productive. They rewarded him by moving him to his own custom-built house on a small lake south of the Kama River, but still within the city of Perm. He was also given access to a new Mercedes with a driver. Of course, the house and the car were wired for surveillance and the driver was former KGB who was still on the FSB, the new KGB, payroll.

Yuri was an investment the government needed to control. His research needed to remain a guarded secret. One of the methods they had used during the Cold War to keep information from getting out was still an effective method today. Yuri was not allowed to leave the Perm area, let alone go out of the country or even to St. Petersburg or one of the resorts like those in Sochi Gagri on the Black Sea. He was allowed to visit an old Communist party resort outside of Perm on the Silver River. At one time it must have been quite a getaway for the upper party members and their wives, or possibly their mistresses. However, today the camp showed the decay of dereliction that so much of Russia was showing since the fall of Communism. No longer was there any running water and the cottages and banya were all in need of repair or razing. The pool was no longer usable and Yuri knew the Silver River was too polluted to chance swimming in. Even here Yuri was never alone. His driver was always there watching and waiting. Yuri had become a prisoner whose cell was a twenty mile radius of Perm. Worst of all he had no access to his secret Swiss bank account or to outside companies that would pay him handsomely for his research notes.

17

Yuri longed for the western way of life he had tasted while attending Kansas State University. The fast-life he liked to call it. Or living large he would sometimes say. It's hard to imagine any kind of fast-life in Manhattan, Kansas. It was more just a desire for freedom and opportunity to make as much for yourself as possible. That's what Yuri wanted. That's what he thought he deserved. Not that Perm was still lost in the previous century. Quite a night life had developed along the Kama Riverwalk near the old Perm 1 Rail Station. Every summer dozens of discos and bistros would spring up along the river catering to those upwardly mobile Russians with enough money to waste on overpriced beer and overpriced prostitutes. On any night of the week dozens of these putanka could be found parading their wares and offering their services to the men along the Riverwalk. That is, until around 11:00 p.m. when the police would shoo them back to their usual place of business along Revolution Street where they would join a hundred others hoping and trying to make enough money to supply their habits for another day. And usually they all succeeded.

The summers were called the White Nights. That was because the sun wouldn't set till after midnight and would rise again by 3:30 a.m. It would be like this for less than two months and then the opposite would occur. For five months out of the year it was almost always dark. Dark and cold! And Yuri hated it! But now it was summer and the Riverwalk had come to life. White Nights! It was Yuri's chance to experience that fast-life he so dearly craved... and deserved.

Yuri would go early to the Riverwalk. He wanted to arrive before the police ushered the prostitutes back to Revolution Street. His driver refused to allow Yuri to pick up prostitutes along Revolution, but allowed him to do so at the Riverwalk. The driver would then reluctantly drive the two of them back to Yuri's house on the lake. Later that night, or in the early morning, the driver would return the prostitute back to the general area and demand to see her papers and then sternly warn her in his scariest FSB voice that she was never to tell anyone where she went or whom she had been with. If she did, she would never be heard from again. And if she doubted it, just look where she would end up. It was then he would push her out of the car in front of Perm's infamous Tower of Terror. This was not like the one you would find at Disney's California Adventure Park. This was the former KGB headquarters where thousands of

18

people entered and were never heard from again. It dominated the skyline in the middle of Perm. It still caused fear in those who looked upon it. The prostitutes understood very quickly of their need to cooperate.

The first few times Yuri picked up women at the Riverwalk they were swallows. The government had planted them there as a test for Yuri. They wanted to see if Yuri talked too much. These women were called swallows for a very obvious reason. And as much as they tried and lived up to their name, they were never able to convince Yuri to divulge as much as even what he did or for whom he worked. After several liaisons with these swallows, the government decided Yuri was going to keep his mouth shut, so they quit subsidizing his sex life.

Yuri knew many of these prostitutes he picked up were, in fact, working for the government, but he didn't care. He knew to keep his personal life to himself and just as long as he got what he was after, who cared. Then one night Yuri met Lyuba.

Lyuba was Ukrainian. Tall, lithe, and extraordinarily beautiful! Her skin didn't have the jaundiced pallor of the usual drug-addicted prostitutes. Her clothes were not the cheap Russian designer knockoffs found at the local bazaar. Lyuba had an air of elegance. Somehow she was different. Very different! At their first meeting Yuri thought she might even be another swallow sent by the government to test him once again. But she never questioned him the way the others had. Either she was very good at what she did or she was just *very* good! Either way, Yuri wanted to be with her again, and soon! Yuri called her his Nochnaya Babochka. His very special Night Butterfly.

The White Nights were coming to an end and, in no time at all, the long, cold, dark winter would have Perm once again in its grip. It was because of this that Yuri's driver was not as careful as usual in checking Lyuba's papers or warning her as to the importance of keeping her mouth shut. Though, had he done so, he would have found nothing amiss for her papers were the best money could buy. He also was not as strict as usual about Yuri repeating his nightly liaison with the same prostitute. For what he did notice was how beautiful Lyuba was and how willing she was to share herself with him as well. She indeed was a very special putanka. Unfortunately, the driver was not as skilled at keeping his mouth shut as Yuri was when the swallow began to sing. In no time at all, Lyuba confirmed the information she had been seeking for her boss.

The Russian government had been very effective at keeping Yuri's research classified information. However, when you have knowledge as important and potentially dangerous as Yuri's GMO research, it is hard to keep it a secret. Many scientists in many countries were doing similar work. Most were still years away from the advances Yuri had made based on his father's experiments during the Cold War. Many knew of his father's research and wondered what had become of it. Even more speculation occurred when Yuri seemed to have come into a financial windfall. At least a windfall according to a Russian perspective of wealth. The fact he was being constantly monitored and that his travel was restricted was known by many intelligence agencies. This led to much speculation as to the importance of his present research. And if the good guys know about it, so do the bad guys.

Yuri's house on the lake was across the street from a Muslim produce market. It was the largest such wholesale market in all of Perm. Hundreds of vendors sold fresh produce grown mostly in the northern caucuses of Chechnya, Osetia, and Kabardino-Balkariya. So there were often many trucks and many people coming and going from the area. That is why Yuri's security never noticed the house was being watched from the market. Actually, since Yuri's security team only consisted of his driver, who had recently been very distracted by Lyuba, it was no wonder he didn't notice anything. At various times Yuri's house was monitored by up to three different organizations. Some spied on Yuri with very sophisticated equipment hidden in the trucks while others spied with only prying eyes trying to catch a glimpse of some telling action that might clue them as to the details of Yuri's research. The past week only one truck had kept a vigil watching Yuri's comings and goings, but that would come to an end tonight. For tonight, The Red Summit would acquire Yuri's services for their next terror campaign.

It was obvious to Lyuba that Yuri wanted to leave Perm in a most desperate way. He had talked about how tired he was of the long winters and how much he missed the warm beaches and bikini clad women he once saw on a trip to the United States. When she told him he should visit there again, he would grow silent and withdrawn. It was her way of teasing him, for she knew he was not allowed to leave the Perm area. When she tried to convince Yuri he should run away with her, he would scold her and remind her people were always listening, so be careful what you say.

Lyuba had grown tired of her most recent assignment. She was tired of Yuri and tired of his driver. Sex was just a tool of her job and it was time for this job to come to an end. She too missed the exciting jet-setting life she had grown accustomed to. Lyuba was actually once a world-class model who years ago was recruited by another model named Niki to work as a courier for a terrorist organization in Japan. A terrorist group called The Red Summit. Niki was the wife of the leader of the terrorist organization. That is until she was murdered by a rogue member of the organization. According to the newspapers and her boss, Niki was killed when a terrorist named Minoru tried to gain control of the group from Taka. He was unable to kill Taka, but he did manage to kill Niki before the FBI in Los Angeles killed him. As Lyuba's modeling career began to ebb, Taka offered her the chance to continue living her lavish lifestyle if she was willing to do more in-depth work for him and his organization. This was one of those in-depth assignments. It was not her first such assignment. Lyuba enjoyed the intrigue and adrenaline rush such tasks had to offer. But she had grown tired of this one and was ready to move on. She always felt safe working for Taka, for there were always several other terrorist operatives there to assist and protect her. She also never had to get her hands dirty. That meant she never had to kill anyone. She often set up many a person to be in a certain situation which allowed them to be killed. But she never had to do the deed herself.

Lyuba sat in the back seat of the Mercedes with Yuri. The drugs she had slipped into Yuri's beer were doing their job and he had grown groggy and placid. The driver kept looking in the mirror at Lyuba who would smile and wink at him in an enticing gesture. As the car approached the driveway to the lake house, a truck was blocking the way. This was not unusual. Many a night Yuri's driver had to get out and scold some truck driver who was parked waiting for the produce mart to open its gates for the next morning's market. It was a narrow road which offered few places for such large trucks to wait.

The driver pulled to a stop and exited the Mercedes. Lyuba smiled and Yuri was too dazed to know what was going on.

"Hey," yelled Yuri's driver to the apparently sleeping truck driver. "Hey, move this damn truck now! You are blocking my driveway." The truck driver acknowledged and started his engine. Whether it was the sound of the starting engine or Yuri's driver's preoccupation with his tryst with Lyuba he had planned for later, he never heard the small Asian man come out of the bushes behind him. As Yuri's driver turned, the attacker in the bushes was already swinging the flattened side of the club towards the driver's face. As the driver jerked his head back the attacker spoke, "Ho! Gadut! Lolo man!" The attacker continued, "da bakatore man ma-ke die dead." Even if the driver had been fluent in English, he still wouldn't have understood the insult and the declaration of impending death the attacker was saying to him in Pidgin. The small Asian-looking man swung the club again, but this time with the side of the club at the driver's neck. The jagged edge of the club ripped viciously into the driver's neck, slashing it to the spine while severing the carotid artery, spraying blood all over the attacker and the ground as the attacker pulled downward on the club almost severing the head from the torso. The driver's body fell limply to the ground. Two men exited the produce truck blocking the driveway and picked up the body placing it on the front passenger floor of the Mercedes. Lyuba exited the back of the Mercedes as a small Russian Lada pulled up next to the Mercedes. Two more men exited the rear of the Lada, one carried towels and a change of clothes for the man who had done the killing. The man carefully wiped the blood from his face and hands then put on a clean pair of Levi's and a Polo shirt. The driver of the Lada waited with the engine running. The assassin next used a bottle of water to wash away the blood and dangling pieces of skin from his club and then placed it under the front seat of the Lada. The killer and Lyuba entered the rear of the Lada and it quickly drove off towards the Perm train station where Lyuba boarded a late night train for St. Petersburg. The Asian man and his Chechnyan driver headed towards a center that housed missionaries where they parked to watch two Russians in a BMW who were watching the center.

The two men who exited the Lada grabbed the now unconscious Yuri from the back seat of the Mercedes and carried him to the rear of the produce truck. There a façade of potato crates hid a rather comfortable seating area. One of the men climbed into the back of the truck pulling Yuri's body into the hidden area behind the crates.

The other man from the Lada closed and locked the rear door of the truck, then jumped into the driver's seat of the Mercedes and headed towards the Silver River Camp that Yuri sometimes would visit with his favored prostitutes. The driver of the produce truck kicked dirt over the pool of blood that had formed next to the slain driver's body in an attempt to mask the grisly murder that had just occurred. He wasn't entirely successful at disguising the scene. As another truck arrived to await the opening of the produce market, the man jumped into his truck in pursuit of the Mercedes.

It was now 3:00 a.m. and dusk was about to turn to full light as the Mercedes approached the bridge spanning the Silver River. Almost no traffic was on the road at that time of the morning. Had there been any checkpoints set up, the Mercedes would not even have been warned to slow, for all the local police would have recognized the special front plate identifying it as an official government vehicle. The produce truck would also attract no attention for this was the time of day they began to travel the roads towards the markets or back to the southern regions that they came from. The driver of the Mercedes had slowed to allow the produce truck to catch up to it. When they reached the center of the bridge the driver of the Mercedes slowed but crashed into the railing, breaking it away but stopping the Mercedes before it plunged into the river. He carefully exited the Mercedes and guided the produce truck as it gently pushed the rear of the Mercedes, shoving it over the side of the bridge and into the Silver River below. He then jumped into the passenger seat of the produce truck where he removed his blood-stained clothes and shoes for fresh ones. Later when they were far from Perm, he would discard these along with the assassin's soiled shirt and pants.

The produce truck pulled away as the Mercedes began to settle to the bottom of the Silver River as it rushed towards its confluence with the Kama River. When the Mercedes hit the water, the battery shorted out interrupting the tracking device located on the car and sending a warning to a small office located at the old Tower of Terror back in Perm. Unfortunately, staff reductions meant no one would see the warning until 9:00 a.m. By that time the produce truck and Yuri would be well on their way out of Russia.

# Chapter Three

**A pang of fear and panic** raced through Haruko's head as she desperately searched the crowded street looking for Taka. She had been following him for almost twenty minutes as he wandered from one familiar place to the next. It was as though he was taunting Haruko by leading her to locations in downtown Tokyo that held some significance for her. What troubled Haruko the most was the heavy bulky coat Taka was wearing today. "What was he trying to hide?" "Could it be a bomb?" "Is it a biological weapon or gas?" The Red Summit had used all of these weapons in the past. These thoughts raced through Haruko's mind as she continued to follow him on his meandering journey.

If her supervisor knew what she was doing she would of course lose her job. Taka had been officially cleared as a suspect in the Red Summit terrorist activities. Her government and the government of the United States both said the Red Summit's reign of terror ended with the death of Minoru Sakura last year in Los Angeles. Haruko had been part of the team responsible for stopping Minoru and his team of assassins both in Los Angeles and on the Big Island in Hawaii. What she did regret was being unable to stop the bombing of the Funabori subway station in Tokyo last year. When it occurred, she was in Hawaii with Ono Saito trying to find out information about the alleged two Takas. She was beginning to believe, as did some others, that Aioka Matsuura, the founder of the Red Summit, was not killed in Lebanon as Israeli intelligence claimed, but was in Hawaii where he replaced his brother Taka as head of the vast Matsuura cattle and restaurant enterprises. She was determined to prove it!

"But where was he now? Where had he gone" Haruko said to herself. Taka seemed to just melt into the crowd that stood on the corner waiting for the light. The light changed and Haruko watched as the massive crowds from both sides dashed into the street meeting in the middle like two warring armies. Then, just as suddenly as the chaos began, it started to ebb as the mass of people separated going in their opposite directions. A few stragglers followed the main bodies of pedestrians as they defied death by racing across the street just avoiding the onrush of cars. Haruko was one of these daredevils. She had to find Taka! She must find Taka! Haruko frantically searched the sidewalks as a foreboding feeling slowly began to cloud her mind. How could she have lost him? How could he just disappear? Then she caught a glimpse of him standing by the entrance to the subway station. It was as if he had been waiting for her to follow. Their eyes met in an ever so subtle acknowledgement of mutual recognition. Taka turned and darted down the steps and into the cavernous underground station. Haruko quickly followed, but again lost sight of Taka when she entered the always crowded station. Anxiety and panic began to overtake Haruko as perspiration beaded on her nose and forehead. A train pulled into the station and a flood of commuters poured out of the doors pushing through the mass of people waiting to board the train. Haruko was being bumped and shoved as the crowd pushed to get by her and continue on their morning trek. Suddenly, as if by magic, Taka again appeared at the far end of the platform and entered the soon-to-be departing train. With all her effort, Haruko pushed against the still onrushing crowd and just managed to get most of her body through the closing door, just catching her right foot. Her attention was diverted from looking for Taka momentarily as she struggled to get her foot free of the closed door. When she turned, Taka stood smiling at her from the far end of the train car with his coat open revealing a large explosive vest wrapped around his upper torso. In his left hand he held a trigger mechanism with a wire leading to the vest. Haruko dared not make a move. She stood frozen in anticipation of the impending massacre of dozens of innocent commuters. Up until that moment, the only person she saw in the train car was Taka. She had focused all of her attention on Taka and everything and everyone else just blended together as part of an unfocused background. Now she began to look around the car at the faces of those who would soon be dead along with her. Suddenly, a fear greater than any she had ever experienced engulfed her body like a rogue wave pounding her into the sand. Sitting right behind Taka unaware of their impending doom sat Jim and Jotty, Haruko's two closest friends. Actually, her only two friends! She wanted to scream, but no sound came out of her mouth as she desperately tried to warn Jim and Jotty of the impending doom that awaited them. As if in slow motion they looked up, recognized Haruko, and both smiled broadly as they began to rise. Haruko tried to run to them, but her feet remained unmoving as if frozen to the train car's floor. Taka seemed not to notice the two men behind him as they began to rise from their seats. Suddenly a roar of bellowing laughter exploded from Taka as he dramatically pushed the detonator clasped tightly in his hand, all the while continuing to smile gloatingly at Haruko. Haruko screamed as a white flash suddenly blinded her. Then all was silent.

The eerie silence was broken as a dog started to bark in the distance. Haruko lay covered in perspiration on the sweat dampened sheets of her bed as she suddenly sat up trembling. It was the same dream she had experienced twice before. Each time she was awakened by her own screams as the Taka in her dream detonated the explosive belt strapped to his torso.

It was only 4:00 a.m., but Haruko knew she wouldn't be able to fall back asleep. She hadn't been able to the other times she had the dream, even though she tried to, so why would this time be any different? She got up and went to her computer to check her e-mail hoping to have a little more information from Jim before she headed out on her trip that day. Jim's last e-mail gave her a lot of information she already knew. She had run every search imaginable trying to find Hiroshi Kurosawa somewhere in Japan, but without success. She already knew about the cousin who purportedly worked at an Aioka Steakhouse somewhere near Tokyo. She hadn't shared that information with Jim or Jotty. In fact, she even knew he worked as a desserts chef. So far, Haruko had been unable to find his cousin working at one of the Aioka Steakhouses anywhere near Tokyo. Not that she didn't try! Haruko had sworn she would never step foot in an Aioka's as long as she lived. However, over the past few months, she had visited almost all of them within a day's drive of Tokyo. She would go in, order a dessert, and then ask to see the dessert chef to thank him for such a wonderful treat. When the chef would come out, she would turn on her charm and ask if he knew where she could find Hiroshi. No luck yet, but with Jim's new information maybe she could end this weekly ritual. At least it would keep her from gaining any more weight. She wasn't used to eating things so full of calories or that contained animal products. The years she had spent being a vegan made it difficult for her body to tolerate such food, and with her busy schedule she didn't have the time to work out. These weekly sweet desserts were beginning to affect her health.

What Haruko's visits to the Aioka restaurants and the questioning of the chefs did accomplish, however, was to allow Taka to know that Haruko had a little too much information after all, and was indeed looking for Hiroshi or at least Hiroshi's cousin in order to get to Hiroshi. Taka had foreseen this as a possibility and had sent Hiroshi's cousin to join Hiroshi at the Aioka's in Phuket. Taka had also instructed the new dessert chef to inform him if anybody came in asking questions about the cousin or Hiroshi. It had become apparent to Taka that he needed to keep a better watch on the movements of Haruko.

What Jim said that really boosted Haruko's spirits was the information about Hiroshi possibly working in Thailand or Malaysia as a head chef at an Aioka's Steakhouse Restaurant. One of the dessert chefs at a Tokyo Aioka's had informed her he had just been promoted to dessert chef, replacing one who had transferred to the Phuket, Thailand restaurant. This just might be the break she needed. Haruko had arranged to take a vacation to go visit Thailand and Malaysia to see if she could find Hiroshi. Being the head of the Counter-Terrorism Unit of the Japanese National Police Agency allowed her to take a vacation whenever she wanted. Up until now, she had never done so, even though her supervisors had urged her to take one due to her exhaustive work habits. She even worked through the typical winter vacation period when most Japanese take time off. So her last minute request was rather surprising to her supervisor but was not questioned.

There were no more e-mails from Jim. She had received one from Jotty exhorting her to be extremely careful on her vacation to Thailand. Haruko had told Jotty what she was planning on doing. Jotty didn't like the idea of Haruko wandering alone around Phuket trying to find Hiroshi. He knew she could take care of herself, but he still cared for Haruko greatly and wanted no harm to come to her. That was why he arranged for one of the clandestine CIA agents in Thailand to keep an eye on her. Of course he would never let Haruko know. Now that he was a boss at the National Counter-Terrorism Center, he could do things like that. Of course he couldn't tell the agent the truth about why he wanted Haruko watched, but Haruko had told Jotty she was going there to look for Hiroshi and, if it involved the Red Summit, Jotty could justify assigning the agent the task of monitoring Haruko's movements. He would just have to be careful how he wrote it up in his reports.

Haruko sent an e-mail to Jim reminding him to e-mail her if he found out any more information about Hiroshi or the photographer. She also told him about her planned trip to Thailand. She had previously told Jotty about the trip, but had neglected to tell Jim. She knew Jotty would be too busy with his new assignment at the National Counter-Terrorism Center to try to interfere with her planned trip. Jim she wasn't so sure of, so she waited till the day she was to leave before she told him how she planned to follow up on his information. She also told him about Jotty's new job. She knew from talking to both of them that they never talked with each other. "Some kind of macho power struggle, positioning thing," Haruko thought to herself.

Even before Jotty had heard about Haruko's planned trip, Taka had received information about it. He had a paid informant in the National Police Agency who contacted him the minute Haruko put in for her 'yasumi'. It wasn't too difficult for Taka to find out it was Thailand she was headed for on her resting time, as the Japanese liked to call their vacation periods. Taka knew better! He would make sure Haruko and Hiroshi would never get the opportunity to meet. One way or the other!

Had Jim known about Haruko's trip to Thailand, he just may have flown there to be with her and keep an eye on her. That is, he may have up until the time the weaponized anthrax was discovered on the dive boat off the Big Island of Hawaii. And, as enjoyable as it may have been, his little tryst with Emma would have had nothing to do with him not joining Haruko. Jim would do just about anything for a chance to be alone with Haruko. The fact was, Jim never even saw Haruko's e-mail until several days after she had left for Phuket.

Taka wished he could send Satochi Yomane to Thailand to handle the Haruko problem. Something this important Taka hated to contract out to an ancillary terrorist cell. Satochi was Taka's most reliable and trusted assassin. Unfortunately, Satochi was still working on a much more important assignment in Russia that he couldn't leave just yet. The head of the embedded terrorist cell in Thailand at least had been trained by Taka in a terrorist training camp in Lebanon. That was many years ago when the present Taka, still known as Aioka, had killed his brother, the real Taka, and took over his business empire, his identity, and his wife.

Haruko was anxious to find Hiroshi but also curious to see the damage Phuket suffered from the tsunami. She had heard that within a couple of months most of the businesses had rebuilt and were open again for tourists. Phuket really wasn't hurt by the tsunami as were several other islands in the area like Ko Phi Phi which was directly hit by the tidal surge while Phuket beach being on the east side of the island escaped relatively unharmed. Still, more than five thousand people lost their lives in Phuket. She actually felt good about going there and helping to support the country's economy. She was also pleased such a trip was now much more affordable than before. Thailand needed tourists and most seemed reluctant to return so soon after such a horrendous disaster. That made both the plane fare as well as the hotel room very reasonably priced. It allowed Haruko to book a much nicer hotel than she would normally be able to afford. Haruko was booked into the Sheraton Grande Laguna Phuket. It was one of the highest-, if not the highest-, rated hotel in all of Thailand. However, it paled in comparison to the finer hotels in Tokyo or even the ones Haruko stayed in when she visited Hawaii. That was a trip she hoped to make again very soon. There was something very relaxing about the Waikoloa Hilton, even though the man she went there with, and had made love with, was murdered. There was also that nasty little business where she had to fight and kill one of Minoru's ninjas in the Malolo Lounge to save Jotty and Jim's lives. All that not withstanding, she really did love the islands and hoped to visit there soon. The fact that Jim now lived on the Big Island made it even more tempting to return. "I wonder what Jotty would have to say about that?" Haruko said softly to herself as a smile crept across her face and surprised her. It was very exciting having two such handsome and wonderful men both desiring her company. It had been quite a while since such lustful thoughts had entered her mind or since she had even smiled. When she returned to the National Police Agency she had been all business. There was no time in her life for thoughts about men or love. Those fantasies would have to wait until after she proved Taka was the power behind the Red Summit. At least that was how she thought it would be.

This was Haruko's first visit to Thailand. She was pleasantly surprised to find Phuket was indeed very similar to Hawaii. The tropical island of Phuket had great natural beauty- - white powder sand beaches, incredible underwater scenery, lush forests and

plantations, plus warm sunshine and delicious seafood just like
Haruko had experienced in Hawaii. At least just like Haruko had seen
and wished she had experienced in Hawaii. She did treasure that one
wonderful day and night she spent with Byron Downing enjoying
Waikoloa before her world seemed to crumble around her. She knew
how wonderful paradise could be and hoped the paradise Phuket
appeared to be would prove more relaxing. More importantly, she
hoped to find some answers in Phuket that so tragically and cruelly
eluded her on the Big Island of Hawaii.

Jotty had contacted a CIA agent in Thailand who had been
assigned to the NCTC much in the same way Jotty had been assigned
there. In other words, his superiors told him of his new assignment,
yet reminded him just where his loyalties would lie. He was now
working for the NCTC, but it was made clear such a technicality as
that shouldn't stop him from filtering all his information through the
CIA first. Pretty much the same advice Jotty was given when told of
his new assignment. This was a covert agent who had been assigned
to keep an eye on known terrorists in Thailand. This Jotty knew!
What Jotty didn't know was that the CIA was aware of an increase in
communication between suspected terrorist cell members and an
unspecified contact from Japan whom they presumed was the cell
controller. They also knew that several of the cell members received
instructions to discretely make their way towards Phuket. This
information was all obtained from monitored cell phone conversations
intercepted by what the military like to call an 'Elephant Cage'. Near
the border where Thailand, Laos, and Cambodia all come together is
what the Thai government believes to be a cell phone transmission
center operated by a US subsidiary. It is a complex of buildings
surrounded by several dozen large antennas sticking up out of the
ground in a giant circle around the buildings, looking somewhat like a
giant pen or cage to hold in a heard of elephants. These antennas
make it possible to listen in on any ground, radio, or cell
transmissions within five hundred miles. There are a few satellite
dishes that do assist in cell phone transmissions, but it is really
nothing more than a ruse designed to fool local officials who happen
to drop by. Jotty's call to the agent asking him to keep an eye on
Haruko while she was in Phuket raised some red flags at the CIA
when they heard about Jotty's request. Someone in the chain of

command at the CIA recognized Haruko had been part of the team that took down the Red Summit in the attempted bio-terror attack in Los Angeles. They also were aware she was head of the counter-terror division of the National Police Agency in Tokyo and that she was still harboring beliefs that the Red Summit was a viable threat to the world. The movement of a known Thai terror cell to Phuket at the same time Haruko was going to be there was too coincidental to ignore, but not important enough to worry Jotty or the NCTC about just quite yet. Several CIA assets were moved to Phuket to keep watch on the cell members who had moved there prior to Haruko's arrival. They all were under strict instructions to watch, but to keep their hands clean. That is, see what developed but wait for instructions before any action was taken. These terrorists were only gophers for more important terror operatives whom the CIA were anxious to find. They had invested too much time already following the actions of this cell to have it screwed up by some female Japanese cop trying to prove a point. She was expendable as far as the CIA was concerned.

The instant Haruko landed in Bangkok she was under observation by both the CIA and by the terrorist cell Taka had arranged to handle his little problem. When she boarded the plane for her flight to Phuket, there were two CIA operatives on board to keep an eye on her. Upon her arrival in Phuket the CIA had three operatives on the ground waiting for the arrival of the plane. There were also four terrorists waiting for Haruko as well. It became obvious the terrorist cell planned to waste no time in dealing with Taka's little problem. The CIA had to decide if they were going to protect Haruko or if indeed she was expendable. The agent in charge contacted Washington and was awaiting a decision when Haruko disembarked from the plane. Shear luck-- and the onrush of a crowd of locals trying to get the autograph of some famous pop star who was also on the plane-- allowed Haruko to escape the terrorists planned kidnapping of her at the airport. She entered a cab and was on her way to her hotel before the terrorists would have a chance to grab her. This was very fortunate since the CIA agents at the airport were still awaiting instructions from Washington on how to proceed. The terrorists regrouped and all climbed into their waiting car and began to follow the taxi. The CIA agents in turn followed the terrorist's car.

Haruko arrived at her hotel, checked in, and immediately headed to her room to call the local Aioka Steakhouse. "Front desk" was the response she received when she picked up her phone. It was the type of phone that required the switchboard at the front desk to dial the number for you.

"Could you please connect me to the Aioka Restaurant please?"

"If you like, we can make those reservations for you ma'm."

"No, thank you, I would rather do it myself." Haruko insisted.

"Yes ma'm." came the quick reply and the phone began to ring.

"This is Aioka's, may I help you?" the restaurant receptionist inquired.

"Oh, I'm just calling to see if you are open," Haruko responded.

"Of course, would you like to make a dinner reservation?"

"Yes I would. How about 6:15 p.m. for one person? Under the name of Ono Saito," Haruko replied trying to sound genuinely interested in dining there.

"Six-fifteen would be fine. Is there anything else I can help you with?"

"Why yes there is," Haruko continued trying not to sound like a police officer. "Is your head chef in tonight?"

"Which chef are you looking for?" the receptionist replied in a somewhat more cautious tone.

Haruko realized she had said too much already and needed to shut up before she alerted Hiroshi that someone was asking about him. "No chef in particular," Haruko said trying to cover her misstep, "I'm just tired of going to restaurants and not getting the best they have to offer."

"Let me assure you that at Aioka's you always get the finest meal available in all of Phuket."

"Thank you very much. I look forward to dining with you this evening then," Haruko said and hung up the phone. She just hoped she hadn't already screwed up.

Downstairs at the switchboard one of the terrorist cell members was asking questions of the desk clerk while his partner watched and listened to the switchboard operator as she placed a call for Haruko's room number. He knew it was to a restaurant from what the operator said and it wasn't much of a reach to deduce that it was probably Aioka's they were talking about.

At Aioka's, Hiroshi was also being informed about a lady inquiring if the head chef would be in that evening. Hiroshi had asked the receptionist to let him know if any such requests were made. He was actually expecting someone to come looking for him. When Haruko made her first inquiry at the Tokyo Aioka restaurant, not only did the new dessert chef in Tokyo inform Taka of a lady asking too many questions regarding Hiroshi's cousin, he also informed the cousin whom he had replaced. Additionally, he let the cousin know about Taka's request to be informed of all such inquiries as well. The cousin, of course, immediately informed Hiroshi of all the details. Hiroshi made his plans to disappear, for good, this time.

The CIA operatives were still awaiting instructions from Washington when Haruko came into the lobby of the hotel. Two of the terrorist cell members were in the lobby and two others were out in front waiting in a car with the doors open. They appeared to be ready to kidnap Haruko and take her off to her death. Inside the bar adjacent to the lobby sat three of the five CIA agents who were keeping an eye on the terrorists. One of them was also the one assigned to keep an eye on Haruko. The two terrorists in the lobby quickly flanked Haruko as she exited the elevators. One of them flashed a gun at her that he was hiding under a newspaper. "Say anything and I will kill you right here," the terrorist threatened as he showed Haruko the gun. At the same time she could feel the second terrorist grab her arm. She could have easily taken that terrorist down killing him instantly, but the other terrorist holding the gun could stop that with a slight pull of the trigger. Haruko would have to wait for a better opportunity to make her move. She did know it had to be before she left the lobby or her life was over.

"There's the whore who stole my wallet!" A drunken voice yelled as a man rushed out of the bar. Before the terrorists or Haruko could react, the drunk decked Haruko with a savage jab to the mouth knocking her unconscious, then falling drunkenly on her limp body. The terrorists were stunned, not knowing quite what to do. Immediately the two buddies of the drunken man ran to his aid. "Someone call the police." One of the drunk's companions began yelling. "This is the thief, this is the thief." They tried to pull the drunk off of Haruko, but he began fighting with his two friends as he continued to lie across Haruko's still lifeless body. "I'm getting my wallet back from this whore," the drunk continued to yell in a rage as he started ripping through Haruko's purse. The drunk's two buddies started wrestling with the drunken man and before long all three of them and Haruko were lying in a gyrating heap on the floor of the lobby. The two terrorists panicked at the chaos and quickly headed out the door, jumped into the waiting car and headed down the street. Once the terrorists were gone, the wrestling mass of people on the floor quickly separated. The original drunk who had struck Haruko swept her up into his arms and headed through the kitchen door that led into the bar area, through the kitchen, and out through the service entrance to the loading dock area. There he gently placed the still unconscious Haruko in the back seat of his three-wheeled TukTuk cycle. He hopped on the front of the bike and whisked them both away as he radioed instructions to the other agents who were still following the terrorists.

"Hi, I'm Eddie, Eddie Pop, like in the soda, you know soda pop."

Haruko was dazed and just beginning to regain her focus as she looked at the obviously hyper man with his hand thrust out for her to shake. "Are you okay? I was kind of worried about you. You know you've been out for almost fifteen minutes. I didn't think I hit you that hard. I hope that doesn't bruise."

Haruko pulled her hand back quickly. "You're the one who hit me?"

"It was all I could think to do under the circumstances," Eddie replied.

Suddenly it all came back to Haruko. "I was being kidnapped," she said to no one in particular. "How did you know?"

"I saw that guy with a gun threaten you, while that other man grabbed your arm from behind. Did you notice their two friends waiting outside in the car? I wasn't sure what to do, so I decided to hit you. I saw it in a Crocodile Dundee movie once. You know when Dundee had to shoot..."

"Would you be quiet for a minute?" Haruko said tersely, interrupting Eddie in mid-sentence. Haruko looked around. "Where am I now? I need to meet someone."

"I don't think it's too safe for you to be wandering the streets of Phuket. I brought you here to my boat. My dive boat. I'm a diver. I'm Eddie, Eddie Pop." Eddie stuck his hand out again, "like in....."

34

Haruko interrupted Eddie before he could finish. "I know," Haruko responded as she shook his hand, "like in soda pop."

"Yeah, yeah, that's right," said Eddie as his grin grew wider.

"Now please take me back to my hotel," demanded Haruko sternly, yet politely. Eddie was about to explain why that would not be possible when a huge explosion echoed through the city and a fireball could be seen with a small mushroom shape cloud forming above it.

"That was a big explosion, a really big explosion!" said Eddie in awe. Immediately his cell phone began to ring. "No shit! Were any of our people hurt? How many do you think were killed? Good. It's still early for dinner. Did you see them do it? Where are they now? Well, just keep an eye on them until we hear differently."

"Just who the hell are you and who do you work for?" Haruko demanded, but this time not so politely.

"I'm sorry you had to hear that conversation. Now I have to kill you." A look of panic came over Haruko and she swung fiercely with her right fist. Eddie jumped backwards and the blow glanced off of his chin. "Relax, relax, I'm just joking. It was just a joke, alright? Relax? Jeez, can't you take a joke?"

"Well, I didn't find it too funny. Now tell me who the hell you are and what is going on? What was that phone call about and what was that explosion?"

"Let's start with the easy question first," replied Eddie. "That explosion was the Aioka's Restaurant being blown into nonexistence. It and everybody inside of it! Fortunately, it's way too early for most people to be eating dinner in Phuket, so not many patrons were killed. Mostly just the staff. And thank goodness not you. If I'm not mistaken, you had a 6:15 reservation, did you not?"

Haruko looked at her watch. It was 6:25. She would have been one of those unfortunate diners had she made her dinner reservation. "Did the explosion kill the entire kitchen staff as well?"

"I can't say for certain, but my sources tell me there is nothing left but a crater where the restaurant used to be," Eddie responded.

Haruko was dumbfounded. She knew the explosion was meant to keep her from talking to Hiroshi. "God, it was meant to kill me," Haruko thought to herself. "How did they know I was here in Phuket to see Hiroshi? Taka and the Red Summit must be behind this." "Just who the hell do you work for? Who are these so-called sources?" Haruko asked Eddie again.

Things weren't quite going the way Eddie expected they would or should go. He knew he did the right thing by saving Haruko from the terrorists, but he wasn't sure how much he should he tell her. At least for right now! Should they have stopped the bombing of the restaurant or could they have even prevented it? Eddie was sure they could have stopped it by taking out the four terrorists at the hotel, but that would have blown the entire CIA operation here in Thailand. "Not a good thing," Eddie said to himself.

"What's not a good thing?" Haruko said interrupting Eddie's thoughts.

"You returning to your hotel would not be a good thing. Those men are probably waiting for you there. We have got to get you out of Phuket."

Haruko stared at Eddie, trying to decide just who he was and what was going on. Eddie was about six feet tall, excellent physical condition, and very tan. "That was probably from being on the water so much," Haruko thought to herself. "Actually, not too bad looking if you like the shaggy-haired, blond surfer type." Haruko didn't care much for the surfer type. Especially one so cocky! Haruko stood up and pretended to lose her balance. When Eddie reached out to steady her, Haruko grabbed his arm and flipped him to the ground, putting him in a control position with his windpipe in jeopardy of being crushed.

"Now would you please tell me who you work for and why I'm here before I crush your larynx," Haruko said in her most pleasant voice yet. Eddie pretended he couldn't breathe and started gasping for air. Haruko loosened her grip just enough to allow Eddie to reverse the hold and gain control over Haruko.

"You are a live one, and pretty, just like Jotty said," Eddie told Haruko as he released his grip on her neck, "but a little too compassionate! You should never have loosened your grip the way you did. If I was a bad guy, I could have killed you."

"Who's to say you're not a bad guy?" Haruko replied tersely. "What does Jotty have to do with this? Do you work for Jotty?"

"Let me just say Jotty and I, by a happenstance of politics, are momentarily working for the same organization."

36

"So you got stuck in the NCTC too?" Haruko began to laugh. "You're not FBI though. What are you-- CIA, Military Intelligence?"

"Now there's an oxymoron," Eddie replied. "I'm CIA. Or at least I was CIA, just like Jotty was FBI. Jotty asked me to keep an eye on you while you visited our tropical paradise and it's a good thing I did."

Are there others watching out for me too? Or are you the only one assigned to my well being? Who were you talking to on the phone?" Haruko had several questions she wanted answered now.

"No, I'm it, Eddie Pop at your service!"

"I know," Haruko replied, "just like the soda." Eddie smiled.

"That phone call came from one of my dive buddies who I have help me out now and again. He followed the men who tried to kidnap you after they left the hotel. They went to that restaurant that just blew up and dropped off a few packages. Needless to say, we now know what was in those packages. They were probably hoping you would be there for the fireworks, especially since they missed you at the hotel. I guess they're going to be very disappointed. By the way, who were those men?" Eddie asked, pretending to be clueless.

"Don't bullshit me, Eddie. You know damn well who those men were. They were terrorists working for The Red Summit."

"I thought you and Jotty put an end to that Red Summit group last year in Los Angeles. At least that's the rumor I heard."

Haruko just glared at Eddie. "Okay, okay, settle down. Yes, I had an idea they were terrorists but I didn't know anything about The Red Summit connection." Eddie had to be careful with what he said so as not to let Jotty know he was still working for the CIA. He knew everything he said was about to be screamed at Jotty from Haruko. "Don't blame me, I was just doing my job. Here's a secure satellite phone. Go call Jotty if you want more information. He's the boss."

Haruko grabbed the phone out of Eddie's hand. "Don't think I'm through with you. There's a lot more you are going to have to answer for," Haruko said as she headed out of the cabin and onto the deck for some privacy.

"I sure hope so," Eddie said softly to himself as he stared lustfully at Haruko as she stormed out of the cabin.

# Chapter Four

**"It's just a potato,"** Gladys emphasized and elongated the word "just" as she lectured her husband.

In his best sleazy advertising voice, Howard lifted the potato into the air and took a demur Vanna White pose as he responded with a gleam in his eye, "It's not 'just' a potato. It's much, much more." His voice rose in crescendo as he elongated and emphasized each consecutive word. "This is the new and improved Russian super-tater."

The clerk behind the counter just stared in utter confusion at Howard. Like most Russians she understood no English whatsoever. Gladys laughed out loud at Howard and at the clerk's cold stark reaction to her husband's antics. This was the first sign in three days that Howard was beginning to act his normal silly self. Gladys felt some relief and was able to genuinely laugh along with him. "Maybe his paranoia is beginning to ebb," Gladys thought to herself. Howard had been a nervous wreck since the second day after their arrival in Perm. That was the day they had visited Orphanage #2 in Gajva, just north of Perm. It was one of the orphanages they visited every time they came to Russia on their bi-annual humanitarian missions. They had become friends with several of the workers at the orphanage. Besides the clothes, toys, and hygiene supplies they regularly brought to the orphans, Howard would always bring the orphanages boxes of fresh fruits and vegetables that he had purchased at the local produce marketplace in Perm. Even in the winter, Howard was able to find fresh fruit and vegetables shipped from the most southern reaches of Europe and Asia. That was the greatest treat the orphans could wish for. Rarely did the Russian bureaucracy supply the orphanages with any fresh fruit or vegetables. If the orphanage wanted those, it was up to the orphanage to purchase the items themselves. The budget always seemed to have no room at all for such an extravagance. Howard's generosity in supplying these treasured commodities had made him the best friend of every cook in every orphanage the team would visit. The cook at Gajva Orphanage #2 was no exception. Over the years the cook and Howard had become quite good friends. That was what had led to Howard's present paranoid state. That was the day the cook gave Howard the potato.

"Hadn't you better finish paying for your purchase there, Vanna?" Gladys said jokingly to her husband, although she couldn't understand why Howard would pay such a premium price for a large seven-piece matryoshka that he could easily get for one fourth the price at the marketplace in Moscow. Actually, she was rather surprised Howard was even able to find such an item in Perm. This was not your typical tourist city with your typical tourist items. In fact, this was the first store they had ever seen in Perm that carried tourist items. This store even carried postcards, though none of them featured pictures of any Perm attractions. As if there were any! They were in one of the many Perm shopping complexes that were pretty much indistinguishable from all the others. It was the first floor of a large seven story building with several small shops, kiosks, and tiny designated areas where various vendors all plied their wares. On the upper floors of the building were other small businesses and stores that dealt in computers, appliances, travel, insurance, shipping, and a variety of other services any up-and-coming free trade economy needed. That was what had brought Howard to this particular complex. He needed to ship his new matryoshka to the United States as quickly as possible and, if Howard's ability to read Russian was correct, there was a FedEx shipper on the third floor.

Howard pulled a wad of rubles out of his pocket and paid the clerk the exorbitant price she had demanded without question. This made Gladys begin to worry again, but she knew better than to question her husband in the store. Howard was normally not the sort of person to spend money frivolously. In fact, he was considered by most people to be quite frugal.

"I will need that in a box so I can ship it," he explained to the clerk in broken Russian. The clerk sighed as though feeling very put out, but knew she had taken this tourist for a lot more money than the silly Matryoshka was worth, so she handed Howard a box and didn't even ask for the extra rubles usually charged for bagging or boxing an item. Howard gladly accepted the box, then he and Gladys headed out of the shop.

"I know you probably have a very good reason why you paid so much for that matryoshka," Gladys told her husband, "and I would like to hear it."

"For peace of mind," Howard replied to a now very confused Gladys. "Let's get in the elevator and I will tell you."

Most Russian elevators don't work and haven't worked since before the fall of Communism. As a matter of fact, not much of anything seems to work properly in Russia. Especially elevators! The elevator in this building was the exception to that rule. Someone had managed to scavenge enough parts to keep this elevator functioning, but just barely. You could walk up and down all seven flights of stairs before the elevator traveled three floors. The lighted numbers displayed above the door showed the building to have eighteen floors although, in fact, the building was only seven stories tall. Inside the elevator the control panel had buttons to take you to twenty-four different floors.

"Are you sure you want to get in this thing?" Gladys questioned Howard.

"Of course I'm sure," Howard responded. "Just trust me, I have my reasons."

"Uh, oh," Gladys said to herself. "He's starting to sound paranoid again."

When they got into the elevator and the door closed, Howard pushed the button for the third floor.

"Where are we going?" Gladys asked. "What's going on?"

"I need to mail something," Howard responded. "Here hold this."

Howard opened the matryoshka and removed all inside pieces of the doll and handed them to Gladys. "Hide those in the bag." He ordered her. Gladys did as she was told. Next, Howard pulled the potato from his pocket and placed it inside the large matryoshka. He then pulled out a letter he had written and placed it inside the box with the potato. He grabbed some tape he had hidden in Gladys' shopping bag and sealed the matryoshka closed. Then he wrapped the matryoshka in some newspaper and placed it in the box the clerk had given to him.

As Gladys watched, she was at first more upset at her husband's paranoia. Then she realized that maybe sending the potato away also meant sending her husband's paranoia away. She began to feel relieved that things would soon possibly return to normal.

"Are you sending it back to our house in Canada?" Gladys asked.

"No! No, I think that would be too dangerous. I need to send it to someone who can analyze it for me and tell me what makes a

40

potato so damn important that we are being followed because of it," Howard responded.

Even Gladys had to agree that indeed someone did seem to have been following them for the past two days. She had noticed a car follow them from the center where they were staying, at the orphanages and then back to the center. She had also seen the same car follow them to the shopping mall today.

"I'm sending it to my nephew Jim in Hawaii. He works for the USDA and will be able to have it checked out," Howard replied. "I just can't understand how a potato could last so long without spoiling." Gladys was about to ask more questions when Howard continued, "I just hope they don't ask me to open it at the FedEx shop."

The elevator door finally opened and Howard and Gladys headed into the store. "Let me do the talking," said Gladys. "You sound too suspicious when you are trying to hide something." Howard had to agree with that. He could never be a poker player because he was the worst bluffer in the world.

"Do you speak English?" Gladys asked the clerk, even though she knew someone there had to be able to speak English if they were a worldwide shipper.

"Yes, a little bit," the clerk responded in halting and heavily accented English.

"We need to ship these two matryoshkas. They had a box for the big one," Gladys explained as she opened the box and folded back the newspaper so the clerk could see what it was then wrapped it back up, "but I will need a box for this one," she continued explaining as she pulled the inside matryoshka dolls from her bag. As she did so, she pulled the outside doll apart spilling the assorted inner dolls out on the counter in hopes of both irritating and distracting the clerk at the same time. Her ploy worked and the clerk paid no further attention to the already wrapped matryoshka.

"I want to send the big one to Hawaii, USA, and this smaller one to Canada," Gladys explained to the clerk as the clerk wrapped, then typed, the information into a computer. Gladys was relieved when the clerk placed the big box in an official FedEx shipping container and stuck the label on the package.

The clerk passed the receipt for the cost to Gladys who almost called the whole thing off when she saw it was costing them almost

700 Canadian dollars to ship the two packages. Howard saw her hesitate, but he grabbed her hand and gave her a wink. She tried to smile as Howard reached into his pocket and removed the money from his wallet.

"How long will it take for those packages to reach their destinations?" Howard asked the clerk in Russian.

"Six to nine days," the clerk replied in English. "More likely nine days for the one going to Hawaii," she continued as she stared towards the doorway. Howard and Gladys turned quickly when the two other men entered the FedEx office. One was dressed shoddily and looked to be of Chechnyan decent. The other appeared to be Asian and was dressed in Levi's and an expensive Polo shirt. The clerk showed much disdain when they walked in. Chechnyans are much despised in most of Russia. In Perm they seem to be a little more tolerated than in other parts of Russia, but are still thought of as second-class. The Asian man looked very out of place. For even though the Ural Mountains were the dividing point between Europe and Asia, few Asians were seen in this part of Russia. Howard and Gladys' initial fear subsided when they realized neither of these men could be the man they thought had been following them.

"We will be home before the package gets there." Gladys turned back to her husband and said. "Oh well," she continued, "at least it's over with."

Howard stuffed the two receipts into his pocket and he and Gladys headed out of the shop. This time they decided to take the stairs.

Howard and Gladys Rikey had been coming to orphanages in the Perm area of Russia since the fall of Communism. Howard was a retired professor of Sociology from the University of Alberta in Edmonton. Gladys had spent her life as a housewife, Sunday school teacher, and as the local piano teacher. They first came to Russia as part of a church mission to help orphans in the areas around Moscow. They soon learned hundreds of churches sent teams of missionaries to these areas. They were easily accessible by road from Moscow and safe to travel to. The real need was in the more remote Ural mountain region. That was where many of the prisoners who had been shipped off to Siberia settled after their release. It was a very poor area with severe alcohol, unemployment, and unplanned pregnancy problems.

That is why there were so many orphanages scattered throughout the region. Hundreds of them in fact! So that is where Howard and Gladys ended up volunteering their time. Every summer and winter they would join a team of missionaries from churches around Canada and come to the Perm region to work at the orphanages. Sometimes they actually did physical work, but mostly it was just holding and caring for babies and children who had no one else to love them. It was a life-changing experience.

Perm was a thirty hour train ride from Moscow. Unless of course you caught the express train and then it was only a twenty-five hour trip. It was possible to fly into Perm, but taking the train was a whole lot cheaper and probably a whole lot safer than flying. Aeroflot is not known for their safety record or their maintenance standards, though it is said Russian pilots are the best in the world.

When the fall of Communism occurred, somebody forgot to let the people in and around Perm know about it. There is still a mistrust of authority in the hearts of most of the people. Checkpoints are still active throughout the countryside. The infrastructure is crumbling as are the state-built apartment high-rises that dominate the landscape. Driving the roads and expressways in and around Perm is a death-defying act. There is no skilled labor. The only people making money are those affiliated with organized crime. But worst of all…, nobody smiles. You really cannot blame them for not smiling. They have no reason to. Several families are crammed into tiny two-bedroom apartments that rarely have hot water or heat. In fact, many don't even have consistent-running water. The buildings themselves are unsafe and in danger of collapsing. Huge blocks of cement can be seen missing from the sides of buildings. Balconies are crumbling with some dangling precariously, held only by pieces of rebar that are dangerously close to rusting through. The unemployment rate is staggering and there are hardly any social services provided. What is provided is alcohol. Lots of alcohol! Any time of the day or night you can find dozens of people wandering the streets drinking or lying on the sidewalk passed out from drinking. It has become an epidemic that affects the young and old alike. With nothing to do but wander the streets and drink, the youth have made baby proliferation their pastime. Hence, the drastic increase in orphanages. With no social agencies preaching birth control and with the orphanages sending their charges back to the streets when they turn fifteen, the problem increases exponentially. Alcohol-damaged babies making more alcohol-damaged babies.

That was up until five years ago. That was just about the time Howard started to notice a change in the ratio of boys to girls in the baby orphanages. With every trip he and Gladys made to Perm, he had noticed a decreasing number of male babies being given up to the orphanages. Howard was both troubled and intrigued by this statistic. He first tried to find out if it the same thing was happening all over Russia or if it was a localized phenomenon. Acquiring that information was difficult, but Howard's background as a sociologist made the task somewhat easier. It did draw some unwanted attention to him from the Russian bureaucracy and made getting his humanitarian visa renewed a little difficult a couple of years back. That was solved simply by obtaining a new passport and sending his visa application to a different embassy. There is not much networking yet between the Russian embassies on such non-priority items. What he did discover was that the decreasing birthrate of male babies was a regional phenomenon and not just limited to the Perm region. It was much more significant in the breakaway republic areas of Russia than it was in the Perm region. Howard had acquired much of his information from missionaries like himself doing work in orphanages in those areas. Something was up, but Howard wasn't sure what was causing this sudden change in population growth. He speculated about several possible natural explanations, looked into chemical or nuclear contamination possibilities, but up until three days ago had given no thought to any conspiracy theories. That was the day the cook at Gajva Orphanage #2 gave Howard the potato and told him a most peculiar story.

When Howard and Gladys reached the first floor of the shopping mall, the rest of their team were already in the Mercedes van waiting for them. The Mercedes seemed to be the van of choice for the humanitarian organizations. They held up well to the disintegrating Russian roads. They also had large windows all around, giving the passengers and driver an awesome view of the incredible Ural Mountain countryside. But more likely, because they were expensive and the only decent vehicle available, the missionary organizations seemed to come up with the money to buy them.

Howard could tell something was wrong as they approached the van. The team leader was outside talking on his cell phone and looked very distressed at whatever was being told to him over the phone. Right as Howard and Gladys arrived, he ended his call and opened the van's side sliding door to speak to the team.

"I'm afraid I have some tragic news I must tell you," he said softly with pained eyes. "It seems there has been a horrific fire at Orphanage #2 in Gajva this morning. Many of the orphans were killed as well as several of the workers there."

Stunned cries and moans came from the team members. "My God," Howard said not thinking. "How did it happen? What can we do to help?"

"I don't know if there is anything we can do right now," the leader continued, "but we do have the clothes and food we were going to deliver to Mosni. Maybe we should take them to Gajva to see if they are needed there. It's possible everything was lost in the fire and the orphans now have nothing but the clothes they were wearing."

The team members nodded their agreement and it was decided they would return to Gajva to see if they could be of any help there. As the Mercedes van pulled away, the two men who had been following the team for the past three days jumped into their BMW sedan and began to follow the van. Howard was too pre-occupied as to whether his friends at the orphanage were still alive to notice the men continuing to follow them. He had also forgotten all about the potato.

As the van crossed the Kama River, it turned right off of highway P242 and followed the river road as it wound its way through the birch tree forest. In this part of the Ural Mountains, the rolling hills are covered with a thick dense forest of birch. The roads are hacked out of this forest, as are the villages and cities interspersed throughout. There are few if any signs distinguishing one road from another and, in fact, few roads seemed to even be named. They just exist. You relate your destination to the village it is nearest to and drive using landmarks to find it, if indeed you are lucky enough to ever find it. At least on the first or second try!

The team passed several crossroads where local vendors stood along the road selling firewood and switches for the banyas or freshly caught fish from one of the many streams and rivers in the area. Some of these crossroads were nothing more than dirt roads heading to secret fishing spots along the Kama or Silver River. Others were well-paved and hid secret military installations no one was welcome to visit. The team had traveled this road often and more than once was caught up in the traffic of some military convoy. Last summer it provided them quite a bit of amusement as they were stuck for almost half an hour behind a military personnel transport truck carrying several uniformed soldiers carrying machineguns, drinking vodka, and playing a gigantic tuba. At first it was worrisome because vodka and machine guns don't seem to really go well together and everyone seemed a little uncomfortable staring back and forth at each other. Then Howard offered them some beef jerky to go along with their vodka and they in turn entertained the missionaries by playing the tuba. A pretty funny interaction between two cultures that not many years back were sworn enemies. At least the two governments made it sound as if they were enemies.

"There must be a checkpoint up ahead," Sasha the driver informed the team. "Watch the car approaching us. See how he flashes his headlights. He's warning us about a military checkpoint ahead. The people still fear and hate the government. You would think with the fall of Communism they would stop harassing their own people."

Most of the team already knew about the checkpoint signal, because they had been signaled the warning by angry citizens and required to stop at them dozens of times before. Usually nothing came of the checkpoint stops and often the van was waved through without being checked or even so much as stopped, but every so often the van was stopped and searched. Sometimes a small bribe was needed to speed up the passport check by the soldiers so the team could quickly continue on their way. It was just part of life as it had been for generations in this part of Russia.

As the van approached the checkpoint, two soldiers signaled the van to pull to the side and stop behind a military transport truck. The BMW that had been following the van pulled ahead and stopped about fifty yards further up the road where the driver had a rather animated conversation with what appeared to be the officer in charge of the checkpoint. The officer seemed upset and walked away from the BMW and made a call on his radio. Moments later he returned to the BMW and saluted. The driver returned the salute and the BMW headed on down the road. The officer-in-charge called several of his men over to talk with them. Many of them glanced down at the Mercedes van as the officer spoke to them.

46

"What do you think the holdup is?" Gladys asked the team leader.

"Probably some kind of training exercise. One thing for sure, these are not your typical weekend warriors we usually see out here," the leader responded.

"You mean like those ones we were stuck behind last summer on this road?" Howard answered.

"Yeah," the leader laughed. "The tuba, vodka, and machineguns-don't-mix soldiers." Then his voice took a more serious tone. "No, these are the first line goose-stepping soldiers like those you see outside the Kremlin in Moscow. These guys don't fool around."

As he spoke, eight of the soldiers boarded the truck parked in front of the van. One of the officers walked up to Sasha and explained in Russian that maneuvers were taking place up ahead and the van would be escorted through by the truck in front of them. They were also told they may have to stop a few times in the next ten kilometers. Just stay behind the truck in front of them and be prepared to stop.

As the truck and van pulled away, two other military vehicles pulled out of a side road and blocked the river road from the direction the van had been coming. Sasha noticed this in his mirror and informed the team leader about what was taking place behind them. Sasha spoke in Russian so as to not worry the team members. Howard spoke enough Russian to understand Sasha was concerned about something behind them and he turned to see what was going on but said nothing. The soldiers at the checkpoint were now forcing cars to turn around and head back towards Perm. The winding road quickly turned and Howard could no longer see the checkpoint behind them and it appeared no other cars were following behind them either.

The team sat silently as the van followed the slow moving truck. It wasn't as if anyone didn't have anything they wanted to say or ask. It was just that it felt as if the world needed to be silent for a few minutes. It felt like everyone was being given a moment to reflect on their life and what they had accomplished in that life. It was as if the whole world was holding its breath.

The soldiers in the back of the truck sat rigid on the side benches looking straight ahead and not speaking. Each held an automatic rifle on his lap in the identical position as the soldier next to him. The truck began to slow as it approached the BMW parked sideways across both lanes. Someone in the front of the truck moved a curtain and spoke to the soldiers seated in the back. Immediately the soldiers were off of the benches and out of the truck before it had come to a complete stop. They moved to the right-hand side of the road next to the Mercedes as it came to a stop.

"Please turn off your engine while we wait," One of the officers called to Sasha. The passenger from the BMW approached and stood next to the front passenger side of the military truck. The silence screamed louder as time seemed to slow down, almost coming to a stop. Several members of the team sensed what was about to happen and began to pray. The man from the BMW nodded his head slightly and the bullets began to tear through the side windows and steel frame door of the Mercedes van, ripping into the bodies of the missionaries inside with a series of rapid sucking thud sounds. In a manner of seconds it was all over. The eight missionaries along with their team leader and driver lay sprawled chaotically in the van. The entire interior of the van was awash in blood and the silence of the birch forest deep in the Ural Mountains once again began to scream.

The man from the BMW, Viktor Cheznov, was on the phone giving further instructions even as the noise of the last rounds fired by the soldiers echoed off the birch trees. Within moments a white produce truck came from around the trees following the bend in the road. Written on the side of the truck in Russian were the words "fresh vegetables". The license plate identified the truck as coming from the Chechnyan region. Two soldiers were in the front of the truck and the back roll-up door was chained and locked. The truck pulled to a stop in front of the Mercedes van as if it was there to block it from trying to escape. One of the officers unlocked the padlock holding the chain, while the soldiers who had been along the side of the van now positioned themselves behind the produce truck with their machineguns raised and ready to fire. The soldiers who had done the initial shooting of the Mercedes passengers returned to their truck to retrieve new weapons, piling the still warm automatic rifles they had just used to assassinate the missionaries near the front of the troop carrier truck.

The rear door to the truck opened and one of the guards yelled for the occupants to exit the truck. Very hesitantly three men and one woman, all Chechnyan, jumped down to the ground and stood silently

48

in a state of confusion shielding their eyes from the sudden bright sunlight. Finally, one of them spoke.

"What, what do you want from us? We've done nothing wrong. We are but peasants that came to the marketplace to sell our cucumbers and potatoes."

Viktor had strolled leisurely from his BMW to where the peasants stood.

"Well, how fortunate it is then we have found you. We need someone with knowledge of potatoes to assist us. Tragically, terrorists have just murdered these unfortunate visitors to our great republic. It seems they had something the terrorists needed. A potato!" Viktor smiled a very evil smile. "My men do not wish to soil their uniforms with all of that messy blood. So we need you to search through the van and find us the potato the terrorists were after."

The peasants stared in disbelief back and forth between the arrogant Russian standing before them and the bloodied bodies of the missionaries inside the Mercedes. The scene made no sense. Why would anyone commit such an atrocity over a potato? How could a potato be worth all of this? A feeling of impending doom came over the peasants.

"What if we refuse?" responded the peasant who seemed to have been put in charge by default.

"You don't wish to do that," Viktor replied. "That would make things so very unpleasant for all of us. Besides, you may take whatever money and jewelry you find on those poor souls. Just find me the potato and any cameras, film, or paperwork that may still be in one piece. Once I have my potato you are free to go. So please give us a hand. My men need to head out to try to catch whoever is responsible for this ugly massacre."

The Chechnyan peasants realized if they wanted to survive, they really had no choice and grudgingly agreed to search the van for the potato. They knew their chances of survival were still slim at best for no terrorists had done this. This was done by the cold, ruthless Russian standing before them. They all knew this to be true. What was hardest for them to understand was why anyone would kill so many for just one worthless potato.

"You might find your task to be easier if you first remove the bodies from the van," Viktor suggested. "That way you can search each one individually and then have room to search the van."

As distasteful of a task as it was, the leader of the Chechnyans agreed with Viktor and grabbed the arm of the passenger closest to the side-sliding door of the van. It was a female who had been riddled with bullets. As she was pulled from the van, the wounds from the bullets in her abdomen caused her bowels to pour out onto the Chechnyan leader's shoes. He in turn vomited as he stumbled to his left and fell to the ground next to the first lifeless body. He stared at Viktor with contempt. No one else made a move.

"Well, what are you waiting for?" Viktor demanded. "Search her pockets and drag the rest of those bodies out of there."

Slowly the Chechnyans started the arduous task of dragging the bodies from the Mercedes and searching through the pockets and bags of the bloodied corpses. As they were told they could do, they removed the rings, watches, bracelets and necklaces from the dead missionaries. All papers that were found in the pockets or purses were turned over to one of the soldiers who wore latex medical gloves. The soldier stood next to Viktor and would read aloud the contents of the paper and then place it in a box as Viktor commanded. At least the papers that were not too soaked in blood! Those blood-soaked papers that Viktor had were placed by the peasants in a plastic bag. He would instruct his staff to analyze those papers back at the laboratory after they had dried.

When they pulled Howard's body from the van, his clothes were completely saturated in blood. One of the Chechnyans reached into his front pocket to see if it held any papers. The Chechnyan's hand had to force the sticky pocket apart, in turn making a sickening sucking sound.

"There's no potato in this poor soul's pockets!" the Chechnyan said under his breath. He looked at Howard's other pocket and decided there would be no potato in that pocket either. Nor would there be any papers that needed to be removed. Howard's pants were so soaked in blood the peasant chose not to place his hand into Howard's other front pocket, thus he failed to find the shipping receipts that were pasted with blood to the inside of the pocket. He did manage to remove the Seiko watch from Howard's wrist along with Howard's wedding ring. He removed the wallet from Howard's back pocket and handed it to one of the Russian soldiers standing next to Viktor. Fortunately for Viktor, Howard died lying on his stomach and bled out onto the front of his clothes leaving his back pocket and his wallet relatively free of blood. The soldier removed the money and handed it to the Chechnyan who smiled and placed it in his own pocket. The soldier then placed the wallet into the box of papers to be searched at a later date.

Once the bodies were clear of the Mercedes van, the peasants searched the interior but were unable to find any potato. As the search lingered on, Viktor became more anxious and surlier. Viktor eventually realized no potato would be found and ordered the peasants out of the van.

The Chechnyan peasants stood solemnly by the pile of massacred bodies along the side of the road. Viktor paced back and forth in a furious anger at not having found what he was seeking. The soldiers remained silent with their rifles at the ready as Viktor ranted quietly to himself. Then suddenly Viktor stopped his pacing and turned and smiled at the peasants.

"Thank you for your help," he said politely. "I apologize for bringing you here to perform such a ghastly task, but I hope the spoils you removed from these poor victims will be adequate compensation. The Russian Federation thanks you for your assistance and you are now free to leave."

The Chechnyan peasants stood staring dumbfounded at Viktor. Were they really going to be allowed to leave?

"We are going to need your truck for a little longer. We will need it to transport the bodies back to the city. So I would suggest you leave on foot. In fact, I think you had better run as fast as you can for the woods before I change my mind."

The Chechnyans looked at each other puzzled as what to do next.

"I really think you should run," Viktor repeated as a smile began to grow across his face. The peasants still didn't move.

"RUN NOW!" Viktor screamed at the dazed peasants.

The three men broke into a run heading straight for the thick birch forest not fifty feet from where they stood. The female peasant burst into tears and fell wailing to the ground. Viktor pulled his Yarygin "Skyph mini' pistol from its holster. He kicked the woman and told her to look at him. As she raised her head, Viktor fired one shot directly into her left eye killing her instantly. The three men did not look back. They knew what had happened to their friend and understood the slightest hesitation could cost them their lives.

Before the three remaining peasant men were halfway to the forest, the soldiers opened fire. The Chechnyans bodies were ripped apart by the barrage of automatic weapon fire.

Then once again, the forest screamed its silence.

"Place the rifles used to kill the missionaries in the hands of the Chechnyans." Viktor ordered. The soldiers did as they were told.

"Today you are heroes," Viktor told the soldiers. "You killed the Chechnyan rebels who so savagely murdered these foreign missionaries."

Two men had appeared with cameras. One was taking digital still photos of the grisly scene, while the other made a video recording of Viktor's speech to the soldiers.

"Make sure you edit my face out of that video," Viktor ordered the cameraman. "And I want to see all of the still photos before anyone else."

Both the men nodded their understanding.

"Clean up this scene and bring the bodies and the Mercedes back to the laboratory. We need to get this road back open," ordered Viktor.

Viktor stared at the commotion taking place in front of him, but heard only the silence of the forest. He sensed his problems were greater than they presently seemed. Viktor knew somewhere in this mess he would find what he was looking for and he was sure it was not the potato. He turned and entered his waiting BMW as his cell phone began to ring.

# Chapter Five

**"Who passed gas?"** the teacher asked and several students began to laugh. "No, I'm serious, whoever is passing gas needs to step outside. It smells terrible in here."

Several of the students started to complain about the acrid odor as well.

"Somebody better cut it out or I'm going to kick their ass." One of the classroom bullies shouted out. Several students began to complain they were going to throw up. The odor was getting worse and worse. The teacher told one of the students to open the back door while he went to the front door and opened it.

"Jesus Christ! It smells even worse outside," the student shouted to the teacher.

"There must be a gas leak somewhere," the teacher told the class, trying to remain calm. "Shut the door and I'll call the office." Several students were starting to panic and a couple of students were very close to throwing up. Just as the teacher picked up the phone, the fire alarm sounded. That meant everyone needed to head to the field immediately. Most teachers and students routinely ignored the warning bells. They were always going off by accident or being set off by some prankster.

"This is stupid," the teacher remarked. "They want us to go outside where the gas leak is even worse. I guess that is better than getting blown up in here." That's all the teacher needed to say. Instantly, the students were out of their seats and headed out the door into an even more potent odor. Several students started cursing and complaining while a few even began to gag the smell was so bad.

Outside on the street in front of the school sat a non-descript white delivery van. The van was solid with no windows except for the driver and passenger door and the windshield, but even these were heavily tinted. On the top of the van, in a strip along the center, were several scientific weather instruments. These were impossible to see from ground level, but very apparent if you were looking down on the van from above. These instruments were capable of reading the exact wind speed and direction in real time and could record the slightest changes. It also read barometric pressure, temperature, humidity, and several other random weather-related observations. There was also one of the most sophisticated E-nose's available with the most sensitive sensors yet invented. The electronic nose had been around a long time, but NASA engineers had recently taken its capabilities to a whole new level. Twenty other identical vans were located throughout the Los Angeles basin. An additional eighteen vans were located in the San Fernando Valley and the Pomona Valley. There were even other vans located in all of the passes that led out of the Southern California region. Each of these vans had identical equipment and was equipped with synchronized computerized clocks accurate to the millisecond. All of this data from the mobile labs would then be compared to the information gathered by the fixed E-noses located throughout the city. Most were in the port area and downtown Los Angeles, but with the monies finally filtering in to all the areas in southern California, other cities were beginning to install their own E-noses. Even many industrial plants were using the new technology in hopes of avoiding potentially devastating mishaps in the workplace. Even with all the devises now in place, there was no software technology to interface them to create a viable warning system.

Even as all of the classes made their way out of the classrooms and to the physical education field, the odor had begun to dissipate. It was as though an invisible toxic cloud had just passed through the school and community, then headed inland to the next city. Which, in actuality, was exactly what was occurring and what was expected to happen. The only difference was it wasn't a toxic cloud, just a smelly one. A United States Navy ship lying just outside the Long Beach Harbor released a large quantity of Mercaptan. Mercaptan is the chemical added to natural gas and gives it the odor. Without Mercaptan, natural gas is odorless and almost impossible to detect until it explodes in your face or knocks you out and kills you.

This was the third release of the gas in the past two years in the Los Angeles area. It was always big news in all the local papers, after the fact. Each time it was blamed on an accidental release of the gas at some unnamed facility in the harbor area. And everybody was supposed to believe that! Most people probably didn't care enough to give it a second thought. Nobody was hurt, no reason to worry. It was just one of those industrial accidents that seem to happen daily in Los Angeles. Even though nobody came out and said it, there were the conspiracy theorists who knew it was some secret government experiment designed to control the minds of the masses. They really weren't too far off in their theory. It was a secret government experiment designed to see how vulnerable Southern California was to a chemical or biological attack. The possibility of using these findings in controlling the population was definitely not being overlooked by certain sectors of the government intelligence agencies. In reality the real purpose wasn't a big secret. The same tests were being conducted in New York City. They admitted what the purpose of the experiment was and even warned police, schools, and city agencies before the test took place. For some reason, the powers that be thought the residents of California either didn't need to know, or shouldn't know, the true reason for the Mercaptan release.

In spite of this semi-secrecy, it was still possible for just about anyone, at least anyone with the right connections, to get a copy of the results of these tests. Taka had these connections. He knew that with the usual Catalina Eddy shore breeze it took only five hours for the gas to travel from San Pedro to San Bernardino and only four hours for it to reach Woodland Hills. Traces of the gas would eventually reach all the desert regions and valleys that surrounded all of Southern California. Taka smiled when he received the results of the latest test. He knew it was only a matter of time.

## Chapter Six

**"Bam, bam, bam!"**

"Go away!"

"Bam, bam, bam!" The pounding continued. "Wake u-u-up," someone said in a sing-song voice.

"I said go away," Jim answered as he shook his head trying to get the champagne that clouded his mind to allow him to clearly focus. Actually Jim was amazed how well he felt after drinking so much champagne. "Maybe $200 a bottle champagne doesn't give you nearly the hangover that $2 a bottle champagne does."

"Wake up Jimbo, it's me." Jim jumped out of bed and pulled on his pants.

Emma smiled coyly at Jim as he got dressed.

"The last person who called me Jimbo got punched in the mouth," Jim yelled at the voice on the other side of the door. Jim quickly flung open the door and swung savagely at the person who so rudely awakened him. Unfortunately, for Jim, the visitor was expecting just such a move and sidestepped to avoid the punch. He then planted a solid jab into Jim's stomach doubling Jim over, knocking him back into the room.

"Hello Jotty," Jim gasped as he tried to get his breath back. "Long time no see. Seems you are in a little better shape than I remember since the last time I saw you."

"A little quicker too, don't you think?" Jotty replied, laughing as he entered the stateroom.

"Emma, I would like you to meet my good friend, Jotty Joplin. I've been told he's some kind of honcho with the NCTC back in Virginia these days." Emma had pulled the covers of the bed up to her neck frightened by the exchange of punches between the two supposed friends. "Jotty, this is Emma, Lady Farrelton's handmaiden."

"Pleased to meet you sir," Emma answered sheepishly. "You will forgive me if I don't get up."

"That's okay," Jotty replied, "I can wait," he said with a smile, then sat down and paused as if waiting for her to rise. "Just kidding!" Jotty said and laughed as he stood back up, "it's a pleasure to meet you also."

"So this is how the really rich live," Jotty said as he looked around the lavish Presidential stateroom of *the Grand Maui*.

"Yeah, I know it's a tough life, but I guess I have to suffer through living in these conditions," Jim replied trying to sound serious.

"In your dreams, buddy!" Jotty responded. "That's for sure" Jim replied and they both laughed.

"By the way," Jotty remembered, "the Captain told me to let Emma know a helicopter will be here in…," Jotty looked at his watch, " oh my, in just twenty minutes. It's to take you to join Lady Farrelton at the naval base in Pearl Harbor."

"Oh my goodness," Emma replied, "I must get prepared at once." She leaped out of bed oblivious to the fact she was still naked and ran through the suite and through the door to the adjoining room.

Jim and Jotty just looked at each other and smiled.

"Welcome to *the Grand Maui*, Jotty. The most luxurious ship cruising this part of the high seas," Jim spoke up.

"I want to know just how the hell you can afford this rich man's paradise?" Jotty asked in amazement.

"I'm here as a favor for Haruko. You know that! I'm sure she told you."

"Yeah I know," Jotty answered, sounding rather frustrated. "I do a lot of things for that girl too. A lot of things I probably shouldn't do. What can I say, I'm in love,"

"Take a number, buddy. We are both still in love with Haruko," Jim replied.

Jotty wasn't going to dispute that nor was he about to point out the fact Emma just jumped out of Jim's bed. He hadn't exactly been faithful in his love for Haruko when he was back in Washington either. "Do you think either of us really has a chance with her?" Jotty asked Jim.

"Not until she gets this Taka thing settled in her mind. And that may take a while! That's why I'm on this damn ship," Jim answered, sounding put out.

"I know, she told me all about it. It's your fault she's in Thailand right now," Jotty said accusingly.

"What are you talking about? I didn't know she was in Thailand. When did she go there?" Jim asked rather upset.

"Check your e-mail buddy. She left yesterday. Don't worry, I got somebody keeping an eye on her. Nothing's going to happen!"

Jim wasn't so sure. "You should have let me know. Hell, you never even told me about your promotion. I heard about it from Lord Farrelton yesterday. Did Haruko know?"

"She's known for almost a month. I thought for sure she would have told you. But then again, the only reason I knew you were on this boat is because Lord Farrelton contacted the President and the shit hit the fan at my office."

"How the hell does this Lord Farrelton know so much about what's going on around here?" Jim asked.

"You know I asked the same question of my boss. He told me Lord Farrelton, besides being one of the most prominent Royals in Parliament, owns some company that is testing a new invention or weapon in the South Pacific. I heard he is a close personal friend to the President and several of the big dogs in D.C."

"Well that explains why he knew so much about our little run in with the Red Summit last year," Jim replied. "By the way, I hear you got a new boss at the NCTC."

"That's news to me," Said Jotty. "Well that's what I heard from the good Lord Farrelton, so it must be true." They both just shook their heads in disbelief. At that moment Emma rushed out of the adjoining room. Both Jim and Jotty stood as Emma walked over to Jim. It was a very awkward moment. "I truly had a most wonderful evening with you last night, Jim Rikey. I certainly hope we will meet again very soon." Before Jim could respond with his "aw shucks, it was nothing ma'm" Texas drawl, Emma kissed him on the cheek and ran out of the stateroom to catch the now-waiting helicopter.

"You must have made quite an impression on her," Jotty said jokingly as Jim slugged him on the arm.

Jotty and Jim hadn't seen each other since the two of them and Haruko all parted ways last year at the vegan restaurant in Los Angeles. At that time Jotty was still in pretty bad shape trying to recover from the beating he received from Minoru. Since then, he had been working with a physical therapist and several trainers and instructors. He now was in better physical condition than he was when he left the military. Jim had been living on the Big Island supposedly working for the Farm Service, but still spending a lot of time trying to track down the source of the weaponized anthrax. Up until yesterday he was having no success at all. They had both religiously kept in touch with Haruko and she had been fairly good at keeping each of them informed about the other. That is until recently. The past few weeks she seemed to have a renewed focus trying to prove Taka was the real power behind the Red Summit terrorist organization. Officially, both the Japanese and United States governments said the Red Summit was a defunct group and Taka had nothing to do with it. However, several high-ranking officials in both governments believed Haruko was on the right track and pretended not to notice or interfere with her continued investigation.

"You probably guessed the anthrax found on that dive boat is the same weaponized type found at the Paleaka Ranch," Jotty said getting down to business. "I'm here to let you know you are going to be working for me for a while again. The NCTC is now pulling your strings. Finding the source of this anthrax has become a high priority operation. Thanks to Lord Farrelton, I'm sure."

"No doubt!" Jim responded nodding his head in agreement. "We also have an appointment with the good Lord Farrelton at the Navy base at Pearl Harbor. The Navy will be sending a chopper for us within an hour."

"What does he want with us?"

"Jimbo, your guess is as good as mine, but I'm sure whatever he has to say has been cleared with Washington."

"I told you not to call me Jimbo," Jim responded with a feigned anger that made Jotty smile.

"Oh by the way, I'm also bringing in a dive specialist with the CIA to help us out with this anthrax problem. A nice guy. I think you'll like him. Actually, it's the same guy I have keeping an eye on Haruko right now in Thailand. His name is Eddie. Eddie Pop. You know, like the soda."

# Chapter Seven

**It took two days** for the technicians at the Tower of Terror lab in Perm to find the blood-soaked FedEx receipt in Howard's pocket. The U.S. Embassy and the Canadian Embassy in Moscow were very troubled that the Russians refused to release the bodies for so many days. That fact, along with the method of death suffered by the missionaries, caught the attention of several intelligence agencies in the United States. The name Viktor Cheznov also sent up several red flags with the agencies. Viktor had been a very effective agent in the KGB in the old Communist regime in Russia. He was an old school KGB man who was a favorite of Russian President Putin. If Viktor had any part in the investigation of the killing of the missionaries then there was a lot more to the story than the Russians were telling the embassies or the world press.

The Russians found the Mercedes in the Silver River within a few hours after the office staff found the warning light that signaled the tracking device had shorted out. They found the driver's body, but were unable to locate Yuri's body. Determining the method of death for the driver took a little longer. They knew he was murdered and it was assumed Yuri had been kidnapped or ran off on his own. Yuri running off on his own was not too likely. Viktor knew Yuri desired a more western lifestyle than Russia was able to offer him, but Yuri was watched too closely and was too frightened to think up such a scenario on his own. Especially one that involved committing such a gruesome murder as was done to Yuri's driver. No, Yuri would have needed a lot of help to pull something like this off. He had to have been kidnapped. It was something Viktor had feared might happen for a long time. Viktor would have to get a couple of his agents to find out just what had been going on with Yuri the past month. They would have to talk to everybody who worked with Yuri and those who worked with the driver as well. The swallows would also have to be questioned. Viktor knew Yuri was spending a lot of time with the putanka he picked up at the Riverwalk or on Revolution Street. He would have them questioned. Somebody had to know something!

"A tiger shark? Don't be ridiculous. There are no tiger sharks in the Silver River. That's absurd!" Viktor bellowed at the medical technician.

The technician was very afraid of Viktor and rightly so. Viktor was known as an extremely ruthless man with a fiery temper. Someone you would go out of your way to avoid if at all possible. Unfortunately, today that wasn't possible. "As absurd as it sounds," the technician replied weakly, "the tooth fragment we found embedded in the spinal chord is from a tiger shark."

"Are you serious?" Viktor shouted. "Are you seriously telling me a tiger shark is responsible for almost decapitating that man?"

"No, I didn't say that. There are no bite marks of any kind on his neck. It was as if someone sawed his head off with a very sharp but jagged saw. I'm just saying we found part of a tiger shark tooth lodged in his spine. How it got there I can only guess," the technician replied.

"Then please guess. Why do you think the shark tooth is there?" Viktor tried to sound calmer.

"I believe somebody sawed his head off with a saw made out of these tiger shark teeth and one of them caught on the spine and broke. There are signs of blunt trauma on the neck and face. It is possible he was struck on the face first and then the saw teeth were used to rip the neck away. A very messy and bloody way to kill someone! As far as the blow to the face, it appears he was struck by some kind of flat club which broke his jaw. That happened before the neck blow." The technician paused to see if Viktor had any questions. He was feeling a little less scared than when he began. He was confident in his analysis and was beginning to get excited as he anticipated his next comment that he was sure would impress Viktor.

"I actually believe I know what the weapon is. I have a picture of it here to show you." The technician handed the picture he had downloaded from the internet to Viktor.

"That's a nasty looking weapon," Viktor replied. Where is it from and what is it called?"

"I'm not sure of its exact name, but I believe it is sometimes called a Lei O Mano. It was used in the South Pacific islands by ancient warriors in combat. Places like Fiji, Tonga, Hawaii...."

Viktor interrupted, "Did you say Hawaii?" Viktor thought it quite a coincidence Hawaii was also where the potato may have been sent. Either there or Canada according to the two FedEx receipts found. Could the kidnapping of Yuri and the discovery of the GMO potato be linked somehow? It didn't yet make sense to Viktor that they were, but it was worth checking out.

"Yes, they were widely used in Hawaii and even today are available to tourists as souvenirs. Very expensive souvenirs I might add. That picture is of one for sale in an art gallery at the Ritz-Carlton Hotel in Kapalua on Maui. Five thousand dollars!" The technician accented the cost as he spoke. "I cannot even imagine spending that kind of money on such an item. But as you can see from the description, it is a solid piece of Koa wood which has a flat side used for striking an opponent, and the jagged edge made of twenty-three tiger shark teeth for slashing and ripping. A weapon like that is exactly what could have caused those injuries to the driver."

Viktor didn't respond. He was already making his plans to head with a team of agents to Hawaii. Just in case, he would send two of his men to Canada to follow up on the FedEx package there, but his instincts told him Hawaii was where he would find Yuri and the potato.

# Chapter Eight

**It was a brief period of mourning**. A very brief period of mourning! When Taka's wife Niki was killed by the terrorists last year, the people of Japan rallied behind Taka and shared his grief. At least for about three days! That was how long the newspapers kept the story on the front page. Now, Taka was pretty much forgotten. Even the tabloids stopped writing stories about him after only two weeks. With the death of Ono Saito there was no one dedicated to writing the wild speculative stories that had plagued Taka for so long. No longer was he a celebrity warranting the interest of the freelance paparazzi. He had become a person of no interest. That is, a person of no interest to everyone but Haruko. She still devoted most of her free time to keeping tabs on Taka's every move, both his social activities and his business decisions. That did not always prove to be the easiest task for Haruko. Haruko was very dedicated to her job with the National Police and it kept her very busy. Taka was spending more and more of his time outside of Japan. Haruko tried to keep track of his travels and movements as much as possible by accessing his credit card purchases as well as his visa applications and passport usage notifications. She began to religiously read the Yomiuri Shimbun, Tokyo's equivalent of the New York Times, following any possible merger, sale, or acquisition that even remotely mentioned Taka or any of his business holdings, past or present. She had to be careful not to allow her colleagues to know of her activities trying to track Taka. He had been exonerated of any connection to the Red Summit and Haruko had been told officially that Taka was no longer a suspect in any of the past Red Summit terrorist activities, so drop it! That was something Haruko just couldn't do. She had a hard time giving up on anything she believed in. Especially something that had consumed her thoughts for so many years. She was often troubled when she had no idea where Taka was or what he was doing.

Taka, on the other hand, gave little thought to Haruko or the trouble she had once caused him. He was focused on his future terrorist plans and worked diligently at bringing them to fruition. That was until he started receiving reports of her visiting the Aioka restaurants searching for a particular dessert chef. He knew she was looking for Hiroshi. It troubled him to think how his act of kindness in sparing Hiroshi's life could come back to cause him grief. He should have had Minoru kill Hiroshi along with the ship's photographer when he had the opportunity. That was the past and Taka refused to think about errors he had made in the past. He was too busy preparing for the future. A future that would show the world American imperialism was finished. Too long had the robber money barons in the United States pushed around the other countries of the world, raping their resources, enslaving their people, and then leaving them to suffer in poverty and desperation. They even did it to their own people and country. The thought of it was appalling to Taka. How could so few be so greedy? It was this very greed that would allow Taka to launch the next phase of his terrorist plot. The big corporations run by these power brokers controlled the policies of the United States government. Just like with the poor oversight in the cattle industry, there was no oversight in the thriving transgenic seed and food production industry. These large corporations saw to that. There were massive sums of money to be made in the new biotechnology field of genetic modifications of organisms and it was all in the name of humanity. Feeding the starving masses of the world through science. Right!

Taka may not have been the business visionary his brother, the real Taka, had been, but he did have a vision on how he thought the world should be and a plan on how to achieve that vision through terrorism. Like his brother he understood immediate rewards were not always the best rewards. Sometimes true happiness was found when you began the changes that would achieve your goals for future generations to realize. That was what Taka had tried to do with his tainted cosmetics and meat. That is what he would accomplish with the second part of his terror plan. Taka did recognize trends in the world and knew how best to capitalize on them to achieve his terror campaign. He had been busy shifting the focus of his business away from the cattle industry and his ranching operations. He still owned most of the Aioka Steakhouses throughout the world but was beginning to franchise some of the operations. He sold most of his interest in the Paleaka Ranch on the Big Island to the Island Cattleman's Association which was more than happy to pay a premium to once again gain control over who could and couldn't own a major ranch on the island. Even before his and Osama's terrorist plot began to unravel last year, Taka had begun inquiring about coffee plantations available to purchase in the Kona area. Taka was looking for a large coffee plantation with mature trees and a good yield. A place away from prying eyes and unwanted visitors! The more he looked in the Kona area the more frustrated he became. Kona coffee is considered one of the finest coffees in the world. The reputation is well deserved. To be called Kona coffee, the coffee must be grown within a very limited geographic area. Unfortunately, that area is mostly hard black lava with very little dirt. To grow coffee the plantations must truck in most of the dirt. Just south of Kona in the Captain Cook area, most coffee must be grown using hydroponics since practically no dirt is available. Not worth the trouble when you can't even call it Kona coffee. The Kona Coffee Council makes sure of that. The Council oversees all the coffee plantations in the area awarding its seal of approval, assuring the plantation has met federal and council regulations in growing, roasting, and labeling all the coffee produced and packaged in the Kona area. If you do think you have found a suitable area for growing the coffee, you soon discover the reason there isn't a plantation there already. Water! The county water is only available in certain areas and they have no intention on increasing the area they currently supply, mostly because there is just not enough water on the Kona side of the island to supply the present needs let alone the needs required by the huge number of new homes being built in South Kona. With those new homes come a lot of new people who need water. Water that is just not available!

All the regulations and oversight combined with the ground and water supply problems convinced Taka that Kona was not the place to buy a coffee plantation. He may have dealt with those problems had he found a large enough plantation to buy, but most of the coffee plantations in Kona were small boutique plantations with very limited production and sales. Not what Taka was looking for! But even with all that going against his buying in Kona, he did have a safe house and the hidden laboratory in Hawi on the northern part of the island which was still operable and he could have used. He would have bought several of the smaller plantations had it not been for George Fujii. George was the deal breaker! George was Kona Coffee Council's expert in transgenic research. He made sure no GMO coffee seedlings or plants came anywhere near the Kona area and he was avid in enforcing the Big Island regulations that stated as much. Kona Coffee had such a great reputation, and high price, that the local coffee industry could collapse if cross-pollination between the Kona Tipica coffees grown there and a genetically modified version of the plant were to occur. Taka would have to look elsewhere, so he looked to Molokai.

Molokai did offer the privacy Taka was looking for as well as plenty of land. There were no more than seven thousand residents on the island and very few tourists. There were two small airports on the island, but one went to the old leper colony in Kalaupapa. That part of the island was basically inaccessible from the rest of Molokai unless you took a mule or hiked down a very steep and dangerous trail. Those tourists who did venture down the trail to where Father Damien had tended the sick and dying lepers usually were flown out to the other small airport on the island. There was also a small port area on the island. It was built far out into the channel past the huge coral reef that barricaded access to most of the south facing part of Molokai. Kaunakakai is Molokai's largest town and the location of the port. This is where all the supplies and tourists entered the island. Three times a day the ferry would leave the manmade port facilities in Kaunakakai on its two-hour journey to the Lahaina Harbor on Maui. The morning crossing was usually full of residents heading to Maui to do their shopping. Some were going to work while others went to visit family. There would be a few tourists who spent the night at one of the sparse accommodations available on Molokai, most of them anxious to get back to Maui and the activities, restaurants, and shopping much lacking on Molokai. This first ferry of the day was also popular because that was when the wind was the calmest, blowing off the ancient volcanoes of Maui and Molokai and combining to form a powerful wind tunnel between the two islands. When the wind was strong, the waves were at their highest and roughest. This channel, called the Pailolo Channel, is arguably the roughest and most difficult to cross among all the channels separating the eight largest islands making up the Hawaiian archipelago. It was the later ferries that kept tourism at such a low. By the time the ferry would arrive in Molokai on the two later crossings, most of the tourists were too seasick to even begin to want to explore the island. All many of them did was try to relax and lament the fact that "Yes, they did indeed have to return to Maui on the same boat through the same rough seas." Nobody would tell them the return trip was usually rougher than the trip to Molokai.

Taka was interested in purchasing a coffee plantation on Molokai, but there was only one small one that operated in Hoolehua. It was not large enough to meet Taka's needs. He looked at property on the western part of the island along Highway 460, but ran into much the same problem he encountered on the Big Island. Forty percent of the island was owned by the Molokai Ranch Corporation and they had no interest in selling off a large portion of it to a Japanese businessman so he could build a large coffee plantation. Smaller sections of land were offered to Taka as was a large area off the Kalua Koi Road near Kepuhi that was once a large condominium and hotel complex that had been ravaged by both the elements and vandalism. The locals claimed it closed down because the expected influx of tourists never materialized. In reality, that section of the Molokai suffered the same shortcomings as did the Kona area on the Big Island. That being a significant lack of water! The problem of insufficient fresh water was even worse in this part of Molokai than in Kona. Even if Taka did purchase the land and somehow dug wells and found water, it would still take several years before he would have mature coffee trees. Taka was a patient man but could not wait that long for the next phase of his plan to begin. He needed to put his plan in motion while coffee was still on its upward trend in popularity.

Taka found what he was looking for on Kauai. Actually, what he found couldn't have suited his needs more. Several coffee plantations were located in the southwest portion of the island near Port Allen. The largest plantation on Kauai was actually the largest producer in the entire state of Hawaii. It was a large facility with thirty-four hundred acres of land planted in coffee trees. They also bought the coffee cherries from several other growers in the area. What made this the most productive plantation in all of Hawaii also made it the most controversial of all the plantations. Kauai allowed genetically altered coffee to be grown there. Taka couldn't have been more pleased. These plantations were already using a genetically modified coffee plant that caused all the coffee cherries on the plants to ripen at the same time. This allowed mechanical harvesting of the cherries. On unaltered plants the coffee cherries, or beans, ripen at various rates requiring the cherries to be hand-picked when they are ready. This ripening could take place over several weeks, necessitating many man hours of the tedious harvesting. In Kauai, large modified blueberry picking machines are used to harvest all the ripened cherries at one time saving hundreds of man hours and tens of thousands of dollars. Like most successful businesses, the owners were trying to increase their profits by lowering their expenditures. One of their methods was to charge the smaller plantations for the transgenic coffee plants they required them to plant if they wanted to sell their cherries to the large plantation. Then they would pay the smaller plantations less for the cherries claiming the harvesting expense of the machinery used. It was a ploy to force the smaller plantations to sell their fields to the larger producer. It was Taka's good fortune to be in the market for plantations when this was occurring. He was able to buy all of the smaller plantations in the Port Allen area that were being taken advantage of by the major producer. Almost two thousand five hundred acres of mature coffee trees! It was an offer they could not refuse and one the major coffee plantation was unable to match.

It was a perfect location for Taka. Port Allen was a small port, but capable of handling Taka's cargo ship. Port Allen also had an airport that could accommodate small corporate jets. This would make it easy for Taka to get in or out of Kauai relatively unseen. There were tourists on the island, but not in the numbers one would find on Maui and Oahu, or even the Big Island. Port Allen was not on the scenic side of Kauai, although the large coffee plantation located there did cater to the tourists. It was a popular stop for tour buses and visitors who had seen the island's other highlights and were still seeking something to do. Also, Port Allen was just off the Kaumualii Highway which was the only road to reach the Waimea Canyon State Park and Koke'e State Park, which are one of the biggest tourist attractions on Kauai. That is where you will find the "Grand Canyon of the Pacific" as it was called by Samuel Clemens. The board of tourism for Hawaii likes to call it the "Grand Canyon of Hawaii". This too led to tourists stopping by for a cup of free coffee at the plantation. However, this didn't trouble Taka. There were too many positive advantages to the location to be concerned about a few tourists. Or so he thought!

# Chapter Nine

**Satochi Yamane was a cold-blooded assassin**. He had been recruited by Taka's previous ninja assassin, Minoru, when Minoru first came to the Hawaiian Islands in search of property for the cattle ranch. A hatred for the white Americans who stole his native islands burned deep inside Satochi's heart, which was quite a contradiction since he himself was a descendant of Japanese immigrants who had been brought to the islands to work in the sugarcane fields and who were no more native Hawaiian than the white Americans he now hated. Yet he felt the islands belonged to him and his people. He had spent his life studying the history of the Pacific Islanders and promoting their culture and traditions. Minoru had heard about Satochi, recruited him, and sent him to Pakistan where he was trained in terrorist techniques. Satochi was already a skilled martial arts black belt and was capable of killing with numerous weapons, including his hands, but it was his preferred weapon of assassination that set him apart. He had mastered the ancient fighting weapons of the Pacific Island warriors and used these weapons as they were meant to be used, which was as an extremely bloody and gory message to any enemy who saw the aftermath of such an attack. It was not a pleasant way to die and for most people not a pleasant way to kill someone. The assassin would be covered in blood when he used his shark-tooth club to viciously slash the jugular vein of his opponent. Satochi loved the feeling of the blood spraying from his victim's neck onto his own body. It was as though he was absorbing the life of his victim into his own, making him more powerful as the blood dripped from Satochi's head, arms, and hands.

Satochi was raised in the shadow of the "Sleeping Giant" in the hills above Kapa'a. The "Sleeping Giant" is a jungle-covered mountain that appears to be in the shape of a reclining man. The area is an older one comprised of locals who had purchased small plots of land where they were able to carve a small open area out of the jungle to build their modest houses. These were the children of the immigrants who had been brought to Kauai to work the sugarcane fields from Japan, China, the Philippines and a hundred other places. They were workers who could be bought like slaves to work for the huge sugar industry that thrived on many of the islands generations ago. Now these small plots of land backed up to the huge expanses of ranch land owned by the rich Japanese businessmen who bought them thirty years ago when the Japanese economy surpassed all others. They were selling off large lots to the white mainlanders who were desperate to escape the fast life that for so long had sucked the life right out of them. Now they could build their mansions in paradise and bring that mainland fast life with them to the islands. Satochi hated this trend and swore he would do everything in his power to bring an end to it.

Growing up, Satochi acquired quite a reputation as a powerful young man always getting into fights, and always winning them. This along with his passion for native Hawaii and Pacific Island traditions made him popular with the local youth who shared his dislike for the hoales. Satochi was a hero to the Samoan, Tonganese, Fijians, and other Pacific Islanders who immigrated to Kauai. They looked upon Satochi as their leader. Even though Satochi had gone to college he was still able to speak the local Pidgin that most of the Kapa'a youth spoke. Many times he was challenged by the much larger Samoan or Tonga young men who were trying to establish their own reputation in the immigrant ghettos that lay on the outskirts of Kapa'a. Without exception all of these challengers were beaten by the much smaller Satochi, winning him many loyal followers. Minoru heard about Satochi and recruited him and several of Satochi's loyal companions to work for Taka. They were paid well and trained in many terrorist tactics. They returned to Kauai and were called upon at various times to perform tasks for Taka. Finding the coffee plantations and convincing the owners to sell was one of those tasks. Satochi assigned several of his men to work and guard Taka's new investment. He chose two very large Tonganese men as his seconds in command when he was off performing tasks for Taka, which had become more and more frequent since Minoru's death. They were now the leaders of the terrorist cell that resided in Kauai, although most of them failed to realize they were indeed employed by a major terrorist organization. They looked upon their organization as a well-organized crime family dedicated to stopping the Americanization of Hawaii and preserving Hawaiian traditions. Satochi knew better! He knew he was an impeccably trained terrorist assassin and would support Taka and his terrorist goals at all costs. That was why he was now in Russia.

70

Taka had read about Monarch Chemical's transgenic potato and saw the possibilities genetic modifications had for his terrorist goals. He had one of his men contact the scientist who claimed to have made the genetic modifications. The scientist admitted, after receiving a hefty amount of money for copies of his research, that the real scientist behind this type of genetic modification was a man named Yuri Rastsanov in Perm, Russia. He also explained how Yuri was no longer able to speak with outsiders and was being well-protected and compensated by the Russian government. He had heard rumors Yuri had taken genetic splicing to a whole new level that the rest of the scientific world was years from reaching. He also told Taka's man that Yuri was not happy living in Russia and longed for a more western lifestyle with lots of money and freedom. Yuri sounded exactly like the type of scientist Taka was looking for. That was why Satochi was sent to Russia.

Satochi was a very careful and thorough man. He spent several weeks in Perm observing and planning the best way to recruit Yuri. Information about Yuri was easy to obtain with a relatively small bribe. Actually, just about anything was available in Perm for the right amount of money. That is, everything but a nuclear weapon. Those were being carefully monitored by the United States and the European Union. Acquiring one of those was something Taka was going to work on in the future. For now, the focus was getting Yuri safely out of Russia and to Kauai. Satochi learned a man called Viktor Cheznov was in charge of keeping Yuri and his research safely in Russian hands. Satochi also learned there was some concern about a possible breach in the secrecy of Yuri's research and it had something to do with orphanages and a certain Christian missionary group that often visited Perm. This also troubled Satochi, because he knew Taka would not want Yuri's research made public as much as Viktor would not want that to happen. It seems Satochi now had two assignments in Russia. Satochi called in several sleeper cell members from the southern regions of Russia. He also requested Lyuba be sent to assist him in what he decided would be a kidnapping of Yuri. That would be the simplest way. Once they had Yuri in their control it would be a simple matter of getting him to cooperate with Taka, for Yuri was a greedy man and Taka had the money to keep Yuri happy.

It wasn't too difficult for Satochi to discover that Viktor was concerned about a genetically modified potato one of the orphanage cooks gave to a missionary. It seems the potato never seemed to spoil. He also found out from his paid source that the potato also had some rather nasty side affects Viktor and Russia did not want anyone else to find out about. That meant Satochi wanted no one to find out about it either. That was why, even before his successful kidnapping of Yuri, he began following Viktor who in turn was following the missionary who supposedly had the potato. The potato became of prime importance, especially if for some reason Yuri decided not to cooperate. As unlikely as that was, if it did occur, then another of Taka's researchers may be able to decipher the potato's potential affects and the reason for it causing so much concern for Viktor.

Satochi and his driver had been watching Viktor's BMW since early in the morning. When the missionaries' Mercedes van left in the morning, Satochi followed Viktor who was in turn following the van. When it stopped at the shopping complex, Viktor remained in his car, but Satochi and his driver quickly entered the complex to keep an eye on the missionary whom they guessed had the potato. It was really a simple deduction as to whom they needed to follow. The one they called Howard acted extremely nervous and kept looking as if he knew someone was following him.

"He must know he is being followed by the men in the BMW," Satochi said to his companion. "Did you see how he looked for it and spotted it when they got out of the van?" The driver only grunted in agreement.

"I guess surveillance was not something the FSB needs to do very often because those two sure don't know how to do it."

Satochi watched as Howard bought the matryoshka. It was obvious what Howard had in mind, especially when he and Gladys got in the elevator. Satochi and his driver quickly ran up the stairs waiting at each floor's stairwell to see if the elevator stopped. When it finally did stop, they watched from behind the open stairwell door as Howard and Gladys entered the FedEx office. They waited a few minutes before they entered to try and see where the potato was being sent. Satochi had planned on stealing the two packages the clerk had prepared for shipping. Satochi was taken aback when he saw the package that obviously held the potato was being sent to the Big

Island of Hawaii. He paused for a moment as he memorized where and to whom the package was going. Before he could grab the package, several other customers entered the office and a second clerk came from a back room and removed the packages ready to be shipped. Satochi and his driver hurried out the door as the clerk stared at them in disgust. They had missed their opportunity to take the package and now Satochi would have to acquire it when it reached Hawaii. "At least that will be convenient," Satochi said to himself.

He and his driver hurried back down the stairs and jumped into their Lada just as the Mercedes began to pull away. They waited for Viktor to begin his not-so-covert pursuit of the van and then they followed, keeping well back. Traffic began to slow and suddenly Satochi was caught at the roadblock the military had set up. Neither the BMW nor the Mercedes van was anywhere to be seen. The soldiers were forcing all the cars to turn around and go back the way they had come. When Satochi and his driver reached the front of the line, they were told there were terrorists in the area and they must turn around and go back. Satochi told the driver to put up an argument and tell them this road was the only way to reach their destination. They would wait until it was clear to pass. The soldier insisted they turn around and the argument began to grow when in the distance considerable machinegun fire was heard. Both the driver and the soldier turned when they heard the weapons. Satochi motioned to his driver to turn around before the confrontation escalated and the soldiers began asking to see their documents. Satochi had some of the best documents money could buy. You really couldn't even call them forgeries, because they were the real thing, only everything on them was made up. He still thought it best to bring as little attention to himself as possible, so they turned around and traveled about a half-mile down the road and waited to see what transpired.

The soldiers continued to turn cars around for about a half-an-hour. Suddenly, Viktor's BMW went speeding by and Satochi could see Viktor screaming into his cell phone. The BMW turned in the direction of the Silver River. A smile came across Satochi's face as he realized that Viktor had just received really bad news. Satochi and his driver headed down the now open road to see what happened to the van. Satochi already knew, but wanted to confirm his suspicions. As they drove on they saw several military vehicles parked along the road surrounding the bullet-ridden Mercedes van. Soldiers were picking up the bodies of the missionaries from the side of the road and placing them in one of the military trucks. Traffic had once again come to a stop as the loading of the bodies continued. Satochi caught the attention of one of the military truck drivers.

"What happened?" Satochi asked the driver. "We heard something about terrorists in the area." The driver looked at Satochi, trying to decide if he should answer or just ignore the foreigner. Finally, he did respond.

"Terrorists killed and robbed a van load of missionaries. Our soldier comrades arrived just in time to kill the cowardly Chechnyan terrorists before they could get away." The soldier then recognized Satochi's driver was Chechnyan and glared at him with a despicable hatred.

Satochi saw the anger in the soldier's eye. "It looks to me like your comrades got here a little too late," Satochi said with impudence. The soldier quickly switched his stare to Satochi and was about to say something when traffic began to move and the Lada pulled forward away from the military driver. Satochi looked at his driver and they both smiled.

"Now I need to know if Viktor found out what happened to that potato," Satochi said out loud as he began to dial the number of his informant at the Tower of Terror.

# Chapter Ten

**"What do you mean you can't tell me where he is?"** Haruko shouted at the person on the other end of the phone. "This is his private line at the NCTC. How would I have this number if he didn't want to talk to me? You better get a hold of him fast or there will be hell to pay. Your agent here just interfered in a Japanese National Police investigation on foreign soil. This is a serious matter that your President is going to hear about unless Jotty calls me in the next ten minutes." Haruko pressed "END" on the cell phone before the secretary on the other end could even answer. Haruko had made her point and hoped she had scared Jotty's secretary enough to call Jotty and give him the message immediately, even though she and the secretary both knew it was a hollow threat. Besides, Haruko had forgotten that she also would be in big trouble if the Thai authorities became aware that she was following leads regarding a terrorist cell without notifying them of her presence in their country.

Eddie was also on the phone to the NCTC in McClean. He thought it best to inform the office about the terrorist cell that the CIA had been following before somebody realized that the CIA was withholding pertinent terrorist information from the NCTC. He knew Jotty would figure that out once he talked to Haruko, but if the information was time-stamped into McClean, he and the CIA would at least be able to somewhat cover their asses and assets. Eddie was also informed by the NCTC that the small terrorist cell the CIA had been watching in Thailand was taking credit for the bombing of the Aioka restaurant in Phuket. They claimed it as a victory for the Red Summit. This made absolutely no sense at all to Eddie. He hoped Haruko could clear up what the Red Summit had to do with her attempted kidnapping. The bombing was undoubtedly meant to eliminate her. And just how was this Thai terrorist cell connected to the Red Summit? They both were going to be answering a lot of each others questions.

One thing that Eddie did know was that he needed to get Haruko out of Phuket as quickly as possible without being seen. Actually, that would be fairly simple given the fact he had his own dive boat and she was already on it and it was well on its journey away from Phuket. Eddie called one of the agents to find out the status of the terrorists they had been watching. Two of them were still watching Haruko's hotel while the two other terrorists had somehow managed to find Eddie's abandoned TukTuk in the harbor area near where the dive boat had departed. "That's not good," Eddie said to himself.

"What's not good?" Haruko asked Eddie.

"It seems the terrorists traced us to the harbor and now know we left together in my dive boat," Eddie explained. "We really need to get you back to Tokyo."

"And what if I don't want to go back?" Haruko responded in a challenging tone.

"Then I guess I'm going to have to knock you out again, tie you up, have my way with you, and hi-jack you back to Tokyo," Eddie said with a grin.

Haruko just glared at Eddie as every muscle in her body began to twitch in anticipation of an all-out fight for survival.

Eddie saw the look in Haruko's eyes and knew he had overstepped his bounds. "Relax, relax, I'm just kidding."

Haruko did not relax. This was exactly the type of arrogant egotistical typical macho male she had grown to despise. Just like all the men at the National Police force that treated women as second-class humans. At least in Japan the men had the excuse of blaming their culture for the low esteem which they had for females. What excuse did this pathetic blond-headed white bimbo-of-a-man have for his ignorant arrogance? She wanted nothing more than to pummel Eddie into oblivion and was preparing to do so when her cell phone began to ring. Haruko continued to glare at Eddie as he stood in front of her with the idiotic grin still on his face.

"Well, aren't you going to answer it?" Eddie asked puzzled. "It's probably Jotty calling you back."

Haruko suddenly snapped out of her fighting frame-of-mind, but was still wary as she backed away from Eddie, refusing to turn her back towards him as she entered the cabin to speak with whomever was calling. "And that whomever had better damn well be Jotty!" Haruko thought to herself.

Eddie had never been happier to hear a cell phone ring. This Haruko was a lot different than any woman he had ever met before and he liked it. He liked it a lot. He could see the agitated Haruko yelling into the cell phone. "Thank God it was someone else suffering the wrath of this vixen," he thought as once again that silly grin crawled across his face.

# Chapter Eleven

**The Navy helicopter was hovering** off the starboard side of *the Grand Maui* waiting for the helicopter that came for Emma and the Farrelton's luggage to depart. That gave Jim and Jotty a chance to speak with the head of the Navy haz-mat crew.

"What's the situation?" Jotty asked.

The Commander was surprised that a civilian was questioning him. That is, until he saw Jotty's credentials. "Sorry sir, I was told you were in charge of the investigation, but I had yet to meet you. There has been no trace of anthrax found on *the Grand Maui* or to its shore boat."

Jim had expected as much.

"We have secured the dive boat in the dry dock vessel and are preparing to take it to a secured location to continue the decontamination," The Commander continued.

"This doesn't look like a Navy vessel," Jim commented.

"It's not, sir. It is a privately-owned ship the Navy leases for just such situations. The Navy has found it much more economical to pay private dry dock vessels to handle such emergencies rather than pay the fortune to build and man their own."

"When will it get back to Pearl?" Jim asked

"It shouldn't take more than a couple of days to thoroughly clean her, sir. Then the dry dock vessel will bring the dive boat to Pearl Harbor and return to its berthing."

"Thanks for the information," Jotty responded.

Jim and Jotty boarded the Navy helicopter that was finally cleared to land. Even with a two-copter landing platform, several helicopters waited for their turn to land in this developing saga. Jotty and Jim thought they must rank pretty high up, for their' copter bumped several others in the landing rotation. Actually, it wasn't Jim and Jotty that warranted the special treatment, but Lord Farrelton who was waiting to meet with the two agents back at Pearl Harbor.

When their helicopter landed, Jim saw Emma as she entered a waiting SUV being packed with the Farrelton's luggage from the ship. She was too far away to talk to, but they did manage to quickly wave at each other before Jim and Jotty were whisked away. A sedan was waiting to take them to the VIP quarters located inside a restricted area on the base.

"Rikey, it's good to see you again. I hope you were able to keep a close eye on Emma for us?" Lord Farrelton laughed at his own comments. "You must be Joplin. I've heard quite a bit about you. Like I told Rikey, that was some damn fine work you two did solving that Red Summit nonsense. I even spoke with the Queen about your heroic deeds."

"Well, thank you very much Lord Farrelton," Jotty replied. "It's truly a pleasure to meet you. Jim told me you knew about what happened with the Red Summit, but it just wasn't Jim and I....."

"Yes, yes, yes," Lord Farrelton interrupted impatiently, "there was that Japanese police woman as well. I heard she is quite deadly with her hands. But I didn't ask you here just to exchange pleasantries. I thought you might be able to use a little help in your investigation of this dive boat affair." Farrelton waited anxiously for them to ask the obvious next question.

"What kind of help might that be?" Jotty finally asked.

Lord Farrelton was excited about what he was about to tell them. "I checked with Washington to make sure both of you had the necessary authorized clearance to hear what I am about to tell you. You, of course, have a top secret clearance, Joplin. You, Rikey, they had to check on to see if you had the correct security authorization, which in fact you do have. As I told you Rikey, I have been here in the Pacific monitoring tests of some new equipment that my family company, Hydrogen Solutions, has been developing for your military and, of course, eventually for my country's military as well. It's just your Navy has a larger budget for such things, so they get the first crack at it."

"Well, how will this help us in our investigation?" Jotty asked.

"Patience, Joplin, I'm getting to that," Lord Farrelton replied politely. "I'm sure you are aware that a military surveillance satellite has very limited capabilities as far as the time it can track a designated target. Usually within two hours a satellite's orbit forces its surveillance of a target to cease and another satellite must take over that surveillance. This is all well and good if you have enough satellites to dedicate to tracking the same target over time. But, of course, you Yanks don't have enough satellites to do that. Neither do we! No country does! And what satellites you do have are already heavily scheduled as to what they will monitor. Then of course there is the problem of having to shift a satellite's orbit in order to acquire a target that lies out of the normal orbit. That can cause a real problem." Farrelton paused to let Jim and Jotty think for a moment about what he was saying. "Hydrogen Solutions has come up with a way to eliminate this satellite problem altogether. We have created an unmanned high altitude aircraft with surveillance capabilities superior to most satellites. It can stay in the air circling a designated area for up to three weeks at a time before it needs refueling. We have been testing it here in the Hawaii area for almost a year."

"Well, just how in tar nation will that help with our investigation of the anthrax on the dive boat?" Jim asked in a drawn out puzzled tone.

"Our hydrogen plane has been in the air for the past ten days and has recorded everything that occurred within a hundred miles of every Hawaiian Island. With the technology at the control center here at Pearl, we can isolate the dive boat and follow it backwards tracing its exact movements. Don't you agree that would be of some assistance?" Farrelton smiled proudly.

"Indeed it would!" Jotty replied.

"It will take a little work on your part to master the computer program, but Washington has cleared both of you to work in the secure control center to see what you can come up with."

"That would be a great help to our investigation," Jim replied.

"The only problem is that I can't let you have access to the control center for a couple of days. We need to finish up another little test of one of our newest research projects. This one is brilliant. Someday it will help out considerably with those big hurricanes that always seem to ravage your southern states. But that is more than you need to know. I have already said too much. Now tell me, Rikey, did you get as fine a "rogering" as I imagine?"

Jotty looked at Jim trying to figure out just what exactly Farrelton was asking. "Lord Farrelton, you must forgive me, but in Texas I have an impeccable reputation as a gentleman. And sir, in Texas, a gentleman does not kiss-and-tell." Jim spoke slowly and drew out his words as if to accent his point.

80

"Damn you, Rikey!" Lord Farrelton responded dramatically and the two of them began to laugh boisterously as Jotty looked on wondering just what the hell they were talking about.

"Gentlemen, you must excuse me. I have to prepare for a luncheon with the governor and the Lady Farrelton insists that I be back at least an hour before we need to leave. Unfortunately, that was ten minutes ago. If you have any questions just speak to the Navy liaison officer Mr. Bonner. He will take good care of you. I do hope I will see the both of you again soon. I will be spending quite a bit of time in this area over the next couple of years. I'm sure Emma will be pleased about that, Rikey. Here is my secretary's number if you ever need to reach me. You can also leave a message for Emma at this number if you so desire, Rikey. Now I must bid you farewell."

Before either Jim or Jotty could respond, Lord Farrelton was out the door and Jotty's phone began to ring.

It was his secretary informing him of Haruko's angry phone call and the situation report from the CIA regarding what all had transpired in Thailand. Jotty was told about the attempted kidnapping of Haruko, the bombing of the Aioka restaurant, the claim of responsibility by the Red Summit, and the phone call to the terrorists from Japan the CIA had intercepted.

"Damn," Jotty paused to listen. "Where is she now?" Again he waited. "Good, she will be safe there. Make arrangements to fly her by helicopter from Ko Phi Phi back to Bangkok, then on to Tokyo. Make sure it is first-class. Book me on a flight to Tokyo tomorrow night out of Honolulu." Another pause as Jim waited anxiously to find out just what was going on. He knew it was about Haruko. Obviously she was safe, but he didn't like the tone of Jotty's voice. There must have been trouble in Thailand. "I know, she's probably furious, but I can handle it. I'm going to call her right now. Also, make arrangements to have Eddie Pop fly to Oahu to help out here. We may need someone with diving expertise." Jotty closed his cell phone as Jim waited for an explanation.

"The damn CIA has been holding out on me. I'm going to raise hell when I get back to McClean." Jotty was mad and his voice showed it.

"Who gives a damn about the CIA," Jim interrupted, "Is Haruko okay?"

"She's fine, but really pissed off. Eddie is with her right now. I had him keeping an eye on her. Good thing I did. A terrorist group tried to kidnap her. Eddie broke it up. Then they tried to kill her by blowing up the Aioka restaurant where she was supposed to talk to the chef. Fortunately, she wasn't there, but a few dozen others were and now are in little pieces scattered around Phuket. The bad part is the Red Summit has claimed responsibility."

"That's not good." Jim said, shaking his head. "Sounds like Haruko may have been right all along about the Red Summit."

"It gets worse!" Jotty said solemnly. "The damn CIA has been holding out on the NCTC. It seems they have been monitoring calls and listened in on a call from Japan telling the leader of the Thai terrorist cell to take Haruko and the Aioka chef out. They must have had that information for quite a while, but never passed it on until the shit hit the fan. Then it was only to cover their butts. You can bet I'm going to have a few words to say to Eddie when he gets here."

"You and me both, pal," Jim responded. "I don't care much for somebody putting my friends in danger. Especially when it's a friend like Haruko!"

Both men were quiet as they thought about Haruko, each knowing how much the other one cared for her.

"What's the plan?" Jim finally spoke up.

"I need to head to Tokyo to talk with Haruko and find out just how much she does know and hasn't shared about the Red Summit," Jotty responded.

"Are you going to tell her about what the CIA knows?" Jim asked.

"Only if I have to," replied Jotty. "You do know I'm going to try to get her back on our team."

"Good luck with that," Jim replied laughing. "You got about as much of a chance of that as you do teaching a hound dog to fly. All you are going to do is waste your time and irritate the dog."

"You calling my woman a dog?" Jotty said as he pushed Jim as if challenging him to a fight. They both began to laugh. "I want you to look into this hydrogen plane surveillance that Lord Farrelton offered. Then when Eddie gets here you will have some idea where to begin."

"That won't be for a couple of days, so if you don't mind, I think I'll head back home to the Big Island to check my mail, feed the dog, and water the garden," Jim told Jotty. "I am sure glad I'm not the one that has to call Haruko. You my friend are about to get an earful. I'll give you a call when I get back to the control center here. Now I need to find that liaison officer and have him fix me up with a ride back to the Big Island. Keep in touch," Jim said as he headed out the door.

Jotty stood quietly as he prepared to make a very dreaded and difficult phone call.

# Chapter Twelve

**It was six in the morning.** Taka was waiting for Lyuba at the St. Petersburg train station when her thirty-hour trek from Perm came to an end. It came none too soon for Lyuba. She had shared her compartment with four different travelers, but only with three at a time. The fourth compartment companion replaced one of the passengers that boarded at the train's origin in Yekaterinburg on the opposite side of the Ural Mountains from Perm. That change took place in Kirov. It was not a pleasant change! Lyuba's new compartment companion reeked of rotting fish and alcohol and had no interest in trying to sleep. His only interest was in keeping the others in the compartment awake with his complaints about the fall of Communism. That was a common complaint shared by most of the working class poor throughout Russia. The only people who seemed to benefit from the fall of Communism were the rich, organized crime, and Muscovites. Now, even the rich were starting to question the benefits of its collapse with the arrest and trial of several of the wealthier entrepreneurs in Moscow and St. Petersburg. Still, the rich got richer and the poor continued to suffer.

Lyuba was very glad to see Taka. He always treated her like she was very special. Which of course she was! Taka knew Lyuba was a very valuable asset to his organization and plans, though he kept her uninformed about much of the logistics of the terrorist operations as well as his business enterprises. Lyuba was content in her role. She didn't need to know and she didn't want to know why Taka had her perform the duties he did. She was good at what she did and was well-compensated for it. It was an adventure for her that she hoped would last forever. At least, that was how she felt about her life working for Taka at the present.

Taka had arrived in St. Petersburg the previous day. He had been in Helsinki negotiating with several pharmaceutical companies trying to find one that was in need of an influx of considerable cash. Taka of course would require a controlling interest in the company for his assistance, but as a silent partner. No one was to know that it was Taka who now was in control of the company. Taka would assign a close confidant to represent his interest in the company until the time was right in the future to again exploit another company and industry as part of his terrorist goals. For now, that was several years in the future, but never too early to prepare for. That was the one lesson he had learned from his ojiisan. Change would occur in time, just as long as you arranged and prepared for that change. It may not directly benefit you, but it would benefit your children's children. For Taka, he knew there would be no children from him to reap those benefits. His desires and plans were for the good of the Japanese people and others who were oppressed by the Americanization of the world. He would achieve that goal through his terror operations and his foresight of American trends. Much as his grandfather had done with his foresight of Japanese trends.

Taka had been successful in accomplishing his goals while in Helsinki. He looked forward to spending a few relaxing days in St. Petersburg enjoying the pleasures that Lyuba knew so well how to provide. He had caught the overnight ferry from Helsinki two days ago, arriving in St. Petersburg the previous morning. He had wanted to stay at his preferred hotel, The Grand Europa, but it was undergoing some remodeling and Taka could not be bothered by the inconvenience that the construction might cause. Instead, he booked one of the luxurious nineteenth century suites at the Astoria Hotel just across the street from St. Isaacs. He spent the rest of that day relaxing and preparing for Lyuba's arrival. That included the purchase of a full length "minka" as the Russians called the popular fur coat worn by the aristocrats. He knew Lyuba would love such a gift, even though the white nights of summer had not yet come to their end and the days were still warm.

Taka was somewhat troubled that Satochi had not yet arrived in St. Petersburg to debrief him as to how things had gone in Perm. The last time Taka had heard from Satochi, he expressed some concern about a former KGB agent interfering with his task at hand. However, Satochi had assured him that all would go as planned, although he may need to stay a little longer to handle some business related to Yuri's research. Taka was unclear as to what that actually meant and was anxious to have it cleared up. He hoped Lyuba would be able to tell him what Satochi's concerns were, though he knew Lyuba would have asked no questions of Satochi.

Lyuba was happy to see Taka when she exited her train car. Taka's bodyguard had hired a porter to carry Lyuba's small bag to the waiting car. Most of her clothes were left in Perm and were destroyed by Satochi so there would be no record of Lyuba having been in Perm and no chance of any incriminating evidence being found. Taka would take Lyuba shopping later that evening for new clothes. Taka had done this for Lyuba before after she had successfully completed a mission. She was looking forward to visiting the exclusive shops in St. Petersburg, although she couldn't wait until she could visit Milan or Paris to buy some of the new fall fashions that were coming out. For now, the only clothing Taka wanted to see on Lyuba was her new minka and only the minka.

Later that day, after Lyuba had time to relax, and Taka had also been relaxed, Satochi arrived from Perm. Taka sent Lyuba shopping with his bodyguard so Satochi and Taka could discuss the Yuri mission in Perm and the complications that Satochi had alluded to. It seems that a Canadian missionary stumbled upon an FSB cover-up of some of the results of Yuri's research and experiments, the same research that had drawn Taka's attention and interest to Yuri's experiments, that being, the genetic modification of an organism resulting in future male gendercide for any man who ingested that organism. It seems that male sperm production could be halted in any male who ate as little as one bite of Yuri's GMO potatoes. The Russian government had used this research as a means of controlling the orphan population in the Perm region. They also sent it to select regional areas of Russia that tended to cause grief for the present Russian administration. It was discovered that the affect was even more pronounced when the potatoes were used to produce a local Perm-manufactured vodka, a vodka that had grown very popular because of its inexpensive government subsidized price.

A former KGB, now FSB agent named Viktor Cheznov, had been assigned the task of making sure this information did not become public. Satochi described Viktor as a man as coldhearted and bloodthirsty as he himself. A man who would stop at nothing to fulfill and perform his assigned duties for the Russian government. Satochi described in vivid detail the massacre of the missionaries to Taka, who actually smiled at the description of the carnage. He reminded Taka that all of this information came from his informant at the Tower of Terror in Perm, but Satochi assured Taka that it was entirely accurate.

Satochi told Taka about the potato that was sent to Hawaii. He had been able to get the address, but not the name of the recipient

86

from the FedEx office. He was sure that it was this information that Viktor was looking for when he had the missionaries assassinated. According to his informant, Viktor had not yet discovered any information about the potato or where it may be. Satochi knew that it was only a matter of time till Viktor did discover what he was looking for. It was quite possible he already had discovered it. This troubled Taka greatly and he asked Satochi to return to Hawaii to collect the potato before any information regarding its importance became known to the Americans. Taka wanted to keep the consequences of ingesting the GMO potato a secret as badly as Viktor did. Viktor was undoubtedly a man who would stop at nothing to obtain his goals. Taka knew that somehow he could use this knowledge to his advantage if he could get to the potato first.

Satochi also told Taka of his concerns about the sudden transition of pulling Yuri out of Russia and putting him to work for Taka. They all knew Yuri wanted to leave Russia in the worst way, but Satochi feared that without a familiar face to reassure him, no matter how well he was compensated or treated, they risked Yuri either fleeing or going to the authorities. There would be guards around him but that in itself would not be conducive to easing Yuri's fears. Satochi recommended that Lyuba go with Yuri to the house and laboratory in the compound on the coffee plantation in Kauai. As much as Taka had desired to spend a few relaxing days with Lyuba in St. Petersburg, he had to agree with Satochi. He would arrange for a jet to take the two of them to Hawaii that evening. He first would have to break the news of her new assignment to Lyuba. It really would all work out for the best. Once the jet picked up Satochi and Lyuba it would stop in Bahrain to collect the very frightened Yuri. Then it would quickly head on to Hawaii, so Satochi could attend to the potato collection business before Viktor could interfere. Taka knew Lyuba wouldn't be happy about having her vacation in St. Petersburg cut short. At least he hoped she wouldn't be happy about it.

As Satochi left the room to make the arrangements, Taka looked at the bed and smiled. Lyuba's new minka lay open on the bed where she and Taka had made love just hours before. "I don't think Lyuba will need that any time soon where she is going." He began to laugh.

# Chapter Thirteen

**Jotty was calmly trying to explain** why he was having
Haruko watched while she was in Thailand. The conversation wasn't
going well. Not well at all! He was very thankful that his office gave
him the information Eddie supplied about the terrorist organization in
Thailand. He also told her about the call to the terrorists from Japan
picked up by the Elephant Cage along the Thai border. She was still
furious that he hadn't told her about any of this. How could he have?
He had just heard about it himself. He explained that in his position
with the NCTC he was unable to share the information with foreign
agencies without oversight committee approval. He hoped this
mumble jumble sounded believable to Haruko. He assured Haruko
that he would meet her in Tokyo in two days and discuss new relevant
information the NCTC had acquired regarding the Red Summit. He
also beseeched her to share with him any new information she may
have about the Red Summit when they officially met. Haruko did not
respond to this request. "What new information?" Haruko thought.
"Every time I'm close to getting some lead about Taka someone is
killed or something blows up." She was distracted from Jotty's
conversation by her own thoughts as well as the stupid grin that was
once again on Eddie's face.

In mid-sentence Haruko cut off Jotty. "What is with this
brainless CIA agent you have watching me? I'm close to killing him.
He has threatened to tie me up, rape me, and take me back to Tokyo.
He even knocked me out."

"He what?" Jotty shouted even though he had already heard
the story about what happened in Phuket.

"He knocked me unconscious and kidnapped me," Haruko
complained. "Now he won't let me return to Phuket so I can finish my
business."

"I'm afraid your business in Phuket is finished," Jotty
explained calmly. "As for why he hit you, I will take that up with him
personally. I guarantee he will not touch you again, but you will have
to go with him to Ko Phi Phi where we have arranged a helicopter to
pick the two of you up and take you to Bangkok. There you will board
a return flight to Tokyo before the Thai authorities figure out you and
my agent were involved in the terrorist happenings in Phuket. I will

meet you in Tokyo in two days and bring you up to date on what we know."

"What do you mean bring me up-to-date?" Haruko asked. "Is there more going on than I am aware of? Just where are you right now?"

"I'm with Jim back at Pearl Harbor. It seems that there has been a return appearance of the weaponized anthrax. Are you continuing with your series of anthrax shots?"

"You know I hate needles," Haruko responded. "And thirteen shots seem like an awful lot of shots for one stupid disease but, yes, I am still getting my anthrax shots. Do you think the Red Summit has anything to do with this new anthrax incident?"

"That's something we will discuss when I get to Tokyo. Right now we need to get you safely home. I will have somebody collect your things from the hotel. They should arrive in Bangkok not long after you do. And don't be concerned with Eddie. Put him on the phone so I can have a few choice words with him. I will see you in Tokyo." Jotty made it clear to Haruko that any other questions she had would be answered in two days. She had a thousand more questions, but knew she would get no further answers. Haruko exited the boat's cabin and tossed the phone at Eddie like a fast ball pitcher trying to bean a batter. Eddie was much quicker than Haruko thought and easily caught the phone. He smiled that stupid grin Haruko already had grown to detest.

Eddie wasn't smiling for long.

# Chapter Fourteen

**Hiroshi and his cousin** were well on their way to Bangkok when the Aioka Restaurant in Phuket was vaporized by the terrorist bombing. They did not hear about the bombing until they arrived in Bangkok and saw the television coverage in the airport lounge. It was a live broadcast from Phuket and the announcer was reporting that a Thai terrorist cell was taking claim for the bombing in the name of the Red Summit. Hiroshi and his cousin sat in a dazed stupor as the reality of their good fortune due to Hiroshi's foresight began to sink in.

Hiroshi had always expected that someday Taka would come after him. He did not believe the newspapers or the television news when they reported the end of the Red Summit with the death of Minoru in Los Angeles. Nor did he believe that Taka had been the innocent pawn deceived by the terrorist mastermind that everyone now believed Minoru to be. When Haruko started making inquiries as to his cousin's whereabouts at the Tokyo Aioka Restaurants, Hiroshi knew trouble was on the horizon and began to prepare for it. He was not surprised when he heard that someone was asking about the chef at his restaurant earlier in the day. He knew that the time to move on was now. He had hoped to save up more money before what he knew was inevitable occurred, but sometimes your actions are dictated by current events.

They both sat nervously afraid to speak as they waited for their flight to Tokyo. Each of them was suspicious of anyone that glanced their way or came too close to their table in the lounge. Hiroshi was not sure what to do. Was the terrorist bomb meant for him and his cousin? Or was it meant for the lady with the 6:15 reservation who asked too many questions? It had to be for him. Taka knew that was where Hiroshi worked. Taka had arranged the job for him. At least Hiroshi thought it was Taka who had arranged for him to safely leave *the Grand Maui* and go to Phuket. Could Minoru really have been the power behind Taka? Should he and his cousin continue on their journey to Tokyo? Their names will show up as passengers on the flight from Phuket to Bangkok, as well as on the passenger list for the flight to Tokyo scheduled later that night. And what about money? Where could he and his cousin ever find another chef position without Taka finding out? It would be impossible. What would they do to survive? Much of the money Hiroshi had saved went to pay for the plane tickets to Tokyo. Of course neither of them had time to sell their possessions before they left. Maybe Taka would not check the passenger lists and would assume that they both died in the explosion. If someone was watching their apartments, they would think that they were killed when no one ever returned. Too many questions were flooding Hiroshi's already taxed and paranoid mind. His cousin was too scared to talk and sat quietly crying, refusing to even look up. Hiroshi had to decide what to do. So far their fortunes had been good. They had escaped before the bombing and were now safe in Bangkok. The terrorists must still be in the Phuket area, which should guarantee their safe departure for Tokyo. Then, hopefully, no one would check the passenger manifest until they had landed in Tokyo and cleared customs.

But then what? Should they go to the police when they arrived in Tokyo? What good would that do? Hiroshi had no proof as to who did the bombing and why they did it. For that matter, he couldn't even say for sure that the bombing was meant for him and his cousin. Then the police would question why they left Phuket. How did they know to leave before the Aioka restaurant was destroyed? Maybe the police would even blame them for the bombing. No, they couldn't go to the police. They needed to disappear in Japan. Change their names and change their occupations. But that would take money. Where would they get the money to safely hide for the rest of their lives? Suddenly Hiroshi had an epiphany. He would threaten to sell his information to the tabloids if Taka didn't pay them an exorbitant amount of money. Of course Taka would pay. He had too much to lose not to pay. When he did pay, Hiroshi would still sell the story to the tabloid newspaper that he had talked to before. It was a good plan. At least Hiroshi thought it to be a good plan in his traumatized paranoid state of mind. First, he and his cousin just needed to get back to Japan safely. With a plan in mind, Hiroshi began to feel more at ease and that in turn brought comfort to his cousin.

The flight from Bangkok to Tokyo was uneventful. Hiroshi and his cousin waited until almost everyone else had boarded, checking out each passenger trying to determine if that particular passenger was there to finish what the terrorists had failed to accomplish in Phuket. However, they were not the only ones that kept looking over their shoulders during the flight. Haruko had also been added to the flight for her return trip to Tokyo, although Jotty made sure hers was a first-class ticket after what she had been through. She also had been one of the last to board the flight having barely arrived by helicopter from Ko Phi Phi. It was ironic that after missing each other twice in different parts of the world, and after several dozen people had been killed to keep them from meeting, they sat within a few rows of each other on the flight to Tokyo, not knowing that each could have been the other's salvation.

It is strange how severe stress can sometimes cloud a man's mind to make him believe what he wants to believe and not what is real based on fact and history. That had become the case with Hiroshi. He spent his time on the flight writing down all the facts he had concerning the two Takas. He wrote about the scheduled meeting between him and the ship's photographer with Ono Saito from the tabloid in Tokyo. He told of the photographer's death from the suspicious fire aboard the ship and the threat he received from Minoru warning him to leave the ship immediately before such a fate befell him. He then related the story of Ono Saito's death, though he had only heard about it from the news and read in the tabloids. He also told of the lady who had searched out his cousin in the Tokyo Aioka restaurants in order to find Hiroshi and how she had come to Phuket to find him. He told of the attempt to kill him and his cousin at the Phuket Aioka restaurant. He told that the lady who was searching for him must have died in the explosion. He added some details that were not exactly true to tie Taka to the murders of the photographer and journalist in Hawaii. He told that it was Taka who told him he had better leave the ship and who had offered him the position as head chef in Phuket to keep him quiet. When Hiroshi had finished his story, he smiled and felt at peace for the first time since he had left *the Grand Maui* back in Hilo. Ever since that day he had lived in fear, knowing that death could be waiting for him around any corner. No more! He and his cousin had survived so much already that he was now sure his plan would lead to wealth beyond his dreams and a safe obscure life with no more fear of retribution from Taka. How little he really understood about the mind of a terrorist and assassin!

Taka had planned to stay several days in St. Petersburg but, now that Lyuba and Satochi were on their way to Hawaii, he felt no need to waste the time there. He had accomplished the business transactions and now could return to Japan to refine his plans for his current terrorist plot. He was sure Yuri would work out fine, with Lyuba there to help his transition to a new life. Soon he would have Satochi find Yuri a replacement for Lyuba so Taka could use her special talents for a better purpose that he had been thinking about.

Taka had not heard from his terrorist cell in Thailand for two days. He was not too concerned for he knew the head of cell was a well-trained diligent man who had yet to fail in any task Taka had requested of him. Yet a nagging doubt had been gnawing at Taka's stomach since Lyuba and Satochi had left the previous night. One other time Taka had to use someone other than his top assassin to handle the elimination of a serious problem. Things had not gone well! All his men managed to do was draw more attention to the Red Summit while getting themselves killed, the exact opposite outcome of what Taka had desired. Because of their bungled performance, an international counter-terrorism task force was formed with the sole purpose of eliminating the Red Summit. Haruko was a major part of that task force and now once again it was Haruko that was causing Taka concern. Fortunately, it was only Haruko that still seemed to believe that Taka was the mastermind of the Red Summit. With her eliminated, along with the chef Hiroshi and his cousin, there would be no one left that could prove or even wanted to prove that the Red Summit was still an active terrorist organization, let alone that the great Taka Matsuura was its leader. Only when the time was right would Taka announce to the world his two-phase plan that would spread terror to tens of millions of Americans and then to millions more throughout the world as his plan progressed.

Things began to fall apart! At least it looked that way on the surface. Taka had just left St. Petersburg on his private jet, when he heard on the news about the bombing of the Aioka restaurant in Phuket. "A little extreme," Taka thought to himself, "but if they eliminated the problem, one restaurant was a small price to pay, although the bombing would bring a little unwanted attention towards…." Taka's thoughts were interrupted by what the announcer said next.

"Associated Press has learned that a caller claiming to be a member of the previously thought defunct terrorist organization, the Red Summit, has taken responsibility for the bombing."

"What did you just say?" Taka said to the television as if he expected an answer. "The Red Summit has claimed responsibility? Someone will pay dearly for that remark."

The announcer continued giving details of the bombing with estimates about the possible number killed. He explained that there were no survivors and that the blast had been so large it was even difficult for rescuers to find body parts. Taka was glad to hear that. He just hoped that his problem was eliminated. The announcer started talking about how Taka owned the Aioka restaurant chain and the troubles he previously had with the Red Summit killing his wife and trying to ruin his businesses. The announcer speculated that this might possibly be the continuation of some vendetta that the terrorists had against Mr. Matsuura.

"Maybe this won't be so bad after all," Taka thought. "This could just be what I need to separate my name even further from the Red Summit." Still, someone was going to have to pay dearly for that phone call. No one but Taka spoke for the Red Summit.

For the rest of his flight to Japan, Taka watched the various news channels trying to find out as much as possible about what had happened in Phuket. He continued to try to reach the Thai terrorist cell leader on his global cell phone. Each attempt was carefully noted by the computer at the Elephant Cage located along the Thai border. The number had been designated as hot by the CIA and it received priority attention whenever someone dialed it. The NCTC now also received this information directly from the Elephant Cage as well. Eddie made sure of that. The CIA was able to identify the incoming number, but was having difficulty getting a fix on its location. The GPS reading kept changing dramatically with each call. It took a few calls for them to realize that the incoming call was coming from a jet flying east across Russia.

When Taka did get in touch with the leader of the terrorist cell, he was not happy with what he learned.

"We lost our primary target. My men are still searching for her throughout Phuket," the leader explained.

"What about the chef?" Taka asked.

"We are certain we removed both the targets at the restaurant. We had hoped she would be there as well, but she failed to show for her reservation." That was a guarantee that the terrorist leader would soon regret having made.

"Who made the call to the media?" Taka asked.

The leader was hesitant to reply for he knew it more than likely meant death for the caller. "It was one of my men who claimed the bombing as the work of the Red Summit. I am very sorry."

"I too am sorry this occurred. Do not let it happen again. I will deal with this matter later." Taka knew the phone was not secure so he kept his conversation short.

"I want you and your team to come to Tokyo. Follow the instructions as before. I will contact you as planned."

No names were ever used, but both the NCTC and the CIA knew Haruko was the primary target that was being discussed. Jotty would not be happy when he received the information from the monitored call.

Taka had much to consider when he arrived back in Japan. He would wait for Satochi to complete his tasks in Hawaii, then have Satochi join him in Japan to deal with the Thai cell. Taka remained confident in his path towards his goals. If all continued as planned, this nonsense in Phuket would be but a bump in the road on the Red Summit's journey of terror.

When Hiroshi and his cousin arrived back in Tokyo, their fears had been overcome by their foolish greed. Though they were still cautious as they left the airport, they were careless in their actions. They gave no thought to the cameras located everywhere that followed and recorded every detail of their movements, from the exiting of the plane to the baggage area, through customs, and eventually to the cab they entered. Nor did they think to give a false location to the cab driver and then walk to their eventual destination. These things most people, like Hiroshi, never thought of.

Hiroshi and his cousin had gone to the apartment of a trusted friend who still worked for one of the Aioka restaurants in Tokyo. It was the same friend who had warned them that a lady had come in asking too many questions just as Hiroshi had predicted someone would do. They had called their friend asking if they could stay at his apartment while they made arrangements to move far from Tokyo. They had told the friend that they were in some danger, but no trouble would befall their friend. A very hollow promise indeed! The friend of course would let them stay for as long as necessary, which Hiroshi assured him would be no more than two weeks. That agreement was made before the friend heard of the bombing at the Aioka Steakhouse in Phuket. When he did, the friend would only allow them to stay for one week claiming that a relative had called and needed to stay the following week. Hiroshi knew this to be a lie, but understood the fear his friend must have after hearing of all the deaths at the Phuket Aiokas. It was too much to ask of anyone.

The next day Hiroshi typed his letter to Taka that included all the facts he had written down on the airplane. He also made a request for an exceedingly large sum of money, the receipt of which would guarantee that Hiroshi would not send a copy of the information to the police or the tabloids. And of course, if any harm were to befall Taka or his cousin in the next fifty years or so, Hiroshi claimed to have arranged for an attorney to deliver the information on his behest. He made three copies of the information, but typed separate letters to the Japanese Police Agency and to the tabloid. In the letter to the police he explained that he was going into hiding, but that he had pertinent information regarding Taka Matsuura's connection to the Red Summit. He also wrote of Taka's involvement in several murders and the recent Aioka restaurant bombing in Phuket. He placed that letter on top of one of the three copies of information. He would decide what to do with it later.

The letter to the tabloid was basically the same, although it included a request for a large sum of money for the information. He also included some details about Ono Saito's death which Hiroshi was sure would peak their interest. Hiroshi told them that he would be in touch with them very soon. He told them when he called that he would use the name Shogun so they would know it was him. He took the letter to the closest mailbox and sent it on its way.

He placed the copy of the letter and information for Taka in a large envelope and wrote on it:

For: TAKA MATSUURA
PLEASE DELIVER IMMEDIATELY
VERY PRIVATE AND PERSONAL

96

TO BE OPENED ONLY BY TAKA MATSUURA
THIS IS A MATTER OF LIFE AND DEATH

Hiroshi had wanted the friend to deliver the envelope to the Aioka restaurant manager claiming that he had found it in the kitchen when he arrived at work. The friend refused, wanting nothing more to do with Hiroshi and his cousin's dilemma. He said it was stressful enough allowing them to stay the week in his apartment. Hiroshi could understand his friend's fear and decided to have his cousin leave the envelope in the doorway of the restaurant so the manager would find it when he arrived to prepare for the day. It wasn't the safest way, but Hiroshi and the cousin could watch from a distance to insure that it was the manager who found the envelope. At the last minute, Hiroshi decided he should put a seal on the envelope to show Taka that no one else had opened and read the information inside. Hiroshi hoped that this would help protect any other innocent person from getting killed for knowing too much about Taka and the Red Summit.

As they watched the restaurant that morning, Hiroshi's confidence began to ebb. "Was this really what he should be doing?" he thought to himself.

Just then the restaurant manager walked up to the door. Hiroshi could see him lift the envelope, read it and then turn looking to see who might have left it there. Hiroshi quickly ducked inside a doorway to avoid being seen.

When the manager turned and entered the restaurant Hiroshi instructed his cousin to keep watch to see if anyone came to pick up the envelope or if the manager left the restaurant with the envelope. Hiroshi knew that the manager would call the corporate office and inform them of the peculiar envelope he had found when he opened that morning. They in turn would attempt to contact Taka's secretary who in turn would contact Taka. This could take several hours, but Hiroshi had a feeling it would happen much quicker. Nobody would want to upset Taka!

As Hiroshi headed back to the apartment, a shiver ran down his spine as a vision of Minoru came into his head. "Thank goodness he was killed in Los Angeles," Hiroshi whispered to himself. "Nobody could be as cold and evil as that man." As they say, ignorance is bliss and Hiroshi had yet to meet Satochi.

# Chapter Fifteen

**Jim convinced the Navy liaison officer** to helicopter him back to the Big Island. It wasn't so much Jim's convincing as it was the instructions from Lord Farrelton to help Jim and Jotty in every possible way. The helicopter dropped Jim on the Kailua pier in Kailua-Kona. His arrival attracted quite a crowd of onlookers curious as to why a Navy helicopter would be landing on the pier. It was actually one of the safest spots to sit the copter down that was reasonably close to where Jim had parked his car. The copter really never landed. It just hovered near the ground long enough for Jim to jump out with his suitcase and gun case. It wasn't that much to carry, but the gun case was a little awkward and it did draw quite a bit of attention as Jim walked back to his car.

It was a good hour drive back to Waimea this time of day. That is a good hour if you drive the speed limit and about the only people who do that are the tourists and the locals that are a little too high to be driving in the first place. The roads in Hawaii are not the safest in the country. Jim took Highway 190 towards Waimea. It wasn't the most scenic way to Waimea, but it was shorter and avoided all the tourist traffic going along Highway 19 to the expensive resorts located along the Kohala Coast.

Jim lived on the side of the volcano just a few miles up Highway 250 overlooking Waimea. It was one of those small vacation houses built by a Japanese businessman back in the eighties, when owning a vacation home in Hawaii was what every up-and-coming mid-level Japanese corporate executive had to do. Then in the nineties, when the Japanese economy hit the skids, local residents were able to buy these houses for practically nothing. It was one of those locals, who just so happened to be a real estate agent that had bought several such houses before they came on the market, whom Jim had leased his house from. It wasn't big, but it was large enough for him and his dog. It also had plenty of room for his garden. The house could be easily secured to keep visitors out when he was away. He had added a dog run that was accessible from the street so he could have one of the local kids feed his dog when he had to be out of town.

When Jim arrived home he went straight to his message machine to see if Haruko had tried to call or if Jotty was trying to reach him. Jim purposely hadn't taken his cell phone with him on vacation aboard *the Grand Maui*. If he had his way he wouldn't take that damn phone anywhere. As far as he was concerned the cell phone was one of the worst and most annoying inventions known to mankind.

There were three messages on his answering machine. The first one was from FedEx telling him a package sent to him by a Howard Rikey from Perm, Russia, had been confiscated by the Hawaii Department of Agriculture. They gave him the Agriculture Department's number to call to see why his package was being held. Jim didn't need that number. It was one he called often. In his position with the USDA he worked closely with the Hawaii Department of Agriculture. Many of the new friends he had made since he moved to the Big Island worked there. "Probably some kind of practical joke," Jim said to himself. "Those guys do stuff like that when they are bored. And that is one boring place to have to work." Jim realized that couldn't be it. Nobody there knew about his uncle who was always going to Russia to work at those orphanages and FedEx did say it was shipped by Howard from Perm, Russia. "Just what in the world was this all about?" Jim thought.

The next message was from one of his friends at the Agriculture department building located by the Kona airport. "Hey Jim," the message started. "You won't believe what we have here for you. It seems Pete the Beagle sniffed out something that shouldn't be coming into Hawaii that was headed your way. It must have come from one of your relatives, because they have the same last name as you. I didn't know you had family in Russia. Anyway, Pete sniffed out a potato hidden inside some kind of wooden doll or something." Jim could hear another voice call out in the background, "it's called a matryoshka." "Yeah, that's it," his friend's voice continued, "a matryoshka. The potato was hidden in a matryoshka. Can you believe it, a potato? We didn't even know Pete could sniff out tubers. We thought he just did fruits and vegetables. Go figure! Anyway, there is this letter with it that seems kind of serious. Some guy named Howard is really concerned about this potato. He thinks something's not right with it, but I'll let you read the letter for yourself. You should know, though, that this Howard guy thought someone was following him and trying to get a hold of the potato. Pretty weird, huh? I called your office and they said you were on vacation, so I thought it best just to leave you this message. We will hold on to it until you get back. Hope you had a good time. See you soon."

Jim stopped the answering machine so he could think about the message he just listened to. Why would Howard be sending him a potato? The only time he heard from Howard and Gladys was around Christmas. They kept inviting him up to their place in Canada, but Jim just never seemed to have the time or inclination to go there.

Jim restarted the answering machine for the final message.

"Hello, this message is for Jim Rikey. My name is Lewis Foster. I'm with the State Department. Please forgive me for leaving this message, but we have tried to call several times and have always gotten the answering machine. I'm afraid I have some very bad news. You were listed as the contact person if anything were to happen to a Howard and Gladys Rikey. I'm very sorry to have to tell you this but they along with several others, were killed by Chechnyan terrorists outside of Perm, Russia, earlier this week. The State Department is looking into just what exactly occurred, but has been getting the run-around from the Russian government. They have yet to release the bodies, but assure us it will be as soon as their investigation is complete. We have lodged a formal complaint with their ambassador in Washington regarding the delay. In accordance with the papers filed with the missionary organization, the bodies, upon their release, will be returned to Edmonton, Canada. Arrangements for their dispositions are in place. They also list a Mr. Frederick Allen as their estate attorney in Edmonton. I would suggest you contact him regarding their estate. Again, I am extremely sorry for your loss, but assure you that the State department will do everything in its power to…."

Jim shut the machine off. He walked to the refrigerator, grabbed a beer, and headed outside to look down on the Kohala Coast from his favorite chair next to his organic garden and do a little thinking.

Most times the death of a friend or family member makes a person wish they had been a better friend or more caring relative. Jim had never spent much time with his uncle. They exchanged Christmas cards and talked a couple of times a year on the phone, usually on the anniversary of either the day Jim's parents were killed or the day

Jim's brother died. Howard was Jim's dad's brother. He left Texas to attend school back east somewhere and never moved back home. He met his wife Gladys when he went to graduate school. They married as soon as Howard received his PhD in Sociology and got that job teaching at the university up in Canada. That was the only job Howard ever had. He retired from the University a few years back and he and Gladys had been traveling ever since. Howard and Gladys never had children, whether by design or by some physical problem keeping them from it, Jim never knew. Maybe that is why they went to Russia so often to work with the orphans. Howard and Gladys were both very religious people. Much more so than Jim! They were always going on some mission or involved in some fund-raising activity with their church. They were always trying to get Jim to come up and visit them in Canada. Jim always had some excuse as to why he couldn't do it. A little late now!

As much as Jim wanted to just sit, relax and reminisce about Howard and Gladys, he was just too troubled by the coincidence of Howard's letter. Howard's concern about being followed and now hearing that he and Gladys were killed was just not right. And what was so important about a potato? None of it seemed to make any sense. Even the State Department couldn't figure out just exactly what was going on. Jim sat his beer down without having even taken one sip and got back in his car either forgetting or just forgoing unloading his guns or luggage. He had to see what Howard had to say in that letter. The only way that was going to happen was if he drove back down to the Agricultural Office at the Kona Airport. Gravel flew from the spinning tires as Jim raced out of his driveway forgetting to close the security gate.

# Chapter Sixteen

**"Lyuba!" Yuri shrieked with delight**. Yuri had never been happier to see anyone in his life.

"Privyet, Yuri. Did you miss me?" Lyuba smiled as she walked into his room at the Bahrain safe house. Taka had sent someone to stay with Yuri and explain to him that a large Japanese-American research company had coordinated his escape from Perm. They were willing to guarantee his freedom and pay him more money than he could ever have imagined. They promised to supply him with a new identity. Still, Yuri was extremely frightened and nervous. Had he been conscious to see what Satochi had done to his driver back in Perm that night, he would have had more than enough reason to be so concerned.

Lyuba told Yuri the same story and made him the same promises he had already heard. Coming from Lyuba, it sounded much better. "We have built a new laboratory for you in Paradise. You and I are going to live in Hawaii. My boss has a very secure compound where you will be completely safe. Once you are acclimated to the surroundings, you will be free to travel around the island at your leisure. Of course you will always have a bodyguard in case one of Viktor's men from Perm happens to come looking for you. But of course, that will never happen," Lyuba assured him.

"I will stay there with you for a while if you like," Lyuba said seductively.

A mischievous smile appeared on Yuri's face as another part of his anatomy also seemed to smile. Lyuba took notice and gently caressed Yuri.

"I too cannot wait to be with you again, but not quite yet. A private jet is waiting to take us immediately to Hawaii," Lyuba seemed to purr as she spoke. "The quicker we leave this part of the world, the safer you will be. Then the sooner you and I can be together."

"But I have no clothes, no toiletries, no anything," Yuri said, sounding bewildered.

"We have a change of clothes and toiletries for you on board the plane. When we arrive in Hawaii, you and I will both shop for a new wardrobe," Lyuba said excitedly, "but we must leave at once."

"With you I will go to the ends of the world," Yuri replied joyfully, and they headed for the airport.

It was fortunate that Lyuba had been able to raise Yuri's spirits from the paranoid state he had been in since his abduction. For when they arrived at the airport and boarded the jet, Yuri came face-to-face with the coldhearted Satochi. Satochi seemed to emanate evil as Yuri and Lyuba made their way past him to the two empty seats toward the front of the jet. Yuri's willingness to go to Hawaii seemed to quickly diminish under Satochi's burning glare and would have probably completely dissolved had it not been for the reassuring caresses of Lyuba.

"Don't be afraid of Satochi," Lyuba said softly. "He is just another employee of the company. When we arrive in Hawaii he has other things he must do. We won't see much of him."

Yuri wasn't so sure he wanted that kind of protection. Satochi really frightened him. Satochi frightened many people. Yuri slept for most of the flight to Hawaii. That was due to the sedatives Lyuba had mixed in his drinks. He did awaken for a moment when the jet landed for refueling, but soon fell asleep again still groggy from the sedatives.

About an hour from the islands both Lyuba and Yuri were awake. Satochi never slept. At least that was how it appeared to Yuri. In fact Satochi did get plenty of rest on the long flight. The first stop on the islands was at the Kona airport on the Big Island. One of Satochi's henchmen was waiting for him at the airport. Satochi told Lyuba and Yuri that the jet would take them on to the airport in Lihu'e on Kauai. There a car and driver would be waiting to take them to the compound at the coffee plantation near Hanapepe. Satochi also recommended they stop for more appropriate clothes for the Hawaiian climate at the Hilo Hattie's in Lihu'e. Maybe tomorrow or the next day they would have the opportunity to shop at a more upscale store for some nicer clothes.

Yuri was glad to see Satochi go. He felt much more at ease as he watched Satochi's car pull away as the pilot began to close the jet's door.

A car was waiting for Satochi when the jet landed at the Kona airport. "Ba, gon Waimea," Satochi said to the driver in a mix of pidgin and English. "Eh, one box wen come to me, ka?"

"Nobody stay, no mo one box," the driver replied. "Tree mokes wen come ova, dem wen spak da hale, dey wen talk to one keed. Dem still looking at house."

"Eh bra, wat, wat, which one, which braddah?" Satochi asked sensing trouble.

"Mainlander, kook, joj, military brat, not local haoles," the driver replied.

At once Satochi knew who this man was. The Russian! The one they call Viktor must have found the address on the dead missionary. He knew where the FedEx package was being shipped and was here to intercept it. Satochi would not let that happen!

# Chapter Seventeen

**Viktor and two of his men** arrived in Kona the day before Jim returned from Pearl Harbor. They arrived on different planes coming from different departure destinations, so as to draw as little attention as possible. They appeared to be typical tourists getting away to enjoy the pleasures Hawaii had to offer. Just like all the other tourists that inundated the islands this time of year. Viktor's two men were able to arrive in the United States unnoticed. For Viktor that was an impossible task. When Viktor's passport number showed up on the computers, a message was sent instantly to several government agencies informing them that a known former high-ranking KGB officer had entered the country. During the days of Communism, something like this was unheard of and would have warranted immediate attention by the CIA and the FBI. There would have been a constant watch and documentation of every movement Viktor made while on American soil. Now that the Cold War was over and tensions had eased significantly between the two countries, Viktor's arrival only warranted a fifteen minute delay in clearing Customs while a low-level State department bureaucrat asked a series of questions listed in some seldom used manual.

Even though the three Russian agents came on separate flights, they all stayed together in a large three bedroom condominium at The Bay Club at the Waikoloa Beach Resort. This time of year it was mostly families that stayed in the condos. There were several conventions scheduled in Waikoloa, so three men staying in a condo on a golf course seemed perfectly normal. With the weekly turnover of guests, no one would be likely to even notice them. The house cleaner would only clean the condo once a week, instead of the normal daily cleaning they would have had, had they chose to stay in a hotel room. The less contact with outside visitors or workers the better. The hotels also tended to have sophisticated video security monitoring that the condos did not have. It was the perfect base for Viktor's team to work from.

After unloading their baggage at the condo, Viktor met with a former Russian KGB agent who had been living in Oahu for several years. He had come to the Big Island when Viktor requested some special equipment for his team. That special equipment was, of course, weapons and disposable cell phones. His old friend had performed several jobs, some clean and some quite dirty, for Viktor since he had retired and moved to America. Actually, there were several such retired KGB agents or previously embedded Russian spies living throughout the United States. Many still performed specific tasks for the Motherland when called upon.

Once the team had their equipment and maps of the island, they headed to Waimea to find a Mr. Jim Rikey's residence. When they arrived at Jim's house, they found it well secured. No one appeared to be home, but a large dog locked inside a dog run adjacent to the street barked incessantly at Viktor and his men. They decided not to break in just quite yet and drove up the road to keep watch to see if anyone came home. As they were watching the house, they saw a young boy walk up the road pull out a key and unlock the gate to the dog run. He went inside and began to play with the dog. One of Viktor's men walked down the road towards the house.

"That's a mighty fine-looking dog you have there son," the man said.

"Oh, he's not mine. Mr. Rikey just pays me to feed and play with him when he has to go out of town for business."

"What's his name?" The man asked. "Sandy. She's a yellow lab," the boy replied stressing the "she".

"Why don't you take her into the big yard so she can run around?"

"I can't get into the main yard. It's secured. That's why Mr. Rikey had the dog run built over here so I could get in without setting off the security alarms."

"That Mr. Rikey sounds like a pretty smart man. What kind of work does he do?"

"He works for the Department of Agriculture. Not the state one down by the airport, but the United States Department of Agriculture." The boy looked around like he was in trouble, then spoke a little softer as if whispering a secret. "You know my dad told me that Mr. Rikey is also some kind of secret agent or something. My dad says Mr. Rikey once killed a whole bunch of terrorists."

"No kidding," the man replied. "Maybe that's why he is out of town so much."

"I never thought about that," the boy replied excitedly.

"How long you going to be feeding Sandy?"

"Oh just for another couple of days. Mr. Rikey took a seven day cruise on that fancy ship that goes around the islands."

"Well, you take good care of Sandy," the man said waving his hand as he hurried away.

Viktor was pleased with all of the information his man had been able to get from the young boy. That gave them at least one day to go inside and see what they could find out before Jim Rikey was to return home. Viktor knew that the package had not yet been delivered. It would only have arrived within the last couple of days.

It appeared that FedEx had not yet tried to deliver the package from Howard. If they had, they would have left notice of their attempt to deliver on the security fence by the driveway. The three agents kept watch on the house for the next several hours, but no FedEx truck arrived. Viktor decided they would continue to watch the house for the rest of the day and then they would break into it that night. He left one of his men to keep an eye on the house. He and the other agent headed back to the condo where Viktor could access his computer to find out as much as he could about Jim's security system. There wasn't too much traffic on the road nor were there any real close neighbors, so Viktor thought it safe to leave his agent on the side of the road. He was near a small bridge where he could conceal himself if necessary.

Not long after Viktor had left for the condo, the car carrying Satochi and his driver passed by Jim's house and then by the Russian who was keeping watch on the house. They continued to drive until the road turned and they were out of sight. Satochi was determined to get into the house and collect the package before the Russians could do so. Satochi was no expert at security systems, but he did have wire cutters and knew he would have at least fifteen minutes before the security firm could get a car up there to check on the triggered alarm. Plenty of time for him to search the house for the package! That also meant it would be necessary to kill the Russian. That would undoubtedly alert Viktor that the same people who kidnapped Yuri also knew about the potato. But if Viktor was half as good as Satochi was at their chosen professions, Viktor already knew this. He would also know that Yuri was here. Satochi smiled as he thought that for the first time he may have a worthy adversary.

As Satochi silently moved through the trees and bushes along the stream that led to the bridge where the Russian was watching, he heard another car approach the house. The car stopped and a tall lanky man jumped out, unlocked the gate, and punched a coded number into the keypad of the house's security system shutting it off. The Russian agent watched as Jim entered into the house. When Jim was inside the agent pulled out one of the untraceable throwaway cell phones and called Viktor.

"The owner of the house has returned. He just opened the gate and turned off the security system," the agent told Viktor.

"We will return at once. Continue to watch and keep us informed."

"I will do as ..." the Russian stopped his response in mid-sentence. "Viktor, he has just come out of the house and has gone into his garden to sit down and drink a beer. Wait a moment, now he is getting up and is headed back to his car. The Russian watched in silence. Viktor did not speak. "He is leaving in a hurry and did not close the gate or set the alarm."

"How fortunate for us," Viktor said. "He may not be gone for long. Hurry inside the house and have a look around. See what you can find. Check his message machine. We will be there in twenty minutes. What kind of car is he driving?"

"It was an older green Jeep Cherokee. It looked like a government vehicle."

"Good, we will watch for it as we return. Now hurry," Viktor stressed the urgency of his order.

Satochi watched as the Russian made a call on his cell phone. Satochi knew the man was calling Viktor to find out what to do. He also watched the movements of Jim going to his garden then suddenly jumping up and hurrying away. Satochi thought he could read anguish on Jim's face as Jim hurried to his car then sped down the road.

Even before Jim's Jeep was out of sight, the Russian was hurrying down the road and through the unlocked security gate. Satochi was seconds behind him, but remained hidden along the side of the road. The crunching of the gravel beneath the Russian's feet startled Sandy and she began barking furiously at the man as he entered Jim's unlocked house. Satochi entered the gate, but no sound came from beneath his feet as he snuck up to the rear of the house.

With both men out of sight, Sandy stopped barking and went back inside her doghouse. The Russian agent immediately went to the answering machine as Viktor had instructed and sat down at Jim's desk to search the drawers as the machine began to play.

The agent stopped his search of the desk when he heard that the first message was from the FedEx office at the airport. Unfortunately, he never heard the end of that message.

Satochi had silently entered the rear door of the house and came up behind the Russian agent.

"Ho! Lolo man," Satochi yelled out. The agent was reaching for his gun as he turned to see who was behind him. Satochi smashed the gun out of the Russian's hand with the flat side of his shark tooth club breaking four of the tiger shark teeth in the process. On the backswing he smashed the opposite flat side of the club into the Russian's jaw knocking loose six of the Russian's teeth. The Russian, like all the others, reacted to the blows by instinctively lifting his head back exposing his neck.

"You ma-ke die dead," Satochi said to the Russian as he turned the club handle in his hand ever so slightly then swung savagely at the Russian's neck severing the jugular vein. Satochi's club cut deep into the spine as it had done with Yuri's driver. The blood splatter reached across the room covering the wall and door. Blood continued to pulsate out of the Russian's neck as his knees buckled, collapsing him into the chair he had just raised out of. Satochi too was covered in the Russian's blood. Satochi knew that was how it should be. That was how it had to be.

Satochi continued to listen to the messages on the answering machine. When the third message came to an end, he understood why he saw the anguish on the face of this Jim Rikey. He thought about removing the tape from the machine, but decided to allow Viktor to stay in the game a little longer.

Satochi's club had been damaged beyond repair in this attack. He had previously chipped one of the shark's teeth when he caught it on the spine of Yuri's driver in Russia. When he hit the gun out of this Russian's hand, he broke several more of the shark teeth. He even felt the integrity of the Koa wood that the club had been painstakingly carved from begin to fail when he struck the Russian's face. It had been a good weapon, but was no longer of any use to Satochi. He would leave it on the desk as a warning to anyone who was foolish enough to pursue him in this game. He had other clubs as fine as this one once was. He would order another when he returned to Kauai. He knew it would be at least a year before Larry could make another. Satochi would stop in Maui on his way back to Kauai. The gallery at the Ritz-Carlton had one of Larry's weapons for sale. He would buy that one and have Larry adjust it until a new one could be made to meet his personal needs.

Satochi left quickly, knowing that Viktor would soon be arriving. As he headed back to where his driver waited, he thought about Jim Rikey. He must have gone to Kona to read the letter from this Howard that was talked about on the message machine. The same Howard that Viktor had so coldly murdered. Then Satochi thought about the potato. "What made the potato so valuable that Viktor had killed more than a dozen people trying to get it?"

When he arrived back at the car, the driver was waiting with a towel. Satochi wiped the blood from his face and hands. The driver also had a change of clothes waiting. They had both been through this before. As they drove down the hill headed for Kona, they passed Viktor and the other Russian agent hurrying towards Jim's house.

"Welcome to the game," Satochi said as Viktor's car sped past them. "Too bad you are going the wrong way."

# Chapter Eighteen

**When Haruko arrived back in Tokyo,** she was still furious at Jotty for having assigned an agent to watch her in Phuket. She was more than capable of taking care of herself. She prided herself on her self-reliance. She needed no babysitter to watch after her as though she was some helpless female. It would be at least another day until she calmed down sufficiently to realize what Jotty did probably did save her life, although Jotty could have at least assigned some agent besides Eddie Pop to keep an eye on her. That man was nothing more than an arrogant, egotistical, chauvinistic pig. Haruko hoped she never saw him again. If she did, she just might do something she would regret.

Haruko's unexpected return to her duties at the National Police Agency only three days after she had begun her holiday drew some curious speculation among her colleagues. Most assumed she canceled her vacation because of the statement by the Thai terrorist cell claiming the Red Summit was behind the bombing in Phuket. Fortunately, she had told no one it was Phuket where she had gone on her holiday. Had her supervisor been aware of what had occurred in Thailand, she would surely be in trouble. Even though she was spending her own time investigating Taka, the Japanese Police could not afford to be accused of carrying on an illegal investigation in a foreign country. Haruko would at the very least be demoted for her actions. Several of her colleagues would like nothing more than to see Haruko removed from her position as head of the counter-terrorism division.

Several issues of the Yomuri Shinbun newspaper had collected on Haruko's desk while she was away. She was diligently reading through them, searching for any reference to Taka, when she came upon a story about the grand opening of a new Aioka Restaurant in Kashiwa. Kashiwa was a suburb in Ikebekuro Province a little east-northeast of Tokyo Center. The opening was not for another week. The article said Taka would attend the opening. Haruko too would be there. She had to see Taka face-to-face.

Taka had returned to his home north of Tokyo. He was making plans as to how best put Yuri's talents to work for him in Kauai. He had called for Satochi at Taka's house in Kona. That was where Satochi would be staying on the Big Island until his business there was concluded. It was the house Taka had built that held the secret passage through the lava tube to the hidden laboratory which was still usable at the Paleaka Ranch. The tube also led down to the ocean ending somewhere below the Alenuihaha Channel. The channel separated the Big Island from Maui. It had a very swift current which kept most boats from venturing a crossing from Maui to the Big Island. Taka knew that the tube opened into the channel because the water level in the tube would rise and ebb with the tide outside. He had Minoru explore the entrance and now kept scuba equipment hidden near the waterline of the tube. What he didn't know was that some cave divers had discovered the lava tube. They were unfortunate enough to venture up it to the point were Satochi had spilled some weaponized anthrax. When scientists were hurriedly evacuating the upper lab at the Paleaka Ranch during the FBI raid of that facility last year, they had been very messy filling the canisters. Minoru had spilled anthrax at that time in the lava tube just as Satochi had spilled it recently. The divers thought they had stumbled upon a hidden drug lab and picked up some of the powdery anthrax thinking it was cocaine. Within three hours they were dead, as were the captain and crew of the dive boat. The divers brought some of the fine powder on board to see what the captain thought the substance could be. A very poor choice indeed!

Satochi did not answer the phone at the house nor was he responding to calls to his cell phone. That was fortuitous because the CIA had targeted Taka's cell phone as one of interest ever since the call to the Thai terrorists. Taka knew how easy a cell phone could be traced. Like most government spy agencies, he too used throw away cell phones to avoid detection. As he waited for Satochi to contact him, something told Taka it was time to dispose of this phone. He needed to send it far away from him and his home.

Fortune sometimes seemed to shine on Taka. As he tried to decide how to deal with the Thai terrorists who had bungled the job in Phuket, one of his bodyguards came into his study to inform him that a courier from one of the Aioka Restaurants in Tokyo had just arrived with an envelope.

"Who is the courier?" Taka questioned the bodyguard.

"He is one of the waiters at the restaurant. He said the manager found this envelope when he opened up this morning. He had the waiter immediately drive here to bring it to you personally."

"Tell him to come in," Taka instructed.

When the waiter came in, Taka took the envelope and looked it over carefully but did not open it. Taka could see that the envelope had been sealed with a wax seal. He then took out over fifty thousand yen and handed it to the waiter.

"Share this money with your manager."

"Yes sensei," the man responded smiling sheepishly. Taka pulled out another wad of yen and again handed it to the waiter. "This is for a task I wish you to perform for me." Taka paused and the waiter was smart enough not to respond. Taka pulled out the cell phone from his pocket and grabbed a large brown envelope from a drawer in his desk. He carefully wiped the cell phone clean of any possible fingerprints with his handkerchief and dropped it into the envelope. "I want you to drop this phone into the sewer when you return to Tokyo. Do not be seen doing it and make sure that you do not touch it. Then take the envelope back to the restaurant and throw it into the garbage. Tell no one about this. Not even your manager. Do you understand?" Taka asked sharply.

"Yes sensei," the waiter responded even though he didn't understand. Taka waved his arm as a sign that the waiter was free to go. The bodyguard came up next to the waiter grabbing his arm to escort him out of the house. It was meant as a sign of intimidation to encourage the waiter to do exactly as Taka had instructed him.

Taka picked up the envelope and slowly turned it around looking at all sides before reading the label. He grabbed a letter opener off of his desk and carefully cut the seal making sure that he was the first to break it. He pulled out several printed pieces of paper from inside the envelope, laid them on his desk and began to read.

A scowl came across Taka's face. As he read further the scowl turned into a smile. "I thank you Hiroshi Kurosawa," Taka said out loud. "You have just given me the solution to cure all the grief that has been troubling me. You have made it possible for me to put all suspicions and allegation of my connection to the Red Summit behind. And in the process eliminate all of those who have let me down or hounded me, including you, Hiroshi Kurosawa. I knew I had allowed you to live for a reason."

# Chapter Nineteen


**It was not like Jim to leave** his house without locking his
security gate. He thought about it as he was driving down the road
and almost turned around, but he had to be back at Pearl Harbor the
day after tomorrow and he needed some answers about just what in
tar nation was going on with this damn potato. It had to be related to
the deaths of his aunt and uncle, but how? Jim knew he couldn't even
start to figure out this mystery until he read that letter. Jim called the
FedEx office on his way to the state agricultural office located near
the airport. FedEx told him that they had turned the package over to
the state. They were able to tell him the date it was sent from Perm.
That wasn't much help, but it might be when he found out exactly
when his uncle and aunt were murdered.

When Jim got to the Agriculture Office, most of his friends
were out doing their jobs at the airport or running around the island.
The place was practically deserted except for a few secretaries and
bosses who just sat behind desks talking on the phone, eating, and
getting fatter all day long.

"Hello Mr. Rikey, how was your vacation?" The smiling
receptionist said greeting Jim.

"I'm not much for fancy vacations," replied Jim.

"I heard you were on that high-class cruise ship. Forgive me
for saying so, but it did seem a little out of your league," the secretary
continued. "By the way, rumor is something bad happened on the
ship. People saw lots of helicopters and Navy ships in the area. It sat
off the coast for a couple of days without moving. It shouldn't have
done that, should it?"

Jim just smiled without answering and the secretary got the
hint.

"I bet you're here about that FedEx package. We didn't know
old Pete was a tuber sniffer." The secretary laughed out loud at her
own joke. When Jim didn't respond, she got serious. "I think Mr.
Laval has your package in his office. I'll tell him you are here."

Within minutes Jim was upstairs in Mr. Laval's office. Mr.
Laval was the supervisor of this facility and was a friend of Jim's.
Normally, such incidents as this were handled by one of the low-level

pencil pushers on the first floor. Since they recognized Jim's name and it was a rather curious set of circumstances, Mr. Laval decided to handle it.

"Jim, it's good to see you. Tell me, what the hell is all of this about anyway?" Greg Laval asked.

"That's exactly what I'm here to try to find out and I only have a day to do it," Jim replied. "Can I see that letter that came with the package?"

Greg was quiet while Jim carefully read the letter that had been included in the FedEx box. Greg had already read the letter so he knew the seriousness of its contents. When Jim finished he looked up with a worried grimace.

"Let me tell you what else I just found out," Jim said to Greg. For the next twenty minutes, Jim told Greg about the call from the State Department and about the apparent lack of information coming out of Russia concerning the deaths of his uncle and aunt. Greg sat silently as Jim told the story.

"What could be so damn important about a potato that someone is killed over it?" Greg said in frustration.

"Well, I damn well guarantee you I intend to find out," Jim responded.

Up until then, Jim had not even seen the potato or matroyshka. Greg reached into a file cabinet behind his desk and pulled out the wooden doll with the potato hidden inside.

"Your uncle sure made it a point to try to hide what he was sending," Greg commented.

"Jim picked up the doll, opened it, and removed the potato. He held it up in the air and turned it around and around looking at it from all angles. "Sure as hell looks like a normal potato."

"Yea, but did you read that part in the letter about it being over two years old. That's impossible. No potato can last that long without sprouting or going bad," Greg said in a matter of fact tone.

"Apparently this one has," Jim responded. "It must have been genetically modified in some way so it could stay fresh for so long."

"Maybe that's what your uncle was trying to find out."

"Nahh..," Jim replied. "It's got to be something more than that. Nobody would kill over something like that."

"You never know," replied Greg. "I was reading in this organic food book, by this guy named Robbins, how big companies take some pretty extreme measures to protect their genetic patents. Monarch even bought out this one company and fired the scientist who had discovered that this potato was…." Greg stopped in mid-sentence. "I know who you have to contact. This guy in the book I've been reading. He's some kind of an expert on genetic modifications of potatoes. You should call him. I have the book right over here. I'll find his name and we can search for him on the computer."

"You just get me the name," Jim replied. "I have some friends who can get me that number in no time." Jim picked up the phone and called the NCTC back in McClean.

In less than ten minutes Jim had the address and phone number of the fired scientist and called him immediately. The scientist was a little leery at first, but when Jim explained the circumstances surrounding the potato and his uncle and aunt's death, the scientist soon warmed up.

"Did you say it was sent from Perm?" the scientist asked.

"Yes, why?" Jim replied.

"Perm is the center of Russian genetic research. I hear they are doing some pretty scary things when it comes to genetic modifications. They have a couple of pretty ingenious scientists working for them. Could you send me a sample of that potato? If you do, I will tell you exactly what they have done to it and why it has lasted so long," the scientist explained to Jim.

"I will overnight a piece to you immediately," Jim replied.

"I don't need much, just a tiny slice will do," replied the scientist.

"It's on its way," Jim replied as he hung up the phone. Jim pulled out his pocket knife and sliced a small section of the end off of the potato. They wrapped it in plastic, placed it in a box and had one of the secretaries rush it over to the FedEx office to be shipped out immediately.

Mind if I take another little piece for a friend of mine here in Kona that knows a thing or two about GMOs?" Jim asked Greg.

"You must mean George?" Greg responded. "Sure you can."

"I hope you don't mind holding on to this potato a little longer," Jim said to Greg. "Could you keep it down in the lab for a few days until I hear back from that scientist?"

"Not a problem," Greg responded, as he picked up the potato and the two men headed out the door and down to the lab where it was labeled and placed on the shelf. "Don't you want the doll it came in?" Greg asked Jim.

"I'll pick it up later. If we leave it in the doll your lab technicians are less likely to eat it." Both men laughed and said their goodbyes.

Jim headed to his friend George Fujii's house. When he arrived, he explained what all had occurred with the potato and his uncle in Russia. Jim also told him about the scientist who agreed to analyze the potato for Jim.

"I don't see how I can help," replied George. "You have one of the top genetic researchers in the world analyzing that potato for you."

"Yea…, I know," Jim replied in his Texas drawl, "but I would just feel better about someone I know taking a crack at it as well. Besides, you can't tell me you wouldn't give your eye teeth for a chance like this," Jim said with a smile.

"That's for sure," George replied, as he smiled broadly and shook Jim's hand a little too energetically.

Viktor and the other Russian agent arrived at Jim's house less than three minutes after Satochi and his driver passed them near the intersection where Highway 250 meets Highway 19. They parked up the road where they had left the other Russian to keep watch over the house. They had hoped he would have seen them coming and met them at the driveway to the house. When he didn't, Viktor thought he must still be inside. He would reprimand him for allowing Viktor to approach unchallenged. Viktor left the other Russian agent to keep watch as he walked down the road to the open security gate. He called out, hoping to hear the Russian answer, but the only response was the dog coming out of its house barking. He paused a moment while he called the agent waiting in the car to see if any traffic was coming up the road. All seemed clear, so Viktor hurried to the rear of the house out of sight from the road. He left the phone line open in case he received a warning from the agent concerning someone approaching. When he neared the rear door, he could see it was ajar. Again, he called for the Russian who had been left behind. There was no answer. As he pushed the door open ever so slightly, he saw the blood splatter starting to trail in little rivulets down the length of the door.

He pulled his gun from his waistband and eased through the doorway and into the house. Sitting in a chair behind the desk was his agent with his throat slashed in the same manner as Yuri's driver in Perm. Viktor had no doubt the same assassin had killed them both. He noticed the gun lying on the floor near the dead agent's feet. Then he saw the Koa wood and shark-tooth club lying broken on top of the answering machine. Viktor knew that the placement of the club was a message left for him by the assassin. He reached over and pushed the club off of the answering machine's controls and used his gun to push the "play" message button. He listened carefully to the first two messages. The third was of no interest to Viktor. He already knew how that one turned out.

Viktor was troubled to know that whoever had kidnapped Yuri also knew the importance of the potato and would stop at nothing to possess it. He also knew that whoever this bloodthirsty assassin was, he had now thrown down the gauntlet challenging Viktor. It was now a race to retrieve the potato. Even more, he had dared Viktor to try to find Yuri, or to die trying. It wasn't often that Viktor found a foe that he could respect. But he knew that this assassin was like no other he had ever faced before.

Viktor picked up the gun that lay in blood on the floor near the desk. He could see his agent never had the opportunity to fire the weapon. Viktor knew there was nothing more he needed to see in this house. He had been challenged by this mystery assassin who always seemed to be a step ahead. He would never back away from such a challenge.

The potato was no longer important to Viktor. His goal had been to keep it out of the hands of the Americans. He knew his mysterious adversary would see to that. Viktor knew the assassin would do his job for him. He had no doubt that the assassin would retrieve the potato and keep its secrets from the Americans. That is, if the Americans didn't already know the secrets the potato held. Viktor would find out who this Jim Rikey was and why the potato was sent to him. Then he would focus on his two main tasks, retrieving Yuri and eliminating his new challenger.

Jim was feeling better now that he had some direction for trying to figure out what had happened to his aunt and uncle. It made the drive back to his house a little better, but not much. He mentally made a list of all the calls he would make starting with the State Department to see what the holdup was with the Russians. He would also call Jotty to let him know what had happened and to see what suggestions Jotty might have. He knew Jotty could pull some strings back in Washington to get things moving.

Day was turning to evening when Jim arrived back at his house above Waimea. He had thought about stopping at Merriman's for some grilled Ahi, but remembered he had left his security gate open and wanted to get back to his house before dark. This was the first time he had ever left his house without locking the gate and activating the security system. It felt oddly strange to pull up into his drive without having to get out and perform the security chores that had become second nature to Jim.

Jim pulled into his driveway and knew something was not right. It was that same strange inkling that Jim had felt several times in the past when a situation was about to turn upside down and Jim's life was in the balance. He turned around, reaching in the back seat and opened his gun case. He pulled out one of his Colt 45s. He grabbed some bullets out of a box of ammunition and carefully loaded his six-shooter. He knew that if there was anyone in his house they of course had heard the car pull into the driveway. Sandy had come out of her doghouse at the sound of the car and was barking for Jim's attention. Jim opened his door and waited for a moment, then got out of the car and stood behind the open door pretending to grab something off of the floor. Like a flash Jim sprinted to the house and stood silently next to the front door. It was ajar! Had he left it ajar? He couldn't remember. He had too many thoughts on his mind when he left earlier that afternoon. Sandy had stopped barking when Jim had moved out of her line of sight. He listened for the slightest movement inside of his house. He heard none! He moved around to the back door and saw that the screen door seemed to be propped open. He knew he had not done that! He cocked the trigger of his Colt. His body tensed as he listened for any sign of movement. He again heard nothing. He slowly moved towards the opened back door. Then he saw the blood. A lot of blood! He looked through the doorway and saw a body splayed awkwardly in the chair behind his desk. A dark scarlet pool of blood had formed below the chair. He continued to survey the room, making sure whoever left the body in his chair was no longer in the house. He saw no one and entered very slowly and cautiously.

As he approached the body, the savageness of the attack came into view. The neck of the victim was brutally ripped away from between the head and the torso almost to the spine. Jim saw the club on his answering machine. It was cracked and several of the shark-teeth were missing. He had seen weapons similar to this along the hallway at the Waikoloa Hilton. It was in an area that featured Oceanic Art and artifacts just off of the lobby toward the lagoon tower, actually right by where Jim, Jotty, and Haruko had the shootout with Minoru's men near the Malolo Lounge. Several questions were racing through Jim's mind, not least of which was who is this dead man sitting in my house and what was he doing here?

After carefully searching the rest of the house to make sure he would find no more surprises, Jim went to the kitchen and grabbed a dish towel. The house was small and only had one phone. That phone had some blood splatter on it, but not a lot. Jim used the towel to pick up the phone and call 911. He didn't think to use his cell phone to make the call. He rarely thought about using his cell phone. He reported that he had just returned home and found someone murdered in his house. He gave them the address even though they already knew it. Next, Jim tried to call Jotty, but got his message machine. Jim left a quick message telling Jotty to call ASAP and said that the shit had hit the fan on the Big Island. Getting Jotty's answering machine drew Jim's attention back to his own. Why did the murderer leave the broken club on the answering machine? Why didn't he take it with him or just drop it on the floor or on the desk? It was placed there as if to send a message, "but a message to whom?" Jim said out loud. Jim had a funny feeling that he wasn't the first person to come across this dead body lying in the chair. This day was going from bad to worse. It made him wonder what was going to happen next. Jim went into the kitchen and grabbed another beer out of the refrigerator. He went back out to his favorite chair in his garden and sat down to watch the sunset. His first beer was still setting there untouched and warm. He sat his new beer down next to the warm one and stared to the west, waiting for the elusive green flash. When the police arrived both beers still sat untouched. Jim would have to wait for another sunset to see the flash.

# Chapter Twenty

**When Lyuba and Yuri arrived** at the Lihu'e Airport on Kauai, they were met by two of Satochi's most loyal and trusted foot soldiers, Tonga Tonga and Bendo Tonga. They were two of seven brothers who were all born in The Kingdom of Tonga, but moved with their parents to Kapa'a, Hawaii, when they were young. They were very, very large brothers! Like many Tonganese men they were both over six feet seven inches tall. Bendo was slightly taller than Tonga, but Tonga was a little wider at the shoulders than his brother. They both looked as big as a professional football lineman with his pads on. By anyone's standards they were huge muscular men. They both worked out religiously and were surprisingly fast and agile considering they had so great of a mass to move around. They also were not nearly as serious as Satochi. They were usually smiling, but rarely spoke to anyone but each other and that was not very often. When they did speak it was in Pidgin and almost impossible for most people to understand. Pidgin was a local dialect that was designed to say as few words, or for that matter, as few syllables, as possible to get the message across. It consisted of words made up of parts of several other words or phrases that allowed the speaker to say an entire sentence or express an entire concept in one or two words. Basically, it was a language for very lazy people who didn't even want to expend the energy it took to carry on a conversation. It had become a very popular language in many parts of Hawaii!

As Satochi had instructed, Tonga stopped the car at Hilo Hattie's so Yuri and Lyuba could buy more appropriate clothes for the warm Hawaiian climate. The compound where they were to stay was in Hanapepe on the southwest side of the island. That meant it didn't get much rain, so Lyuba and Yuri didn't need any jackets, at least for the time being. They could pick those up later at one of the nicer hotel boutiques or at one of the smaller shopping complexes like Poipu Shopping Village or even Old Koloa Town. The next couple of days Lyuba would spend making Yuri feel at ease while he became familiar with his new laboratory and surroundings. Part of her assignment was to explain why Taka had selected Yuri to be brought out of Russia and what they expected of him. Taka knew very well that Yuri was capable of providing the science needed for the next phase of Taka's terrorist activities, but would Yuri agree to do it? It would be these next few critical days when Satochi and Lyuba would determine if Yuri was going to work out as Taka had envisioned. If not, more stringent means would be necessary to convince Yuri to cooperate.

Their fears were quickly put to rest. Even before Satochi returned from the Big Island, Yuri was busy working in his new laboratory and explaining to his assistants the tasks and duties he expected them to perform. Yuri's research was even more advanced than Taka had thought. It wasn't until Satochi returned to Kauai that Yuri explained the capabilities of his genetic modifications.

Tonga and Bendo spent most of their time at the compound working out and training in various martial arts. It was their job to make sure the rest of the security team stayed alert and prepared for any scenario. Automatic weapons were hidden in various locked vaults around the compound. These vaults could be opened from the master control room located in the main house or at each individual vault. That way the security team could work and walk around the plantation without carrying weapons and raising suspicions from the occasional visitor who happened to be passing by.

Tonga and Bendo also set up a little plan, with the help of Lyuba, to distract Yuri from the pleasures that Lyuba had to offer. The third day after their arrival, Lyuba told Yuri that she had some errands to handle in Poipu. When she left, an incredibly beautiful, young and provocative housecleaner just happened to mistakenly walk into Yuri's bedroom. It didn't take much for this new beauty to seduce Yuri while making it seem like Yuri was seducing her. Nature quickly took its course and in a matter of minutes the two were frolicking wildly in bed. Yuri seemed very pleased with this new, younger mistress. Had Lyuba not been so secure with her own attractiveness, she might have taken offense at how quickly Yuri turned from the pleasures she had to offer to those of the much younger Hawaiian girl. Yet that had been the purpose of the whole ruse and it had worked to perfection.

# Chapter Twenty-one

**Jotty had been in the shower** when Jim tried to call. After Jim left Pearl Harbor, Jotty had the Navy liaison officer arrange for a car and driver to take him to his hotel in Waikiki. Jotty was staying at the Prince Hotel facing the Ala Wai boat harbor just at the northwest end of Waikiki Beach. That was the boat harbor made famous by the opening scene in the television show, "Gilligan's Island". That was from where the ship set sail for its three hour cruise. All the tour guides made sure to tell their customers that fact. The Prince Hotel seemed to cater to a mostly Japanese clientele. Why the NCTC Travel Office booked Jotty there he wasn't sure, but it probably had a lot to do with the price. Jotty's room was nice and had a terrific view of Honolulu. He was on the fourteenth floor and could see the planes coming in for a landing at the airport and the cruise ships docking down by the Aloha Tower. Jotty had taken a nap trying to get his body to adjust to the six-hour time difference. He had a bite to eat in the hotel coffee shop and then had gone back to his room for the shower.

When he heard Jim's message he knew that something serious had happened. He was not prepared to hear just how serious when he returned Jim's call. The crime scene investigation was in full swing by the time Jotty called. Police, FBI, and Customs agents all were on the scene taking Jim's statement, listening to the message machine, and reading the letter that Howard had included in the package. Jotty told Jim he would head to the Big Island immediately and asked to speak to whomever was in charge. He told them the NCTC was now taking charge over the investigation and that a senior FBI officer on the scene was now in charge until Jotty arrived. He told that agent he was now working on temporary assignment to the NCTC. From his run-in with the Red Summit last year on the Big Island, he knew the Hilo FBI office was understaffed, so he called the local FBI office in Honolulu and had several of the agents conscripted for immediate temporary assignment to the NCTC. In his position as head of a counter-terrorism section of the NCTC he had the power to do this but, up until now, had never even thought about it. He also instructed the FBI office to arrange immediate transportation for him and his new conscripts to Kona, Hawaii. They were to leave within the hour.

He also told them to bring their best crime scene investigators with them. Jotty, like Jim, sensed that there was more going on with this murder than it appeared. With what had just happened to Haruko in Thailand, Jotty was taking no chances. He was calling in all the reinforcements on this one.

The plane and the agents were waiting at the airport when Jotty arrived. He knew many of the agents wouldn't be happy to have rank pulled on them by some NCTC bigwig. When he arrived, several of the agents recognized Jotty from the shootout last year at the Paleaka Ranch. Their animosity quickly waned. They did have to wait a few minutes until the CSI technicians showed up, because they had been involved in an investigation on the North Shore.

The plane ride to Kona took less than forty minutes, but gave Jotty the chance to fill the agents in on what he knew and what he expected of them. The main thing was to get the local authorities out of the investigation. As their jet circled for the south-to-north landing at the Kona Airport, a large building fire could be seen out of the left side of the airplane. As the plane neared the runway, the fire could be seen burning out of control just to the east of the airport. Jotty had the pilot ask the control tower what was burning. The tower informed them that it was the State Agriculture Offices and that was going to cause all sorts of problems with delays for incoming aircraft from the mainland. How were they going to process all of those fruit and vegetable importation notices those passengers had to fill out before their arrival? It was going to be one big mess the controller told the pilot.

When the pilot relayed the message to Jotty, he knew things had just gotten a lot more complicated. Jim had told him about the potato being held at the Agriculture Office. It wasn't much of a stretch to connect the murder victim in Jim's house with the fire at the Ag Offices.

Three large SUV rentals were waiting on the tarmac by the public aircraft parking area. Jotty and several of the FBI agents, along with one of the CSI techs, headed to Jim's house in Waimea in two of the SUVs. He had two other agents and the other CSI head to the Agriculture Office to see what had occurred. The fire looked to be out or at least in the final stages. Jotty told the two agents to head to the Ag Offices and find the matryoshka with the potato inside. Jim had told Jotty it was in the lab on one of the shelves, and Jotty relayed that information to the agents.

Satochi and his driver drove directly to one of the many auto supply stores located in Waimea. While Satochi waited in the car, his driver entered the store and bought several three-gallon plastic containers for gasoline. They stopped at a local filling station in town and filled all of the containers. They headed down to the agricultural building near the airport. They circled the building several times looking for cameras that might monitor the coming and going of visitors, but found none. They parked in the lot next store to the Ag offices and watched and waited. Jim had already left the offices by the time they had arrived but Satochi would not have known Jim even if he had seen him. Several people exited the building around 4:30 p.m., getting in the few cars parked in the lot. Satochi got out of the car and instructed his driver to drive to the back. He walked up to the door as a maintenance worker prepared to lock the doors for the night.

"Sorry, everyone is gone for the day. You'll have to return in the morning. They open…." The man's explanation was cut short when Satochi pushed his way inside. With a quick jab, he knocked the man unconscious. Satochi grabbed him before he could collapse and laid him behind the counter out of sight of anyone who happened to walk up to the entrance door. He locked the door with the keys the man still held in his hand. He went to the back of the building and unlocked the back door.

"Brah, bring in the gasoline, then search the building. I want no surprises," Satochi instructed. Satochi went into the lab to search for the potato. The task was much simpler than he had expected. The matroyshka was sitting in plain view on the shelf. He grabbed it and smiled when he felt its weight. The potato was no doubt still inside. His driver returned from searching the building and was holding a well-dressed man from one of the offices on the second floor.

"Tell this thug to unhand me. Just what is the meaning of this?" The man was trying to exert his authority by acting all blustery. "I demand you release me at once."

Had Satochi not left his club in the car, he would surely have used it on this stuffed pig of a man. He bound and gagged the man, then tied him to one of the large metal tables in the laboratory.

The driver placed plastic explosive charges with what looked like cell phones on the containers of gasoline in the laboratory and two adjacent rooms. Satochi and the driver left through the back door, locking it with the keys that Satochi had taken from the maintenance man. He broke the key in the lock just in case someone tried to enter before he could detonate the explosives. He tossed the potato and matroyshka in the back seat of the car as he entered. As the driver pulled onto the Keahole Airport Road, Satochi pressed the button of the garage door opener. The blast was barely audible. They headed back to Taka's house in the hills above Hawi without looking back.

When Jotty's team arrived at Jim's house, they quickly took over and excused all the other police personnel on the scene, but only after they had retrieved any notes that the investigators had taken. Before Jotty's team arrived at Jim's house, he had heard from the agents he sent to the Agriculture building. The fire was not as destructive as it had appeared from the air. It was limited to just one portion of the building which included the laboratory where the matryoshka was located. The agents were quickly able to determine that it was a gasoline-fueled fire ignited by some sort of small explosive. There had been multiple areas where the fire had started, indicating that several containers of gasoline were used. Unfortunately, two bodies were found at the scene. Both bound and burned beyond recognition. It would be a couple of days before there was a definitive identification, although co-workers had already told them who would have been in the building at the time of the fire.

The FBI agents from the Honolulu office were well-trained as were most FBI agents and did not need someone to tell them how to proceed in an investigation. They had already begun contacting gas stations between Waimea and Kona to see if anyone had purchased and filled several containers with gas. With the high price of gasoline on the Big Island, it did not take long for them to find the location where Satochi's driver had purchased the gas. The clerk remembered because the man had paid with a hundred dollar bill instead of the usual credit card. One of the agents was now on his way there to collect that hundred dollar bill and to view the videotape recording which all gas stations had these days. Another of the agents had checked the neighboring businesses and buildings to see if they might have had video monitoring that might prove useful, but had no luck in

126

finding any. The CSI was checking the burned out lab to see if he could find any residue from the potato or matryoshka in the area where it had been stored, but he knew that search would be futile.

"I got bad news buddy," Jotty said as he sat down with Jim. "There's been a fire at the Agriculture Offices."

"From your tone I'm guessing there's more to it than just a fire."

"Two bodies were found," Jotty said.

"Any idea who the bodies are? I've got several friends there."

"One was the night maintenance worker in charge of locking up and cleaning the building."

Jim had met the man but really didn't know him. "Who was the other one?"

"The other was one of the supervisors. Greg Laval."

"Shit!" Jim shook his head and sighed. "I hope I didn't bring this on him." Too many people were dying around Jim and he was starting to get very agitated about this whole affair. "I'm going to need a few days to sort things out here I need to figure out just exactly what the hell is going on."

That meant Jotty would have to postpone his trip to Japan for a few days. He would now have to check out the videos from the hydrogen plane. He knew the Navy liaison would allow only Jim or Jotty to view those tapes and he had to agree that Jim needed to stay here to work on this case. Eddie would be arriving in Honolulu in a day or two so he could give Jotty a hand there. The worst part would be calling Haruko and putting her off for a few days. Jotty was looking forward to seeing her again and knew she would not be happy about being kept in the dark about what was going on any longer than she had to be.

Satochi ordered his driver to take the long way to Taka's house. That required going through Waimea, driving over the volcano and coming into the backside of Hawi. This way he could see what was going on at Jim's house. As they approached the house he was surprised to see what were obviously several FBI agents already working the crime scene. It normally took, at the minimum, a day for the FBI to get involved in an investigation. Satochi realized he needed to be more cautious and to cover his movements a little better. The FBI would learn where the gasoline containers were purchased, as well as the gas used to fill them. That meant they would soon have a picture of his driver and not long after that a name to go with that picture. They would also have the license number of the car. Fortunately, his driver had placed stolen plates on the car before he had picked up Satochi from the airport. He would have the plates changed as soon as they arrived at Taka's house. He would also need to leave the Big Island early in the morning and return to Kauai. Even though his driver was from Kauai and that is where the FBI would look, Satochi knew the driver would be safer there hidden away at the coffee plantation. No one in Kauai and especially no one in Kapa'a, where the driver was from, would do anything to help the FBI find their man. That was a quick way to die in Kauai.

The team at Jim's house was quickly making headway. There was no identification on the dead man's body and his fingerprints were not listed with the FBI. From his face they determined that he looked to be of Slavic descent. His clothes were typical tourist fare, probably purchased here on the island. Their break came when they checked out his tennis shoes and underwear. Both had labels that identified them as having been made in Russia. It now seemed clear that this man was Russian and more than likely come in search of the potato, but why? Jim hoped that his two genetic scientists would give him that answer. He was certain this potato must have been genetically altered and carried in it some secret so damning that the Russian government would go to any extreme to keep it secret, even to the point of murdering his aunt and uncle and the other missionaries killed in Perm. That now made sense, but this dead Russian body now lying on a gurney in Jim's house didn't fit in. Someone else must want that information as badly as the Russians, but who? Jim didn't doubt his own country would go to extremes to get their hands on such information, but he knew that wasn't the case. This seemed more like the work of terrorists. The way the Russian was killed was designed to be a message. Not necessarily a message to Jim but more likely a message to the Russians. Someone else was meant to see this body and Jim was guessing that whoever that was had seen it. If this man was a Russian agent as suspected, there would be others on the island.

Several fingerprints were found on the club, but none that matched any the FBI had on file. It also appeared that these

128

fingerprints had been altered surgically to help disguise the identity of their owner. The placement of the club was also important. It too was a message not necessarily meant for Jim, but for the same person the body was left for. The murderer wanted someone to listen to the answering machine almost as though he was challenging them to a game. A very deadly game!

One of the agents noticed that there had been a gun lying on the floor at some time. You could see its outline in the blood splatter. That meant it was there before the neck was ripped out, but removed sometime after that.

As the FBI agents speculated about the dead man being a possible Russian agent, one of them suddenly remembered an e-mail that had come to his computer earlier that day. The e-mail was a standard one their office would occasionally receive from Customs informing them that a visitor to the islands was yellow-flagged when their passport name or number was put into the computer. A yellow flag just meant a person of interest. In this case, that person of interest happened to be a former high ranking KGB agent. "He just so happens to have arrived this morning here on the Big Island," the agent informed the part of the team working inside the house.

"That means we should have a local address where this former KGB man is staying," Jotty said, emphasizing the word "former". This drew a smile from several of the agents. "Somebody get me that address now," Jotty ordered. The agent already had his computer out and pulled up the e-mail.

"A Mr. Viktor Cheznov, staying at The Bay Club Condominiums in Waikoloa, number 1301," the agent called out while another wrote it down for Jotty.

"What do say you and me take a little ride and visit this Viktor as a gesture of friendship and diplomacy," Jotty said smiling towards Jim.

"Let my grab my six-shooters," Jim responded as he headed for the door.

"You better come with us," Jotty said pointing to three of the agents. They all put on bullet proof vests just as a precaution and jumped into one of the SUVs. The day was about to get much longer!

# Chapter Twenty-two

"**Yes?**" a soft voice said into the receiver.

Taka had finally reached Satochi at the house in Hawi. "How are things going, my friend?"

"I have successfully recovered the potato," Satochi said, without going into detail.

"That is good news. Very good news! I am pleased," Taka responded.

"I am troubled the FBI has become so quickly involved. The Russians have also been here seeking the potato, but of course failed. I had to eliminate one of the Russians at the home of this Jim Rikey. I believe that is why the FBI was so quick to react. They must have identified the man as Russian FSB almost immediately to warrant such a swift response," Satochi explained.

Taka was listening as Satochi was relating what had occurred when he was suddenly struck by the recognition of the name, Jim Rikey. "Did you say the house belonged to Jim Rikey?"

"Yes, a Jim Rikey, you sound like you know this man," Satochi responded.

"I have never seen this Mr. Rikey, but I know him so very well. He is one of the men responsible for destroying my operations on the Paleaka Ranch and foiling the distribution of the tainted cosmetics in Los Angeles. The reason the FBI was there so quickly is that he himself works for the FBI. I was told he moved to the island to try to find the source of the weaponized anthrax that was spilled in the laboratory during the raid," Taka explained.

Satochi could hear the concern in Taka's voice.

"You must make a trip to the hidden lab through the lava tube and bring out more canisters of the anthrax. Store them with the others below the safe house. I will soon put it to good use."

Satochi did not like the idea of having to move the anthrax. He had been inoculated to protect him from the disease, but the scientists had been sloppy when they filled the canisters and he had spilled a pile of the anthrax in the lava tube when he last transported one of the canisters. He had not yet cleaned it up. Every time he transported some of the anthrax, Satochi had to go through a time-consuming decontamination to insure that no anthrax spores accidentally made it out of the lava tube or safe area below the house. If some did it could prove disastrous to Taka's plan and deadly to anyone who came into contact with those spores.

"I want you and Lyuba to come to Tokyo next week. Some issues have come up that require your expertise. I will explain when you arrive. First you must return to Kauai to see how our scientist is adjusting to his new identity and assignment." Taka paused to think. "Have him explain what makes that potato so important."

"I understand Mr. Matsuura," Satochi responded politely. "Would you like me to eliminate this Jim Rikey before I return?"

"That won't be necessary. In time you may have to, but for now I think it best for you to leave the island and return to Kauai."

"As you wish, sir."

Satochi told his driver to change the plates back to the correct ones on the car, return it to the rental agency at the airport and return immediately to Kauai that night. "Braddah, I'm afraid by the morning the FBI will be looking for you," Satochi said almost apologetically. "We were careless and the FBI will be quick to capitalize on our errors. When you get to Kauai, return to the plantation and stay there. I have to make a stop on my way back but will return to the plantation later in the day, ka."

"Whateva." The driver responded and left immediately to change the plates and return to Kauai.

It was best that the driver was gone. Only a few of Taka's and Satochi's most trusted and loyal comrades knew about the hidden laboratory and the lava tube passage from Taka's house to the lab. Satochi waited until the driver had left, then secured the house and entered into the secret passage below. He unlocked the heavy steel door that separated the safe room from the lava tube. It was outside this door that he had spilled the anthrax. He had been in the tube over a month ago. He had not told Taka about having spilled the anthrax and had planned on cleaning it up next time he moved a canister. Unfortunately, he would again have to put off cleaning up his spill. His time was too short for such a task this trip. As he swung the heavy door open, an involuntary gasp escaped from his throat. The majority of the spilled anthrax was gone. Someone had scooped it up and left the remaining portion spread around on the floor. It appeared someone had used their hand to scoop it into some type of container or bag. A torn zip-locked sandwich bag lay on the ground next to where the pile had been. There were also pry marks on the steel door that appeared to be made by a knife. It would take much more than prying to ever break through that door. It also would have been impossible for anyone to have breached the secret door at the lab. That meant someone had come up the lava tube from the ocean.

"This is bad, very bad!" Satochi said out loud. He grabbed one of the powerful flashlights and followed the lava tube down to where it went into the ocean. There he found a wrapper from an energy bar. He was now sure that this was how the intruder had entered the tunnel.

He started to panic, but realized that if the FBI had discovered the anthrax and the ocean entrance to the lava tube they would have already broken through those steel doors. It must have been some divers exploring caves in the channel off the island. Regardless, whoever had accidentally stumbled into the lava tube and taken the anthrax was no doubt dead by now if they had not been inoculated against the disease. Satochi knew that this strain of anthrax had been modified to kill within hours, not days. Chances are they never even made it back to their boat. As soon as he exited the tunnel he would make some calls. An outbreak of anthrax was something that nobody could keep a secret. Someone would have to have heard about some dead divers.

Satochi returned up the tunnel and moved another canister as Taka had requested. He went through the decontamination process and returned back to the house. He decided to postpone informing Taka until he found out more information about what may have happened to the divers who had entered the tunnel. He called several of his sources around the islands and they all said they would get back to him in the morning.

When the next morning arrived, Satochi called for a helicopter to pick him up at a field about a mile from the house. The helicopter was to take him to Kapalua on Maui. There was a certain Koa wood club in the gallery at the Ritz-Carlton that he needed to buy. He would also arrange for a car and driver to take him by Larry's house to see if the one he had ordered a few months back was completed yet. He certainly hoped so. He had not expected to break the other club as soon as he did but, then again, these were busy times.

132

As the helicopter began to rise, Satochi smiled as he wondered what the Russians were up to and if they were still in the game. At least he knew that there was one new player who had joined the game, Jim Rikey. He hoped he would prove to be a worthy opponent for, if not, he most assuredly wouldn't be around long.

# Chapter Twenty-three

**To say that Haruko was not happy** about Jotty delaying his visit to Tokyo was at best a major understatement. When she received the e-mail Jotty had sent her from the plane on the way to the Big Island, she was almost angry enough to fly to Hawaii and confront him on the spot. When he followed up with a call after he had arrived at Jim's, she was much more understanding. The problem now was that Jotty would probably arrive just around the time of the Aioka Restaurant opening in Kashiwa. She was determined to attend the opening but wasn't so sure Jotty would understand. If he was in town at that time he would just have to go along with her. That's all there was to it!

Haruko was disappointed that she would have to wait to get the information regarding the Thai terrorist cell and their connection to the Red Summit. She knew that Jotty had a lot more information than he was willing to talk about. She hoped she could convince him to be a little more forthcoming with the information, but knew she could never lead him on romantically as a means of gaining information. She did care for Jotty, but she was conflicted as to just how much she cared and how to deal with it. Like before, her job came first. Not this daily job at the National Police Agency. That was just a tool to pursue her real job. That job was to prove beyond a doubt that Taka was indeed the real power behind the Red Summit. Someday, and hopefully someday soon, after she successfully revealed the truth about Taka Matsuura, she would be free to pursue the romance and the emotions she kept bottled up inside. Until then her life was on hold and, even though she didn't realize it, it was ripping her apart.

Taka had requested that Satochi join him in Japan after he was assured all was going well back in Kauai. Taka had devised a plan that would finally prove he was the victim of the Red Summit and not its leader. He needed Satochi's help in doing so. The Thai terrorists had arrived in Tokyo over the past couple of days. They had been supplied with excellent false passports and identification papers to insure that their names didn't pop up on the international no-fly list. They were now staying in one of Taka's safe houses outside of Tokyo center awaiting his instructions. Taka had devised a plan for the Thai terrorist cell to blow up the new Aioka Restaurant while Taka was attending the grand opening ceremonies. They would release an announcement saying that they were trying to finish the job that they had failed to complete the previous year when they only succeeded in killing Niki. Taka and his Americanization of Japan was their true target. Of course, Taka would escape unhurt, but it would once again build public sentiment in his favor. It would give him an excuse to sell his Aioka chain of restaurants and move away from Japan. Then he could pursue his terrorist goal of bringing the United States to its knees. He knew Haruko would not miss a chance to see him in person and, if for some reason, she happened to get killed in the terrorist attack, so much the better. Just to be safe, Taka planned on sending an anonymous tip to her office warning of a potential terrorist attack occurring at the opening. Taka knew that she would never be convinced that anyone but Taka was the leader of the Red Summit. He had to admire her for that. She was no doubt a smart dedicated police officer but, unfortunately for her, her dedication to this belief would lead to her downfall. If all went according to his plan, Haruko would actually have to save Taka from the terrorists. If Taka was lucky enough, maybe she would even die in the process. How ironic that would be!

Taka knew that even if he did pay the exorbitant sum of money Hiroshi had requested for the alleged proof Taka wasn't who he claimed to be, Hiroshi would still make it public. Taka expected such and had already put into motion a plan that tied Hiroshi and his cousin to the bombing of the Aioka restaurant in Phuket. He also would make it look as if they were members of the terrorist cell that had carried out the bombing. Taka would make it appear like Hiroshi was involved in several other activities associated with the Red Summit's past violence, including the murder and fire on *the Grand Maui*! It would be easy for Taka to show that this supposedly damning information about him was nothing more than part of the Red Summit's plot to destroy and discredit him. After the attempt on his life at the grand opening, who would possibly think otherwise? That is, who besides Haruko?

# Chapter Twenty-four

**Viktor knew that it wouldn't take long** for the FBI to figure out that the dead man in Jim's house was Russian. They would be quick to determine that the former KGB agent Viktor Cheznov, who had arrived recently on the Big Island, undoubtedly, was somehow involved. That was how the intelligence business worked. Just as it hadn't taken long for Viktor to discover that Jim Rikey had once worked for the FBI as part of that international counter-terrorism task force put together to deal with the Red Summit and who had just within the past two days been asked to work again as part of such a task force under the same leader as before, a Mr. Jotty Joplin. However, now he was part of the new National Counter-Terrorism Center. Information was easy to come by in this business.

He was expecting the FBI to show up at his condominium at any moment. He was looking forward to meeting Jim Rikey and, hopefully, Jotty Joplin. In preparation he had taken all of the weapons and secure cell phones and placed them in hidden compartments in his and the other agent's golf bags. He had taken the bags to the club house of the Waikoloa King's Course to be placed on golf carts for their 6:30 a.m. tee time in the morning. For he and his friend were just visiting the island for a little fun and relaxation which included several rounds of golf. They had been paired with another twosome who just happened to be Russian ex-patriots. They would exchange golf bags with Viktor at the end of their game the next morning, taking the guns and cell phones with them.

Viktor didn't bother to go to the Agriculture offices to look for the potato. He knew it would already be gone. Nor was he surprised when he saw a story on the local news about the apparent arson fire and murders at the Ag offices. He knew that his challenger was a dangerous, bloodthirsty man. He was confident in the assassin's ability to get a hold of the potato and keep its secrets from the Americans. He just hoped the assassin had done so in time. He knew that this assassin already had Yuri, so the knowledge the potato held was already at their disposal. Viktor needed to find Yuri and knew he would find him somewhere in Hawaii.

Suddenly there was a loud knock at the door. Viktor had left it slightly ajar so as not to have the FBI break it down costing Viktor an expensive replacement fee.

"FBI," a voice shouted, "we're coming in. Put your hands in the air."

Viktor and the other Russian agent were standing with their hands in the air wearing nothing but swimsuits to show that they were not concealing any weapons. This was just in case some over-anxious FBI man came storming into the condominium looking for an excuse to shoot. They stood quietly while the FBI searched and secured all the rooms. Viktor stood smiling while the other agent stayed expressionless.

"You must be Viktor Cheznov," Jotty said to Viktor. "I am Jotty Joplin with the NCTC."

"Let me assure you we are not terrorists," Viktor replied. "We are just two Russians here to enjoy a little vacation and golfing in Hawaii. I am Viktor, as you already know, and this is my friend Sergei."

"Just a little golf vacation you say. That's the same thing you told the customs agent when you were questioned at the airport yesterday," Jotty replied.

"That is because it is true," Viktor replied smugly.

"Passport security says that a third Russian arrived on the Big Island yesterday as well. A Sascha Lavrov! Was he with you also?"

"I'm afraid I have never heard of this Sascha Lavrov. Do you know of this man, Sergei?" Viktor asked his friend. Sergei just shook his head no. "I'm sorry we can be of no help, Mr. Joplin. Could we please put our hands down now if you don't mind?"

"I'm sorry, of course you can," Jotty replied politely. "If I didn't know better I'd say it looks like you were expecting us, with the door ajar as it was and the two of you dressed so there would be no doubt that you were unarmed."

Viktor continued to smile without responding. Jotty stared at the two Russians while his team did a thorough search of the condominium. "By the way," Jotty finally said, "here is a copy of the search warrant that authorizes this search." Viktor never bothered to look at the piece of paper Jotty laid on the table before him

"That is a hindrance we do not have to worry about in my country," Viktor replied. "Could you please introduce me to the tall agent behind you, the one that is obviously not an FBI agent?" Jim stepped forward as Viktor continued. "I am quite a fan of the history of your Old West, as I think you call it. I have never seen anyone wearing six-shooters and a holster out of that era. I find it simply fascinating."

"I'm Jim Rikey," Jim stuck out his hand, offering to shake Viktor's hand. Viktor was a little surprised by the gesture, but shook Jim's hand. "I sorta fancy these weapons myself," Jim responded pulling one of the Colts from his holster and spinning it around in his hand like a professional showman.

"Quite impressive, Mr. Rikey!" Viktor replied.

"Just call me Jim," Jim responded.

"And you call me Jotty," Jotty spoke up. Jotty's men had found nothing in the condo or in the rental car to link the dead Russian to Viktor. Jotty had not expected to find anything. He had read the dossier sent from Washington on Viktor Cheznov and knew he was a top flight FSB operative not likely to make such a mistake.

"Mr. Cheznov. .." Jotty started to say but was interrupted.

"Please, call me Viktor. We are on a first name basis already," Viktor replied laughing.

"Well, Viktor," Jotty began again. "I'm sure you know as much about us as we know about you. I have no doubt that the man killed at Jim's house today was one of your men." Viktor pretended to act surprised. "Please, no melodramatics," Jotty said. "I also know that we can probably not prove any connection to you or Sergei, although we will be trying over the next several days, as I'm sure you would do if such a murder happened in your country." Viktor nodded his head. "The difference between our countries, however, is that in Russia you would arrest everyone remotely involved and hold them until you were able to manufacture evidence against them. Here you are free to go until such real evidence is found."

"And your way is more effective?" Viktor replied. "Your courts allow hundreds of rapists and murderers to walk free every year. And you say your way is better?"

"It works for me," Jim spoke up. "Let me just add one thing here. As far as I'm concerned you are welcome to enjoy the freedoms that the United States has to offer, but if I find out you had anything to do with the killing of those missionaries in Perm you had better disappear before I make you disappear."

138

"Is that a threat, Jim?" Viktor asked smiling.

"No sireee, Jim said. "It's just a fact. I've no doubt you are here looking for the potato my uncle sent to me, but I think somebody beat us both to it. Unfortunately, one of your men and two Ag office workers died along with several innocent missionaries in Russia. We intend to find out just who that person is killing people here in Hawaii, just as I hope you find out who did the murders in Russia. It's been a pleasure meeting you." Jim turned and walked out the door.

"You must excuse Jim. He is a little upset by what happened to his aunt and uncle as well as what happened at his house today," Jotty told Viktor. "He is correct in saying we do think you are involved in this somehow. We will be keeping an eye on you while you enjoy Hawaii."

"I would expect nothing less," Viktor replied sincerely. "I do hope we have the opportunity to meet again under less suspicious circumstances. It was a pleasure meeting you both."

Having said their goodbyes, Jim and Jotty drove down to the Ag offices just to confirm that the potato was indeed missing. Jotty made sure that men were in place to continually watch Viktor as long as he was in Hawaii. On the way to the Ag office Jim told Jotty how he had been able to cut slices out of the potato and send them to two genetic experts to analyze. He also told Jotty about what he found out regarding the genetic research going on in the Perm region of Russia. Jim had no doubt that the potato and all the deaths were related but knew that there was a part to this puzzle that they were missing. What it was, he had no idea, but he was convinced that Viktor did, along with this mystery assassin who seemed to be one step ahead of them and one step ahead of Viktor. Jim and Jotty were both surprised by how calm Viktor remained under pressure. He had lost one of his own agents and seemed to have lost the potato.

"You know Jotty, I think that club left on my answering machine was a message. Maybe even a challenge meant for Viktor. I would bet the farm that Viktor was in my house and received that message. I also think Viktor, in turn, left it for me to find."

"I think this case is a little too close to home for you right now, buddy." Jotty replied.

"It's a game. Viktor has invited us to the game in the same way the assassin had baited Viktor into this mystery."

"Well, I'm ready to play," Jotty replied.

"Yep, me too! But you're right about one thing. "As much as I want to stay on the Big Island and work on these murders, it is too personal. I have some work to do back at Pearl Harbor. Finding the source of the weaponized anthrax found on the dive boat is more important. That's where I need to be."

Jotty had to agree. Jim had the expertise with anthrax. "I'll follow up on the murders here until I leave to meet Haruko in Tokyo in a few days. It will also give me a chance to pressure Washington to see what they can find out about the murder of your aunt and uncle."

Jim's house would be a mess for the next few days while the crime scene people went over every inch of it. He would not be allowed to remove anything from the house, but fortunately, he still had not unpacked his suitcase from the cruise ship. He convinced Jotty to have the NCTC pick up the tab for a night at the Hilton Waikoloa. Jotty didn't seem to mind spending the government's money and decided to join Jim and also stay at the Hilton. It gave them both a chance to find out what each other had been up to for the past several months without having to hear it from Haruko. It also gave Jim the opportunity to finally do more than just open a beer.

# Chapter Twenty-five

**Satochi paid cash** for the Koa and shark-tooth Lei O Mano at the gallery in the Ritz-Carlton in Kapalua. He also refused to give them his name for the mailing list. The club turned out to be much nicer than Satochi had expected. It should be for the price he had to pay. Five thousand dollars! It was actually one of Larry's finer pieces of work. Had he been holding out on Satochi? When Satochi confronted Larry with that very question, he found out that particular club had been at the gallery for several years, at least two years prior to Satochi becoming Larry's primary customer. Satochi felt better once it was explained to him. In fact, Larry had advised Satochi that the Ritz-Carlton club was one of his finer pieces and Satochi should purchase it, but at the time Satochi thought the cost to be prohibitive. That was before Satochi was added to Taka's payroll by Minoru.

With his business handled on Maui, Satochi had a private jet take him to Kauai. Waiting for him there was Tonga and Bendo. They reported there had already been inquiries about the whereabouts of Noe Espeleta by the FBI in Kapa'a. Of course no one said anything. That was the way it was in Kapa'a. No one ever said anything. If you did, it could get you and your family killed.

Better news was the news that Yuri seemed to be more than willing to cooperate and had even begun working in the laboratory. He seemed to know what was expected of him, even before it had been completely explained. He knew they wanted him for his expertise in modifying organisms for use in devious ways. As long as the money was right, Yuri didn't care who he did it for. It also seemed fairly obvious to Yuri that it wasn't potatoes that they wanted to genetically alter here in Hawaii. Since the compound was in the middle of a vast coffee plantation, it seemed fairly obvious what organism to begin to work on. It was just a matter as to what degree of potential deadliness did Taka desire for these modifications and were they to be gender-specific or race-specific, or possibly both. For now it didn't really matter. The preliminary work that Yuri needed to do was not specific to the kind of modification outcome required. That would begin next week and, by then, Yuri was sure he would have the specific instructions he needed to continue.

When Satochi showed the potato he had acquired from the Agriculture offices to Yuri, Yuri was more than happy to explain the significance of its modifications to Satochi.

"This looks like one of my prize efforts," Yuri began. "Though it appears someone has spliced out a bit to analyze. Where did you get it? The Russians keep close tabs on these babies. If the Americans were to find out what the Russians were doing, all hell would break loose."

"It was sent by a missionary working in Russia to a USDA worker here in Hawaii," Satochi explained. "We were able to pick it up before he could."

"It must have come out of one of the orphanage kitchens. That's where most of these are sent. There, or the vodka manufacturing plant. Helps control the birthrate by sterilizing all the young boys at the orphanages who eat them. Actually, it just keeps them from producing male babies. Male gendercide! We have been using these and studying the effects for years. It has really slowed down the influx of babies placed as orphans. It all started out as a way to help feed the hungry in Russia. This potato stays fresh for almost three years. Pretty remarkable, wouldn't you say?" Satochi didn't respond. "I kept experimenting with them until I reached the point where I could manipulate them any way I chose. I know the Russians have also been shipping them to the breakaway republics. They are slowly but surely reducing the male population of those areas. I was able to refine these to not only produce the male gendercide affect, but I can manipulate the DNA to only allow the effects to occur in men with specific hereditary traits or to certain ethnicities. I am the master at this," Yuri said, stretching out his arms as if he held the whole world in his arms.

Satochi was truly surprised at what Yuri was telling him. He had no idea the power genetically modified organisms held. Taka was truly a wiser visionary than Satochi had imagined. Satochi was sure even Taka did not know how far advanced Yuri's research was. No wonder the Russians were so anxious to keep the secrets of the potato. This Russian they call Viktor must be desperate to find the one scientist who discovered all of this. "Are you the only scientist in Russia with this expertise?" Satochi asked Yuri.

"There are others that are trying," Yuri responded," but they are years behind me in their research. Of course, I was smart enough to keep false records of my procedures. I wanted no one to be able to copy my work. That way my importance and position was always guaranteed. Something I am sure the Russians are very displeased about today. Of course, they do have my potatoes. They can run the DNA and deduce the effects the potato would have on an individual or ethnicity, but they will be unable to successfully reproduce my modifications. That potato you hold in your hand is very old technology. I have taken my research to a much higher level," Yuri boasted. "I can modify the next crop of coffee beans as soon as you tell me just exactly how and to whom you want those alterations to affect."

"How is that possible?" Satochi demanded to know. "It takes years to cultivate and mature these coffee trees so they can produce the beans."

"I don't need to produce genetically modified trees," Yuri grinned slyly. "I told you I was way past the research that went into that potato. I genetically modify and produce vast amounts of pollen to pollinate the flowers when the trees bloom. That pollen genetically alters that year's coffee bean crop. Of course, every year I must slightly change the genetic modifications. I must take into account any alterations to the genetic makeup to the trees that may have occurred because of the previous year's pollination. But that does provide me with job security."

"Taka will be pleased to hear of your cooperation and of your advanced research," Satochi assured Yuri. "Taka is a very generous man and you will be properly compensated."

"I am sure I will be," Yuri responded smiling. "This man Taka obviously knew what he wanted and knew enough to recruit the best. I have no doubt he will be more than fair with me. Just let him know the sooner I am told of his desired modifications, the more pollen I will be able to produce. Then we have only to wait for the Kona Snow."

"What do you mean, Kona Snow? Satochi questioned.

"You have lived here your whole life and never heard of the Kona Snow?" Yuri replied incredulously. "Even here on Kauai it is referred to by that name. Kona Snow is what they call the time of year when all the coffee trees are covered with the delicate white coffee flower. The trees appear to be covered in snow. I have heard it is a wondrous sight that I look forward to seeing in just a few short months. That is when we will make history."

Satochi was overjoyed at what Yuri had told him. Taka would be pleased. Yuri turned and went back to work in the lab. "What about this potato?" Satochi asked. "Trash, as far as I am concerned!" Yuri responded with a flippant gesture. "Just keep it from the Americans. The less they know about what I am doing here the better, although, I am sure they will learn much from the piece removed." Yuri's last statement troubled Satochi. Just how much did the Americans already know?

At least things were going well at the coffee plantation. Satochi still had to tell Taka how someone had found the water entrance to the lava tube and happened upon some spilled anthrax. He had heard that *the Grand Maui* had stopped at sea for two days while a Navy investigation occurred regarding a small boat with several bodies found on board. Nobody had any details and the dry dock ship that picked up the small boat had not yet returned to Honolulu. As soon as it did, Satochi would be able to find out what had occurred. Rumor is that whatever happened was serious. Several men were seen in haz-mat suits on *the Grand Maui* and on the smaller vessel. *The Grand Maui* had returned to port but none of the passengers seemed to know what had really occurred and they all seemed to be in fine health. Satochi knew that most of the passengers would have died if exposed to the weaponized anthrax. Logically, it figures that the smaller vessel could be the source, but Satochi was still waiting for confirmation. He had his men check with all the dive boat rentals or excursions on the island and had found that one boat out of Lahaina had not returned from a dive trip that headed out four days ago. The FBI was also interested in this particular company. They had been at the dive boat office going over the reservation lists and log books for two days now. It all seemed to add up, but Satochi would wait for confirmation before telling Taka. Fortunately, the boat was found nowhere near the water entrance to the lava tube and these dive boat captains rarely kept records of dive locations. More likely than not, they all would have been too busy dieing from the disease to worry about writing such things down in a logbook.

Jim and Jotty spent a late night drinking in the Malolo Bar at the Hilton. The next morning Jotty and Jim both were fighting off

144

hangovers as Jotty drove Jim to the airport where a Navy helicopter was waiting to take him back to Pearl Harbor. He was to begin his review of the video data collected by Lord Farrelton's hydrogen plane. Jim was curious as to what else Lord Farrelton's Hydrogen Solutions Company was working on for the United States military. He doubted he would find out at the Control Center at Pearl. He would keep his eyes open just in case. When the helicopter touched down a longhaired, very tan man, who appeared to be several years younger than Jim, greeted him.

"You must be Jim. The liaison officer told me you would be on this copter. I'm Eddie, Eddie Pop. You know, like in the soda," Eddie stood grinning at Jim.

"Nice to meet you, Eddie. I want to thank you for taking care of Haruko in Thailand. Jotty told me what you did," Jim said to Eddie

"She was one hot little mama, but once I got her in bed she settled right down, Jimbo," Eddie replied grinning.

Like a bolt of lightening Jim socked Eddie squarely in the jaw knocking him to the ground. "Nobody calls me Jimbo," Jim said tersely, "and nobody talks that way about Haruko. Are you trying to tell me you slept with Haruko?" Jim asked, sounding really pissed off.

"No, no way! I was only joking. It took everything I had to keep from getting killed by that woman," Eddie replied seriously. "She nearly ripped my head right off of my neck."

Jim laughed, "that sounds more like Haruko. She probably could have ripped your head off. I've seen her kill at least three men by crushing their larynx or breaking their necks. You are lucky to be alive, but if you ever call me Jimbo again, I'll kill you." Jim had turned serious again.

"That's the last time I listen to Jotty," Eddie replied, rubbing his jaw. "He told me you liked to be called that."

"Well, now you know," Jim replied and they both faked a laugh.

Jim actually thought Eddie was an okay kind of guy. Eddie reminded Jim a lot of himself when he was younger. Full of energy and brash! Jotty was sure Eddie would prove to be beneficial on this investigation and had ordered him to Hawaii from Thailand. That would also give Jotty the chance to chew Eddie out for keeping information from the NCTC. He didn't want to make any official accusations because all had worked out and everyone was safe.

Everyone, that is, but those poor souls who died in the bombing at the restaurant. That would have occurred regardless of the NCTC knowing what the CIA had been slow in passing along.

Eddie was not welcome in the control room at the Navy base, but Jim had plenty of other work for him. He had the liaison officer fly him out to the dry dock ship so he could have a look at the dive boat and see what he could find. The boat had been decontaminated and was preparing to return to Pearl Harbor for further investigation. Jim wanted Eddie to get a jump on the investigation. It would also keep him busy while Jim looked at the hydrogen plane's information.

When Jim was finally escorted into the control room, he noticed that most of the screens and overlays around the room seemed to be weather-related. Many showed real time readings of wind speed and direction along with water temperatures of the area around Hawaii, Los Angeles, and San Francisco. He was led to a smaller separate area in the room that was surrounded by several large video screens. One of the technicians turned a switch and a live feed from the hydrogen plane appeared on all three screens. One was an overview that showed all of the Hawaiian Islands from a very high altitude. Another was a close up of Pearl Harbor. The third seemed to be some kind of thermal imaging. The technician showed him the capabilities of the controls zooming in and out with both the cameras. On the close-up camera of Pearl Harbor, the technician was able to zoom in on Eddie as he was about to board a helicopter for his trip to the dry dock vessel. If you were a lip reader you would have been able to see what Eddie was saying to the liaison officer as he prepared to board.

"Unfortunately, you don't quite have this much control of the previously recorded video," the technician explained. He then zoomed out with the camera and punched in a different set of coordinates. "Her name is Jenny. At least that is the name on the mailbox. Everyday around this time she comes out to sunbathe naked." Immediately the camera began to zoom in on the coordinates that had been typed in to the computer and Jenny came into focus.

"Wow," Jim said. "That's what everybody says," the technician said, laughing. He then typed in the commands for the computer to play the videos of the day the dive boat was discovered. Someone had obviously been instructed to zoom in on the boat to see what the trouble was, soon after Lord Farrelton was informed of the circumstances. This was the first real view Jim had of the bodies in the water and those aboard the ship.

"That is definitely death by anthrax," Jim said about the close up of the body lying on the deck of the dive boat. "See those sores. That is normally the result of several days' exposure to anthrax without medical intervention. These guys look like this after only a few hours. Amazing!"

"Let me show you how this control board works these cameras and videos," the technician said. "Pay attention because it is a little complicated."

"Tell you what, partner," Jim said in his Texas drawl, "why don't you stay on here and help me out a bit. I really don't have the time to learn how to operate this gadget. I'm sure Lord Farrelton won't mind one bit."

The technician like the liaison officer had been instructed to do whatever Jim or Jotty requested. "I see no problem with that," the technician replied. "I'll handle the controls. Just tell me what we are looking for."

"Well, good," Jim replied. "Let's start with a wide shot of all the islands and then zoom in to where the dive boat was found near the Big Island. Then we will start running the tape backwards."

It wasn't real clear, but they were able to pick out the boat when it arrived at the location where it was found. As they tried to follow its path backwards the task became complicated by several factors. The biggest problem was someone had used the camera for zooming in and out on certain other areas. When the overview would return, they would have to try to find where the boat had moved to. Then there were the times when clouds would obstruct their view. At one point they had hopelessly lost the dive boat and had to start from when it was last seen leaving the Lahaina Harbor. That did help but, after several hours of sifting through the tapes, there were still many blanks in the tracking of the boat. They were able to identify two areas where they believed the boat had anchored for the divers to explore. But according to the timeline they were missing at least one anchorage and possibly two. They did know that those anchorages had to occur somewhere in the Alenuihaha Channel between Maui and the Big Island, but exactly where was anybody's guess. As the technician quickly scrolled through the videotape, Jim noticed on the thermal imaging screen an intense heat source that appeared in the middle of the ocean west of the islands.

"What's that big heat source that you just passed by?" Jim asked.

The technician was obviously caught off guard. "Probably some sort of camera malfunction or volcanic activity."

Jim knew better, but decided not to press the issue. It was just another curious thing he would discuss with Jotty later on.

"You know, if I had enough time, I could probably come up with a more accurate tracking by viewing some of the other cameras that were also on board the plane," the technician explained.

"I'm sure Lord Farrelton wouldn't mind. It would be a huge help in my investigation. Hell, why wouldn't he give the okay?"

"I'm sure he will, but I have to clear it with him."

"I would appreciate that," Jim replied. Jim knew Lord Farrelton would do everything possible to help in the investigation. It was for this very kind of thing that the hydrogen plane was designed. What better way to insure that the United States place a large order with Hydrogen Solutions for several of these aircraft than to prove their value by helping to resolve the mystery as to where the anthrax came from.

Eddie was proving he was well skilled as an investigator when he came aboard the dry dock vessel and started looking around. From the number of tanks on board he was able to determine just how many dives had already occurred before the divers and crew had died. He also found equipment that led him to believe these were not your typical recreational divers, but your more hard core thrill seekers who enjoy the much more dangerous cave diving. He also grabbed the underwater digital camera one of the divers had been using along with a regular digital camera. One of the crew members took pictures of the divers poising on the boat in their dive gear and of them entering the water at various locations. That would come in very handy for trying to discover the exact locations along the coast where the boat had anchored. When the dry dock vessel arrived back at Pearl, the Navy took possession and started their investigation. Eddie was careful not to be seen removing the two cameras when he exited the ship and joined Jim who was waiting on the wharf. Jim was impressed by Eddie's initiative, though he knew that sometime down the line

Jotty was going to have a lot of explaining to do about the missing cameras.

Later that afternoon Satochi received the confirmation he had been waiting for about the anthrax-contaminated dive boat. It was as he thought. Two divers had been found dead tied to ropes next to their dive boat. They, along with the captain and two crew members of the boat, died from acute anthrax disease. According to what the investigators from the Navy told the dry dock vessel workers, both the inside and the outside of everyone on the boat were covered with lesions. A comment meant to keep the civilian sailors out of the way of the Navy personnel assigned the task of neutralizing the anthrax and decontaminating the dive boat. According to the informant on the civilian ship, no records were found of where the dive boat had anchored before it was discovered by *the Grand Maui* crew. They did tell of an FBI man who was flown out to the ship and allowed to go aboard and look around. He seemed to be taking notes and pictures. He also picked up a couple of cameras that he hid in his backpack. The informant had been watching through a closed circuit television that the Navy wasn't aware of. Satochi didn't like hearing about the cameras, but he remained confident that the lava tube entrance was safe from further discovery. He decided not to mention the cameras to Taka.

Satochi would spend the next two days reviewing the security at the compound before he was to leave to meet Taka in Tokyo. Since Yuri had seemed pleased with his new Hawaiian putanka, it was decided that Lyuba would accompany Satochi to Japan. Taka had expressed a desire to see her again since their time in St. Petersburg was cut short. She too looked forward to seeing Taka, but not as much as she looked forward to visiting the high-end fashion and design boutiques in the Ginza shopping complex in Tokyo Center.

On the Big Island the investigation into the murdered Russian at Jim's house and the fire and murders at the Agriculture office were in full swing, but going nowhere fast. They had identified the man who bought the gasoline and the containers in Waimea who they suspected burned the Ag offices. His name was Noe Espeleta. He was a Filipino who had moved to Hawaii with his family as a young boy. Many relatives still lived in the Kapa'a area of Kauai. They even discovered he had flown to Kauai the night of the murders, but so far the FBI had no luck finding him in Kauai. It would still be several days or possibly weeks before either of the two genetic experts would have any answers about the slices of potato they were analyzing. Jotty had arranged for George to use the lab at the Paleaka Ranch. The equipment there was far superior to any other found on the Big Island. Hopefully, that would expedite his research.

Several man hours were spent following Viktor and Sergei around the premier golf courses scattered about the Big Island. They never did anything the least bit suspicious and always were teamed up with a different twosome at every course. One of the agents did notice that at each golf course for at least two of the holes one of the members of the other twosome would ride in Viktor's golf cart. Viktor always seemed to have a lot to say to these people. The agents never thought it significant enough to warrant sending for sophisticated eavesdropping devices located at the Honolulu office. This game of follow the leader lasted for two more days until the two Russians left to return home.

Jotty had followed up on the weapon that was used in the murder at Jim's house. He checked with the curator in charge of the art collection at the Waikoloa Hilton. He had a list of people and companies that made or sold replicas of the weapons. There were several people who made the Polynesian style weapons on Maui, two on the Big Island, and a company that knocked out cheap replicas on Oahu out of Monkey Pod instead of Koa wood. Several of the tourist shops bought theirs wholesale from a company in Fiji, but those were not made of Koa either. There was one guy on Maui who did really high-end work, selecting and carving the highest quality Koa wood and collecting just the right size tiger shark teeth to insert in the club, tying them to the club as was done in ancient times, not superglued like most of the ones found around the islands today. This guy would know who else was making the high end Koa wood weapons. The curator had heard that this guy, Larry--he couldn't remember the last name--sold his clubs in the galleries at the high-end hotels for up to $5000. Jotty thanked the curator for his help and headed out with at least an idea where to start looking. He would head to Maui and start checking out the galleries at all the high-end hotels. He decided to take the broken club that was found at Jim's house with him just in case this Larry guy was as sharp as the curator thought him to be.

Jotty had called Washington to see if the Russians had released the bodies of the murdered missionaries. He was told that they were to be released within the next two days to an Embassy attaché in Perm. The United States and Canadian governments had jointly sent a plane to Perm to bring the bodies back to their respective home countries for burial. The Russians had released a tape and transcript describing what had occurred. According to the report, Chechnyan rebels attacked the missionaries to rob and murder them. Russian troops came upon the roadside slaughter and in turn killed the rebels. Not the most believable story, but the Russians claim to have the forensic evidence to prove it. The State Department said they would forward a copy of the tape and transcript immediately to Jotty. Jotty told them to send it to Jim in care of the Honolulu office. Jotty expected to be on his way to Tokyo before the tape arrived and thought Jim should be the one to hear it first.

Eddie arrived back at Pearl and showed the images on the cameras to Jim. There were several underwater pictures that showed several caves or tubes the divers had explored. Then suddenly there was a picture of a big steel door with one of the divers pointing to a pile of what could easily be mistaken as cocaine or speed.

"That has to be the anthrax," Jim said excitedly. "Just where are they? What do you make of that door?" Jim asked Eddie.

"It looks to me like they followed a lava tube from below the water that led up under the island. That steel door tells me there has to be a land entrance into that tube. Do you think that tube is somewhere down in Volcano National Park?" Eddie asked.

"Not a chance," Jim replied. "Their boat was never anywhere near that side of the island."

Eddie looked quizzically at Jim. "How do you know where their boat was? I found no log on board. Just exactly what were you doing in that secured room?"

"Something I'll tell you about later. But trust me that boat never got close to that side of the island. I can't tell you exactly where it was since it left Lahaina, or everywhere it may have anchored, but I know for sure it was never there," Jim replied, trying not to pique Eddie's curiosity too much.

"Well, if you know where the dive boat was part of the time and even know some of the dive spots, with these pictures taken of the divers before they entered the water, we just might be able to figure out just where this underwater lava tube is," Eddie replied. "Have you ever scuba dived?" Eddie asked.

"I had a little experience with it when I was in the military. But I'm not so sure I'm too interested in exploring caves and tunnels," Jim replied cautiously.

"You'll love it. It's such a rush." Eddie's enthusiasm seemed to just explode out of him.

"Well, I reckon I'm in for a rush then," Jim smiled as he replied in his Texas drawl. "But before we go sailing the high seas, I want you to do a little more investigating." Eddie didn't reply. He had already learned Jim took a while to get to the point, so there was no need trying to hurry him along. "I'm still waiting for some more information from that secure building you're so curious about and that will probably take a couple more days. I want you to fly to California. Huntington Beach. That's where the two divers were from. They were firemen there. Talk to their family and co-workers to see if you can find out where they planned to dive. See if they dived here before. Also make a copy of those camera pictures for both of us. See if you can figure out anything else about where they were. The family has been notified about the deaths, but they were just told it was a diving accident. Just leave it at that for now. When you get back you can arrange for a dive boat and dive gear for us."

Eddie felt like he was being punished and sent away for something he must have done wrong. He would eventually learn that Jim, like Jotty, was very methodical about an investigation and believed the key investigators needed to do the footwork themselves. Jim was actually complimenting Eddie by sending him off. That meant Jim considered him an equal part of the team. It was probably a good thing Jim sent Eddie to California before Jotty returned to Oahu on his way to Tokyo. Jotty was not quite ready to be so generous in his opinion of Eddie. Jotty and Eddie needed to work out that lack of communication problem they seemed to have regarding what was going on in Thailand.

Jotty flew to Maui and decided to start at the top of the island and work his way down checking out the galleries at the high-end hotels. It was a very fortuitous choice. He started with the Ritz-Carlton in Kapalua. When he asked if they ever sold replicas of the Polynesian weapons, the clerk was completely taken aback.

"You know that thing sat in here for over five years with hardly anybody giving it a second look. Now two days in a row a customer comes in asking for one," the clerk told Jotty. "I sold it yesterday. It cost only $5000. It takes the artist over a year to create one in the authentic traditional way. I'm sure if you are really interested we could order another, but it may take up to a year."

Jotty pulled out his badge and identification. The lady looked disappointed. She was not going to make another big commission. "Do you have the name of the person who bought the weapon?" Jotty asked.

"He never said. He paid cash and said just three words. I'll take it," the clerk responded matter-of-factly.

"Could you describe him?" Jotty inquired.

"Not really," she replied. "He was probably of Japanese descent, wore dark expensive looking sunglasses, and seemed fairly well dressed, nice shoes, but no watch. We are told always to look at the shoes and the watch to see if the customer will be able to afford items in our gallery. That's why I was surprised when he pulled out the cash. He had no watch."

Jotty thought about what she said. "Are there video cameras located inside the store and hotel?"

"Of course we have them in here. I'm sure the hotel has several," she replied, getting tired of the questions.

"I will need to have a look at your recording from yesterday. One more question. Do you have the name and number of the artist who made the weapon?"

"Of course we do. I will get it for you as well as the videotape from yesterday." She hurried away seeming rather put out by the entire process.

Jotty took a look at the hotel video from the previous day, but it was of no help. He still had them make a copy so other agents could go through it more thoroughly. From the gallery video it was obvious whoever bought the weapon knew exactly where the camera was located and did an excellent job at not allowing it to get a clear view of his face. The experts at the lab back in Washington should be able to tell quite a bit about the man after their computer programs analyze every second of the tape. Even then, Jotty knew it wouldn't be of much help.

He decided that he didn't need to check any other hotel galleries. He got all the information he needed from the one at the Ritz-Carlton. His next stop would be at this artist's studio. The one everybody just calls by his first name, Larry. Jotty found out the reason they only used his first name was because nobody could make out what his last name was on his business card. His signature was the only way his name was printed on his card and information sheet and it was totally illegible. At least Jotty had an address and phone number that he could read.

He found Larry working in a studio behind his house in Makawao, a little town a few miles up Baldwin Road above the beach town of Paia. Makawao used to be a cowboy town in the upcountry of Maui and still celebrates its Rodeo Days. However, it has turned from that quaint cowboy town to an upscale artisan's village frequented by tour buses and the packs of bicyclists coasting down the volcano from Haleakala Crater.

Larry proved to be not much of a conversationalist nor very cooperative. Most of his carvings and weapons were sent to the higher-end galleries on all the Hawaiian Islands and he had no record of who purchased them from the galleries. He admitted he sold to a few individuals upon occasion, but kept no records as to whom he sold them to, or how many he sold. He stressed that it took at least a year to create one of his Lei O Mano clubs. Finding the right size tiger shark teeth was getting difficult. Larry was no doubt trying to avoid having to pay taxes. When Jotty showed him the picture of the man who purchased the weapon from the Ritz-Carlton the previous day, Larry denied recognizing the man. Jotty sensed that Larry was lying. Whether it was a fear of retribution from this man or a fear of getting caught evading taxes, Jotty was not sure. He decided now was not the time to put pressure on Larry. He would arrange for a phone tap. A phone tap was much easier to get these days with the Patriot Act in effect. He would also have a list of recent phone calls to and from Larry's phone printed and sent to the Honolulu office. Later in the investigation, if necessary, Jotty would have one of his agents put the pressure on Larry.

154

Jotty returned later that afternoon to Oahu to check in with Jim and the Honolulu FBI office to see how things were going. Multiple investigations were taking place on four different Hawaiian Islands regarding the murders on the Big Island and the anthrax discovery. Over a dozen FBI agents had been recruited by the NCTC for the investigations in Hawaii. Agents were also busy at work back in Washington D.C., California, Thailand, undercover in Russia, and soon to be in Japan when Jotty headed there the next day to finally meet with Haruko. Jotty and Jim talked through the complexities of the investigations and of everyone who seemed to be involved. They both got an intuitive feeling that somehow it all tied together. How everything was connected, they weren't sure, but they knew that a few hundred man hours of investigation would bring them a little closer to that answer.

As Jotty and Jim discussed the investigation over a drink at the Officer's Club at Pearl Harbor, Satochi and Lyuba boarded a private jet in Lihue headed for Tokyo. The following day Jotty would also start his journey to Tokyo, but in a much more uncomfortable coach class seat on a commercial airliner. Three days after that, his fate, along with Haruko's and Taka's fates, would become intertwined in a way that none of them would ever have thought possible. That is, no one but Taka!

# Chapter Twenty-six

**Taka was anxiously awaiting** the arrival of Satochi and
Lyuba. He wasn't sure which one of the two he was more pleased to
see. Lyuba, of course, would satisfy his desires that were left
unfulfilled in St. Petersburg. It was true that there were several
women available to Taka who could please him in the same ways, but
Taka had grown to respect Lyuba. Her ability to use her talents to get
information that he wanted earned her the lifestyle she desired and
financial security. Lyuba had been able to save and invest a great sum
of money since working for Taka. She was wise in doing so, for she
knew better than most how age and a fickle society could rob you
instantly of fame and fortune. She knew that her usefulness to Taka
must also someday end.  This time she would be financially prepared
to cope with the change.

Satochi's arrival meant Taka's plans would soon come to
fruition. Taka was very anxious to culminate this next step in his
terrorist vision. He needed to discuss these plans with Satochi and
hear how things were progressing with Yuri at the coffee plantation.
And there was still one problem with executing his plan he hoped
Satochi could solve.

Hiroshi was confident with his plan to extort the money from
Taka. What he had failed to do, in his excitement, was include a way
for Taka to agree to meet Hiroshi's demands. He left no contact
information. He did not realize this until the Aioka employee he and
his cousin were staying with told them that the manager at Aioka's
announced that Taka would pay several thousand yen to whomever
could get a message to the person who left the envelope at the
restaurant. They were to tell that person to either contact Taka directly
by phone, or leave a way Taka could contact him. Taka even left his
home phone number for that person to call. The worker was more
than anxious to try to claim the reward Taka had offered and had
already informed the manager that he could deliver the message. That
would prove to be a fatal mistake! Hiroshi was not happy with the
worker for telling the manager this, but he was even unhappier with
himself for not having thought about how Taka was to contact him to
agree to his demands. Hiroshi took the number from the Aioka worker

and promised he would call from a phone away from the apartment in the morning. Hiroshi's confidence in his plan was beginning to weaken, but he knew he must go through with it. He had no money and would never be able to work as a chef again. His plan was his only hope!

It was a strained meeting between Jotty and Haruko. "At least she didn't punch me," Jotty thought to himself. Haruko had met Jotty at the airport and drove him immediately to her office to talk. She was not overly friendly by any means, which really distressed Jotty. He was still in love with her and had told her so often. That's why he was so troubled by her behavior. Even though Haruko was angry, she did notice what excellent physical condition Jotty was in. He obviously had worked hard in recovering from the beating he received from Minoru last year in Los Angeles. Haruko found this attractive, but would never allow Jotty to know. Never!

"Well?" Haruko said rudely expecting an explanation.

"Well what?" Jotty responded just as rudely. "You should be thanking me for saving you. If Eddie hadn't been watching over you, who knows what would have happened." Haruko just stared without responding. She knew that what Jotty said was probably true, but there was no way she was ever going to admit it. Her demeanor suddenly changed as did the subject.

"So tell me what you know about these Thai terrorists being part of the Red Summit," Haruko said in a much more civil tone.

"You know I cannot tell you everything. It's classified. Unless, of course, you're willing to come to work for the NCTC as part of my team." Jotty thought he had caught Haruko off guard with his offer.

"I expected you to ask me that," Haruko replied. "And as much as I would like to, at the present time I am just unable to make such a change."

"Why?" Jotty responded. "You have told me several times that you hate it here. Your co-workers cannot wait for you to make a mistake. They all want you replaced. No one here supports you. No one here supports women. These are obscene working conditions. Why do you insist on subjecting yourself to this?" Jotty asked, but he already knew the answer: Taka!

"As long as the Red Summit continues their terror campaign in Japan I will stay. This is my job."

"Do you mean the Red Summit or Taka?" Jotty responded. "I believe you stay because you are consumed with the belief Taka is the head of the Red Summit. It is Taka that keeps you in Japan and on your hopeless quest," Jotty said, even though he didn't completely believe what he was saying. Recent intelligence showed that someone in Japan had given the orders to the Thai terrorist cell to kill Haruko. The same voice was heard ordering the terrorists to come to Japan. They were probably already here. Haruko would not be safe here in Tokyo.

"I do not believe it is hopeless," Haruko answered. "I went to Thailand to meet with the chef from *the Grand Maui*, the same chef Ono and I were to meet when we went to the Big Island last year. For some reason Taka had spared his life while killing so many others. I had to find out what he knew."

"Someone had to know you were going to Thailand to find him," Jotty told her. He decided he must tell her some of what he knew. "We have been watching that terrorist cell in Thailand for quite some time. We intercepted a phone call ordering them to kill you and this chef named Hiroshi. The call came from Japan." Haruko was stunned but pleased to hear these facts. "We know it was this terrorist cell that tried to kidnap you. They also bombed the restaurant trying to kill the chef along with you, if you were foolish enough to keep your scheduled reservation. Of course they failed! They failed at everything but destroying the restaurant and killing a few dozen innocent workers and tourists."

"Are you telling me the chef survived?" Haruko asked stunned.

"Hiroshi and his cousin both returned to Tokyo the very day of the bombing. They either were tipped off about the bombing or there is the possibility that they could have been responsible for the bombing."

Haruko was more embarrassed than surprised by Jotty's information. Why hadn't she thought to check the passenger manifests for Thailand to Tokyo flights?

"Before you get too down on yourself," Jotty said, sensing Haruko's embarrassment, "the only reason we discovered them was because we were searching the passenger lists for members of the terrorist cell. Unfortunately, after the bombing in Thailand, they all seem to have disappeared." Jotty was not sure he should tell her the rest of the information, but after a few seconds of thought, decided that he must.

"What I'm about to tell you could get me in very serious trouble," Jotty prefaced. "I hope you in turn will be as open with me as I am now being with you." Haruko nodded. "We know that the Thai terrorists were called here to Japan by the same man or at least the same voice that ordered your death in Thailand. This time the call came from a throw-away cell phone by someone traveling by jet across Russia headed towards Japan. So far we have been unsuccessful at determining who that person was, but we do have some suspicions."

"Is Taka one of your suspects?" Haruko asked almost hesitantly. Jotty didn't need to reply. Haruko could see by Jotty's expression that indeed Taka was considered as the possible leader of the Red Summit.

"This is something you may not share with your supervisors or for that matter anyone in the Japanese government. This is classified information." Jotty was very serious with his warning to Haruko. Jotty knew that with this new information there was very little chance that Haruko would leave Japan. Taka was again a suspect with the American intelligence agencies. "We believe the Thai terrorists are in Japan to finish the task they failed to complete in Thailand. I think you are in very grave danger, Haruko. I would like to stay and be your investigator for the next few days in Tokyo. You may not tell your supervisors what I have told you. I know you will be unable to assign any of your men to look for the terrorists or for Hiroshi. I can help you. Hopefully, in a few days my government will allow me to inform your government of the suspected Thai terrorists we know are here. Until then, let me help you." Jotty was almost pleading with Haruko. He knew she was in danger and he had to help but, unlike what happened in Thailand, he wanted to be completely honest with her.

Haruko had no choice but to agree to Jotty's offer of assistance. In doing so she would also have to allow Jotty to go with her to the grand opening at Aioka's in Kashiwa. She wasn't convinced taking Jotty was the wisest thing to do, but it would finally give Jotty a chance to see Taka in person. Investigating would be difficult for Jotty. He spoke little Japanese, only the few words

Haruko had taught him. He would have to have a translator if he was to be of any assistance at all. He would have access to the sophisticated cell phone interception capabilities provided by the U.S. military, but actually using that information without the knowledge of the country and its culture would be next to impossible. Haruko thought about assigning one of her agents to act as a guide for the visiting NCTC official from America, but there were none in her office she could trust. There was really no one in Tokyo who Haruko could trust except her sensei. He had trained her in the martial arts since she was a young girl. He was the one man in all of Japan Haruko felt would never betray or disappoint her. When she asked if he would do it, he of course accepted. His English was not good, but it was considerably better than Jotty's Japanese. They would make an odd pair as they wandered the streets of Tokyo. Haruko sensed that this concord would prove to be rewarding, if not for the information they might possibly learn, at least for the benefits they would both receive from learning from each other.

For the next few days, as Haruko went about her job with the National Japanese Police Agency, Jotty and Ishiro, Haruko's sensei, followed leads provided to them by Haruko. The U.S. military Elephant Cage monitoring Japanese cell conversations had so far been unsuccessful at acquiring any communication to the identified cell phones belonging to the Thai terrorists or to the phone that had originally contacted them. Some very powerful voice recognition computer programs were in use, but the volume of calls intercepted and recorded was overwhelming to the computer's memory. Specific voice identification could take weeks to be hewed from the millions of calls occurring hourly throughout Japan. Jotty and Ishiro started by going back to the Aioka restaurant which had originally given the lead to Haruko as to Hiroshi's location. They visited the restaurant and asked questions of several of the workers as they took their break in the alley behind the restaurant. Ishiro could tell that something was amiss. Nothing openly was said to Ishiro or Jotty, but much was said without words being spoken as Ishiro put it. Jotty did not fully understand what Ishiro meant by that statement, but knew better than to question it.

In the evenings Jotty and Haruko would dine and discuss any leads Jotty and Ishiro had come across during the day. Ishiro had been spending much time in the alley and had learned that someone had sent an anonymous envelope to Taka. Taka had offered a large reward to whatever employee could deliver a message to this anonymous person. It seemed that one of the employees had claimed the reward. Ishiro said that by tomorrow, Saturday, he would know who that employee was. Following up with Ishiro's information would have to wait till later in the evening Saturday or possibly even Sunday. Tomorrow afternoon was the grand opening of the new Aioka Restaurant in Kashiwa. Tonight, however, they would enjoy each other's company at dinner. Haruko was friendlier than she had been in months with Jotty. Not that she was leading him on, just that her spirits were higher and she was laughing more than Jotty had seen in a long time. It renewed Jotty's hope that once this Taka thing was settled maybe there was a chance that the two of them might someday fall in love. Or more precisely, she might fall in love with him. He was already in love with her and she knew it. She too hoped that someday she would be free of the cloud Taka seemed to hold over her head. She only hoped that it would not be too late to fall in love when that time finally arrived.

Taka discussed his plans in detail with Satochi. Satochi was impressed at how Taka could turn what seemed to be a serious problem into a benefit for his terrorist goals. Taka had received the call from Hiroshi. Taka of course agreed to all of Hiroshi's demands, but insisted that Hiroshi himself deliver the pictures he claimed to have and pick up the money. Of course it had to be in a public place. Taka suggested the exchange take place at the grand opening of his new restaurant. The media would be present as would several hundred people and at least a dozen police officers. What safer and more public conditions could there be? Taka of course could not make the exchange, but he would have one of his men meet Hiroshi at the entrance to the Takashimaya department store next to the new restaurant. Taka's man would be carrying a briefcase and a red backpack full of money. Hiroshi had requested way more than would fit in a briefcase. Taka assured him that no one would try to follow him or ever search for him again as long as the information against Taka never surfaced. Hiroshi of course agreed, but did have second thoughts about sending a copy of the information to the tabloid.

Hiroshi was satisfied and assured Taka he would be at the exchange with the information.

Taka already knew where Hiroshi and his cousin were staying. He had found out easily when he offered the large reward to whomever could contact the person who had delivered the anonymous envelope. Satochi had wanted to kill all three of the men sharing the apartment immediately, but that was before Taka fully explained his plan. Satochi's bloodlust would just have to wait.

Taka had summoned the Thai terrorists to his house. They arrived in two separate limousines that pulled into Taka's below-ground garage to prevent anyone from viewing their arrival. The terrorists were somewhat wary expecting to be thoroughly reprimanded for their missteps in Phuket. Upon arrival they were checked for weapons by members of Taka's security team. None were found. When they were called into Taka's library, the fear in their hearts grew a thousand fold. Standing slightly behind and to the right of Taka stood Satochi. They all had met Satochi and knew what kind of a cold murderous assassin he was. In Satochi's hand was a Koa wood and tiger shark tooth club. They all knew what Satochi was capable of doing with this club and prayed that it wasn't meant for them.

As Taka questioned them about what had gone wrong in Thailand, Satochi walked menacingly behind them.

"Who were the two that allowed Haruko to be rescued by some drunken American in the hotel lobby?" Taka demanded.

Sheepishly the cell leader and another man raised their hands.

"One of you must be punished for such negligence," Taka said solemnly.

Before the severity of what he had just said began to sink in, Satochi reached out with his club and viciously ripped the ear of the man standing next to the leader. He screamed in pain. Satochi quickly handed him a towel so the blood would not soil the room more than it already had.

"That was just a slight reminder that I will not tolerate failure in the future," Taka said sternly. A sigh of relief escaped from all the men, including the one whose ear was still bleeding profusely. They had expected much worse!

For the next hour Taka explained his plan to the Thai terrorists. He told them this would be their redeeming moment for the

162

Red Summit. Taka's plan was to blow up the new Aioka Restaurant during the grand opening celebration. He told them that in the process they would get the opportunity to finish what they had been ordered to do in Thailand. He explained how Hiroshi was attempting to extort Taka by releasing damaging information. Taka had arranged to pay off Hiroshi at the grand opening. One of the terrorists would meet Hiroshi at the entrance to the Takashimaya department store just as the ceremony was beginning. This man was to carry a briefcase full of money and a red backpack full of money. He was to give both of these to Hiroshi in exchange for an envelope. Then he was to join his partner who was to wait at the end of the block with another backpack. There would be no money in the red backpack. Maybe just a little on top hiding the bomb that was hidden beneath, sewn into a lower compartment to conceal it. The black backpack also contained a much larger bomb. The two terrorists were to quickly take it to the rear of the Aioka Restaurant and hide it in the trash can. Once they were clear of the area, they were to call Satochi who would detonate both the bombs destroying the rear half of the restaurant and killing Hiroshi. The two other terrorists were to be on the outskirts of the crowd behind the area where Taka would be standing watching the ceremony. When both the bombs went off, the two watching were to rush toward Taka with guns at the ready. Haruko would be waiting there as an easy target distracted by the explosion. They were to kill her and anyone with her, then disappear into the chaos that was sure to ensue. The Red Summit of course would claim responsibility for the bombings. It would appear that Hiroshi was a terrorist whose bomb prematurely exploded. That way any information he may have sent to the tabloid or anyone else would appear to be nothing more than another slanderous attempt by the Red Summit to disgrace Taka. It was a great plan. Taka would again be thought of as the poor victim of the murderous terrorist group Red Summit. It would distance him forever of any thoughts that he was the power behind the terrorist organization. Especially with Haruko finally dead!

Satochi would watch from the crowd as the plan developed. Satochi was there to ensure things would go as Taka truly wished them to go. Hopefully, he would not have to intervene, but was prepared to if necessary. It was decided that Lyuba would not join them at the grand opening. Taka wanted the crowd to see he was still alone since the death of Niki. It would create more empathy for Taka when the horror of the attack was told by the media around the world.

Saturday morning Hiroshi awoke early. He had promised that he and his cousin would be gone by evening. The Aioka worker who had taken them in was pleased to hear of their planned departure. He was more pleased with the large sum of money he had earned from Taka. Hiroshi told his cousin to pack and be prepared to leave that afternoon. He took the envelope with the information he had gathered about Taka and left early so he could scout the area around the scene of the grand opening before anyone else arrived. He did not want any surprises.

Satochi had risen early that morning also. In fact, several hours before Hiroshi! He was watching from the stairwell as Hiroshi left the apartment and entered the elevator leaving early for the scheduled exchange. Taka and Satochi had expected him to do that. Once Hiroshi had entered the elevator, Satochi left the stairwell and immediately went to the apartment door. He was taking a chance, for Hiroshi could return. It was a chance that he was willing to take. He knocked on the door. Hiroshi's cousin assumed it was Hiroshi at the door returning to grab something he had forgotten. The cousin opened the door and Satochi slammed it hard against the cousin knocking him to the floor. In an instant Satochi had closed the door and pulled a cheap American 25-caliber semi-automatic pistol with a silencer attached from a holster hidden beneath his left arm. He placed the silencer against the cousin's forehead and squeezed the trigger. There was a soft thud as the head barely moved from the impact. Blood began to pour from the hole in the cousin's forehead. The owner of the apartment had heard the knocking on the door and then the louder banging of the door when Satochi slammed it into the cousin. He came hurrying out of the bathroom asking what the all the commotion was. He didn't see Satochi standing behind the wall. The last thing he felt was a tingling sensation of the hair on the back of his head as if someone or something was touching him. His knees buckled and he was dead before he hit the floor. Just to be sure, Satochi put one more bullet through the right eye socket of both men. The 25-caliber bullets were perfect for such a job. They would penetrate the skull and then just ricochet around in the brain. There was not the usual bloody mess

164

associated with a larger caliber weapon where the bullet makes the small hole going in, but tears away the back of the head spilling out the brain as it exited. Satochi dropped the gun on the floor, then quickly left the apartment making sure the door was locked. No one saw him or at least would remember having seen anyone but Hiroshi leaving the apartment that morning.

Haruko and Jotty met that morning for coffee and tea. He had the coffee, she had the tea. They had no real plans other than seeing Taka in person at the grand opening. In the back of their minds they both thought of the possibility of the Thai terrorists being at the grand opening, but neither shared their thoughts with the other. Haruko did take her gun with her. She normally never carried it on weekends, but since the trouble in Phuket she was always armed. Jotty did not carry a gun with him that day. There were stringent laws that restricted foreigners, even supervisors in foreign intelligence agencies, from carrying weapons. There were ways around these restrictions, but Haruko and Jotty decided not to request a variance. They did not want to draw attention to what Jotty was doing in Tokyo.

After breakfast they took the Densha to Kashiwa. It was much cleaner and quieter than the subways or trains Jotty was used to taking in Washington D.C. The hour trip went quickly. They arrived early and enjoyed a leisurely walk to the location of the new Aioka Restaurant. A crowd was already beginning to gather. Free food and drinks always seem to increase attendance at any function.

Hiroshi had also taken the Densha to the grand opening that morning, but much earlier. He had been watching from down the block as the crowd began to gather. He could see that Taka had not yet arrived nor had he seen anyone with a red backpack and briefcase in the area.

Satochi arrived in Kashiwa by car not long after Hiroshi had arrived. However, he didn't go to the area of the grand opening. He met two of the Thai terrorists about six blocks from the new Aioka's. There he gave them the two back packs, the briefcase, and reviewed and stressed the importance of following Taka's plan to the letter. He gave them a phone to call him when the backpack was in place behind the restaurant. They both said they understood and headed towards the ceremony. The other two Thai terrorists met Satochi on the opposite side of the new Aioka's about three blocks from where the ceremony

165

was to take place. There Satochi gave them both 9mm pistols with silencers identical to the one he had used on his small 25-caliber pistol to kill the two men at the apartment earlier that morning. He reminded them not to rush towards Taka until the explosions. He told them he would pick them up at this same spot after they completed their task. Satochi told these two terrorists exactly what he had told the other two. They were to follow Taka's plan exactly or there would be consequences to pay. The terrorist with the bandaged ear reached up and touched his bandage almost unconsciously as he thought about what would happen if they failed again. They left the car and headed to get into position. Satochi too moved to where he could oversee the entire plan unfold. Like a conductor standing before the orchestra, Satochi was about to lead all the players to their destinies.

A limousine came to a stop in front of the large crowd that continued to gather. Jotty and Haruko had worked their way to the front of the crowd in order to get a clear view of Taka and to take several photos of him. Taka had expected Haruko to do this. Taka exited the car and a cheer went up from the crowd, much to Haruko's dismay. At the same moment, the two terrorists with the backpacks separated. The one with the briefcase and red backpack walked down the street and stopped at the entrance to the department store. There were several police around keeping an eye on the crowd, but none paid the man with the red backpack any attention. Hiroshi waited for a moment and then hurried across the street to meet the man. Hiroshi took the backpack and briefcase without looking into either one. He handed the envelope to the man who had given him what he thought was his future. Satochi watched the exchange and a smile came upon his face. Down the street Satochi saw the second terrorist with the black backpack pacing as he waited for the exchange between his companion and Hiroshi to be completed. Taka was heading toward a microphone that had been set up for his dedication speech. Haruko was snapping pictures of Taka while Jotty surveyed the crowd looking for anyone suspicious. Haruko received a call from Ishiro telling her that he had found where Hiroshi and the cousin had been staying. Unfortunately, he had found out too late. He told her two dead bodies were inside the apartment. Neither was Hiroshi. Haruko's attention was diverted back toward Taka. She would deal with the apartment and bodies later in the day. The two other Thai terrorists

166

had made their way behind Taka and were awaiting the blast to make their move. Satochi moved swiftly from across the street and into the huge crowd. At the same instant he pushed a garage door opener he had in his jacket pocket. Seconds before, as Haruko had tried to focus her camera for another picture of Taka, she had noticed a man with a bandage on his ear. He looked familiar to her. As she focused the lens, the face on the screen of her digital camera became clear and she realized it belonged to one of the men who had tried to kidnap her in Thailand. Jotty noticed Haruko's sudden panic as she began to reach for her gun. He turned to see what the trouble was just as two explosions happened almost simultaneously not two blocks away. Jotty and Haruko were both professionals and kept their focus on the man with the bandaged ear as he and the man beside him rushed towards Taka with guns drawn. Taka screamed that the terrorists were going to kill him. Jotty and Haruko also began to run towards Taka. One of the terrorists saw Haruko and raised his pistol and fired two shots just as Jotty stepped in front of her. The first shot struck Jotty in the chest, stopping him in his tracks, while the second ripped into his left shoulder. Haruko returned fire killing the shooter with two quick bullets to the head. As she turned to shoot the second terrorist, she was jostled hard by someone in the panicking crowd knocking her gun beneath dozens of screaming and frightened people running in all directions. It was Satochi who had knocked the gun from her hand. The second terrorist saw her lose her pistol and lifted his own gun, aimed it at her and pulled the trigger, but nothing happened. Taka had dropped to the ground continuing to yell that terrorists were trying to kill him. Haruko knew Jotty had been shot, but she could not allow it to distract her focus. When the terrorist's gun jammed she attacked him with all the fury knotted up inside her for the past year. She used her martial arts skills to both crush the larynx and jam the nose bone into the brain of the attacking terrorist, killing him instantly.

Both backpacks had exploded almost simultaneously. The red backpack that Hiroshi had just placed on his back was the first to explode, killing him, the terrorist who had made the exchange with him, and three other people entering the Takashimaya department store. Several others were injured when the large plate glass windows that made up the front of the store seemed to just explode into a million deadly shards. The black backpack was still on the back of the other Thai terrorist when it was detonated. It was by far a much larger explosion, but fortunately more than two blocks from the large crowd that had gathered for the grand opening. It disintegrated everything within ten feet of the initial explosion and caused considerable damage for up to seventy yards away killing several people and injuring dozens more with the shrapnel that had been packed tightly around the explosives.

Haruko turned and rushed back to Jotty. The first bullet had struck him squarely in the chest. The second had entered and exited his left shoulder just nicking the bone. As Haruko ripped Jotty's shirt open to try to stop the bleeding, she discovered that there was no bleeding from the chest. Jotty had worn a bulletproof vest under his jacket. He had not told her he had done so, but she was infinitely thankful that he had. The first shot to the chest had knocked him down, but would do nothing but cause him to have a very sore chest for a few days and leave a very large bruise. The second shot would require surgery but was not life threatening.

"I always wear a vest when I am in a foreign country," Jotty told her. "Especially, when I am not allowed to carry a gun!" He smiled as he looked up and winced in pain.

Several sirens could be heard as police and ambulances began rushing to the scene to tend to the injured. It would take days to sort through what had happened, but the Japanese police would eventually figure it all out. Several journalists had been present for the grand opening and got a story that could make their careers. Haruko heard Taka in the background as she sat next to Jotty. He was specifically thanking her and the Japanese police for saving him from a certain death by the hand of these terrorists. He hoped that this would finally be the end of the Red Summit that has done so much to ruin his life for the past two years. Then he began to cry as his driver helped him back to the limousine. Satochi was already waiting inside with a glass of champagne poured for the both of them. It all had gone exactly as planned.

Haruko began to cry. How ironic life could be. She had just saved the life of the man she had sworn to prove was the power behind the terrorist organization, the Red Summit. The man she despised more than any other in the world! And, in the process, had removed much of the doubt anyone besides her ever had that Taka was indeed its true leader.

That night Haruko would again have that dream!

# Chapter Twenty-seven

**Back in Hawaii** over a dozen agents were following a hundred different leads on four different islands trying to solve the two major cases the NCTC had become involved with. It was easy to justify spending the man hours on the anthrax case. That was because it was basically just Jim and Eddie working together until Jotty returned from Japan. The "Potato Case" as it had come to be called required many more men and many more man-hours in following the numerous leads that seemed to be constantly multiplying. Unfortunately, most of those leads were going nowhere fast. The most interesting information had come from sources in Russia. Rumor was that a major Russian genetic scientist had mysteriously disappeared from right under the watchful eye of his keeper. A keeper named Viktor Cheznov! The missing scientist was causing quite a stir both locally in Perm where he had worked as well as in the higher offices in the Kremlin. A level of concern had developed within the Kremlin that hadn't been seen since the Beslan School attack. It was this information from American agents in Russia that kept so many agents in Hawaii actively pursuing those many leads.

Lord Farrelton of course had given his technician the approval to spend the time Jim had requested to do a more thorough search of the videos supplied by the hydrogen plane. Jim knew he would! Jim also got the opportunity to spend another evening with Emma. The Lord and Lady were staying in Hawaii and were invited to the governor's mansion for a formal dinner. That freed Emma for the evening and she and Jim enjoyed, as Emma liked to put it, another jolly good rogering. Jim had to agree! He also found out that the Farreltons would be spending considerable time over the next nine to twelve months in Hawaii and on the west coast of California. Jim and Emma should be able to see each other at least two times a month according to the Farrelton's calendar. Jim liked that idea very much. What Jim didn't like very much was the transcript and audiotape he heard by the Russian officer in charge of the murder of the missionaries. Of course the tape was in Russian and Jim knew very few words in Russian. What he did know was that the voice on the tape was that of Viktor Cheznov. The same Viktor Cheznov he had met in Waikoloa who pretended to know nothing about the massacre of the missionaries. Jim didn't like being lied to! He hoped someday he would have the chance to let Viktor know just how much he hated it. Up close and personally!

Eddie had returned from his investigations in Southern California but had found very little information of any use. As they had thought, the two divers were both thrill seekers trying all sorts of adventures that pushed them to the limit. They had been diving for quite some time, but this was only their second cave diving expedition. Their other such dive had been somewhere in Mexico, but none of their co-workers knew for sure where. At least Eddie confirmed they were definitely here to do cave diving. That meant they would have stayed relatively close to the shoreline.

Jim had Eddie checking out the harbor area in Lahaina where the dive boat company had its office and mooring slip. Office might be a bit of an overstatement. More like an adult version of a lemonade stand decorated with framed pictures of past excursions and a pricelist screwed to a plywood front that was in desperate need of a coat of paint. There also was a couple of rusting folding chairs stacked below the stand. Actually, it was pretty much identical to the twenty or so other stands in front of boats advertising their snorkel tours, dive trips, fishing trips, or whale watching and dinner cruises.

As Eddie asked around, it became apparent that it was a close knit community of entrepreneurs trying to make their fortunes from providing similar services to the thousands of tourists. They all expressed their sincere sadness at the deaths of the dive boat captain and crew, but they had a business to run and life goes on. One peculiar item of notice, that several of the longer range fishing boat operators were in a stir about, was the huge number of dead fish they had seen floating to the west of the islands. The fish looked as if they had been boiled. There was much speculation about a volcanic eruption somewhere underneath the ocean in that area, but no one really knew for sure.

Eddie was also trying to arrange for a dive boat that the NCTC could lease for the next several days. Many boat operators were happy to offer their services, until they heard it was to try and retrace the dive spots of the ill fated dive excursion that resulted in the deaths of all on board. And though no mention was ever made as to the cause of the deaths, somehow everyone in the Lahaina Harbor knew everyone on board had died from anthrax. Secrets like that were hard to keep!

On Kauai, Yuri had finally heard from Taka. Satochi had explained to Taka how much more advanced Yuri's research and abilities were than they had even speculated. Taka had thought it would be several years until the GMO coffee would be ready to sell to those caffeine addicted Americans. It came as quite a pleasant surprise to know that within a year his GMO coffee would be in distribution. Taka and Yuri discussed over a scrambled land phone just what the possible modifications were and the consequences of those genetic modifications. Yuri was capable of modifying this year's coffee bean harvest by creating a genetically modified pollen that would lead to GMO coffee cherries being produced. Those GMO cherries, as the beans were called, would become further potent in the modifications during the processing and roasting process. This had been first discovered in Russia when the potatoes were processed into vodka. It seems as the genetically modified organism goes through a transformation it increases the resulting affect of the modifications exponentially. So with the coffee beans, after roasting, it would take but one cup of the coffee to cause the desired affect of stopping the production of any male sperm by the men who drank that one cup of coffee. It would not take several weeks of constant consumption as was first thought. And best of all, the effect was irreversible. The man who drank a cup of the GMO coffee would never again be able to produce the male sperm. Yuri also had developed the capabilities to alter the genetic modifications to make them effective for males with specific ethnic or racial characteristics. This research, however, needed more documentation as to its effectiveness and would require more time in creating and processing the pollen. Something Taka chose not to have Yuri do this time. The key to this entire plan relied on enough pollen being produced to saturate the coffee trees as the flowers first began to open. Coffee trees are self-pollinating, so it would be essential to heavily apply pollen often to the trees during this Kona Snow period to help guarantee it was the GMO pollen that did the pollinating of the flowers. Yuri assured Taka that he could produce the necessary GMO pollen in time.

171

It wasn't only the NCTC and FBI agents that were blanketing the islands following leads. Viktor had several of his present and several of the sleeper and former agents following their own leads searching for Yuri or the assassin with the Koa wood club. Viktor knew he had been challenged and was not one to ignore such a blatant invitation. One of his agents had also visited several of the same sources Jotty had used in trying to track down the seller or maker of the Polynesian clubs. When his agent entered the gallery at the Ritz-Carlton, the clerk was rather upset to again be bothered by the FBI. She had already given them everything they had asked for. She had even called Larry to find out about ordering a new weapon for the gallery, so she knew they had already visited him. The Russian agent played it off, thanking her for her help, but saying he was supposed to follow-up and visit Larry again, but he had lost the address that his boss had given him. He told her he would be in big trouble if his boss found out. The clerk said she understood and once again supplied Larry's address and phone number. When the Russian agent visited Larry, he was not quite as affable as Jotty had been. He could tell that Larry was holding back some information and used the threat of a little violent force to get it out of Larry. In actuality, Larry really didn't know much about his best customer. He didn't even know the name. He did know that he lived on Kauai and was quite the high roller. He always paid in cash and always had a driver bring him to Larry's house. Once Larry had even heard him tell the driver to have the pilot gas the jet before they got back to the airport. The driver would always wait out by the car. The driver was a huge man, much bigger than the man who bought the weapons. Larry described his customer as being a Hawaiian of Japanese descent, not a big man but extremely fit and toned. He usually wore expensive sunglasses but once, when he took them off, his cold, dark eyes almost burned a hole in Larry's heart. He was a very scary man.

"Would you really have broken my fingers like you threatened?" Larry asked as the Russian was beginning to leave.

"I would have broken your neck had you not told me what I wanted," the Russian replied. Larry almost peed in his pants at the man's comment. "Are you sure there is nothing else you can tell me?" the Russian asked, even though he was sure Larry had told him everything he knew.

"There is one thing," Larry said after thinking for a moment. "I did hear him speak Pidgin to his driver, if that helps." The Russian never answered. He just walked out the door, got in his car, and drove down Baldwin towards Paia. The real FBI agent staking out Larry's house across the street wrote down the license number and tried to figure out just what another agent was doing at his stakeout. Would he be surprised when he found out just whose agent it was!

# Chapter Twenty-eight

**The U.S. State Department** was in a frenzy when word came through that a top NCTC supervisor had been shot by terrorists during a terrorist bombing attack in Japan. The U.S. embassy in Tokyo was unaware that Jotty was even in the country. The resident CIA liaison was to always be informed when an agent was operating in their area. He was not happy when he got the call informing him of the attack and the shooting. He couldn't understand why in the world this agent would be wearing a bulletproof vest if he wasn't on an assignment, although everyone at the embassy was very thankful that he did have on the vest. Jotty was initially rushed to a local hospital, but was immediately taken by helicopter to the Navy base hospital at Atsugi. The injury to the shoulder was not serious, but did involve a damaged bone and ligaments that would require a few weeks of rest and healing followed by several months of physical therapy to regain full motion. First though would be several days of paper work that some poor, low-level State Department attaché would be required to fill out for the Japanese Government. He would have to explain just exactly why a U.S. intelligence agent was at the scene of the terrorist bombing. Jotty of course would be of little, if any, help!

Haruko was still in a state of shock at having to deal with Jotty being shot. Even worse was knowing Taka was made to once again look like the victim of terrorism and not the instigator of the terrorism like Haruko knew he truly was. There would be plenty of questions from her supervisor as to how she knew that the Thai terrorists were going to try to kill Taka and set off the explosions. They wondered why she hadn't alerted her office to the threat. And what in the world was an American NCTC supervisor doing there with her? As bleak as it may have seemed, Haruko knew that, in the end, all would work out in her favor. After all, she had saved one of Japan's most famous and favored citizens from a certain death at the hands of these Thai terrorists and once again stopped the Red Summit. Haruko knew better! Taka's manipulation of the events at Kashiwa only solidified Haruko's desire to prove once-and-for-all that Taka was not the man he seemed to be.

174

Jotty was to be sent back to Washington D.C. for recovery and physical therapy. One of the perks of being head of his division was that he could override protocol. He assigned himself to Hawaii as the location of his recovery and therapy. It would allow him to stay on top of the two major developing cases his dozen or more agents were working around the islands. First, though, he would have to spend a few days at the Tripler Army Medical Center Hospital on Oahu while he had a little shoulder surgery to repair the torn ligaments. Tripler is that gigantic pink building on the side of Moanalua Ridge which is visible from anywhere in Honolulu. One day Jotty asked one of the doctors why the hospital was painted pink. He was told it was built during World War II and was painted pink as a form of camouflage to protect it from the Japanese bombing it. "Apparently, it must have worked," Jotty thought, "because the hospital is still standing here."

Jim heard about the bombings and Jotty's injury from the NCTC watch officer in McClean, Virginia. He tried several times to call Jotty's cell phone to see how he was and if Haruko was okay. The watch officer did not yet have the details of the incident, but did know that several people were killed and injured. It was a very worrisome afternoon until his cell phone suddenly rang. It was Haruko!

"Are you all right?" Jim blurted out even before he said hello.

"I'm fine! Jotty will need a little time off, but he will be fine as well. He will be coming back to Hawaii for surgery on his shoulder. It will take him a few months of therapy to recover fully, but he now seems to have the discipline to do it. He wants to supervise the investigations that are underway." Haruko went on to explain in detail what had occurred at the grand opening. "I am more convinced than ever that Taka was behind the bombings and I intend to prove it."

Jim was happy that they both had survived. "Would you reconsider joining us again in Hawaii?"

"As long as Taka is in Japan and free, I will never leave my job at the Japanese National Police Agency," Haruko replied.

"I knew you would say that, but I at least had to try. Actually, I just wanted a chance to see you without Jotty being able to do anything about it." Haruko laughed at Jim's statement, though she knew there was much truth in it.

"I must go now, but I promise to keep you informed about my investigation here," Haruko said, snapping back into her all business demeanor.

"Talk to you soon. I love you," Jim said, as the call disconnected. Jim was shocked at what he had just said. "I love you". That was a phrase Jim didn't take lightly. It just seemed to pop right out of his mouth. The ringing of his cell phone snapped him back to reality.

"This is Jim." It was the technician from the facility at Pearl.

"I've narrowed down the scope of the search area by quite a bit using some of the other digital camera recordings from the hydrogen plane. I need you to stop by to have a look. Security restrictions won't allow me to remove the images from the building. You know, given enough time, say three or four months, I could probably correlate the satellite photos from all the satellites that had crossed that area during that time frame with the digital recordings from the plane and give you an even more precise idea of the dive boats path."

Jim didn't have three or four months. "Go ahead. Just as long as Lord Farrelton is paying your salary."

"I'll see what I can do. Keep in touch!" The technician responded.


Eddie finally arranged for a dive boat and equipment, but he had to call upon the help of the Navy. They offered a crew to go along with the boat, probably to make sure Jim and Eddie didn't destroy Navy property. The only problem was the boat was unavailable for another week while it was being refurbished. That was okay with Jim, for it would give him a chance to go over the investigations with Jotty while Jotty recovered in the hospital. Eddie would also be free to help out with the other investigation of the murders and missing potato. It was going to be a long fall and winter of investigations in Hawaii, Russia, and Japan. Thank goodness they were in Hawaii and not Perm, Russia, where Viktor was not having such a good time or enjoying such pleasant weather.

176

# Chapter Twenty-nine

**For the next five months,** all the investigations around the world seemed to be at a standstill. Most investigations always appear that way until one of those numerous leads turns into the big break. Sometimes it takes several small leads that all seem to add up to a major break. There were agents and investigators constantly following those leads all around the world.

Haruko was now able to use several members of her force to do much of the footwork since the devastating bombing in Kashiwa. Her investigators had actually turned up many interesting and peculiar facts. It seems that the terrorist's gun that misfired had been deliberately tampered with to keep it from firing. Also strange was the videotape made by a local news station showing the two Thai gunmen rushing towards Taka. They didn't appear to be after Taka, but seemed focused on Haruko and Jotty as they ran into the crowd. They paid little attention to Taka. It was also peculiar that Hiroshi was blown up by one of the terrorist bombs. Videotape showed him exchanging some sort of an envelope for a briefcase and red backpack which immediately exploded, killing him and the man who gave him the backpack and, of course, several bystanders. It was odd that the two blasts happened to occur almost simultaneously, killing two of the Thai terrorists that had been part of the attempted kidnapping and bombing in Thailand. The American CIA had confirmed that all four Thai agents were killed in the attack at Kashiwa. Coworkers of the man who was found dead with Hiroshi's cousin in the apartment told how Taka had offered a reward to anyone who knew the person or persons who had delivered the envelope to the restaurant which the manager in turn had forwarded to Taka. The dead man had claimed that reward two days before he was found murdered. When Haruko tried to have Taka questioned, she was told he was out of the country and they were unsure when he would be returning. She could wait! This was the first real evidence that shed not such a pleasant light on Taka. The news video also showed a very sinister looking man in the audience who seemed to be on the perimeter of the event and was continually looking down the street where the eventual explosions occurred. After the explosions, the man rushed into the crowd as the gunmen started towards Taka. It also looked as if this man was responsible for knocking the gun from Haruko's hand. This so far unidentified man seemed to disappear in the direction of Taka's limousine. Was it possible that this man worked for Taka? There was also the information from the Americans about the intercepted cell phone calls coming from a jet crossing Russia. Taka traveled by private jet often and was known to have visited Russia on several occasions in the past. Haruko would investigate Taka's past travel herself. It would be hard to justify to her supervisor just why she had assigned one of her men to such a task. She had much work that needed to be done, but was determined to see it through to the end. Hopefully, the end of Taka!

In Russia, Viktor was not a happy man. Nor were his bosses happy men. In just two days time, the entire top secret genetic program designed as a means of genocide for the males in the ethnic groups of the Northern Caucuses region had collapsed with the real possibility of the world being told of this Russian designed holocaust. Dozens of Russian politicians were actively trying to distance themselves from any possible connection to the research project or the facility in Perm. This did not go unnoticed by foreign agents from several countries working undercover in Russia. Viktor was under a lot of pressure to find Yuri and get him back. Preferably alive! They needed Yuri to continue his research. His skills were far beyond those of his fellow researchers who were unable to come close to replicating Yuri's results. Even more unfortunate was the fact that the genetic modifications had to be constantly updated each year. The plants would cross pollinate changing the resulting effects of the genetic modifications requiring Yuri to adapt new alterations in the genetic code to maintain the desired consequences. Without Yuri, the program would cease to exist which, in itself, might not be such a bad thing, but who knows what the consequences would be if the GMO potatoes were allowed to cross-pollinate without controls. Entire crops would have to be destroyed in several regions if it came to that.

It had taken several months, but in Hawaii Viktor's agents were starting to make some progress in their investigations. It was made more difficult by the large number of American agents continuing with the same investigation. It was looking more and more like Kauai would be the focus of their search for Yuri and for the search of the assassin with the tiger shark tooth club. Viktor now had more than a dozen of his own men searching and watching anything that may be of interest in every part of Kauai. Soon he would get the break he was waiting for.

Jotty had recovered nicely from his injury in Oahu. He stayed in close contact with Haruko giving her pertinent American intelligence information to assist in her investigation of both the Thai terrorist bombings. He also helped her as much as he could in her personal investigation of Taka. He did so with NCTC approval, for not everyone believed Taka was the innocent victim as he claimed to be. He was disappointed in the anthrax investigation, but things were looking better in the investigation of the murders on the Big Island. Much of the evidence was beginning to point to Kauai as the location of the murderers. He had decided to move his headquarters and many of his men to that island to continue the investigation. He moved into a suite at the Princeville Hotel on the north side of the island near Hanalei. It wasn't the most central location for his headquarters, but the Sheraton had a deal with the NCTC and offered them a substantial discount, something the accountants back in Washington D.C. were very pleased with. The Princeville was actually one of the premier hotels on the islands. Jotty definitely found it to his liking. He had met the most incredibly beautiful women in the bar one night. They hit it off nicely and had spent just about every night together since he had moved to the Princeville Hotel.

Taka had left Japan, but not nearly as soon as Haruko had been told. He had been avoiding her inquiries. Not only had he left Japan, but he didn't plan on returning. He, Satochi and Lyuba all left several weeks after the terrorist bombing. Taka spent this time preparing to move all of his assets out of Japan. Before they left, Taka put all of his Aioka Restaurants on the market. His financial advisors told him that he would make more money selling them off individually rather than selling the company as a whole. Discreet inquiries would be made to potential local buyers before the sale was to be made public.

Taka was finally able to meet Yuri and congratulate him on what a fine job he was doing. Those congratulations included a hefty contribution to Yuri's new Swiss bank account. Yuri was pleased that

Taka had arrived when he did. It was just about time for the Kona Snow to arrive. Yuri had prepared an adequate supply of pollen to begin spraying on the coffee trees. It would take several applications, but there was more than enough pollen to ensure this year's coffee crop would be no less than 80% GMO coffee beans, guaranteed to create the male gendercide as Yuri designed them to do. And not only was there sufficient pollen for all of Taka's coffee trees, but Yuri had created enough to fully pollinate all of the trees of the other producers on the island. Taka was very pleased with this news.

Satochi had learned from his men in Kauai that there was a build-up of both NCTC agents and what they believed to be Russian agents on the island. The NCTC had even set up their headquarters at the Princeville Hotel on the opposite side of the island. Taka was pleased to hear that. He knew just how to find out what they were up to. Still, he didn't feel Kauai was necessarily the safest place for him to be right now.

Satochi also learned about the agents searching for the ocean entrance to the lava tube that connected Taka's house to the secret laboratory. Taka was not so pleased to hear this news, for Satochi had to tell him about the spilled anthrax and its discovery in the lava tube by some recreational divers. Satochi said he had cleaned it up thoroughly, then decontaminated the area of the spill and the passageway down to the water. Taka was happy to hear that all on board the dive boat had died, but he was very concerned about the security of the anthrax and of his safe house. According to Satochi's sources, the agents had tried several times to find the entrance to the lava tube but had finally given up. At least for the time being! Taka wanted to make sure that enough of the weaponized anthrax was removed from the secret laboratory for the coup de grace of his planned terrorist attacks. He also decided that he needed to buy a large yacht and explore the ocean exit from the lava tube. He knew it was best to always be prepared.

Jim and Eddie had spent several weeks scuba diving in the areas they believed the dead divers had visited, many of the areas several times! Still, they had not found the entrance to the lava tube that they were searching for. They also spent several weeks driving every road and walking every trail on the Big Island hoping to find a land entrance to the lava tube, or possibly some sign of the anthrax or lab were it could come from. They had no luck!

They were both tired and edgy and decided they needed a break.

"We're getting nowhere fast," Jim told Jotty over the phone. "This search is beginning to really wear on me and Eddie."

"I think we need a couple of days off," Jim told him.

"This wouldn't have anything to do with Emma, would it?" Jotty laughed. He had already heard the Farreltons had given Emma three days off to enjoy Hawaii on her own.

"Of course not!" Jim replied, trying to sound sincere.

"Jimbo, you lie like a dog, my friend."

"Don't call me Jimbo, unless you intend to give me time off, then I will forgive you this one time," Jim replied.

"I've already booked you a room at the Princeville Hotel. It will give you time to relax, but also let me bring you up to date on all the investigations. Besides," Jotty told him laughing, "it is a very romantic place to bring Emma. I would love for the two of you to join me and my new friend for dinner one night at the Cafe Hanalei and Terrace. You won't believe the great view."

"Your new friend?" Jim asked puzzled. "I would have bet money that you were going to save yourself for Haruko."

"Yeah," Jotty replied. "The same way you always planned to."

"So much for those plans!" Jim replied.

"Tell Eddie I have a room for him here too! I need to have a talk with that boy," Jotty said.

Haruko had continued to read the business section of the Yomiuri Shimbun religiously every day searching for information about Taka. She was stunned one day to read an article that reported of Taka's liquidation of all of his Japanese assets, including all of the Aioka Restaurants throughout Asia. They also reported that he had already sold his large estate and moved out of the country, far from the terrorist group-the Red Summit-that seemed so determined to destroy his life. The article went on to talk about his new investments in farming, but did not elaborate as to what type of farming or where these investments were. That information would take Haruko several more days to discover and was she ever surprised at what she learned.

# Chapter Thirty

**The rains came early to the coffee fields** along the southern coast of Kauai. That meant the Kona Snow also came early. That was very good news for Taka who was now staying at the compound on the plantation in Port Allen, although he was beginning to feel less and less secure staying there. He kept a helicopter at the plantation that could speed him quickly to the airport in either Lihue or even to Honolulu, where he kept his corporate jets at the ready. His new yacht was anchored in Lahaina and was maintained by a crew made up of several of Satochi's trusted soldiers. It too was always available to leave at a moment's notice.

"I think it is time we remove a potential problem," Satochi said to Taka. "The FBI has been asking too many questions around Kapa'a about Noe Espeleta."

"He is the one wanted for the fire and murders on the Big Island. Is that not so?" Taka asked.

"He is," replied Satochi. "Eventually, someone will say too much. They are questioning everyone remotely related or acquainted to the man."

"I agree. It is better to remove the inconvenience before it festers into a much larger problem. I want you to handle it personally." Taka told Satochi to make it public and away from the coffee plantation so there would be no chance of a connection being made. "Do it somewhere in Kapa'a. Place the potato and a gun on his body. That might take the pressure off. Besides, we don't need that potato anymore. We know what it can do. Let the Americans try to figure out what that potato is all about. They already have those slices so it won't matter. By the time they do discover its power, it will be too late. Then they will know what real terror is." Satochi understood and immediately went to follow Taka's orders.

Jotty was spending his days coordinating the investigations on Kauai and his evenings and nights with his newfound lady friend. He was completely captivated by her beauty and her sexuality. Just like he was supposed to be! Lyuba had once again masterfully found her assigned mark and was using her special skills to acquire daily information about the progress of both investigations that involved

Taka. Each day she would pass on the newly learned information to Satochi, usually in the lobby or by the pool of the Princeville Hotel, but if Taka so requested she would deliver the information to him personally. Jotty was completely oblivious to the fact that he was being used, but that was the point. Lyuba was an expert at her job.

Seventy-five miles off the southern coast of Kauai, a large Russian commercial fishing ship was pretending to be working. The Americans knew what the ship really was and why it was there, but they were mistaken about what its true purpose was. They assumed that the ship was there to monitor or discover what caused the massive intense heating of a large area of the ocean. The Americans and Hydrogen Solutions knew the experiments could not be kept a secret. The blasts and residual heat would be visible on infrared satellite images for several days. Jim had even noticed them when he was working in the secured room back at Pearl. The technician had tried to pass it off as underwater volcanic activity. That explanation may have worked for all those fishermen asking why so many dead fish were seen floating in the ocean, but not for anyone trained to notice things and ask questions, like Jim, or the Russian government or, for that matter, several governments! Imagery from the hydrogen plane reported several countries had sent their so-called fishing trawlers to the area to investigate. The Pacific Missile Range on Kauai was also tracking all the ships in the area. They were providing data for the Hydrogen Solution's project that had drawn all the international interest. The assumption by the Americans was very fortuitous for the Russians. They had another agenda for their ship. On board were Viktor and a team of his best commandos. They believe they had located Yuri and were planning on taking him back alive. It was just a matter of confirming their intelligence before making a full-scale attack on a residence on American soil. There was absolutely no room for error in such an undertaking. It could be considered an act of war. Viktor was confident his men would be in and out before anyone knew what was happening. He just had to be sure Yuri was there before staging the assault. Timing had to be perfect and Viktor was confident it would be. He had agents with very sophisticated equipment at the Princeville Hotel monitoring Jotty's investigations. They, like Lyuba, knew as much about what the NCTC was planning and doing as the NCTC itself. What they were just about to discover was Lyuba's connection to Taka and Yuri which, in turn, would lead Viktor to Satochi and that would put Viktor back into Satochi's game in a big way.

One of Viktor's agents watched as Satochi picked up Lyuba. The agent followed them to the coffee plantation where other agents were watching the coming and going of personnel. After Satochi dropped off Lyuba, one of the men that both the Russians and Americans had been looking for from the gas station video on the Big Island exited the house and joined Satochi in the car. The Russians tried to follow Satochi's car, but lost it in the back streets of Kapa'a. When they finally found the vehicle, only Satochi sat in the rear seat. The other man was now missing. They followed the car back to the coffee plantation where Lyuba was waiting to be returned to the Princeville Hotel. As she was saying goodbye to a man that the Russians had identified as Taka, Yuri walked nonchalantly out of an adjacent laboratory, came up to Lyuba and gave her a friendly kiss goodbye. This was the confirmation that the Russians needed. Yuri was indeed where they thought he was!

Satochi decided to stay at the hotel for a while to see if Jotty was notified about the body of the man they had been looking for along with the stolen potato. He and Tonga parked the car after they dropped off Lyuba and headed into the lobby.

When Lyuba arrived back at the Princeville Hotel, Jim and Emma were sitting with Jotty in The Living Room enjoying some champagne. The Living Room was what they called the hotel bar. It was located to your right as you entered the vast spacious lobby area. To the left was the hotel check-in and to the immediate right was the hallway leading to the hotel shops and some of the room elevators. In a panoramic view directly in front of you as you entered was Jurassic Park. At least that was what it looked like. The opening scenes of the movie Jurassic Park, with all of the waterfall and jungle covered cliffs, were the cliffs directly across Hanalei Bay from the hotel. The entire west-facing side of the lobby was solid glass from floor to ceiling and it was indeed a very high ceiling, creating one of the most spectacular vistas imaginable. There was a terrace outside some of the windows and the glass-framed view was broken only by a hallway with elevators that went down to the hotel's rooms built into the cliff.

It was truly a breath-taking sight the first time you walked into the lobby. Actually, just about every time you walked into the lobby!

"Lyuba," Jotty called across to her as she entered. "Lyuba, I would like you to meet my very good friend, Jim Rikey."

Jim was up out of his chair in a flash like any gentleman should do. "It's a mighty fine pleasure to make your acquaintance, ma'm," Jim said in his Texas drawl. Jim was dazzled by Lyuba's charm and beauty. Emma, as pretty as she was, was not even in the same league as Lyuba when it came to beauty, but then of course that was why Lyuba had been a world class model when she was in her late teens and twenties. By thirty that career was over, but the real beauty still remained "Let me introduce you to my friend Emma," Jim said to Lyuba making sure Emma would not feel slighted. Emma was still by anyone's standards a very pretty girl. Both of the women were well-trained in proper etiquette and knew just what to say in any social situation and seemed to hit it off just fine. This was very fortunate because neither Jim nor Jotty were much good at carrying on a conversation. Just as the conversation was beginning to ebb, Eddie walked into the lobby and straight towards the two couples. Like always he had a huge grin on his face like he knew something no one else knew.

"Hi," Eddie said to both the women at the table. "I'm Eddie, Eddie Pop, you know, like in soda pop." He stood waiting for them to respond as he obviously sized up the physical attributes of both women.

"Emma, Lyuba," Jim spoke up, "allow me to introduce you to my chauvinistic friend, Mr. Eddie Pop. Eddie is helping on my investigation."

Both women nodded politely then Emma spoke up. "Is that the anthrax investigation you are talking about?" Before Jim could answer Eddie spoke up. "Yeah, that's the one! Jim and I have been diving all over the place looking for that lava tube entrance."

Jotty intervened, "I don't think we need to discuss such droll things in such a lovely setting with such lovely ladies, do you Jim?"

"I reckon we don't," Jim responded catching on to Jotty's desire to keep confidential information confidential.

"Well, I better go check in," Eddie said. "It was a pleasure to meet you ladies." He turned and hurried off towards the check-in line that had formed while he was visiting with the two couples.

Jim and Jotty both sighed in relief as Eddie headed to the other side of the hotel to check-in. Several Japanese tourists had arrived and received the traditional lei greeting from the Princeville which signified that a connecting flight from Japan had landed at Lihue within the past couple of hours. The Princeville was the first hotel stay of their tour. Eddie was stuck in line behind about two dozen Japanese families ready to check in.

If Eddie's little visit had caused Jim and Jotty to sigh, what happened next left them gasping for breath as though they were both having simultaneous heart attacks. Actually, heart attacks might have been more preferable. They were both being very affectionate with their respective dates when Haruko entered the lobby of the hotel. She immediately recognized Jim and Jotty and hurried towards them. Her pace slowed as she grew closer in her approach and became aware that both of them were kissing the woman sitting next to each of them. Jim and Jotty seemed to notice Haruko at exactly the same instant and both leaped to their feet leaving their dates sitting there with their lips still puckered in mid-kiss. The three of them stood staring at one another in embarrassment, not knowing what to say. Suddenly a voice called out.

"Haruko baby, it's great to see you again." Eddie had seen Haruko enter the lobby and head towards Jim and Jotty. He immediately followed. Hearing her name and recognizing the voice, Haruko quickly turned to face Eddie who now stood directly in front of her. In a flash, all of the anger and jealousy of seeing Jim and Jotty with other women exploded inside her and she caught Eddie by surprise with a vicious roundhouse punch with her right hand to Eddie's left jaw. The punch knocked him across the table of a young couple from Oregon celebrating their first anniversary, shattering their champagne glasses and breaking the bottle of cheap champagne.

Jim was the first to speak, "Eddie always seems to bring out the best in women." Haruko turned and glared at Jim. "What a surprise to see you, Haruko," Jim continued.

"I bet it is quite a surprise," Haruko replied coldly. Jotty was helping Eddie up off the floor and was apologizing to the young couple. He also was doing some fast-talking with the hotel security who rushed to see what the trouble was. "Just a slight misunderstanding," Jotty told them. "Please let me buy you more champagne." He ordered them a very expensive bottle hoping they would not make trouble. It seemed to work, but they moved far away from the now-three couples.

"I hope you are not hurt too badly," Haruko seemed to be apologizing to Eddie, "but you did deserve it for knocking me out in Phuket and for the things you said on the boat."

"Emma, Lyuba, I would like you to meet Haruko. Haruko works for the Counter-terrorism division of the Japanese National Police Agency."

"A pleasure to meet you, ladies," Haruko responded. Both Emma and Lyuba could sense Haruko's jealousy. "But Jim is not completely correct. I used to work for the Japanese National Police. Now I hope to be working for the NCTC if the offer is still open," she said looking at Jotty.

"Of course it is Haruko," Jotty responded, "what made you change your mind?"

"Taka, of course!" Haruko responded. Lyuba flinched when Haruko said Taka's name, but no one in the group seemed to notice. "I always swore I would never leave Japan as long as Taka was there or until I could prove he is the true leader of the Red Summit."

"And you did that?" Jim asked.

"No, but I will soon," Haruko replied. "Taka has left Japan and sold all of his businesses and property. I no longer need to stay there."

"Where has he gone?" Jotty asked, for Jotty also felt that Taka was likely involved with the Red Summit if not their leader as Haruko claimed. "Here in Hawaii. In fact, on this very island! He has purchased a large coffee plantation on the other side of the island near a place called Port Allen. I don't know if he is actually living there now, but I intend to find out."

Just then Jotty received a page from one of the agents in the field in Kauai. He needed to speak to Jotty on a secured line.

"Haruko, why don't you and Eddie get checked into the hotel,…" Jotty began to say when Eddie interrupted.

"Separate rooms no doubt," Eddie said, trying to be funny as he continued rubbing his jaw where Haruko had slugged him.

Haruko and Eddie headed towards the line that had now grown even longer.

Jotty turned to Emma and Lyuba. "Jim and I need to handle a little business but it won't take too long. Emma, why don't you let one of the bellhops show you to your and Jim's room. That will give you a chance to freshen up and you can meet us back out here in about twenty minutes." Jim almost winced when Jotty said your and Jim's room to Emma. He was hoping Haruko was already far enough away not to hear the comment. "Lyuba, I hope you can also join us again in about twenty minutes."

"Of course I can," Lyuba replied. She had already seen Satochi and Tonga enter the lobby. This would give her the chance to tell Satochi the FBI now knew Taka owned and was probably staying at the coffee plantation. She also saw Bendo sitting in the lobby. He was always around to keep an eye on the coming and going of the agents when Lyuba was otherwise occupied.

Jim and Jotty headed for the room that had been set up as the command post for the investigations. When they got to the room, Jotty called the agent that had paged him. The agent told Jotty they had found the body of Noe Espeleta, the man they had been looking for from the gas station video from the Big Island. He had been shot at point blank range in the back of the head with a small caliber gun. They also found a potato in his pocket. They were guessing that it was probably the one stolen from the Agriculture offices.

"This sounds like it was staged," Jim said to Jotty. "I think whoever killed that Russian agent at my house is inviting us back into the game. They know we already have a sample of the potato and that it will take us months to figure out what it can do. At least that is what both of my experts that are working on it have told me. The Russians already know what it can do because they developed the damn thing. I would bet whoever sent us this potato also has the missing Russian genetics expert who created it. It sounds as though Russian agents are here looking at many of the same clues and leads we have looked at. At least that is how I interpret the report of that mysterious questioning of that artist and gallery worker on Maui. We seem to be a step behind everybody. Even Haruko found out that Taka was here on his new coffee plantation and..." Suddenly Jim stopped talking and looked at Jotty with a strange smile. It was as though a light had been turned on in Jim's brain.

"It's Taka," Jim said excitedly. "Taka is the one who kidnapped and brought the genetic scientist here. He's going to use him to alter the coffee crop."

"That would take years," Jotty said interrupting.

"Yes, I know, but Taka has the time and money to wait years," Jim replied. "Taka was willing to wait for years for the tainted cosmetics to kill all of those women. I'm sure he is willing to wait years for the GMO coffee trees to grow and produce tainted coffee. That has to be it."

When Jim and Jotty went to respond to the emergency page from the agent, Lyuba headed for the bar to talk to Satochi. She had to let him know that Jim and Jotty knew about the coffee plantation and that Taka was staying there. When Lyuba came into the bar area Tonga headed towards the hallway to keep a watch out for Jim and Jotty. Bendo was also watching Eddie and Haruko and anyone else who may be an agent with the NCTC or with the Russians.

Eddie and Haruko were arguing back and forth as they waited in line, annoying many of the other guests who came to paradise to get away from just such a thing. Haruko turned toward a Japanese woman who made a rather rude comment in Japanese about her and Eddie thinking they wouldn't understand. Haruko was about to respond a little rudely in return when she saw Lyuba speaking to Satochi in the bar. She immediately recognized him as the mysterious suspect from the news video at the Kashiwa terrorist bombing. What was this Lyuba woman doing talking to him? Haruko grabbed Eddie's arm pulling him out of the check-in line once again and they began carefully making their way towards Satochi and Lyuba. As they slowly crossed the lobby, Haruko explained what was going on to Eddie and he became acutely alert. Bendo also began moving in the same direction. He had seen Haruko's sudden change when she recognized whom Lyuba was speaking to. He moved into position to protect Satochi and Lyuba from any attack by Eddie or Haruko.

Neither Haruko nor Eddie were carrying a gun, but each felt confident with their martial arts ability to subdue Lyuba and Satochi as they continued to approach. They failed to notice Bendo as he too moved into position.

Satochi was aware of Haruko's approach, but did not tell Lyuba. He did not wish for her to react which would in turn let Haruko and Eddie know he was aware of them stalking him. He also knew Bendo and Tonga were in position to assist him if necessary. Satochi had the upper hand! Satochi reached below his table and grabbed his briefcase. Inside was his new Koa and tiger shark tooth Lei O Mano. He was very anxious to test it on one or both of these agents. The thought of the kill excited him! He decided he would kill the man and take Haruko as a gift to Taka. He would allow Taka to decide what was to be done with her.

Jim and Jotty had left the hotel room that was serving as the NCTC command center and were headed back to the lobby. Jotty was unarmed, but Jim had one of his Colt 45 six-shooters strapped in a shoulder holster under a light jacket he had worn to hide it. Tonga saw them coming down the hall, but could not warn Satochi and Lyuba without Haruko and Eddie knowing.

Just as Haruko and Eddie sprung what they thought was a surprise attack, Satochi reached into his briefcase and grabbed his Koa wood club. He swung it viciously at the side of Eddie's head, dazing him but not completely knocking him unconscious. Eddie dropped to his knees, but Satochi grabbed him by his long blonde hair holding him upright with his neck exposed for the final kill. Haruko tried to grab Satochi from behind, but Bendo grabbed her tightly pinning her arms to her sides making it impossible for her to even move.

Satochi smiled at Haruko. "It is time to watch your friend die. What is his name?" "Eddie, Eddie Pop," Haruko responded. "How ironic that he is called by the same name that will soon bring massive devastation to America. Catalina Eddie will bring the American government to its knees." Satochi lifted the club into the air with the razor-sharp tiger shark teeth poised to rip Eddie's head away from his torso. "Lolo man," Satochi began speaking in Pidgin, "da bakatore man ma-ke die dead."

At that very moment, Jotty and Jim turned the corner from the hallway and heard the screams of several of the women in and around the bar area. Jim saw the weapon in Satochi's hand, the same type of weapon he had seen sitting broken on the answering machine in his home. He knew what this weapon could do to a man's neck and would not allow that to happen to his friend Eddie. In a flash Jim pulled his Colt from its holster and began to fire. What Jim had failed to see was the giant body of Tonga hurtling towards him as he prepared to fire. Tonga hit Jim as the first bullet left the gun. Jim was an expert speed shooter so five shots were fired before the gun was knocked from his hand by the tremendous body blow of Tonga slamming into him. Five shots had indeed been fired, but only one would hit its mark, shattering the club in Satochi's hand before it could deal the death blow to Eddie's exposed neck.

The second bullet would have hit its mark had Lyuba not panicked and bolted from her chair. She stepped into Jim's second shot that was meant for Satochi. The bullet ripped through her neck as she was rising from her chair, smashing her spinal cord and killing her. Had she not begun to rise, the bullet would have found its mark in the center of Satochi's cold heart. The third and fourth bullets hit the massive glass window behind Satochi, Haruko, and Bendo, cracking it into giant spider webs but not shattering it. That would be the job of the fifth and final bullet to exit Jim's gun. That bullet struck a tourist squarely in the chest, killing him instantly and knocking him through the already cracked window breaking it into a flurry of shards. There was no terrace behind this window, only a cliff that plummeted sharply to the beach below. The horror of this final shot was made worse by the fact it happened in front of the now dead man's wife and two children who had come with him on what was to be a vacation of a lifetime for this Kansas family. It would no doubt be a vacation none of them would ever forget.

Satochi was infuriated that his bloodlust was denied him. His wooden club was shattered and blown from his hand by Jim's first bullet. Satochi let go of Eddie's hair and Eddie's limp body dropped to the floor. He struck out angrily at Haruko who was still being held by Bendo, knocking her unconscious. He looked toward Jim and Jotty and saw that they both were entangled with Tonga. That would give him and Bendo the opportunity to escape with Haruko as their hostage. They slipped out through the kitchen area behind the bar. Several people had run that way when they heard the gunshots, so they did not raise any undo attention. They quickly got into the car and headed for the coffee plantation.

Jim and Jotty continued to wrestle with Tonga. Tonga was well-versed in the martial arts, but so were Jim and Jotty. He could not defeat them both and soon the police would arrive to arrest him.

Tonga could not allow that to happen. As he broke free from Jotty's grasp, Tonga sprinted towards the opening that was once the window providing the bar patrons with an exquisite view of the Kauai sunsets. Without hesitating, Tonga dove to his death through the broken window and onto the beach below, joining the other body that laid there in the gently lapping surf of Hanalei Bay.

Jotty collapsed on one of the several couches that were placed at various locations around the lobby, too exhausted from fighting with Tonga to try to find Satochi. He had not yet seen Lyuba lying dead on the floor next to Eddie nor did he yet realize that Haruko had been taken by Satochi.

Jim did realize that only one of his bullets had hit the intended target. He rushed to Lyuba to see if he could save her, but she was already dead. He had killed her with his second bullet. What was he going to say to Jotty? He had just killed his best friend's girl. Then he saw Eddie on the floor next to Lyuba; He was still breathing. At least the first bullet had done what Jim expected when it shattered the club in Satochi's hand, saving Eddie's life. That's when Jim heard the screams. The screams of two small children calling for their father who was no longer there! The screams of a wife calling for a husband who would never again answer her call! The fifth bullet from Jim's gun had taken the father from those children and the husband from that wife as they all watched his death in stunned horror. Jim wept! He had never before killed an innocent man or an innocent woman. Of course it wasn't intentional! Tonga had knocked into Jim causing the shots to go astray. Yet it was still Jim's gun, they were still Jim's bullets, and it was Jim who had pulled the trigger. That was all that mattered. Jim had taken the lives of two innocent people.

Jotty struggled off of the couch, battered and sore from the terrific blows Tonga had pummeled him with. He saw Eddie starting to stir from the floor and next to him he saw Lyuba. His beautiful Lyuba! Blood had stopped pouring from her lifeless body and pooled onto the cold marble floor beneath her. Jim saw Jotty kneeling by Lyuba's body and wanted to go to him, but couldn't. He did not know what to say or what to do. It was as though a cloud had engulfed his body and spirit, weighing down his arms and legs, making it impossible for him to move. All he heard were the screams of the now fatherless children as the words "I killed them" repeated like a broken record in his mind. Eddie was finally conscious and was the first to notice Haruko was gone.

"Where's Haruko?" Eddie said to no one in particular. Both Jim and Jotty seemed to be shocked out of their immediate grief by Eddie's question. Jotty and Jim had forgotten about Haruko. Panic set in!

"They took her," the bartender said. "That man with the club hit her, knocking her out, and that giant man with him carried her out. They went through the kitchen."

Neither Jotty and Jim nor Eddie ran to try to catch them. They knew the men had left the area by now.

"Someone needs to call the police. We need to have roadblocks set up immediately," Jotty yelled to one of the hotel employees to make the call. Of course the call had already been made.

Jim had come to where Jotty was standing next to Lyuba's body. "Jotty, I'm so sorry. I didn't mean to kill her. It was an accident. I....." Jim started crying and couldn't speak anymore.

"I know Jim," Jotty replied, trying to comfort his friend. "I don't understand what she was doing here," Jotty said to anybody who would listen.

"I know," Eddie replied. Both Jim and Jotty turned to look at Eddie. "I know what she was doing here," he repeated. "Haruko saw her talking to that man with the club. When you and Jim left, she hurried straight to him and began talking very excitedly and animated like she was telling him something important. Haruko recognized the man from videos of the terrorist bombing in Japan. He was considered a suspect and a possible terrorist. Haruko thought he was with Taka when Taka left Kashiwa. What we didn't see was the huge man that was apparently with him standing somewhere behind him. They must have seen us coming. That's how they got the jump on us. Your girl Lyuba was with them."

The accusation made Jotty sick to his stomach. It couldn't be true! Jotty was too smart to be taken in by a swallow! But the more he thought about it, the more sense it began to make. He had told her much about the progress of his investigations. Way too much!

Police and paramedics began to arrive and filled the lobby of the hotel. The police secured the scene and the paramedics began treating Eddie and Jotty for their injuries along with several people who were cut by the shattered glass window. Several people were in shock. The most serious of whom was Jim. Jim just sat on the floor shaking his head in disbelief at what he had done. He was severely traumatized by his actions and the screams directed at him from the newly widowed wife made it all the worse. However, the fact that Haruko had been taken was kicking in his adrenalin and his training would soon block this horror from his mind. At least for the moment!

Jotty had taken command of the situation and was giving instructions to the police about setting up roadblocks. He knew these men were smart and would expect roadblocks and no doubt avoid them. He needed to contact all of the agents working the case on the various islands and get them to Kauai immediately. It would make sense that if Haruko was correct about Taka owning a coffee plantation near Port Allen, that would be the likely place to look for her and the two men who kidnapped her. As much as he would like to, Jotty knew that they just couldn't storm the plantation without probable cause. He did want to stake it out as soon as possible and get his men in place by the morning. With the new Patriot Act, he was sure he could find some sort of probable cause to secure a search warrant and go in by the time his team was together in the morning.

Satochi called the plantation from his car and requested the helicopter pick them up at the Princeville Airport. Within minutes the helicopter was in the air and on its way. It would arrive just minutes after Satochi's car reached the small airport down Highway 56 towards Kapa'a. Lyuba had told Satochi that Haruko knew Taka owned the coffee plantation and told Jotty and Jim that she believed he was now staying there. Satochi called Taka from the helicopter to tell him what Lyuba had learned before she was killed. Taka was not as concerned as Satochi expected him to be. He took Lyuba's death and the discovery of him being at the plantation as though he had been expecting the news. In fact, Taka had predicted this may happen. He made it a point to think about all the possibilities and was prepared when one of the scenarios came true. To Taka it was just another move in his terrorist game of chess to be countered by the next move. However, he preferred to be the one forcing the countermoves.

When Satochi arrived at the compound, located inside the plantation, Taka had Satochi take Haruko into the wine cellar below the house and tie her up. He did not want Haruko to see him, in case

194

he needed to prove these actions were not of his doing but that of the Red Summit still trying to ruin his life. The Kona Snow was ending and all of the coffee trees at Taka's plantation, as well as the trees at all the other plantations in the area, had been generously covered with the GMO pollen ensuring a good harvest of GMO coffee beans with Yuri's male gendercide enhancements built in. Yuri had been very busy continuing to refine and develop masking techniques to hide his modifications to the organisms he altered. He had served Taka well and hopefully would continue to do so. If all went as Taka hoped, Yuri would. If not, Yuri had given Taka what he wanted and Taka had other means of creating terror in the very near future that didn't require Yuri's expertise.

Satochi was about to order the guards at the plantation to be on alert when the security sensors on the outskirts of the coffee fields sounded a warning. Immediately, Taka and Satochi headed to the helicopter on the roof of the compound. Satochi ordered Bendo to keep the intruders from entering the compound at all costs. Taka told him not to let any harm come to Haruko. He also had him videotape Satochi holding a gun on Taka and pretending to force him into the helicopter. This was added to some previous video that Taka had staged to make it appear he was being held captive. He instructed Bendo to leave the camera and video where the police or FBI would find it. Then he and Satochi headed for a private jet on Oahu that was waiting to take them to the Big Island. As his helicopter headed east away from Port Allen, two other military helicopters came low across the water from the south avoiding the Pacific Missile Ranges 75 foot precision-tracking radar site.

The irony was that it was nothing more that two wild pigs that had triggered the security sensors at the plantation. When Bendo's security team reached the area, they found the two pigs running among the coffee trees. Bendo ordered the sensors shut down until his men could kill the two pigs. They would make a fine dinner for several days to come. Taka would never know how fortunate he was that those two pigs tripped the sensors. Had he waited another five minutes, all possible means of transportation for his escape would have been rendered useless by Viktor's team. Taka had always been lucky! At least so far!

# Chapter Thirty-one

**Viktor had been monitoring** Taka's coffee plantation for several days. He suspected that Yuri was working inside the laboratory at the compound using his special talent to create his Frankenstein GMOs for this Taka Matsuura. Viktor knew that Taka once was thought to be the leader behind the terrorist group, the Red Summit. He also knew that several counter-terrorism agencies around the world still harbored that belief. After what had occurred with the kidnapping of Yuri, Viktor was now sure Taka was the leader. When one of Viktor's agents finally spotted Yuri that afternoon, it was the green light that Viktor had been waiting for. He and an elite team of Russian Special Forces soldiers had been waiting off the coast of Kauai in the Russian trawler for several days. They were well-equipped and -versed in exactly what they were to do. Their primary goal was to retrieve Yuri, unharmed if possible, and destroy the laboratory and all evidence of his research. They had equipment that could instantly fry all electronic circuitry on the entire plantation that was plugged in. This equipment was designed to take out computers and security systems. They didn't even need to be turned on to be destroyed. Any cell phone turned on would be turned to a useless piece of plastic and blown circuitry. They even had the capability of destroying the electronic systems of any automobile, truck, helicopter, or plane that happened to be turned on in the area when they fired up their device. They were to kill as few as possible in accomplishing their goal, but if they must kill they were free to do so. All of their weapons were silenced and they were counting on the darkness to make their task that much easier.

Viktor's men had identified Satochi as the assassin who killed Yuri's driver in Russia as well as the agent at Jim's house on the Big Island. One of his men that had been watching the movements of the NCTC team at the Princeville Hotel had witnessed what had occurred. He was quick to notify Viktor. Viktor even received pictures of Haruko, Lyuba, Eddie, Satochi and Bendo from the agent's cell phone camera as the fight was about to begin. There was even one shot of the Koa wood club in Satochi's hand, before it was shattered by Jim's first bullet. He was also notified when the helicopter arrived back at the plantation with Satochi and Bendo carrying the still unconscious

196

Haruko. Viktor had researched the American agents well and had brought in the necessary equipment to eavesdrop on all of their conversations. He knew who Haruko was and knew how important she was to Jim and Jotty. He told his men to make sure no harm came to her. He also told his men that he wanted Satochi dead. He would prefer to be the one to kill him, but if the opportunity presented itself to any team member Satochi was to be taken out. Viktor also wanted samples of anything Yuri was working on in the laboratory before his men destroyed it.

Back at Pearl Harbor in the secured building Hydrogen Solutions and the Navy were using to monitor the hydrogen plane, the technician who had been helping Jim track the anthrax-contaminated dive boat was distracted by an audio signal signifying that the plane had detected what appeared to be the signature of an electronic pulse weapon being fired on Kauai. It wasn't a very strong signal, but it definitely had all the characteristics of such a weapon. The technician notified the Pearl base commander and the commander at the Pacific Missile Range located near where the pulse was detected. It was a serious enough threat that the Missile Range went on high alert. He next tried to contact the NCTC team that was on Kauai, but there was no answer. He was going to request they investigate, for if it truly was a pulse weapon, it would have the ability to take any helicopters or planes out of the air by killing all the electronics on board. The technician adjusted one of the cameras on the hydrogen plane to show a close up of the area where the pulse was detected. What he saw was truly remarkable. The hydrogen plane gave him a live video account of two helicopters staging an attack on some sort of farm or plantation. The technician's first thought was that it was some sort of federal drug raid, but he knew that the DEA would not have access to the pulse weapon that was first detected. There were no markings on either helicopter to help identify who the commandos were. He saw what appeared to be muzzle flashes indicating weapons were being fired. He called Lord Farrelton to ask what to do. Farrelton told him to call the NCTC team on Kauai, which he explained he already had tried but got no answer. Without hesitation Farrelton rambled off a cell phone number to him. "Call this number, tell them it is an emergency, and ask to speak to Jim. Then explain everything to him.

He will know what to do." The technician said he understood and made the call.

"Hello, this is Emma."

# Chapter Thirty-two

**Emma missed all the action** in the lobby of the hotel. She was watching the bellman unpacking her and Jim's suitcases in their room. It was a job she was used to doing often for Lady Farrelton, so found it very pleasurable to have someone do the same for her. It was a lovely room with huge floor-to-ceiling windows at its end, offering a great view of Hanalei Bay and the waterfalls cascading down the cliffs across the bay. However, the highlight of the room was what the bellhop called the "Good Boy, Bad Boy, Wall". Like most hotel rooms, the bathroom is either to your right or left immediately upon entering the room, as was the case here. The bathroom door was about five feet down the room's entrance hallway on the left. It was a beautiful bathroom with all the amenities, including a Jacuzzi tub and shower that was separated from the rest of the bathroom by a glass partition. Opposite the glass partition that separated the shower from the rest of the bathroom was a white wall whose reverse side faced the rest of the hotel room. That was the Good Boy, Bad Boy Wall. Inside the bathroom was what appeared to be a normal light switch, only this light switch turned the white wall of the shower into a clear glass wall with a simple flick of the switch, offering the person in the shower the same spectacular view of Hanalei Bay and, offering whomever was in the hotel room a spectacular view of whomever was in the shower. So how good of a boy, or how good of a girl, you were, whatever the case may be, would determine which way the switch was turned. Emma could not wait to surprise Jim with this special amenity provided by the hotel.

Emma walked back into a lobby in total chaos. Police and firemen were everywhere and she was kept from entering until she was able to get Jotty's attention. He gave the okay to allow her to enter. She wished Jotty hadn't when she saw the body of Lyuba still lying in the pool of blood. Jim had moved to a couch and was sitting very still and quiet. Jotty stopped Emma before she could go to Jim.

"Jim is in shock. He accidentally killed Lyuba and a bystander. He was trying to save Haruko and Eddie, but was hit just as he fired. Eddie survived, but Haruko was kidnapped."

Emma was in utter shock and disbelief. She stared at Jotty.

"Lyuba was bad! She worked for the terrorists," Jotty said embarrassed.

"Oh my God!" Emma replied.

"It's the tourist that hurts Jim the most. He killed him in front of his own wife and kids. It was awful."

Emma went slowly to the couch and sat next to Jim, but didn't say anything. She reached out and pulled Jim to her as if he was a child in need of comforting. He didn't resist!

Several of Jotty's NCTC agents had arrived at the hotel and were making plans for their visit to the coffee plantation in the morning. It was beginning to get dark when he sent two of the agents to the plantation with night vision goggles to keep watch and report immediately if they saw Haruko or anything out of the ordinary, especially, if it gave them probable cause to invade the plantation before they could obtain the warrant in the morning. Jotty's men would be in place within the hour.

The bodies of Lyuba, the tourist from Kansas, and Tonga had all finally been taken away from the hotel and to the morgue located at the hospital in Lihue. The crime scene investigators gave the okay for the hotel personnel to begin clean-up of the blood that had drained from Lyuba's body and the thousands of shards of glass from the shot-out window. Jotty had briefed his agents and sent them all to dinner. He walked to the couch opposite from where Emma was still cradling Jim. Jotty had finally found the words that he wanted to say to Jim in hopes of removing some of Jim's guilt, when a cell phone began to ring. It was Emma's. She didn't want to answer it, but Jim pulled away from her arms and told her that it may be Lord Farrelton and she was obligated to answer.

"This is Emma," she said as she answered the phone. She listened for a moment and then passed the phone to Jim. "It's for you. He said it is an emergency."

Jim took the phone from Emma and listened intently as the caller described the scene he was watching on a live feed from the hydrogen plane. He explained about the electronic pulse weapon and how they were afraid to send planes or helicopters into the area. He described the action to Jim as he watched the commandos invading the plantation. They needed the NCTC team to get there as quickly as possible. The technician said that military personnel would be sent as well, but Lord Farrelton wanted Jim to be told about it first. Jim thanked the caller and handed the phone back to Emma, telling her he must leave but would be back in the morning. Jim grabbed Jotty's arm, pulling him up off of the couch and began explaining what he was just told as they headed out the lobby door. Jotty told one of his agents, who was still questioning Eddie in the lobby, to get the other agents and immediately head for Taka's coffee plantation near Port Allen. "Jim and I will meet you there. Give me your gun. I left mine in the office, pick it up for me. Eddie, I want you to have Emma get Jim's other gun from their room. Don't forget plenty of ammunition. We may need it. Remember, get there as fast as you can," Jotty yelled as they jumped into their rental car. "Head for the Princeville airport," Jim told Jotty, "we'll take a helicopter."

"I thought you said that pulse weapon could knock down a copter?" Jotty asked.

"It can," Jim responded, "but if the commandos are now moving in, they won't be using that weapon again. Trust me on that," Jim said reassuringly to Jotty. He only hoped he was right!

# Chapter Thirty-three

**Satochi and Taka landed** without incident at the Oahu
airport. The jet was there and prepared to take them immediately to
the Big Island where one of Satochi's men was waiting with the car to
drive them to Taka's safe house in the hills above Hawi. Taka did not
intend to spend much time here. He had already ordered his new yacht
to head to the boat harbor at Kawaihae. He knew it wouldn't be long
until the Americans discovered either the lava tube entrance in the
channel or the safe house itself. His plan was to pick up as much of
the weaponized anthrax as possible and take it to his boat. Then he
would head for his target and unleash the greatest terrorist attack yet
on American soil.

As Viktor's team approached the coffee plantation in the
helicopters, one of his men, who had been staking out the plantation
on the ground, fired an electronic pulse weapon at the main building
of the compound. Immediately, all of the lights went out as the
electrical wiring in the building shorted out and any electronic
equipment that happened to be on had its circuitry fused rendering it
useless and beyond repair. Once the weapon was fired Viktor's man
on the ground gave the all clear for the helicopters to move in. The
first helicopter dropped its commandoes on the helipad on the roof of
the house. The second helicopter dropped its men on the ground in
front of the laboratory. Bendo thought Taka and Satochi were
returning for some reason and went out with two of his men who had
flashlights to help the helicopter land. He had assumed it was an
island power outage, but became very confused when none of the
portable radios seemed to work. He sent men to start the generators to
power the equipment back up. He soon learned it was not Taka
returning when the first man through the door leading onto the roof
was blown back into the second man by what was undoubtedly
silenced automatic weapon fire. The man directly in front of Bendo
began to return fire randomly spraying the doorway with his own
machine gun. In a matter of seconds he too was dead. Bendo hurried
back down the stairs locking the heavy doors behind him as he ran to
alert the rest of the plantation security team, which wasn't necessary
since they had all heard the machinegun fire on the roof of the house.

The two men sent to turn on the generators were taken captive by the commandoes who had landed and dispersed in front of the laboratory. Several other commandoes had stormed the sleeping quarters of the compound taking the lab personnel captive, as well as several security guards who Bendo had not yet ordered to work as Satochi had instructed him to do. Bendo knew there were too many commandoes and the plantation would be taken over. What he didn't yet realize was that the commandoes were Russian and not the FBI. As Satochi had instructed, Bendo placed the video camera on the table in the library of the main house. Before any of the invaders came into the library, he hid behind a secret wall designed to keep the occupants of the house safe in just such circumstances. What he failed to notice as he moved into his hiding place was the now conscious Haruko slowly coming through a rear door .She had slipped out of her restraints and picked the lock to the adjoining room where she had been confined. She quickly stopped her entrance when she heard someone else coming into the library.

The compound and laboratory on the coffee plantation had been secured by Viktor's men with ease. Only two members of Satochi's security team had been killed and both of those deaths had been deemed necessary. Yuri was found in bed in the main house with his Hawaiian putanka. He put up no resistance. When he saw Viktor, he became resigned to his apparent fate. He had expected death, but Viktor told him that was not to be his destiny. Yuri was to return to Russia and continue his research, but not with the freedoms he had enjoyed before. He would be confined to his laboratory until he once again proved through his experiments that he was a loyal patriot. Then maybe he would reap some modest rewards for his work and service for the good of Russia.

Viktor's men were placing charges in the laboratory to destroy it and all equipment and records relating to Yuri's research. They had removed several containers of Yuri's GMO coffee pollen along with other GMO products he was working on. The men were searching the house for laptops and computers that may not have been destroyed by the initial electronic pulse weapon. Viktor entered the library where the video camera had been placed. He looked around the room and saw it appeared to be empty. He assumed it had already been secured by his team. As he picked up the camera to see what was recorded, Bendo silently left his hiding place and made his way behind Viktor.

He prepared to slash Viktor's throat with the large Bowie knife he always carried with him. Just as Bendo was about to strike, Haruko ran from behind the doorway where she had watched Viktor pick up the camera. This time Bendo would not get the best of her. With a mighty kick she threw her entire body weight into the side of Bendo's knee snapping it with a sickening, crunching noise. Bendo toppled toward the floor. As he fell, he lashed out with the Bowie knife at Haurko just nicking her arm as she swung at his throat with all of her might crushing his larynx. Viktor whirled around as he grabbed the Yarygin Skyph mini-pistol from its holster, raising it to fire. He got off one shot into Bendo's chest almost simultaneously with Haruko's crushing blow to Bendo's throat. Bendo collapsed in a heap on the floor as blood poured from the hole in his chest and a shrill wheezing sound came from his throat. Viktor had turned the gun towards Haruko and was aiming it at her head as she breathed heavily from the ferocity of her attack on Bendo.

"Thank you for saving my life," Viktor said to Haruko still aiming his gun at her head. "You must be Haruko. My men have told me much about you. My name is Viktor Cheznov."

"Are you with the NCTC?" Haruko asked, rather puzzled, wondering why the gun was still aimed at her head.

"I am not, but I do belong to similar organization to this NCTC that your friend Jotty is in charge of." By this time several of Viktor's men had run into the room having heard the gun shot. They said something to him in Russian that seemed to concern him.

"I must leave for a few moments. Please cooperate with my men so they do not have to kill you. Just do as they say. I believe your friends are about to arrive." Viktor was out of the door before Haruko could reply.

Jotty and Jim were approaching the plantation on the helicopter they had commandeered at the Princeville Airport. The pilot was not happy about it, but Jotty assured him the NCTC would pay him more than an adequate fee for the use of the copter and him as its pilot. What Jotty and Jim hadn't counted on was that the Russians had a small radar unit and saw the helicopter coming towards the plantation at a very low altitude. It was this information that Viktor was given as he stood speaking to Haruko in the library.

204

The copter had slowed and was coming over the coffee trees at a very low altitude and low speed.

"Use the pulse weapon," Viktor ordered. He knew that at this altitude the helicopter would crash, but it would be a controllable crash. At least it would be if the pilot was any good.

"You had better set it down in the driveway over there and we can sneak in through the trees," Jotty was telling the pilot, when all of a sudden the copter suddenly shook and lost all power.

"Hold on, we're going down," the pilot shouted as he struggled to control the dead helicopter. It only took a few seconds for it hit the ground. Fortunately, it landed upright and no one seemed hurt.

"I thought you said they wouldn't use that weapon anymore..." Jotty said to Jim.

"Guess I was wrong," Jim said in his slow Texas drawl.

As they climbed out of the helicopter, Viktor and his men headed toward the site where the copter went down. One of Satochi's security team members who had originally gone out to see what had set off the remote sensors saw the copter going down and was already there. He had heard the automatic weapon fire come from the house and thought that the plantation was under siege. Which indeed it was! He thought the helicopter must also be part of that attacking force and came upon the copter as Jotty, Jim, and the pilot began to climb out. He lifted his gun and started firing at the copter. Jim had already exited the copter and was standing safely behind it. Jotty and the pilot were in the line of fire and were ducking the shots of the security guard.

"Jim! Shoot the son-of-a-bitch! Jim shoot him!" Jotty was yelling frantically at Jim. Jim had pulled his gun from his holster, but froze as thoughts of the tourist he had killed at the hotel filled his brain. He couldn't pull the trigger! Even to save his best friend, he just couldn't pull the trigger. The security guard saw Jim and turned to fire. Jotty saw the man take aim at Jim as he struggled frantically to get out of his jammed seatbelt. Suddenly there was a burst of automatic weapon fire from the other side of the helicopter. One of Viktor's men shot the security guard as he took aim at Jim. Jotty and the pilot had exited the copter and were staring at several commandos aiming machineguns. "Throw down your weapons," one of the

Russians ordered. Jotty and Jim both complied. Jim seemed happy to throw his gun to the ground.

"So we meet again, my friends," Viktor said as he stepped from behind his commandoes.

Viktor lifted his pistol and fired it towards Jotty's head, just missing Jotty by a few inches, but hitting the other security guard who had been sent to check the alarms. Viktor saw him taking a position to attack the group that had gathered. "Sorry if I frightened you, but I did need to save your life." Viktor ordered his men into the trees to make sure no more security guards could sneak up on them.

"You, like I, were called into this game by a man named Satochi," Viktor explained to Jotty. "Unfortunately, he and his boss, Taka Matsuura, seem to have left the plantation prior to my arrival. I am told they left rather quickly in a helicopter and headed toward the east. This Satochi was the one who killed the man at your house, Mr. Rikey," Viktor said turning to Jim. "The same way he killed one of my men in Russia. He took something that belonged to us and we have now taken it back. I apologize for having not been more forthright with you when we met before."

Jim seemed to snap out of his trance and spoke up. "You lied about the killing of the missionaries in Russia. I heard your voice on the recording. I know it was you. You said you knew nothing about it when I questioned you before."

"Actually, Mr. Rikey, you never once asked me if I knew about the murders of the missionaries. You only threatened to kill me if I was involved in those murders. Had you asked, I would have told you what I did know," Viktor calmly replied. "By the way, Mr. Rikey, you seem a little gun shy at the moment. It is fortunate for the three of you that I came along when I did."

"Don't forget you are the one who brought down our helicopter in the first place," Jotty spoke up. Viktor just smiled. One of his men had just whispered something in his ear. "I have a gift for you before I go," Viktor said to Jim and Jotty. "It is one that I am sure you will appreciate." As he spoke, one of his men brought Haruko up from behind some trees.

"Jim, Jotty," Haruko gasped in surprise as she ran to the two of them. They both hugged her and stood her behind them intending to protect her. She sensed that something was wrong with Jim and started to ask, but Jotty motioned for her to stay quiet.

206

"Now if you all would please duck down behind the helicopter, there is about to be a small explosion." No sooner had Viktor finished speaking, when a large explosion reverberated from the main compound and the laboratory building burst into flames. "I am afraid that there will be nothing left of the laboratory, but the main house should be fine as long as your local fire department gets here soon. I have one other gift for you," Viktor added, turning to take a large glass jar from one of his men. "You may want to have those two genetic scientists you have looking at those potato slices start trying to figure out what this stuff can do," Viktor said handing the jar to a somewhat surprised Jotty. "Are you surprised that we know about your scientists?"

"Not really," Jotty replied trying to act much cooler than he actually was. "Just as we know it is Yuri that you came to retrieve. The business that we both have chosen is one of knowing what the competition is always up to. There are rarely surprises." Jotty took a chance saying what he did, for he didn't know for sure that Yuri was what Viktor had come to retrieve, but it made sense.

"Both of our countries have many secrets in our closets that we do not wish people to know about. It is better for them not to know. And as I am sure you know, we are aware of many of each other's secrets. Yuri's research is one of those secrets that I have now shared with you. Have your scientists study what I have given you and in a year or so you will understand what it can do," Viktor paused for a moment. "I hope we have the chance to meet again someday, Mr. Rikey, Mr. Joplin. I would love the opportunity to try out those Colts you are so fond of," Viktor said to Jim, "but now I must depart before your reinforcements arrive. By the way, I also took a video that I believe Taka had left for the NCTC to find. It is a feeble attempt to make him look innocent in this whole affair. I don't think you need this clouding the truth any longer. I am sure with the information you gather from the workers we left secured in the main house, you will have everything you need to prove Taka is truly the leader of the Red Summit." Not waiting for a response, Viktor and his team ran to the two helicopters that had landed in front of the main compound. Yuri was already on board, being held by two of Viktor's men. Within seconds the rest of the commandoes were on board and the copters were speeding south back to the fishing trawler still in international waters. Just to insure their safety, two other Russian naval vessels were heading full speed to the area as a show of force if necessary. Viktor and his team, along with Yuri, would board one of these Russian naval ships for their return to Russia. It seems the trawler still had more business in the area trying to figure out what created those areas of intense heat and for what purpose. Soon everyone would know!

# Chapter Thirty-four

**As Jotty, Jim, Haruko, and the pilot watched** the
helicopters disappear to the south, they began to hear the wailing of
sirens. Police, fire, military, and Jotty's NCTC team all began to
arrive at the plantation. The electronic pulse weapon had knocked out
all of their radios and cell phones, so they were unable to contact
anyone. Jim hoped that the technician back at Pearl had seen the
Russian copters leaving and had called for military support, which of
course he had done. When the first police car arrived, Jotty
commandeered the radio and contacted Hickam Airbase trying to get
some planes to intercept the helicopters, before they could reach the
Russian trawler. Unfortunately, by the time his call made it through
the proper channels, the copters were safely aboard the trawler. Jets
were still sent to let the Russians know we weren't too happy about
what they had just done. The Pacific Missile Range as well as the
technician for the Hydrogen plane both reported Russian MIGs were
in the air as a counter-show of force and two Russian warships were
fast-approaching the area. This caused several U.S. Navy ships to
leave Pearl and go on alert just as a precaution. It was another one of
the dances the two countries always seemed to be involved in. Both
partners trying to lead and nobody ever coming out ahead and always
stepping on each other's toes!

Just as Viktor had predicted, the main house was untouched by
the intense fire that completely destroyed the laboratory and all of its
contents. The fireman stood and watched as the laboratory burned
itself out. Inside the house there were only three dead bodies: the two
who were initially killed in the stairway to the roof and, of course,
Bendo's massive body that either Haruko or Viktor, or possibly a
combination of the two, had managed to kill. There were also the two
security guards that Viktor had to kill out in the trees to protect Jim,
Jotty, and the pilot. All in all, it was a very clean operation by
Viktor's team, leaving well over two dozen guards and workers
unharmed but incapacitated with plastic ties restraining their arms and
feet. When the guards were finally questioned, several of them were
more than happy to point the finger at Taka as the leader of the
terrorists. They named Satochi as Taka's right hand man and chief
assassin.

Eddie arrived at the plantation with Emma who had stayed in touch with the technician back at the Hydrogen Solutions facility in Pearl Harbor. They were given a running account of all that occurred during the battle at the plantation from the technician watching it unfold on the video feed of the hydrogen plane's infrared camera. When the technician received the signature of the pulse weapon being fired again, it generated much concern as he watched the helicopter going down. It also forced the military air support to pull back until the situation stabilized on the ground and the weapon was neutralized. Eddie and Emma had never been more relieved to hear the technician report that three people had exited the helicopter and seemed unhurt.

Jotty took command and control of the situation on the ground at the plantation. It would take several days to sort out exactly what had occurred and who was involved and to what extent. Jim was still suffering from the post-traumatic stress of having killed Lyuba and the tourist in the Princeville Hotel. It didn't seem to help Jim's spirits to learn that Lyuba had indeed worked for Taka as a swallow assigned to gather information in her own special way. Jotty told Emma to take Jim back to the hotel. It was obvious he would be of no help in the field until he had some serious counseling to overcome his trauma. Jotty knew that could take quite a while, but he hoped with Jim's past training his recovery would be quick. Jotty gave Jim the container of genetically modified organisms Viktor had removed from the lab. Viktor wanted to even the playing field between their two countries. Why, Jotty wasn't sure, but assumed Viktor felt guilt for some reason. Jotty wanted Jim to get samples of the material to the two genetic scientists he had looking at the potato slices, as well as to other top research geneticists around the country. They needed to know what was so special about those GMOs. Jotty knew he still needed to keep Jim focused on work to help him get over his stress syndrome. He hoped putting him in charge of the sample would help. Just as Jim and Emma were preparing to leave, the technician from the Hydrogen Solutions lab called again with some new information.

It seems that soon after Jim first went to the secured facility at Pearl to view the videos from the hydrogen plane, the technician had refocused one of the cameras on the Big Island. The camera had picked up the fire at the Agricultural Office. It also showed a car hurrying from the parking lot of the building just seconds before the explosion and fire began. Since the camera from the plane stayed focused on that area, the technician had a software program that enabled him to mark that car and follow it to its destination up near Hawi. It stayed there for a short time before returning to a rental agency at the airport. By reversing the video and applying the computer software program that marked the car, we were able to determine that this same car was near Jim's house several times during the day. It also stopped at a gas station on its way to the Ag Office. The house in Hawi has to be related to the murders at the Agricultural Office. At least that was the conclusion of the technician.

That also was the conclusion that Jotty reached when he heard the information. He already knew from questioning several of the captured plantation guards that Taka had a safe house somewhere on the Big Island. The return of the rental car on the video was just prior to when the NCTC knew that the driver had left the airport to return to Kauai. It all seemed to add up. Jotty was still on the phone listening to the technician's theory trying to decide his next move.

"That brings me to why I am now telling you this. I know you are really busy with everything happening at the coffee plantation, but I just happened to check that camera on the Big Island and what do you think I found?" The technician didn't wait for a reply. "A car had just arrived at that house. Three people got out and entered. I'm guessing it would take just about this much time for those two guys who flew out of the plantation in a copter to get to the Big Island. I am running a check on commercial flights, but I did discover that three or four private jets flew into Kona in the past couple of hours."

Jotty couldn't believe their luck. It had to be Taka and Satochi going to the safe house on the Big Island. Lord Farrelton's technician had gone far beyond what Jotty had expected of him. His research was far better than what Jotty's own NCTC researchers and team had come up with. A smart move by Farrelton that would no doubt guarantee the United States would place a very large and lucrative order for several of Hydrogen Solution's new hydrogen powered unmanned observation planes.

Jotty shared this information with Jim, Haruko, and Eddie. They were all very anxious to head to the Big Island and capture Taka and Satochi before they could slip through their grasp. Jotty had to forbid Jim from joining them. Jim had frozen under fire from the security guard at the plantation. Jotty could not afford to take the chance of that happening again and putting the rest of his team in jeopardy. Jim would have to stay behind!

# Chapter Thirty-five

**Satochi and Taka were preparing** the canisters of the weaponized anthrax for transport to Taka's yacht. They had made several trips from the secret lab hidden below the Paleaka Ranch Laboratory to the tunnel area off the lava tube just below Taka's safe house. They had labeled the canisters as to where each would be unleashed on the United States. There were over three dozen canisters, each of which was sealed along with three identical canisters in a bio-safe carrying case to protect against accidental contamination. It also protected the canisters from any moisture or other chemicals that could possibly neutralize or taint the anthrax. When the full canisters were placed inside the cases, the cases became heavy and awkward, allowing but one case at a time to be moved by a person. Taka was also packaging much of the cash and bearer bonds he still had stored in his safe. Most of it had been previously removed, but several million in the bonds remained as did almost a million in cash. A million in cash took up a lot of room, so it would be impossible to move it this trip. Hopefully, if the safe house remained undiscovered, one of Satochi's men could retrieve the cash at a later time, although a million dollars was of little significance to Taka compared to the value of the bonds or especially to the value of the anthrax to Taka's future plans.

Jotty, Eddie, and Haruko were on their way to the Big Island. The technician had forwarded a picture of the house to Jotty's laptop that Eddie had brought to the plantation. He also sent directions on to how to get there. Jotty still had two members of his team on the Big Island and sent them to stake out the house.

"Don't let them know you are there," Jotty stressed to the two agents. "Wait until we arrive before you make any move. Call us if anyone leaves. Got it?"

The two NCTC agents, of course, knew to follow Jotty's orders exactly. They would park their car on the road above the house and walk down to where they could keep watch without being seen. At least that was what they thought!

It was a very soft bell that began to sound. It would always sound when someone walked by Taka's house along the road. A series of motion detectors had been placed above and below the safe house to warn when pedestrians were walking by. If it was the occasional pedestrian that walked along Highway 250, the soft bell would have changed pitch as each consecutive sensor recognized the pedestrian continuing on his way. Today, the pitch remained steady signifying that whoever was there was not moving from that spot. That was not good news for Taka and Satochi!

Jim was too traumatized by what had occurred at the Princeville Hotel to stay there with Emma. When they returned to the hotel, Emma instructed one of the bellhops to pack her and Jim's luggage and send it to the Princeville Airport. Emma was very disappointed that Jim never got the opportunity to see the Good Boy, Bad Boy window. "Hopefully, there will be another chance to show Jim just exactly what he missed out on sometime in the future," Emma thought to herself, "but only after he gets better." She knew that was going to take some time.

Emma had arranged with the liaison officer at Pearl to have a Navy helicopter sent to pick up the two of them. If Jim was not to be allowed to participate in the action at Taka's safe house in Hawi, he at least wanted to watch it unfold on the video screen at Hydrogen Solution's building back at Pearl. It had all been arranged by Emma, no doubt with Lord Farrelton's approval. Jim would get to see first hand just how good the hydrogen plane's surveillance systems really were. He would also learn just exactly what that other project was all about that Hydrogen Solutions and the military were trying to keep so secret.

Taka knew that it was no coincidence that the security sensor continued to register someone's presence on the highway. Unfortunately, it was a little sooner than he had expected. His plans would have to change, but like always he was prepared for just such a scenario. He told Satochi to contact his yacht enroute from Lahaina Harbor to the harbor at Kawaihae. He gave Satochi GPS coordinates of where he wanted the yacht to wait for them and told him to contact the captain immediately with the information. Taka would be unable to take but eight of the Anthrax canisters he had sealed in the containers. The eight canisters would be more than sufficient for Taka's immediate terror plans. He would also take the bearer bonds. They were easy to carry and worth tens of millions of dollars, money Taka would most likely need very soon. The million or so in cash and the remainder of the anthrax containers would be left behind. Hopefully, they would stay hidden in the tunnel until it would be safe to return for them. Taka instructed the driver to wait for fifteen minutes, then leave the house taking with him the laptop computer Taka kept in the safe house. He also took several hundred dollars that Taka had given too him. He of course would be stopped by the authorities and questioned. He was to admit that he was a burglar and was there to steal the money and computer that he heard was there. If questioned about his companions, he was to tell them that his companions left overland after a dispute erupted over who got the computer. He left them behind and wasn't sure what they took from the house after he left. Taka told him it was important to make the house appear that it had been ransacked. He was to unlock the gate behind the house that was out of the view of their visitor up the highway. He was to make it appear his comrades went that way. He was also to leave the gate to the highway unlocked to give the appearance he was in a hurry to leave. Once Taka was sure the driver understood the instructions, he and Satochi went back down into the tunnel. They made sure the entrance from the house to the tunnel was well disguised. Taka and Satochi grabbed the containers, which held the Anthrax and the sealed bag of bearer bonds, then headed down the lava tube towards the ocean. Taka had carefully hidden behind a false wall several sets of scuba gear. In a few minutes they would be safely on board Taka's yacht and on their way to the mainland with enough weaponized anthrax to kill ten million people or more.

As Jotty and his team were heading from the Kona Airport for Hawi, his cell phone chimed. It was one of the agents who were staking out the house.

"What's the status?" Jotty said, immediately upon answering.

"One man is leaving the house and driving towards Waimea. How should we proceed?"

"Leave one man watching the house. You follow the man driving away. I'll notify the local police to pull him over in Waimea. Two of my agents will meet you and the police agent there. Arrest him and take him to the local jail. Don't let him out of your sight! The rest of us will continue to the safe house."

"Affirmative," was the only reply.

Jim and Emma had arrived at Pearl Harbor shortly after Jotty's team arrived in Kona. Jim was taken directly to the Hydrogen Solution's secured facility, while Emma and the luggage were taken to VIP quarters. Lord Farrelton had arranged for them to stay there until Emma needed to come back into his service. Jim arrived just as the driver was leaving the safe house. He was amazed at how clear and detailed the picture from the hydrogen plane actually was. You could see the driver carrying a laptop computer in his hand along with what appeared to be a pillow case full of something else. The technician had called Jotty to tell him about the driver, but Jotty was on the radio getting the information from an agent on the ground near the house. By the time Jotty, Haruko, and Eddie reached the area above the safe house where the second agent had continued his vigilant watch, the police had pulled over the lone driver who had left the house earlier. The driver claimed to be no more than a burglar who had broken into the house to see what he could steal. He at first claimed to have acted alone, but later admitted that he had two accomplices in the crime. He told them the story just as Taka had instructed him to do. The NCTC agents with the police passed the information on to Jotty, who in turn told Jim back at Pearl.

"No one else has left the house," Jim told Jotty. "I saw the tape. Three people went in, but only one came out. There has to be at least two more people in that house," Jim said emphatically.

Jotty and the four other agents remained outside the house on the highway. They had pulled their car down to block the driveway, though there were no other vehicles at the residence. Jotty hailed for anyone in the house to come out, but there was only silence. He called for back-up from the local police and requested that they bring in a police dog to enter the house first. After more than forty-five minutes several policemen had surrounded the house and the police dog had arrived.

Back at Pearl, the technician had focused a special instrument on the house that could read heat sources located within it. The instrument was so precise that it could identify pilot lights on water heaters and recognize heat generated by refrigerator motors or other

216

appliance motors. This instrument did in fact recognize both the water heater and the refrigerator, but identified no other heat sources, including humans within the house. Jim passed this information on to Jotty who still sent the police dog in as a precaution. Of course, neither the dog nor anyone else found any sign of the two other men who had been seen entering the house.

"They have to be there!" Jim told Jotty over the phone. They can't just disappear into thin air." Jotty could sense Jim's frustration, but he had personally searched every inch of the house and he was positive no one was there. That was a fact! Jim and the technician couldn't believe it. They knew for certain that two of the men never left the house. "There must be another way out of the house," Jim insisted. "Like a tunnel that leads to another house or building in the area," Jim continued, almost pleading with Jotty. "That has to be it!"

As much as Jotty wanted to agree with Jim, he just couldn't. He had searched the house meticulously and found no such hidden passages. There was nothing there! The imaging from the hydrogen plane had to be flawed and missed the other two men leaving. That was the only explanation.

The technician was beside himself with frustration. There was no possible way the equipment was flawed and missed them leaving. There had to be another way out of that house that Jotty and his team of agents had missed. The technician had called Lord Farrelton to report Jotty's accusation of a flaw in the equipment. Lord Farrelton was beside himself with anger.

"We can't afford for anyone, and I mean anyone, to even have the vaguest whim that our equipment is fallible. What do we have to do to prove there is another exit from that house?" Lord Farrelton asked.

"Well," the technician thought as he replied, "we could send in a portable penetrating radar unit that could identify open space behind walls or floors. That may tell us if there is a hidden crawl space or tunnel leading away from the property. We could even scan the whole area all around the house for up to a mile to see if there might be a possible tunnel or shaft of some sort anywhere in the area."

"Then do it!" Farrelton said decisively. "No one questions the accuracy of our hydrogen plane's surveillance capabilities. Get it done now!" Farrelton was adamant in his demand.

"Jotty, we're sending in a ground-penetrating radar unit. The same type of unit they used to find Saddam in that spider hole. Lord Farrelton will not allow anyone to have the slightest doubt regarding the veracity of his hydrogen plane's abilities," Jim explained to Jotty. "The Navy is flying it to your location as we speak! This will tell us where the other exit is from the house."

Jotty wasn't convinced that there was another exit, but he was willing to give anything a try at this point. Men just don't disappear into thin air.

# Chapter Thirty-six

**This was Taka's first time** on his new yacht. He had named it *Kona Snow*. It wasn't named for the flowering of the coffee trees in the late winter on his plantation, but for the snowfall of anthrax created at his lab near Kona that would soon blanket America. Just as he had instructed, Satochi contacted the captain giving him the GPS coordinates that corresponded to the outlet of the lava tube in the Alenuihaha Channel. The yacht was waiting to take Taka and Satochi aboard with their precious cargo. Once on board, the yacht headed for the Southern California coast. That would be where Taka would unleash his greatest act of terror yet. There he would release the weaponized anthrax into the on-shore flow that dominated the weather pattern this time of year. Within hours his weaponized anthrax spores would be inhaled into the lungs of hundreds of thousand and possibly millions of unsuspecting Americans. It would be a terror triumph unprecedented in history and it would be Taka, leader of the Red Summit, that brought this hell to America. The same hell America had forced on peoples all over the globe for decades. It was time for a change and Taka, no, Aioka, was about to bring it to American soil. Taka was dead! Aioka had killed him on the Big Island over two years ago. Once again Aioka would be called by his real name. Aioka was the true power behind the Red Summit! There was no more Taka! It was time for the world to know and to fear the name, Aioka!

Lord Farrelton did not like to be bothered when he was working on one of Hydrogen Solution's research projects funded by the United States military, especially when it was not good news! Lord Farrelton had been forced to move the test site for his company's newest experimental hydrogen research project from an area west of the Hawaiian Islands to an area offshore of the mainland United States. Too many foreign intelligence gathering vessels had moved into the area near Hawaii where they had first tested their new idea making it impossible for a second test as scheduled. They could not ensure that these foreign ships would stay out of the test area, which could and certainly would cause serious damage to the ships and possibly kill the crew on board. That was why Lord Farrelton had moved all of his equipment to the new location west of the Southern California coast. It had taken several days to move the equipment and would take several more days to set it all up and run the necessary tests to insure all would be ready for the next trial. Most of the recording and data analyzing equipment was set up at Western Launch and Test Range at Vandenberg Air Force Base on California's Central Coast. The equipment was still linked to the secured facility back at Pearl Harbor. Unlike his hydrogen plane, this project was in the early stages of testing and would require a lot more refinement before it could be safely used. It took a lot of Lord Farrelton's attention and any distraction, like someone questioning the hydrogen plane's surveillance capabilities, was not well received.

As Jim sat with the technician at the secured facility at Pearl, he noticed the maps and weather charts that had been on the walls during his last visit had been changed. No longer did they show the Pacific Ocean area west of Hawaii, but now it detailed the Pacific Ocean area off of the California coastline. Specifically, the area northwest of Catalina Island. Jim knew that this area was designated as restricted airspace and was off limits to surface vessels. There were several markers on one of the maps that Jim didn't quite understand. They looked like giant buoys in a large circle with an approximately fifteen or twenty mile radius. On another screen there was a live video feed from what had to be another hydrogen plane showing several ships working around some of the buoys. A great deal of activity seemed to be taking place. The technician watched as Jim continued to look from screen to screen. He knew it would be only a matter of minutes before Jim would have to ask what all those maps meant and just what exactly was going on. The technician smiled in anticipation trying to predict just how long Jim's curiosity could be contained. Lord Farrelton had previously given the technician the go ahead to explain the project to Jim, but only if Jim asked. Which of course Jim finally did!

The helicopter arrived with the ground-penetrating radar unit that Jim and the technician requested the Navy fly over. It didn't take long to discover that there was indeed a hidden passage from the basement of the house down into some sort of underground room. The volcanic rock made it difficult for the unit to penetrate more than a few feet, so the lava tube remained hidden. With the state-of-the-art high security equipment found in the safe house, it was easy to assume that the entrance to this passageway could very well be booby-trapped in some way. It would be necessary to fly in experts from the mainland to access the passageway. This would delay Jotty's search for several more days until the men and equipment arrived. Until then, he would keep busy sorting through evidence at the safe house and coffee plantation.

The technician described Lord Farrelton's other research project to Jim and why it had been moved to the area off the California Coast. Jim wasn't real knowledgeable when it came to the physics of hydrogen or thermonuclear explosions, even though they weren't technically considered explosions. Nor did he know much about weather patterns and high and low pressure areas, but it all did kind of make sense. The technician told him all about the first test and the results it produced. "There was a significant shift, at least temporarily, in the trade winds, but the explosions were not that powerful," the technician continued. "It did heat the ocean up considerably in that area. That is why all the spy ships are out there trying to figure out just what is going on."

"That would explain all the dead fish that Eddie said the charter boat captains couldn't stop talking about," Jim responded.

"Of course, it probably killed millions of fish," the technician replied. "Lord Farrelton knows that we can't keep this project a secret much longer. There are some military applications, but for the most part he's hoping it will be able to do something about these terrible hurricanes that are costing your country billions of dollars every year. But when those animal rights people hear about the fish, who knows what will happen to the testing program. I think they made a big mistake moving it so close to the mainland. We are asking for all sorts of trouble testing it so close to all those crazy Southern California liberal whackos!"

Jim and the technician watched as the radar unit arrived and deployed. They were glad it had been successful, but they too didn't care for the delay in searching the area under the safe house while they waited for the experts to come out from the mainland. The way the two men had just seemed to disappear reminded Jim of the person who killed the two scientists at the Paleaka Ranch lab two years ago had vanished leaving only the traces of weaponized anthrax behind. David Paleaka's Ranch was a couple of miles up the road. It got Jim starting to think! He asked the technician for a map of the Big Island and a ruler. After about two minutes of drawing lines on the map and comparing those to the possible locations where the dive boat could have found the anthrax in the lava tube, Jim almost leaped out of his chair and called Jotty.

"Jotty, I know where the anthrax came from, and I think I know how Satochi and Taka got away. Tell Eddie to get his butt to the Lahaina Harbor now. The Navy dive boat will meet us there with our scuba gear. Eddie Pop and I are about to do a little underwater investigating."

Emma's vacation away from Lord and Lady Farrelton was not turning out anything like she had planned or even imagined. At least Jim took the time to come by the VIP quarters to tell her that he had to leave.

"I'm sorry I have to go," Jim said softly, "but I think I have found the source of the weaponized anthrax. I need to make sure no one else dies."

"I understand," Emma replied, kissing him gently on the cheek. "I will be staying in Southern California for the next few weeks. Maybe you can come visit me there."

"I promise I will," Jim responded and turned to leave.

Emma saw Jim's holster and Colts setting on the bed. "Don't forget your guns," Emma called to Jim as he was about to leave.

Jim paused for a moment and looked towards the bed where his pistols lay. A pained expression came across his face and he turned to leave without responding to Emma. She knew it would be a long time before Jim ever carried his guns again, let alone fire them. She would be sure to have the liaison officer put Jim's things someplace safe. Emma packed and quietly left to join the Farreltons in California.

# Chapter Thirty-seven

**Eddie left to meet Jim in Lahaina,** leaving Haruko and Jotty to return to the coffee plantation to question the workers Viktor's men had captured. It also gave Jotty a chance to talk to Haruko and find out just exactly what had happened in the lobby at the Princeville Hotel. He was also hoping to apologize for being with another woman. He knew he was still in love with Haruko. He just had to convince Haruko!

"I can't believe I fell under the spell of and was used by that woman, Lyuba," Jotty said, trying to confess his sins to Haruko, hoping that she would forgive him for his transgressions.

"She was a very beautiful woman and no doubt skilled at knowing how to get the information she wanted," Haruko responded, causing even more embarrassment for Jotty. "I could see how disappointed you were in yourself when I arrived and found you with Lyuba. You thought I would be hurt and hurting me is the last thing in the world that you would ever want to do."

Haruko was saying exactly what Jotty was thinking, but didn't know how to put into words.

"I was hurt," Haruko said, and paused, "but hurt wasn't the only emotion I felt. I was also jealous and angry at myself for spending all of these past years denying my feelings for you. I've been obsessed with proving to the world that Taka was the true leader of the Red Summit. Now, the world will soon know just how evil he is. All I have to show for the past ten years is an empty, hollow life. When I saw you with her, I never felt as alone as I did at that moment."

"You will never have to feel alone again," Jotty said, taking Haruko into his arms and kissing her. Haruko did not resist.

"I was so afraid when Satochi hit Eddie with that club," Haruko said. "I was afraid that I would be next and then I would never get the chance to tell you how I felt." She began to cry. The sudden and persistent ringing of Jotty's phone jarred them aware as though they had been dreaming.

Eddie was waiting on the Navy dive boat when Jim arrived. He had double checked all the scuba gear to make sure they were ready to go. Jim gave the coordinates to the captain as he filled in Eddie on how he discovered the lava tube entrance. Once they were in the vicinity, Jotty pulled out a chart that showed the coast of the Big Island. He had drawn a line straight from the Paleaka Ranch down through Taka's safe house and on into the channel.

"If that lava tube goes straight, as I'm betting it does, somewhere along this line we are going to find the entrance to that tube," Jim explained.

"Let's start about twenty yards off shore and swim straight out then," Eddie suggested. "Just pay attention to the current. It's a strong one and could pull us off that line easily." Jim agreed, as they got into their diving gear.

What Jim thought would be an easy task took them a full two days to accomplish. There was a slight turn in the lava tube leaving the safe house causing Eddie and Jim to miss the entrance. It turned out to be about fifty yards off of the line Jim had drawn on the map. Had they looked a little closer at the pictures that the dead divers had taken while inside the tube, they would have noticed the slight turn in the tube's path.

The experts from the mainland were due to arrive the very day that Eddie and Jim discovered the entrance. Their task would be made a lot easier now that Jim was on the other side and could see that, although there were explosives in place designed to go off if someone tried to force open the door from the safe house into the lava tube, they had not been activated for detonation. Just as Jim thought, the lava tube did go all the way to the Paleaka Ranch. What he didn't expect to find was an entire second laboratory hidden under the known laboratory at the Paleaka Ranch. This was where the weaponized anthrax was manufactured. He also found an activated self destruct system with an enormous amount of explosives, enough explosives to blow up the hidden lab and the Paleaka lab, if anyone had been unfortunate enough to find the hidden entrance in the Paleaka lab. This would give the experts plenty to keep them busy for quite a while.

Back down at the tunnel below the safe house, Eddie discovered the million dollars in cash boxed and ready to go.

"Oh look," Eddie said to Jim smiling, "Taka left us a gift! Think he would mind if I helped myself?" He held up a huge handful of hundred dollar bills. Jim did not notice. He was too concerned with what was obviously missing from the storage area in the room below the house. On a shelf were several sealed cases with labels designating specific population areas around the United States.

"I'm guessing this is the weaponized anthrax I've been looking for," Jim said to Eddie who let the money fall from his hand back into the box. "A whole lot of weaponized anthrax!" Jim said in an amazed tone. "I would bet it is meant for the areas listed on the outside case labels."

"Well, thank goodness its still here," Eddie said with relief.

"That's the problem. It's not all still here," Jim replied. "There are two empty spaces on this shelf where cases have been removed." Eddie knew that was not a good thing!

Jim opened one of the cases. "Boy, howdy!" Jim said, pulling a canister out of the case. "There's enough anthrax in one of these canisters to wipe out a whole city and there are four canisters in each case. That means enough anthrax to kill several million people in each of these cases. That is, if you had a way to effectively dispense it."

"What do we do?" Eddie asked. "First thing is that you need to tell everybody in that house that hasn't had their thirteen anthrax shots to get the hell out of here now! Then we need a bio-hazard clean-up crew to check this place out before anyone comes in. I've got to give Jotty a call."

# Chapter Thirty-eight

The *Kona Snow* **was well over half-way** through her journey to the mainland when Jim and Eddie discovered the entrance to the lava tube. They had traveled almost 2,300 miles at a much faster rate than the 134' C.B.I. Navi's standard cruising speed of 15.5 knots. The yacht was almost six years old, but had been impeccably maintained by the previous owner who happened to be a prince from Saudi Arabia. He had purchased it new in Monaco and used it to entertain his lady friends. It was a place to stay when he visited the casinos and nightclubs along the French Riviera. He had decided to take an around-the-world cruise and got as far as Hawaii. He had tired of the boredom of the voyage and decided to have his private jet pick him up and return him back to the French Riviera. He left the C.B.I. Navi with a Hawaiian Yacht broker and bought a newer and bigger yacht when he returned to Monaco. Aioka had purchased the yacht at an extraordinarily discounted price of seven million dollars, almost four million dollars less than the going rate for a similarly equipped vessel. Of course it wasn't Aioka who actually made the deal, but Satochi, who had negotiated the purchase. The yacht's old name had been removed from the stern by the brokerage agent and Aioka had waited to have the new name put on until they were on the way to California. He wanted it to remain as inconspicuous as a 134' luxury yacht could possibly be. Unfortunately, there were not a lot of high-end private yachts of that size in the Honolulu area and rarely was one seen at the Lahaina Harbor. People took notice when a vessel like that came into or went out of the harbor. The tourists, the local fishermen and, of course, all the other boat owners!

Jim told Jotty about the discovery of the lava tube, safe-house entrance, the hidden anthrax lab, and all the anthrax and money they had found. What bothered Jotty the most, were the two missing containers that each held four canisters of the weaponized anthrax. Jotty and Haruko immediately headed back to the safe house at the Big Island. Their new confessed love for each other would have to wait a little longer! On the way back to the safe house, Jotty questioned Haruko as to if anything was said at the coffee plantation that might give them a clue as to where Taka and Satochi were headed with the anthrax. She recalled nothing being said at the compound, but did remember that Satochi said a few things right before he was about to rip out Eddie's throat.

"He said some words in a language I didn't quite understand. Something like, yoyo or lolo, and then macky die dead man. I have no idea what it meant," Haruko told Jotty. "Nor do I," Jotty replied.

"Sounds like Pidgin to me," the agent driving the car interjected.

"What's Pidgin?" Jotty asked.

"It's the local Hawaiian slang. A very, very lazy way to talk using as few words as possible to get an idea across. Lolo means very stupid man. Ma-ke die dead means to really kill you. Kind of like getting hit by a cement truck and then the truck backs over you again to see what it hit. That's ma-ke die dead. He was telling Eddie what he was about to do to him," The driver explained.

"Did Satochi say anything else?" Jotty asked Haruko one more time.

Haruko thought for a moment. "You know he did. He asked me what Eddie's name was and when I told him he said how ironic it was that, that..." Haruko couldn't quite remember the exact words. "I don't know, something about Eddie bringing destruction or... devastation to, no, no, I remember, Catalina Eddie bringing America to its' knees. That was it. He said something like that," Haruko explained to Jotty. That was all Jotty needed to hear to know where the anthrax attacks would occur.

Before Jim exited the storage room under Taka's safe house, he made a list of all the cities and areas listed on the remaining containers of anthrax. It wasn't too difficult to figure out which major metropolitan area along a coastline belonged to the two missing containers. Taka had been very methodical about storing the anthrax canisters. They were in order as to geographical locations starting with Seattle and moving south, down the west coast. After San Diego there was a break and they began once again at Houston, Texas, and continued across the Gulf of Mexico, around the tip of Florida and up the eastern seaboard ending with Boston. All major coastal metropolitan areas were designated with at least one container full of anthrax dedicated to each area or region. Several of the larger cities had two containers with the cities name emblazoned on the label. Jim had no doubt where the two missing containers of anthrax were destined!

When Jotty and Haruko reached the Big Island, Jim and Jotty simultaneously told each other that they knew where Taka planned his first anthrax attack. They both had come up with the southern California coast. Specifically, the Los Angeles basin! Now the question was how and what they were going to do about it. Jim already knew the how.

"I'm guessing that they are going to use a ship or boat to access each of the areas," Jim began to explain when Jotty interrupted.

"And they are going to use the prevailing sea breezes to act as their means of dispersion," Jotty added. "In L.A. that sea breeze is sometimes called the Catalina Eddy. They are going to release the anthrax and let the wind do the work."

"How in tar nation did you figure that out?" Jim asked Jotty in a surprised voice.

"Satochi told us. Well, at least he told Haruko back at the Princeville Hotel," Jotty responded. Jim visibly flinched at the mention of the Princeville Hotel. The post-traumatic stress was still very evident in Jim's behavior.

"Well, what are we going to do about it?" Eddie asked the group. Jim was the first to respond.

"Obviously, Taka and Satochi made their escape from the safe house by going down the lava tube and into the water. That means a boat had to be waiting for them. Eddie, I want you to head to the harbors and marinas and see if any boats large enough to motor to the mainland left in the past week. If so, try to get the name of the boat. I'm going back to Pearl to have a look at the hydrogen plane videos to see if I can find a picture of any boats that may have been moored near the lava tube entrance the day Taka and Satochi disappeared." Jim turned to Jotty to see if he was okay with Jim giving Eddie orders and making decisions as to his own assignment.

"How long would it take for a boat to sail from here to the mainland?" Jotty asked.

"It wouldn't be a sail boat," Eddie responded. "There would be too much uncertainty in your travel time. Taka would have a large cruiser of some sort with added fuel tanks. That way he could control his time schedule. A motor yacht of that size could get them to the mainland in six to eight days, unless of course it has been souped up. If that was the case, they could be there by now but, hopefully, we have two more days to find them before they reach their destination."

"I'll contact Washington and let them know what we have found out. Then Haruko and I will head for Los Angeles to set up a command center. Find out what you can, but I do want the two of you in Los Angeles no later than noon tomorrow. You got it?" Jotty said firmly. There was no need for Eddie or Jim to respond, they understood what had to be done.

Jim headed back to Pearl to see if any boats appeared on the hydrogen plane video. Since the camera had been focused on that part of the island the day Taka and Satochi escaped, the boat they used appeared at the proper coordinates just as Jim expected it would. The problem was that the majority of the time the high power video camera was adjusted for a close-up of the safe house so no close views of the boat were available. The computer was able to determine from the long distance camera picture that the boat was about 132'-140' feet in length and could tell that it had twin engines from the wake it produced. The boat could be seen leaving the Big Island not long after the driver left the safe house. The boat headed northeast after it left the island and soon went out of the frame of the hydrogen plane's vision. This was because the plane was focused on the several spy ships far to the southwest of the Hawaiian chain of islands near where the test of Hydrogen Solutions other research had taken place. The computer was able to determine that the boat was traveling at almost twenty knots as it left the islands.

Eddie was able to find out that a large C.B.I. Navi yacht had been moored outside the harbor on and off for the past several weeks, but no one seemed to know who it belonged to or what its name was. In fact, there was no name painted on it. Nor was a crew ever seen coming to shore from the yacht. When he checked, he found that either that yacht or one just like it, had been bought sometime in the last six months from a yacht broker in Honolulu. Eddie questioned the broker and learned all the modifications that had been made to the yacht, but not who bought it. The name the purchaser had given to the broker had turned out to be fictitious. The broker knew it at the time, but if someone has cash in their hand, not a lot of questions were asked. At least they knew just what kind of vessel they were looking for and exactly how fast it could travel, which was not good news. The yacht could reach the California coast by that night!

Aioka had been on his cell phone making arrangements for when the *Kona Snow* reached its destination of Avalon Harbor on Santa Catalina Island. Just twenty-six miles across the sea was the target of Aioka's next terrorist attack, the attack that he hoped would bring America to its knees. He also had one of his terrorists in Japan release a manifesto of the goals and past terror activities of the Red Summit. In this manifesto Aioka denounced Taka and told how he had killed his own brother and taken over his empire to further his terrorist campaign. It had not been Taka these past few years, but Aioka who had fooled the Japanese people and the people of the world. He bragged of the tainted lipstick and how thousands of women and girls would begin to die an awful death in the years to come from the Mad Cow-tainted lipstick. He also lied and said how thousands of pounds of prion-affected meat products had been distributed throughout the United States just as he had done in Atlanta over two years ago. Tens of thousands more people were destined to die from this as his manifesto declared. A sure way to start another Mad Cow panic! What wasn't mentioned in the manifesto was the GMO coffee beans that would be sold within the next year to hundreds of thousands of unsuspecting coffee drinkers. That information he would release at a later date when the coffee was sold and in circulation. The manifesto did go on to say that the worst was about to happen on American soil and there was nothing the United States or anyone else could do to prevent it. Like most manifestos, it also gave Aioka's reasons for his terror campaign and how America's actions around the world had brought this terror to its own citizens.

Aioka had arranged for one of his cell members in the United States to meet him in Avalon with the final piece of equipment necessary for this step of his terrorist plan. It was the method of dispersion for the anthrax. When Aioka and the *Kona Snow* arrived in Avalon all would be ready for what was to be the Red Summit's greatest triumph yet! The world would never forget the name Aioka!

# Chapter Thirty-nine

**Jim asked the technician** if he could view the video from the second hydrogen plan that he knew was flying over the west coast of the mainland United States. As much as the technician wanted to help, and knew how important it was to find that yacht, he just could not allow Jim to see the video without Lord Farrelton's approval. He tried to contact Lord Farrelton, but the Lord was not answering any of his pages or phone messages.

"He's not responding to any of my messages," the technician told Jim. "That means he is getting ready for another test and does not wish to be interrupted. I've waited as long as two days for him to return my calls when he is involved in the preparations."

"You've got to keep trying," Jim pleaded with the technician. "Eddie and I have to get to the West Coast tonight. He says the yacht may already be there and preparing to disperse the weaponized anthrax. It could kill millions of people. You've got to try to reach Farrelton. Call me if you hear anything." Jim hoped he had scared the technician enough to break the rules and see what he could find out regarding the location of the yacht. At least Jim prayed he had!

Jotty established his command center at the Ventura County Naval Base in northern Ventura County. It was about an hour north of Los Angeles. Here he would have access to both sea- and aircraft if necessary. He had heard from both Eddie and Jim about what they had discovered. It was worse than he had expected. The yacht could already be in the California coastal area. Jim told Jotty he had tried to get in touch with Lord Farrelton, who Jim thought was at the Vandenberg Missile Range preparing for a secret test within the next couple of days. So far he had been unsuccessful! Jotty told Jim he would have his Washington sources try to reach Lord Farrelton, but not to be too concerned. Jotty already had two Navy E-2 Hawkeyes from one of the VAW squadrons that were stationed at the Ventura base up and searching the ocean, what the Navy calls their big eye in the sky. If the yacht was still moving, these planes would see it. Unfortunately, the yacht was already moored outside the harbor at Avalon and would be very difficult to detect. The Homeland Security terror alert level had risen to red indicating a severe risk of terrorist activity. Several emergency medical teams were enroute to Los Angeles with hundreds of thousands of doses of 500mg tabs of Cipro to fight the Anthrax spore infections. It would take a lot more than that if Aioka was successful in his attack. Every person exposed would need to take two of these tabs each day for probably six months. The media was frantic trying to find out why the terror level had been raised to red, but no information was being released by the government. They feared a mass panic in California. That would interfere with the NCTC and military's ability to manage the crisis. Jotty had several of his agents calling every harbor master in the area inquiring about luxury yachts that had recently arrived. So far none of the harbor masters contacted reported seeing any new ones. There were several yachts of that size moored in many of the boat harbors up and down the coast, but no one had reported any that seemed out of place.

It was early morning when Eddie and Jim arrived at LAX. A Coast Guard helicopter was waiting to take them up to the Ventura Navy Base. When they arrived, they found Haruko and Jotty had been up all night coordinating the assets that were moving into the Southern California area. Aioka's manifesto had hit all the major media outlets and was fast becoming big news. The American media was claiming it was the reason for the increased terror-level alert. Haruko was finally feeling vindicated for all her years that people thought she was chasing ghosts, swearing Taka was not who or all that he claimed to be. The command center was abuzz in what seemed like organized chaos. Jim was about to call the technician back at Pearl when his cell phone began to ring.

"Sorry Jim, but I have not been able to get through yet to Lord Farrelton. However, I have this premonition that you will find what you are seeking if you look just outside the harbor in Avalon on Santa Catalina Island," the technician told Jim in a hangdog tone.

"I truly appreciate you sharing your inkling with me. I will always be in your debt," Jim replied showing true appreciation. "Keep trying Farrelton, keep in touch and keep an eye on us!" Jim closed his cell phone.

"I think we found our ship," Jim said to Jotty, Eddie and Haruko. "Let's go pay Taka, I mean Aioka, a surprise visit."

There were two Coast Guard helicopters that had been made available to the NCTC team. Jotty thought they would look less menacing when the team found Aioka's yacht. One of the helicopters was larger and could hold several people. Eddie and Haruko, along with six Navy seals, boarded this copter. The other was smaller and faster. Jim and Jotty joined the pilot in the smaller copter. It would be used to coordinate the attack on Aioka's yacht. Both copters lifted off simultaneously and headed across the sea.

Avalon has become a port-of-call for many of the cruise ships that leave Los Angeles, San Francisco, and even Seattle for their three-to fourteen-day cruises down to Mexico. Avalon has the feel of a different time and world. Some people compare its feel to that of European seacoast villages. There are numerous shops and restaurants for the many tourists and a lot of history to keep them occupied for several hours in a very limited and closed area. Perfect as a port-of-call for the cruise ships! It was on one of these ocean liners that Aioka's terrorist cell member brought the final piece to Aioka's terrorist puzzle. He had brought aboard the cruise ship, and then transferred to the *Kona Snow,* a mortar with several shells specifically designed to hold the anthrax canisters. The mortar would be placed on the yacht and the canisters would be shot up into the sky like fireworks. They would explode, releasing millions of anthrax spores into the prevailing sea breeze. There, they would be caught in the marine air, which is often full of fog or low stratus clouds, then spiral around a low pressure center creating the Catalina Eddy. Eventually it would blanket the entire southern California coastal and inland areas with spore laden fog killing millions of people in the process. Avalon and the rest of Santa Catalina Island would bask in sunshine within the clear low pressure area at the center of the Eddy. After delivering the final piece of Aioka's puzzle, a Japanese man left the luxury yacht. He joined his stand-in wife back in Avalon where they collected her purchases. They boarded the cruise ship as it pulled up anchor and headed to Acapulco, Mexico, for its next port of call.

As the two helicopters flew over the yacht and into the harbor area there was no mistaking it to be anything but Aioka's yacht. It fit the profile of the size and type that they had been searching for. Emblazoned on the stern was the name *Kona Snow.* A small boat had just left the yacht heading towards the pier. On board were what appeared to be two Japanese men along with the skipper of the shore boat. As the first helicopter flew over, Satochi looked up to see Haruko looking down at him. He quickly started talking on a radio and the powerful twin diesel engines of the yacht fired up. The luxury yacht immediately began heading away from the outer mooring area of the harbor at a very high rate of speed.

"That's Satochi," Haruko screamed over the roar of the helicopter's engine. "The other man may be Aioka, but I can't be sure."

"The boat is departing." Jotty's voice could be heard through the headset that Eddie and Haruko were wearing. "We need to get those Navy Seals on that boat now," Jotty ordered.

"Put us down first," Haruko begged. "We can't let Satochi and Aioka get away. Let Eddie and I out, then send in the Seals."

Jotty was reluctant to wait, but agreed to Haruko's request. The helicopter turned sharply to the right and hovered above the boarding area by Floats 1 and 2 of the passenger terminal. There were just too many tourists on the streets to allow the copter to drop Eddie and Haruko any closer. The shore boat saw what was happening and veered away from the pier and to the right toward Middle Beach. Fortunately, there were few swimmers in the water in front of the beach this time of the morning. The skipper gunned the small boat's engine running it up onto the sand causing several sunbathers to scatter to avoid being rundown. Jotty and Jim's helicopter had continued to follow the departing yacht. Suddenly, the yacht fired its first mortar shell.

"They're firing a cannon at us," Jotty yelled into the headset microphone. Jim was intensely watching the action on the yacht through his binoculars.

"They're not firing at us," Jim said excitedly, "They're launching the anthrax canisters into the air and exploding them to disperse the anthrax spores. The wind will spread them all along the coastline. That's how they are going to do it. It will kill millions unless we can stop them." Two more shells exploded sending their spores of death into the breeze that would within two hours reign down upon the unsuspecting multitudes in southern California.

"Sink that damn ship," Jotty ordered the Navy Seals whose helicopter was now hovering above the yacht. "Instantly, a barrage of automatic weapon fire ripped through all portions of the luxury yacht, tearing through the huge fuel tanks which had just been refilled from the long journey. The yacht erupted in a massive fireball incinerating everyone and everything on board the ship. "Look for survivors," Jotty ordered the crew of the other copter. He knew no one could have survived such a horrific explosion.

On shore, Haruko and Eddie were making their way along Perry Beach Road toward the pier trying to keep an eye on the small boat that was about to run ashore. They did not wish to lose sight of Satochi and Aioka. It was difficult to follow Satochi's boat when it went behind the pier. Haruko and Eddie would catch an occasional glimpse of it through the pier supports, but only when another boat of the hundreds that seemed present that day were not blocking their view. They knew they had to be extremely careful for Satochi was a bloodthirsty warrior who lived for the battle and would love nothing more than to complete what he had failed to do in the lobby of the Princeville Hotel.

"We have to get down there and help Eddie and Haruko!" Jotty said to Jim.

"We can't!" Jim replied. We have less than two hours to stop those anthrax spores from killing millions of people and I know how to do it. Eddie and Haruko can take care of themselves."

Jotty knew Jim was right, but he also knew that Satochi was a heartless assassin. Was he letting his love for Haruko get in the way of reason? "You're right, Jim. Tell me what we have to do." The helicopter turned sharply and headed off at full speed toward the northwest.

# Chapter Forty

**As the shore boat ran aground** onto the beach, Satochi and the other passenger quickly jumped out of the boat and onto the sand. Satochi could see Eddie and Haruko in the distance approaching Crescent Avenue and its pedestrian walkway. The skipper of the shore boat refused to run as Satochi instructed him to do. In what seemed like a flash, Satochi had pulled the Koa wood and tiger shark tooth club from a holder under his windbreaker, smashing the skipper in the face with the flat end of the club. The skipper was very fortunate that the blow knocked him back into the beached shore boat, where he laid unconscious saving him from Satochi's next swing that would have ripped out his throat. The other man, who Haruko believed to be Aioka, was already running toward the shops on Sumner Avenue directly in front of Middle Beach.

"I'll follow Aioka," Haruko yelled at Eddie as they ran down the street. "You take care of Satochi, but watch out for that club he uses. He is deadly with it!"

Suddenly their attention was diverted as the first mortar shell containing the anthrax exploded in the air less than a half-mile off shore. Two more explosions followed within seconds. The next thing they heard was the sound of several machine guns all being fired at once, echoing off the surface of the water and bouncing off the surrounding hillsides sounding more like the staccato drone of a dozen drummers all playing a drum role simultaneously. It was quickly followed by a massive explosion that echoed with a deafening roar throughout all of the streets and canyons of Avalon, prefaced by the spectacular fire ball of the exploding yacht.

Tourists poured from the shops and restaurants to see what was going on, causing Eddie to lose sight of Satochi. As Eddie ran with his gun held in the air, some of the tourists began to scream and the entire pedestrian walkway was on the verge of mass panic. Those sunbathers and swimmers that had been on the beach when the boat ran ashore were now running from the area having seen Satochi strike the shore boat skipper wanting to be nowhere near a crazed man with a shark-tooth encrusted club. As Eddie ran, he yelled "FBI", holding his NCTC credentials in the air with his other hand, hoping to avoid being shot by one of the Los Angeles County Sheriffs that patrolled

236

Avalon. Had he been yelling NCTC agent as he ran, no one would have known what he was yelling about and probably would have been even more afraid than they already were.

Aioka was desperately looking for a way to get away from the fast-approaching Haruko. He had run inland up Sumner Avenue, not knowing that the sheriff's station was located just a short distance up the street. He could see several L.A. County sheriffs hurrying out of their building upon hearing the explosions and gunfire. Had he been thinking clearly, he would have continued running as several other people were doing, trying to get away from the trouble on the beach. Instead, he ducked quickly into the lobby of the Glenmore Plaza Hotel. As he was going through the entry, he turned and saw that Haruko had spotted him and was just seconds behind. She now too was yelling "FBI" to get people out of the way. Unlike Eddie, she was not carrying a gun. She did get the attention of two of the sheriffs who joined her chase as she quickly summarized the situation as she continued the pursuit. By the time they entered the lobby, Aioka was gone. One of the sheriffs headed through the lobby and out towards the rear of the first floor of the hotel. Haruko stopped to listen for a moment. She could hear footsteps running up the stairs to the second floor above her. She vaulted up the stairs in hot pursuit, listening for the footsteps above her as she followed. At each floor she would stop and listen, then hurry on as she would hear the telltale thumping of someone running up stairs in a hurry. When she reached the fourth floor, she slowed before opening the door and entering the hallway. This was the top floor leaving few options for Aioka, either fight or somehow continue to flee. As she started to push open the door, the full body weight of the man slammed into the other side of the swinging door knocking Haruko down the steps she had just climbed. Her caution had paid off! Although she was knocked down a few steps, it was not nearly as bad as it should have been had she not anticipated trouble.

Aioka ran down the hallway towards the two suites at the end, the Clarke Gable Suite and the Amelia Earhart Suite. Both doors were locked, leaving him no option but to climb out the window to the fire escape. He climbed out and began to head down the steps, but saw a sheriff looking up at him. His only option was to climb the ladder that led to the roof and hopefully another escape route. By the time he started up the ladder, Haruko was climbing through the window after him. She began to climb the ladder right behind him. He paused to allow her to catch up and then savagely kicked downward with his left foot smashing two of her fingers and causing her to lose her grip with her left hand as well as her footing. Haruko hung precariously as she swung to the right side of the ladder dangling by one hand. Her prey saw his chance to finish her off and lowered himself two ladder rungs. He was confident that another well-placed kick was all that was necessary to cause her to lose her grip and hurtle the four stories to the alley below. As he tried to deliver the finishing kick to Haruko's head, they made eye contact for the first time. Suddenly, Haruko felt numb as she looked at his face, the face that was trying to kill her. Then, just as suddenly, her numbness turned to an anger she had rarely ever felt before. As her opponent kicked, Haruko grabbed his ankle with her smashed left hand. With a strength that only an uncontrollable rage could produce, she twisted his leg using the force of his kick to leverage the blow far to his left causing him to also lose his footing and grip on the fire escape ladder. Unfortunately, he was not in the top physical condition that Haruko kept her body in and he lacked the strength to hold the weight of his body with a single hand. He plummeted like a rock the four stories down, landing with a sickening crunch as though someone had dropped a watermelon from the roof. By now several sheriffs had gathered below and quickly cordoned off the alley. Haruko breathed a deep sigh of relief as she gripped the fire escape ladder with both of her hands, placing her feet safely on the supporting rung. She was still too shocked to move. Another sheriff deputy had reached the fire escape and secured her as he slowly helped her down the ladder and back into the hotel hallway where she sat on the floor with her back against the wall and began to cry. "It wasn't Aioka, it wasn't Aioka," she repeated in a teary voice to the deputy who had absolutely no idea what she was talking about.

Satochi had turned at the sound of the explosions just as Eddie and Haruko had and watched as Aioka's yacht was incinerated by the Navy Seal automatic weapon fire. He turned back and saw Eddie fast approaching as Haruko turned to follow Satochi's companion up Sumner Avenue. Satochi quickly turned to his right and began running down the beach towards the massive pier-like wooden infrastructure that supported several restaurants along the waterfront.

238

All of these restaurants featured outside eating areas that protruded far out over the Avalon Harbor. The tide was in, providing Satochi with poorer access to the area than was normally available. As he got closer to the restaurants he could see that, if he continued under the wharf, his way would soon be blocked by the incoming tide and rocks. Eddie was just about to Middle Beach and was headed down to the area where Satochi had the skipper beach the shore boat. Satochi saw Eddie was committed to chasing him along the beach. Satochi leaped upon the huge rocks that provided the protection to the underside of the restaurants. He was then able to jump up and grab a support pulling himself onto the patio of the Busy Bee Restaurant. He ran to the back of the restaurant in an attempt to traverse the expanse of all the restaurants, putting distance between him and Eddie. He hoped to lose Eddie in the chaotic crowd.

When Eddie saw Satochi climbing up to the restaurant he raised his gun to fire but had no clear shot, bystanders would be at risk. Jim's bout with post-traumatic stress also weighed heavily on Eddie's decisions. He followed Satochi's path and climbed his way to the patio of the Busy Bee. Eddie turned toward the back of the restaurant as Satochi had as dozens of patrons watched in curiosity. That curiosity changed to fear when they saw the gun in Eddie's hand. What was unknown to both Satochi and Eddie was that there was no clear pathway along the back of the several restaurants. At one time there may have been, but it had long been broken up into several very segregated areas. When Satochi turned to his left at the rear of the Busy Bee all that was before him was a bar and no further outlet. Satochi stopped and waited for Eddie.

As Eddie made the same left turn with his gun in his hand at the rear of the Busy Bee, Satochi was waiting. With a powerful downward swing of his Koa Wood club, Satochi knocked the pistol from Eddie's hand breaking Eddie's wrist and several hand bones. Satochi kicked Eddie's gun into the ocean. As he was about to administer the killing stroke of the tiger shark, toothed-edge of his club to Eddie's throat, he was once again denied his lust for blood when a rather large restaurant patron ran at him to intervene. Satochi saw the man coming and swung his club towards him intending to severely injure if not kill the misguided Good Samaritan. What he didn't take into account was the actions of another diner who panicked and jumped out of his chair, pushing it into the path of

Satochi's intended blow of the patron intent on interfering with his assassination of Eddie. As the club hit the chair, Satochi had not yet fully gripped it tightly as he would when he was about to make contact. The club hit the chair, jarring it from Satochi's hand, forcing him to use his martial arts skills to fend off his attacker. A simple task! However, this extra confrontation took too much time and Satochi knew he had to flee. He turned to run out of the restaurant, but two sheriff deputies were approaching the entrance and his club was nowhere to be found. He turned to run back into the restaurant, planning to dive into the ocean in hope of escaping. Satochi failed to see Eddie had picked up his Koa Wood Lei O Mano in his unbroken hand. As Satochi sprinted past, Eddie swung the club, viciously ripping into Satochi's thigh and knee. The wound was severe and deep, tearing several ligaments from the knee. Satochi barely flinched as he hurled himself into the Plexiglas sheeting that surrounded the patio protecting the diners from inclement weather and winds. The Plexiglas snapped as Satochi's body burst through the protective barrier and landed in the water below, leaving a large smear of blood on the Plexiglas that remained.

It was Satochi's good fortune that there was a huge Billfish fishing competition taking place at Catalina Island that week. The harbor was overflowing with fishing boats, with several moored illegally close to shore and dozens more in constant motion in the harbor area. Satochi swam towards the confusion of boats leaving a trail of blood as he swam. The water was clear, making it easy to follow his progress, but soon he was lost in the commotion of the venerable plethora of fishing boats moving about the harbor. Despite several hours of searching by lifeguards, the sheriff's department, and the NCTC, neither Satochi nor his dead body were ever found. There were reports of several Mako shark sightings in the harbor area, which was rather unusual, but no one was willing to attribute this to the blood trail from Satochi's gashed thigh.

Further out in the ocean several burned dead bodies, along with several burned body parts, were removed from the water where the yacht had exploded. None were ever identified as belonging to Aioka. On the beach, several hundred people watched as the Navy Seals, the Los Angeles County sheriffs, and the two injured NCTC agents went about their business, all innocently unaware that, in just a few hours, all but those select few who had been ordered to take the shots would be beginning to suffer the effects of the weaponized anthrax spores.

# Chapter Forty-one

**As the Coast Guard helicopter flew** at full speed towards Vandenberg Air Force Base located on California's Central Coast, Jim and Jotty both continued to try to contact the commander of the base, as well as Lord Farrelton. Neither Jim nor Jotty were meeting with much success. Both men were temporarily unavailable and, no matter how grave the situation, the orders were they were not to be disturbed. Vandenberg was where Hydrogen Solutions had set up the control center for the next test of their other secret weapon, the same secret weapon Jim was briefed on by Lord Farrelton's head technician back at Pearl just a day ago. To Jim it seemed like it had been much longer with all that had occurred in the past few hours and days. Millions of lives now depended on Jim's ability to persuade Lord Farrelton to set off an atomic bomb that, in turn, would ignite a series of small hydrogen bombs putting into motion a massive nuclear fusion reaction designed to generate extreme amounts of heat both above and below the ocean's surface. This time the temperatures needed to be much greater than the temperatures produced by Hydrogen Solutions last test of this device near the chain of Hawaiian Islands in the Mid-Pacific Ocean. Millions of lives hung in the balance. First, Jim would have to convince Farrelton to try the device and then, God willing, it needed to work. But before any of that could happen, Jim had to get in touch with Lord Farrelton within the next few minutes and the prospects of that were growing mighty slim.

"We've got to turn off," the pilot shouted to both Jim and Jotty. "If we go any further, they will shoot us down. We are already in restricted air space."

"No way," Jotty replied. "The only hope of saving millions of lives depends on us getting to Vandenberg. Do not change course!" Jotty ordered, hoping and praying that Jim was right about all of this.

"We'll land at Vandenberg all right," the pilot replied, "but in a thousand pieces scattered all over the ground." Still, he remained on course as Jotty had ordered. "It's a good day to die," he repeated over and over to himself.

"Well, if we do die it will be for a noble cause," Jotty said trying to reassure the pilot.

"Any last minute ideas, buddy?" Jotty said to Jim. As he spoke, two F-16 fighters screamed by as a final warning for the Coast Guard copter to stop.

"We know you are a Coast Guard helicopter and you have told us that you have two NCTC agents on board who claim millions of lives depend on you speaking immediately to Lord Farrelton. What you have told us is highly classified information, but regardless of all of that, if you continue on your current flight path I will order the F-16's to blow you out of the sky. Do you understand?," the commander at the Vandenberg control tower calmly explained over the radio to the three men in the helicopter.

At once the pilot stopped the copter's progress and hovered in the sky. "He will have us shot down!" the pilot told Jotty. "We have to wait."

"We can't afford to wait!" Jim yelled, but then had an idea. He grabbed his cell phone and made a call. The sound of the engine made it impossible for Jotty to hear who he called or what he was saying. The two F-16 jets circled menacingly around the hovering Coast Guard chopper.

"CG-1, you are now clear to enter restricted air space and approach the Vandenberg Facility. You are directed to fly to and land at the following GPS coordinates..."Jotty's cheer drowned out the rest of the control commander's instructions, but the pilot acknowledged receipt and the copter shot ahead.

"How in the hell did you mange to pull that one off?" Jotty asked Jim in amazement.

"I knew no matter how secluded and out of contact Lord Farrelton wanted to remain, he would never refuse an emergency call from his wife. What man would, given the consequences of an action like that? I just called Emma and explained the situation to her. She in turn told Lady Farrelton, and 'wallah'!" Jim explained to Jotty. "Now the hard part will be convincing Farrelton to fire up that new device."

When the copter landed, Lord Farrelton along with the base commander and several armed soldiers were waiting with a perturbed look on their faces.

"This better be damned important, Rikey," Lord Farrelton snarled. "Though I must congratulate you on figuring out how to get a hold of me. Damn sharp thinking there, Rikey. Now, what is this about millions of people about to die that my wife was trying to explain to me?"

For the next five minutes, Jotty and Jim summarized all that had occurred over the last few days, but mostly what had occurred within the last hour or so.

"So as I understand this new device of yours," Jim continued, "there is a large ring of these hydrogen fusion bombs in a big circle. You use a small atomic blast to generate enough heat to set off the first hydrogen bomb, which creates more heat setting off each consecutive hydrogen bomb in what I am sure is some predetermined sequence. These reactions channel the air that is rushing in from all directions to be used in this fusion process, thus creating our own mini-hurricane!"

"Brilliant, Mr. Rikey. You should be working for me."

"I thought that when a nuclear bomb went off, it blew the air away from the blast sight," Jotty said.

"Of course it does to a certain extent, but then most of the damage is done as the air rushes back in to fill the void of air created by the blast," Jim explained. "With a hydrogen bomb it's the heat that does the damage. The atomic bomb is a fission reaction. A mass of fissile material is rapidly assembled into a critical mass, growing exponentially, releasing massive amounts of energy. In a hydrogen bomb, this atomic fission reaction is the trigger that sets off an even more powerful fusion reaction which produces incredible amounts of heat. That's where they get the name thermo-nuclear weapon. All this heat requires oxygen, so air rushes to the spot of the fusion reaction. In theory it can create a hurricane, kill a hurricane, or change the course of winds for hours depending upon how much material is available for the fusion reaction to continue."

"Very well said, Mr. Rikey! Very well said indeed!" Lord Farrelton responded, honoring Jim by using the mister in front of his name. Jim did notice this gesture and nodded his appreciation to Lord Farrelton. "So according to what you have told me, we have less than half an hour before this Catalina Eddy starts blanketing Los Angeles with these weaponized anthrax spores."

"You might call it Aioka's own little Kona Snow," Jim responded.

"Indeed!" Farrelton replied, rather amused. "I am not sure we can pull it off in time, but what say we give it a go."

244

Like a flash Lord Farrelton sprinted to the Hydrogen Solution's control room and began barking out orders and instructions to more than a dozen technicians, who in turn either conveyed those instructions to other workers at the buoys or started making adjustments to the equipment in the control room. "Remember, I need everyone at least three miles from the buoys in twenty minutes. Leave the equipment and slower boats. Use the helicopters or the speed boats, but I want those helicopters on the ground or on a ship when I press that button in twenty-two minutes. Farrelton himself worked with speed and precision as he used a software program of his own design to calculate the exact timing of the explosions on the giant seven mile oblique of buoys he had designed for this project. His devise could in moments heat a large area of the atmosphere and the ocean water hundreds, if not thousands, of degrees for several miles and to a depth of almost four hundred feet creating the perfect conditions for creating a massive hurricane or countering one of nature's mightiest forces. Now he only needed to reverse the winds. He needed to change the sea breeze that normally was found up and down the coast to what the locals called the Santa Ana winds that blow off of the desert and out to sea. This Catalina Eddy was a bit more of a challenge, for it created its own unique wind and fog patterns. Farrelton was sure he could do it but did have some concerns as well as some reservations.

"You do realize that if we can pull this off, the anthrax that doesn't get sucked into the superheated air of the hydrogen fusion reaction will, in all likelihood, fall on the islands off the California coast, including Santa Catalina, which I believe has quite a population," Lord Farrelton stated.

"Not nearly the population of Los Angeles. We have medical teams in the area with more teams on the way. They have an abundant supply of Cipro for treating a limited infected population such as Catalina. What we are going to need is air support that can get to all the private and commercial boats in the affected area whose crews will need medical help," Jotty replied.

"This is assuming Lord Farrelton's device works as we hope," Jim responded.

"Oh ye of little faith!" Lord Farrelton replied to Jim's remark. "I couldn't have asked for a better scenario than this to prove

Hydrogen Solution's weather machine. Why don't you step outside and see how long it takes for the sea breeze to reverse itself."

The first line of E-noses located in the harbor area of Long Beach and on the cliffs of the Palos Verdes Peninsula sent an emergency warning to a small monitoring station manned by two Caltech graduate students back at the Jet Propulsion Laboratory in Pasadena. The E-noses reported the presence of anthrax spores. The two graduate students followed protocol, first contacting the scientist in charge of the project and then the JPL head of security. Both men joined the grad students in the monitoring room to see the warning for themselves. If all went as previous tests had predicted, the next line of E-noses located in the area would soon be picking up the anthrax spores as well. Two of the E-noses located at the Seal Beach Weapons Depot suddenly registered the presence of the spores. These two E-noses were more sensitive than several of the others and would also trigger a military response to the anthrax. However, no other E-noses identified the presence of the spores raising speculation about the accuracy of the E-noses, at least until the news about the sudden wind change reached the scientists monitoring the E-noses.

The activation of Hydrogen Solution's weather device went unnoticed to anyone more than thirty miles from the initial atomic blast, except of course for the dozens of countries who monitored such events from their satellites in space or those spy ships out in the Pacific searching the area of the last such test. The equipment on board these ships identified that a nuclear event had occurred. Within thirty seconds, the sea breeze seemed to die out. Then, suddenly, a fierce wind began to blow towards the ocean unlike any wind that the local Californians had ever experienced. It was more like a giant sucking than a wind. It soon seemed like a strong Santa Ana wind had come without warning. Several sailboats in the ocean channel between Catalina and the mainland were toppled over or had their sails ripped from their masts. The fog that had not yet burned off the morning sky suddenly disappeared as if someone had switched on a giant vacuum somewhere out in the Pacific, which in fact they had. The sudden change in weather and the spectacular affect of the fog being sucked out to sea caused many television stations to interrupt there regular scheduled broadcasts as the news and weathermen began speculating the cause. Everything from a nuclear attack on America,

246

to a phenomenon of nature preceding The Big One, the earthquake that had been talked about for years. Some claimed that the second coming of Jesus was upon the world and the Great Tribulation had begun. People flocked by the thousands to churches around the Southland preparing for the End Days. Looting broke out in many of the poorer areas of the city, but was quickly brought under control by the military troops already in place anticipating the anthrax attack aftermath, which in fact this was part of. It would be several hours before the facts would finally be told to the public in a televised news conference by the President.

In Avalon, Eddie and Haruko sat on the pier being tended to by the paramedics at the lifeguard station. They had not heard from Jotty or Jim and were anxious to know what had caused them to head north at such a high speed. Eddie had his suspicions, but didn't want to share them just quite yet. He believed that there were more to the mortar shells than just trying to shoot down a helicopter. A machine gun would have been more effective if that was what the yacht's crew had intended. Those mortar shells had a much more devious purpose.

Haruko was still extremely distressed to know that the man she had chased was not Aioka. In her heart she knew that Aioka had not been on board the *Kona Snow* when it exploded. Once again Aioka had managed to get away from Haruko and this troubled her deeply.

The clear skies, created by the low pressure cell associated with a Catalina Eddy suddenly turned dark as the fog that the eddy pushed onto the mainland, now swirled in the sky above Santa Catalina. Clouds rushed overhead being pulled by the hydrogen fusion reaction that desperately needed air. A strong breeze seemed to come out of nowhere breaking several boats from their mooring pushing them on shore. The wind seemed to push the ocean, creating a small tidal surge. The winds were stronger than anyone could remember having felt on the island before. The streets quickly emptied of tourists. They ran into shops to avoid the debris that was flying through the air. The wind was in excess of fifty miles an hour. The cruise ship moored outside the harbor had to pull up anchor and point into the wind to keep from listing as the wind continued to roar. This wind lasted for almost twenty minutes and then seemed to begin to slowly diminish, though the breeze remained stiffer than normal and continued to blow from east to west for the rest of the day. As on the mainland, the locals, as well as the tourists, feared it was the beginning of the end of the world. In time, when history looked back on this day when Lord Farrelton used his Hydrogen Solutions weather machine to stop the anthrax attack by the Red Summit on Southern California, historians may just say that this was the day of the beginning of the Great Tribulation. Only time would tell!

After the activation of the hydrogen fusion reaction, Jotty was cleared by Vandenberg security to once again use his phone. He immediately called Haruko to see if she and Eddie were alright and find out what had become of Satochi and Aioka. Eddie and Haruko had taken shelter from the strong wind inside the lifeguard building on the pier. Jotty advised them that the wind was man made and had been generated to reverse the anthrax spores from covering Los Angeles and possibly killing millions. He didn't need to tell her what that implied for the population now on Catalina.

"We have Navy ships on the way there now to limit access in and out of the area. Medical teams will be there within the hour with adequate supplies of Cipro. Everybody on the island will be staying for a while until we can assess the level of contamination and start the cleanup process. Within a few days we should have the people, equipment and facilities in place to start moving the tourists out of there," Jotty explained to Haruko.

"Aioka got away," Haruko said softly. "What did you say?" Jotty was unable to hear her over the excitement of the technicians around him.

"I said Aioka got away! Maybe Satochi as well! Satochi was badly hurt by Eddie. In the fight, Satochi broke Eddie's right hand, but Eddie was able to grab and use Satochi's own shark tooth weapon against him. He severely gashed Satochi's knee and thigh before Satochi plunged through a plastic window and into the ocean below. Witnesses saw him swimming away, leaving a large blood trail as he went. He disappeared behind a maze of fishing boats. So far we have been unable to find his body, but lifeguards are still looking, at least they were before this wind came up. That wind has everyone around here pretty nervous," Haruko explained to Jotty. "As for Aioka, that was not him in the boat with Satochi. It was just some Japanese man that looked like him. I chased him into a hotel, we had a bit of a struggle, and he fell to his death."

Jotty knew that there was probably a lot more to the story, but wasn't going to push Haruko for details. That would come later. He was just happy that she wasn't hurt. At least she hadn't said anything about being hurt.

"Aioka was probably killed when the yacht exploded," Jotty said trying to cheer her up.

"I know in my heart he wasn't," replied Haruko. Jotty didn't like the sound of that. She was starting to sound like the old Haruko, not the Haruko who, just days ago, professed her love for Jotty, but the Haruko that had no time for love or relationships, the Haruko who lived only to bring Aioka to justice! No, Jotty did not like the tone of her voice one bit!

"How's Eddie's hand?" Jotty said, trying to change the subject.

"The paramedic said it's broken in several places," Haruko replied dryly. She knew what Jotty was trying to do.

"I need you and Eddie to be in charge there. Tell the sheriffs and any other authorities what is going on, but in private. We don't want anybody trying to sneak off the island until we get things cleaned up there. Got it?" Jotty was again sounding like the boss. "When the Navy medical team arrives, you and Eddie relax for a day or two until you're cleared to leave. When we hear the okay, I will send a copter and get you back to the command center. Until then sit tight and keep in touch." Jotty did not like having to talk to Haruko in that way. He loved her as much as any man could ever love a woman. He wanted so much just to come hold her and comfort her. It was destined not to be!

# Chapter Forty-two

**When Viktor returned to Perm** with Yuri, Yuri was
immediately put back to work. This time at a secure research
laboratory located inside a highly protected military installation. His
new housing quarters were spartan at best, lacking the luxuries he had
been afforded prior to his kidnapping. Not that he was being punished
for being kidnapped, but more so for how quickly he cooperated with
his kidnappers and fell under the spell of unfettered greed. As before,
the more valuable Yuri's research proved to the Russian Federation,
the more rewards Yuri was bound to reap. It was just a minor setback
in Yuri's quest to live large. Besides, he still had his Swiss bank
account waiting for him. He knew his time would come!

It had been close to one hundred and ninety years since the
Russians had a military presence in Hawaii. Not fifteen minutes from
where the coffee plantation battle had occurred stood the remains of
Russia's Fort Elizabeth, the last remaining Russian fort in Hawaii.
The fort that was built in 1815 by Georg Scheffer, a Russian doctor
who had convinced Kauai's King Kaumuali'i to allow him to build the
fort. Doctor Scheffer claimed to have the backing of Czar Nicholas
and said they would help the Kauai King overthrow King
Kamehameha. In fact, when word of his claim reached the Czar, a
ship was sent to collect the doctor and bring him back to Russia to be
punished. He quickly disappeared when the ship arrived and it is said
he eventually turned up in Brazil.

There were strong protests made by the United States State
Department regarding the Russian invasion of the coffee plantation on
Kauai, but the protests were very discreet and kept out of the media.
Russia thought about making a very public protest about the
accusations, but thought better of it when Viktor reminded the
politicians just exactly what Yuri's research projects in Russia had
involved and how now he was reasonably certain the Americans were
aware of the extent of Yuri's work. He knew this wasn't completely
truthful, but some things are best kept secret even from your own
government. Viktor also sent a few pages of Viktor's research notes
to Jim as a means of helping himself ease his own conscience for the
murders of missionaries the previous year. In the note he asked Jim to

keep this just between the two of them. Viktor had no intention of being a spy. He only wanted to help out this one time. He advised Jim to pass the notes along to that geneticist George Fujii, who the NCTC now had working up at the Paleaka laboratory looking at the potato and at the pollen Viktor had given to them back at the coffee plantation. Even with Yuri's research notes, it would be seven more months before the reality of what the potato and pollen were capable of causing became known. By then it would be too late!

For more than three weeks cooked fish turned up on the beaches from San Diego to San Luis Obispo. All had been boiled alive from the activation of the hydrogen weather device created by Hydrogen Solutions. This sparked massive protests from several environmental groups along with equally fervent protests from several animal rights groups. Not least of which was PETA. They placed billboards around the country condemning the use of the hydrogen weather device and calling for the government to discontinue the testing program and to scrap the idea for the sake of the fish and ocean mammals around the world.

Numerous countries around the world also called for the end of testing, claiming it violated several treaties banning the testing of nuclear weapons. The United States government knew it was walking a fine line in supporting the development of the Hydrogen Solution's device and the testing of it. Like so many other treaties and accords, including the Geneva Convention, the current administration thought that these pacts and treaties didn't necessarily apply to this specific situation. Besides, the device had proved itself a necessity by saving millions of people from the Anthrax spores. Regardless, this would be an argument that would continue in the United Nations and around the world for years to come.

Aioka's coffee plantation was bought by a group of businessmen from Seattle wishing to get a start in the lucrative coffee business. The coffee trees on the plantation were overflowing with coffee cherries that promised to produce a bumper crop. In fact, when the cherries were picked, processed, and roasted, there were almost two and a half million pounds of coffee with sixty percent being the prized Peaberry variety. A percentage unheard of! It was attributed to the special pollination applied by the previous owner. Even the neighboring major coffee plantation reaped the benefits of the over pollination of Aioka's trees. Their crop was larger and of a higher quality than ever before. The Seattle investors were going to do very well indeed!

As the high energy that had driven the investigation over the past weeks began to wind down, Jim became more and more remorseful. He was having a difficult time dealing with having shot and killed the Kansas tourist at the Princeville Hotel lobby. Jotty ordered Jim to take some time off and get away for a while. Lord and Lady Farrelton released Emma from her duties for a week to accompany Jim. Lord Farrelton even paid for the two of them to travel to a villa he owned in Monaco. It was a very generous gesture by Lord Farrelton, but it had come too soon for Jim. The post-traumatic stress made him restless and not as responsive as Emma had hoped. They did enjoy their time together, although Jim often seemed to be straining to have a good time. Emma knew it would take time for Jim to heal. She hoped she would be there when he did recover, but knew that the chances of that were slim. She was part of that traumatic scene at the Princeville Hotel. When Jim could put the shooting behind him, she feared she too would only be another memory of the past, also left behind.

When Jim returned from Monaco he had two important pieces of mail waiting for him. One was the research notes and letter Viktor had sent him, which he read and turned over to Jotty. Jotty would get the information to the proper people. The other letter was from an attorney in Edmonton informing Jim that he was the sole heir of his Uncle Howard and Aunt Gladys' estate. There was a lot of personal property and of course the house that needed to be dealt with. The attorney advised Jim that they could arrange to have a liquidator come in and sell the house and dispose of the personal property, then forward the assets of the sale to Jim, if he would like.

Jim gave it some thought and decided that he would rather come up to Edmonton for a few weeks and handle it himself. Jotty agreed to give Jim the time off as long as Jim agreed to see a counselor while he was there. The NCTC would of course make the arrangements. Jim agreed to Jotty's demands.

Eddie's broken hand would keep him out of the field for at least two months while it healed and he had therapy to regain full movement. Jotty and Eddie had an extended discussion about just exactly to whom Eddie held his allegiance. Jotty was still very upset about what had occurred in Thailand with the CIA and didn't want it to happen again. Jotty had grown to like Eddie Popp, even though Haruko still didn't care much for Eddie's machismo womanizing attitude. Maybe Jotty saw in Eddie some of the carefree characteristics he wished he had. Or maybe it was Jotty just wishing he was younger and free-spirited. Regardless, Jotty wanted Eddie Pop as a permanent part of his team. Eddie kind of liked the action of fighting these terrorists and agreed to be true to Jotty and the NCTC. He agreed to stay and rehab his injuries at Jim's house on the Big Island while Jim handled his business in Canada. Somebody needed to feed Sandy and water the garden. After he recovered, he and Jotty would meet again and discuss where Eddie's abilities could best be put to use.

"Just as long as it has a beach and the water is eighty degrees, I'll go anywhere," Eddie said laughingly.

Over the next few months, Eddie Pop would have the time of his life visiting the bars at the exclusive resorts up and down the Kohala Coast, making friends with all the eager and loving female tourists just looking for a blond-haired surfing Adonis beach boy like Eddie Pop. The perfect boy-toy for their Hawaiian vacation fantasies they could brag to the girls back home about. Just the right kind of relationship for Eddie Pop!

Aioka was always planning ahead and thinking ahead preparing for any possibility. It was one of those plans that had saved Satochi's life. Aioka had two sleeper terrorist cell members pretending to be fishermen in the Avalon Harbor that morning. In fact, it was their boat that Satochi was taking the other Japanese man to when the helicopter flew over and Satochi recognized Haruko looking down at him. The two terrorists in the boat watched the chase and the fight between Eddie and Satochi. They were already heading their fishing boat toward the Busy Bee Restaurant to try to help Satochi, when Satochi broke through the Plexiglas and landed in the water. They positioned their boat to block the view of anyone trying to follow Satochi's blood trail through the harbor. Just at the right

253

moment, they pulled Satochi from the water and then joined several other boats as they headed out to fish for the day. Satochi's injuries were more severe than first thought. He almost lost his leg due to the ragged and deep gash across his knee and thigh. For the next several days they tended to Satochi as the boat headed south deep into Mexican waters. Had a doctor been able to treat the wound, Satochi would have probably retained much of the muscle and ligament function that he lost. He would have a permanent and pronounced limp when he eventually recovered enough to walk.

Soon after the men picked Satochi from the harbor, they almost panicked and headed to the mainland when the clouds seemed to be sucked to the northwest. Even the ocean currents began to pull their fishing boat in that direction. Satochi told them they must continue on to Mexico. They were greatly relieved when they heard the American President explaining what had happened earlier in the day to cause the bizarre weather. The boats destination was Manzanillo, Mexico. Aioka had purchased a safe house on the beach located on Calle del Mar. He had owned it for several years and had it prepared for just such a need. It was a place were neighbors asked no questions and strangers were kept away. Satochi would spend several months recovering from his injury there.

When the mortar was delivered to Aioka's yacht by the man from the cruise ship, it was Aioka who took his place and returned with the actress to the first-class cabin that Aioka had arranged for them. That man from the cruise ship was on his way to the fishing boat with Satochi when Haruko spotted them. He was the one killed in the fall at the Glenmore Plaza Hotel in the scuffle with Haruko. Inside the suitcase, Aioka was returning to the cruise ship with more than just the souvenirs purchased at the shops in Avalon. Aioka had taken with him four of the anthrax canisters he had initially planned on using in the Los Angeles terror attack along with tens of millions of dollars in bearer bonds. Aioka knew he would put these weaponized spores to a good use at a later date along with the money. When the yacht was destroyed by the Navy Seals, the crew had launched and dispersed all but one of the anthrax canisters on board. There would be a massive underwater search for the other container of anthrax, but it would never be found in the wreckage. The government would claim all the remaining weaponized anthrax was

254

destroyed when the boat exploded, but there would be many people who would know better than to believe the government's claim.

As soon as the cruise ship reached its next scheduled stop in Acapulco, Aioka and his companion left the ship and boarded a waiting private jet to yet another villa that Aioka had owned before he killed his brother Taka. This villa was located in a friendly and safe South American country often used as a sanctuary by those with the need and desire to disappear from the public eye. As the jet raced toward their next destination, Aioka made a call to a well-known news service taking claim for the anthrax attack on Los Angeles and promising even more and greater terrorist attacks on American soil in the near future.

"American imperialism will no longer be tolerated in the world. We do not share your values and we do not want your culture. The worst is yet to come for America and its partner nations in your undeclared war to rape the resources of third world countries, just to benefit those select few greedy individuals who now own or control most of the wealth in the world. The peoples of America and its partners will feel the burning fury of Aioka Matsuura and the Red Summit as a plague of terrorism never before imagined will be unleashed on the average citizens until they rise up and put a stop to the crimes of their leaders. This is also a warning to those select few megalomaniac power hungry titans of industry who feel they are above the law and above the rules that govern most men. The Red Summit will especially target you, your families, and your corporations. There is no place you can hide that we will not find you. Be afraid! Be very afraid!" Aioka had thrown down the gauntlet! The world and its leaders, both political and financial, had been put on notice! The fires of Hell would soon rain upon them, as would more of his weaponized Kona Snow anthrax!

It had only been ninety-six hours since Haruko had confessed her love to Jotty in Kauai. So much can change in ninety-six hours! Haruko had experienced the same dream every night since she realized it wasn't Aioka who had plunged to his death from the fire escape in Avalon. The same dream she last had the night after the Kashiwa terrorist bombing. The dream where Aioka detonates a bomb killing himself along with everybody she loves. Once again, Aioka had taken from Haruko her right to be a woman, a woman who can receive love and give herself freely to the one she loves. She did love Jotty! There was no denying that! She loved him more than anyone else in the world. It was the hate that would not let her give herself freely to him and share that love. The hate for Aioka! Her hate for Aioka was stronger than her love for Jotty. She tried to explain this to Jotty and he said he understood, although she knew he didn't. What man could understand? Men had needs! Haruko realized this and hoped that when she was free from the hate she felt for Aioka, Jotty would still be waiting. She knew that was a lot to hope for!

Aioka could never return to Japan. Haruko knew this. If she wanted to continue her quest to bring him to justice, she knew her only hope was to continue to work for the NCTC. After Aioka had issued his manifesto and then followed it up a few days later with his declaration of war on the free nations of the world and the leaders of industry, there was no hesitation in the bureaucracy at the NCTC in giving the approval for Haruko to be assigned to exclusively hunt for Aioka and his Red Summit terrorists. After all, she was the expert on both and had been correct all along in claiming that Aioka was still alive and the leader of the Red Summit. It would also keep her close to Jotty in her new office at the main building back in McClean, Virginia.

Jotty was not surprised when Aioka made the follow-up terror declaration after the failed attack on Los Angeles. He knew to trust Haruko's intuition when she said Aioka had not died in the yacht explosion and was still alive. He expected another declaration from Aioka. What Jotty hadn't expected was Aioka's claim to have more of the weaponized anthrax at his command. They had been extraordinarily lucky in countering the anthrax attack on Los Angeles. Had Lord Farrelton not had his hydrogen device in the eastern Pacific waters off the California coast and had it up and ready preparing for a test, who knows how many thousands or even tens of thousands of people may have died from the spores. And even then, had it not been for Jim and his relationship with Emma, Jotty and Jim would probably have been incinerated by those two F-16s sent to keep them from entering Vandenberg. No, next time, they would not be so lucky!

Less than two hundred people had died from the weaponized anthrax spores. Most of those deaths occurred in the poorer areas of

Long Beach near where the first E-nose reported the presence of the spores. The medical team was in place, with plenty of Cipro, but several people, mostly Hispanic, who were exposed to the anthrax failed to seek help in time. This was most likely due to their illegal entry into the United States or their immigration status. It was not until the medical teams realized this and started going door-to-door with the authorities doing mandatory searches, that the extent of the infection become known. There were random infections in several other areas of Los Angeles, but not in the numbers found in Long Beach. Authorities expected the death toll to rise as the house to house searches continued. On Santa Catalina Island the contamination by anthrax spores and the infection rate to the tourists and residents was almost negligible. The vacuum created by the hydrogen device was so powerful that it allowed very few spores to settle onto the island or into the nostrils of the people on the island. However, the island was still under quarantine that would remain for at least another week until medical and haz-mat teams were assured that the island was free and safe of additional spore contamination.

It was Haruko, in her new assignment as Red Summit specialist, who received the information from the CIA informing her that an Elephant Cage located near the border of Costa Rica intercepted a cell phone call. The computer identified the voice of the caller as matching that of several calls made by an unidentified terrorist from Japan. In this call, however, the cell caller identified himself as Aioka Matsuura. It was the call he made to the news service declaring the start of his new terror campaign. The cell call appears to have originated from an airplane flying in a southeasterly direction across the Caribbean Sea. No satellite or radar assets were available to try to identify the origination or the destination of the aircraft, although the agency was still working on it. At least Haruko now had a place to start looking and Eddie would get his wish. As soon as his hand was healed, he would be assigned to go undercover in the most likely place a terrorist on the run would hide out... Brazil! Haruko's spirits began to rise!

Jotty knew from that first phone call to Haruko after the anthrax attack that things would not go as he hoped with their newfound love for each other. He was not happy about it, but he was willing to wait until she was free from the specter of Aioka that seemed to control her very being. Jotty realized Haruko loved him and wanted to be with him more than any other man, but until Aioka was killed or jailed, their love would never succeed. That made it even more of a priority for the NCTC to find Aioka before he could expand his terror campaign as he promised. At least he and Haruko were now working in the same office and he would see her everyday instead of the once or twice a year as before. As time went on and his unrequited love continued to grow, he didn't know if being so close to Haruko was a blessing or a curse. Only the future would tell!

# Chapter Forty-three

**It was George Fujii** who was the first to discover the awful truth about the consequences of consuming the coffee produced by the GMO coffee beans pollinated with Yuri's GMO pollen. It had taken him almost nine months of daily research and study at the Paleaka Ranch Laboratory for George to reach his conclusions. Those conclusions were soon verified by several other government geneticists working on the same project. There was absolutely no doubt that any man who consumed as little as one cup of coffee made from the GMO coffee beans would be unable to produce any male sperm. The GMO coffee caused a permanent and irreversible alteration of the man's testes stopping all male sperm production. Yet it did not interfere with sexual performance or function in any other way. George and the other researchers sent their findings to the NCTC who in turn advised the scientists that what they had discovered was highly classified information and publishing or sharing their findings with anyone else would lead to a lengthy prison stay. They all got the message!

Aioka's former coffee plantation had produced two-and-a-half million pounds of coffee beans. The neighboring plantation whose trees also received pollination from Yuri's GMO pollen produced almost three-and-a-half million pounds of coffee that year. Of that six million pound total, three million of the pounds were blended with beans from other countries to create twelve million pounds of specialty coffee blends. The remaining three million were mostly the Peaberry beans and were sold to retailers and coffee houses throughout the United States. That meant more than fifteen million pounds of coffee with the GMO beans were marketed and consumed around the United States that year. That translates to six hundred million cups of coffee with the potential to cause male gendercide. According to the National Coffee Association, 54% of the adult population drinks coffee on a daily basis. Twelve percent or around thirteen million of those approximately 110,000,000 coffee consumers are male and in the age bracket of those most likely to actively seek reproduction with a female. If only two percent or 22,000 of those males likely to reproduce ingested a cup of the GMO coffee and did indeed produce an offspring, there would be 11,500 fewer male babies born than statistically should be born that year. How this number would skew future population trends was argued considerably by several prominent sociologists working for the government. They all agreed there were just too many variables to get an accurate determination on the significance of the gendercide over an extended period of time. It was certain, however, that if the GMO coffee continued to be produced year after year, major changes would occur in the American population. Fortunately, it would require Yuri's GMO pollen to produce another crop of the gendercide coffee and that pollen was no longer available. However, what the government forgot to factor in to their equations was that since the last crop the Kauai plantations had harvested had been so plentiful and of such a high quality, thousands of the coffee cherries were saved to produce new seedlings. In just three or four years these seedlings would be actively producing their own coffee cherries, coffee cherries whose DNA would carry Yuri's GMO modification and, when turned into roasted coffee beans, would continue to cause the male gendercide for decades to come!

Somewhere in South America Aioka was smiling!

LaVergne, TN USA
15 November 2009
164161LV00004B/4/P